ABOUT THE AUTHOR

As well as teaching in several English primary schools, Ruth Mason home-schooled her own son in Nigeria, illustrated a school primer, and taught unschooled Igala women to read and write. Returning to England, she taught adult literacy at a local borstal and English classes at Reading Prison and Reading Technical College. She obtained her BA at Reading University and taught at the Summer Institute of Linguistics before gaining a PhD and travelling to Kenya, where she taught Linguistics for seven years. In her retirement she started attending creative writing classes at Reading University's School of Continuing Education and won a local writing competition a year later. She has had five poems and an article published in Christian magazines.

Ruth Mason

Amid the Dancing Shadows

With love & best wishes

Ruth M Mason

31st May 2012

Matador
5 Weir Road
Kibworth Beauchamp
Leicester LE8 0LQ, UK
Tel: (+44) 116 279 2299
Email: books@troubador.co.uk
Web: www.troubador.co.uk/matador

ISBN 978-1848760-721

Typeset in 11pt Book Antiqua by Troubador Publishing Ltd, Leicester, UK

Matador is an imprint of Troubador Publishing Ltd

Printed in Great Britain by the MPG Books Group, Bodmin and King's Lynn

With love to Alec, Liz, and Carol
who shared the experience.

... and the flickering shadows
softly come and go.

G. Clifton Bingham
(1859-1913)

Acknowledgements

On my retirement, I discovered creative writing classes at the School of Continuing Education, Reading University. One led by Leslie Wilson, entitled 'Writing your Lifestory', seemed the ideal place to begin. My thanks go to Leslie for getting me started; and also encouraging me further by anonymously awarding me first prize in a local writing competition the following year.

Special thanks go to David Grubb who spurred me on in a whole series of courses; and then agreed to mentor me, making many helpful suggestions as I worked to complete this book.

Heartfelt thanks go to my husband, Don, for his encouragement and for allowing me to spend hours tapping away on the computer while he sat in the living room alone. Many thanks, too, to my friend, Liz Bailey, for reading the manuscript and for all her practical interest and support. And finally, my thanks to Laura Blackburn Finlay for her expert technical advice and especially for converting my pen and ink drawings into a format suitable for printing.

Preface

Long ago I decided to write this account of childhood days as fiction. This has allowed me to cover moments and events not necessarily witnessed by others, and to get inside the hearts and minds of many characters.

In writing this account, I have been inspired by the writings of Stuart Hylton in *Reading at War*; Alan Jenkins in *A Countryman's Year*; H. J. Massingham in *Chiltern Country*, a school prize from 1949; Nanette Newman in *All Our Love*; Valerie Porter in *Yesterday's Farm*; and Sadie Ward in *The Countryside Remembered*.

Chapter 1

Crowsley

Not many people have heard of Crowsley, hidden as it is from the country road linking Stoke Row and Shiplake Row, near Henley-on-Thames in South Oxfordshire. This little out-of-the-way hamlet is where my story begins. As its name suggests, it is the home of the crows.

In spring, crows build their nests in the tops of the elms, shunning the colonies of rowdy rooks. Bulky bowls of sticks, compacted with earth, each in its fork. I try to imagine those cosy interiors lined with wool and hair, sheltering five blotched, blue-green eggs. The eggs take nineteen days to incubate, the hen caring for her brood by herself. Opportunists, crows take carrion, fruit, seeds, invertebrates, small birds and mammals. Bowing forward on their perches, they croak their ripple of raucous calls; 'kraaar, kraaar, kraaar'.

In summer, crows, much persecuted down on the ley, forage and walk with clumsy, hopping gait among the grasses and clover, dodging out of the way of grazing sheep and cattle.

Rain; dreary, penetrating rain, blotting out the landscape, splattering great drops onto the windscreen, and making the wipers work overtime. I hate rain, and the rhythmic clunking of those blades is driving me crazy with its monotonous refrain:

'Rain, rain go away;
Come again another day.'

But it won't go away. It's here to stay. And all our things will get wet.

Why in the world are we leaving our lovely house in Sonning Common to go and live with Grandpa and Grandma Goodchild in their draughty old cottage at Crowsley? None of us want to go there. Why do we have to leave our best chairs for Dr and Mrs Bourne to use? What are *we* going to sit on, for goodness' sake? The floor?

These were the gloomy thoughts that were going through my mind, although, at three-and-a-half, I hadn't yet acquired the vocabulary to express them verbally. That didn't seem to stop me thinking them, though. My parents weren't interested in what *I* thought about the move, anyway. They had to do their duty. That's what they said.

The weather was atrocious that dark November day, boding ill for the future. Frank, the driver of the old pantechnicon van, was sitting forward in his seat, peering through the murk, fearful of wandering onto the verge or tipping the whole cumbersome load into the ditch.

Suddenly, the removal van lurched precariously to the left as the wheels skidded sideways on the wet surface of the country road. It righted itself again, but Frank was visibly shaken. It was certainly a very near thing. However my mother, Emily, dressed in her brown hat and coat, sat on the seat beside him apparently unmoved. Frank's mate, Bob, had dozed off on the settee at the back of the van. "What the heck was that?" he cried, sitting up with a start.

"A skid; the road's diabolical," answered Frank. "We could all've been in the ditch."

Frank soon recovered his composure, and his thin face

assumed the doleful expression he habitually wore. He was giving his whole attention to the road ahead, and seemed not to know how to make conversation. My mother was cradling two-month-old Jimmy in her arms. He was sleeping peacefully, oblivious to the near disaster and the deluge outside. She was in pensive mood, and glad that Frank wasn't the talkative type. Bob lay down again without another word until we reached our destination.

Wedged in behind the bench seat was my little stool. I was kneeling on it, dressed in my old red coat and matching pixie hat, with my arms and chin resting across the top of the seat. That way I could poke my head between Frank's and my mother's in a vain attempt to see where we were going. I had to hold on very tightly, especially when we skidded or swung around the bends. Any other day I would have found the ride exciting, but not today. Something bad was going to happen, I felt sure. My mother knew it too. That's why she was being so quiet.

Then I slid off the stool as Frank was negotiating a particularly sharp bend. I fell and hit my head on the corner of a tea-chest full of crockery, and I felt a nasty graze on my forehead. It stung horribly. I wanted to cry, but there would be no comforting cuddle for me today. So I slowly picked myself up and returned to my perch.

"Are you all right, Maggie?" asked my mother lethargically.

"Yes, Mumsie. Are *you* all right? You don't want to go to Grandma's, do you?" She didn't say anything to contradict me.

Meanwhile, my father, John, had already arrived at Tudor Cottage. He went ahead of us on his 500cc Norton motorbike to open up the part of the house we were about to occupy. He was dumbstruck at what he found. In the kitchen-cum-living room there was a large square hole in the ceiling, where the staircase should have been. My grandfather came round from his side of the house to greet my father, and found him standing there in his old clothes, staring up at the hole with an expression of disbelief and dismay on his face.

"You *did* say you wanted to take out those stairs, didn't you?" asked Albert Goodchild uncertainly. "To give you more room in here. … th-that it was a silly place to put them in the first place…?"

"Yes, I did. But I haven't *built* the new staircase yet, have I?" fumed John through gritted teeth. "Now, what are we going to do? How are we all going to get to bed tonight?"

Outwardly, John managed to be civil to his father, but inwardly he was seething. A whole string of expletives, routinely used by his workmates, came unbidden into his mind — 'Bloody nuisance! … Damn! … Blast! … Hell!' … and other such taboo expressions for someone who calls himself a Christian. Later, when he had regained his self-control, John was mortified. What if he had actually *said* those filthy words aloud? That didn't bear thinking about.

"I'll get you a ladder," cut in Albert. "The men will need it, won't they? To take up the furniture." He spoke with far more assurance than he actually felt.

"Father, whatever *possessed* you to remove the staircase, even before we'd moved in?" complained John in quiet desperation.

"I thought it would help you. Your mother told me I'd got it all wrong. I didn't believe her, that's all," explained the befuddled Albert. In hindsight, he could see how stupid he had been, and why his wife, Ruth, was so mad at him. What could they do about it now?

"Let's go and fetch the ladder. And have you got some steps? We'll probably need those as well." said John briskly, trying to come to grips with the situation. "The van will be here any minute now." Then, more to himself, "I do wish this rain would give over a bit!"

"It's not a good day for moving, I'll say that," continued Albert, who was suitably dressed for foul weather, in a sou'wester and wellington boots. "… Steps, yes, those are in the barn, too."

"Have you something strong for us to stand on, as we lift the wardrobes into the bedroom?"

"Come and have a look in the barn."

The two men were gazing around the well-kept barn, looking for inspiration, when the pantechnicon drew up at the gates. John hurried out to let the vehicle in, and to inform the removal men of his predicament. "My nincompoop of a father has taken out the stairs between the kitchen and the bedrooms. He's left us a gaping great hole in the ceiling."

"Whatever did he do that for?" they asked in astonishment.

"So, we can't move in after all?" gasped Emily in disbelief.

"Don't worry! We can move your things in all right," said Frank reassuringly. "We have ropes and pulleys, you know. Big items often go through bedroom windows. Those we can't get up the stairs."

Bob looked again at the carefully stacked furniture in the van. "You don't have anything really heavy, only the piano. We'll be able to haul the wardrobes and things up through the hole, I'm sure."

Two hours later, the wiry Frank and Bob, the hulking weight-lifter, had put all the furniture, boxes, tea-chests and bundles where my parents had wanted them to go. The empty pantechnicon was standing on the grass near to the house, the deluge had become a steady drizzle, and my father had lit the fire in the kitchen range. He had also secured Albert's ladder to what remained of a wooden support protruding a few inches above floor level at one side of the hole. Everyone was drinking hot tea and feeling slightly more cheerful.

"John, I'd better get back to your mother now," announced Albert, putting his empty cup on the kitchen table.

"Is she feeling unwell?" asked Emily. "She hasn't been in to see us yet."

"She hasn't said anything to me about feeling unwell," replied Albert. "But then, you never know with her. Maybe, she's expecting you to go round and see *her*. ... Come to think of it, she did say something about lunch; what was it?"

"Tell her we'll be round as soon as the men have gone," said John. Emily groaned inwardly, and vowed that she would endeavour to see her mother-in-law as little as possible. This move had been *John's* idea, not hers.

⌒

Emily Goodchild was afraid of heights and the sight of that ladder in the middle of her kitchen terrified her. There was no way she would agree to climbing it. For once, her mother-in-law took her part, rather than John's, when he complained about Emily's intransigence.

"You can't *make* Emily climb that ladder," declared Ruth Goodchild, "especially as she can always use *our* stairs to get up to your landing. She can go through Maggie's room to your bedroom. Be reasonable."

"Is it reasonable for a grown woman to refuse to climb a ladder?" protested John. "Obviously, she shouldn't try carrying Jimmy up that way, but we can't be traipsing through your kitchen umpteen times a day."

"Well, you know what to do then, don't you?" she answered with an edge to her voice. "You and your imbecile of a father had better get cracking on the new staircase!"

Once up in the bedroom, Emily refused to go anywhere near the hole. Every time she even looked in that direction, she felt herself being drawn towards it, as if it were enticing her, whispering, "Come closer, come closer." She felt dizzy and disorientated. She wanted to scream. She knew she was being irrational, but the panicky feelings persisted; they were out of her control.

My mother's fear of falling down the hole intensified as the days went by. It disturbed her sleep, invading her dreams, and even took over her waking thoughts. Why? Why should she be tormented in this way? Then she remembered ... She was thirteen and had been playing in her grandfather's barn, up in the loft. The ladder she was stepping onto suddenly gave way and she landed on top of some bales of hay lying immediately below her. She wasn't badly hurt, only frightened; but she'd been scared of heights ever since.

Now Emily was fearful of other things too: having to cope with a small baby and a new way of life without electricity, water on tap, or a bathroom; and living with an irritable husband, who was behaving like a man possessed. On top of his eight hours of paid work, my father was spending every weeknight evening, and half the following night, building the new staircase, with an Aladdin oil lamp as his only means of lighting. As well as keeping us all awake, he was also adversely affecting his own health; but Emily's pleas for sanity and a quiet night went unheeded. Where would it all lead?

Then my mother started walking in her sleep. One Sunday night she woke up in the small hours to find herself on the very edge of the hole. The room was in darkness, apart from the moonlight streaming in through the window, illuminating her feet and outlining the black nothingness in front of her. She had the presence of mind to step back slowly from the hole and inch herself out of danger. As she felt her way back to her side of the bed, her husband's mouth fell open, he began to snore and normality returned.

Then there was another time ... She had walked into my pitch-black bedroom, dressed only in her nightie. I was awake and called out, "Hello, Mumsie; is it nearly morning?" But she didn't hear me; she walked right past me, and then turned round and went back the way she had come, shutting the door behind her.

I sat bolt upright in bed when I heard a piercing scream and the dull thud that followed. Oh no! She's fallen down the hole. ... "Mumsie! Mumsie!" I shrieked at the top of my voice. I was too frightened to get out of bed in the moonless darkness. Then, as I listened, I heard my father switch on the torch he kept under his pillow. He jumped out of bed, and hastily lit the candle. "Oh Lord!" he cried out in horror. "She's really done it this time! What *am* I going to do? Oh Lord, help us!"

With bated breath, I heard him climb down the ladder. What would he find? Then I heard his muffled voice from far away, down in the kitchen. I couldn't make out the words, but I could sense his fear and anxiety as he tried to rouse my mother. Was she dead or still alive? I knew about death; I had seen a dead dog; it was horrible. But this was my mother. ... The suspense was unbearable.

All at once, I could just pick out a slight stirring and a rustling sound, and then a low moan. She wasn't dead but she must be badly hurt. What would my father do next?

On the other side of the house, Ruth Goodchild was waking up from a disturbing dream. Someone had fallen down the well, because Albert had forgotten to put the wooden lid on again after drawing the water. She lay there in the blackness, worrying about the dream, and listening to the wind whistling in the trees. Then she heard a faraway cry and a distant thump. Something was

7

wrong next door; had Emily been trying to climb down the ladder?

"Albert, wake up," she commanded, as she roughly shook her slumbering husband. "Something's happened to Emily."

"You've had a bad dream, that's all," grumbled the half-awake Albert. "It's the middle of the night; Emily's in bed."

"No she isn't," Ruth insisted. "She's lying on the kitchen floor."

"Don't be daft. You and your imagination. Go to sleep woman; I'm still tired." With that he turned over and hid his head under the covers like a spoilt child.

Almost immediately, Ruth could hear hurried footsteps on the flagstones. John was coming to her for help. He was soon standing below their bedroom window. She fumbled for the matches and lit the candle.

"Mother, Father, Emily's had an accident," John called out urgently. "She must've been sleep-walking. She's fallen down the hole. I need your help."

Ruth could detect the fear in his voice as she opened the bedroom window. "Is she badly injured?" she asked in hushed tones.

"Yes, she is. It's a mercy she fell onto her face, not flat on her back. Come and stay with her while I fetch the doctor?"

"Of course, John; I'll come immediately. What's the time?"

"It's about half past two."

~~

Ruth Goodchild was horrified when she saw her daughter-in-law's bruised and bloodied face. "I don't think we should try to move her," she said decisively. "But she needs to be kept warm. It's bitterly cold in here. Could you find me some blankets and cushions before you go? Nothing that can't be washed out easily. I'll light this fire." With that, she set to and got the fire going in no time. The paper, matches, and sticks were already at hand in front of the stove, and the coal was in the large metal scuttle in the corner.

John climbed up to the bedroom and hurriedly pulled the covers off their own bed. Then he gently tucked them around his unconscious wife. "I'll be off now to fetch the doctor," he said, rising to his feet with an apprehensive glance at his mother.

"Try not to worry. I'll still be here when you get back. This place is warming up already," she added with a hint of self-satisfaction. Ruth Goodchild had a reputation in the neighbourhood as a formidably capable small woman.

The motorbike soon roared into action, and John flew off into the wintry night towards Peppard Common and the elegant home of Dr Michael Prince. "Dear Lord, may he be there, and not already out on another case," prayed John, as he reached the cross-roads and took the Stoke Row road, towards the common.

~~

Dr Michael Prince was highly respected in the area. He had been the family doctor of residents of Peppard, Sonning Common, and the outlying hamlets, for about twenty years. Dr Prince was a tall, heavily-built man, with greying black hair. He had been known to explode in anger when called out unnecessarily, but would willingly come out at any hour of the day or night to those who really needed him. He had been present when Jimmy was born, because the awkward infant insisted on arriving bottom first. John Goodchild knew he could trust Dr Prince.

"Whatever's that?" muttered the doctor, waking abruptly from a deep sleep. "Who's roaring around on a powerful motorbike at this unearthly hour?"

The motorcycle came to a standstill outside his own front gate and Bessie, his Golden Labrador, began barking excitedly as she bounded up the stairs. "I can answer my own question, Bessie old girl," laughed Dr Prince, patting Bessie playfully on the rump. "It looks as if I've got a patient I must visit ... want to come?"

The doctor donned his red velvet dressing gown and made for the front door.

"I'm sorry to bother you at three o'clock in the morning," said John apologetically. "My wife's had a bad fall, from the bedroom to the kitchen below," he explained. "She's seriously hurt."

"How come?" queried the mystified doctor. "Have you got a hole in the ceiling, or something?"

"Yes, we have, thanks to my crazy father. Couldn't wait for me to build the new staircase before taking out the old one! My wife must have been sleep-walking and just tumbled over the edge."

"Who's with her now?"

"My mother. She's lit a fire, and she's sitting with Emily till you get there. She told me not to try to move her. We've wrapped her around with covers, where she is."

"Your mother's a wise woman. Let me get some clothes on, and then you can lead the way."

~

"You've certainly made the patient as comfortable as possible, Mrs Goodchild," said Dr Prince as he walked into the cosy kitchen. "Has she gained consciousness at all?"

"Only briefly," answered Ruth.

The doctor looked up at the hole and then down at his patient, as he gently pulled off the covers and began his examination. As he worked, Emily slowly regained consciousness. "She's obviously badly bruised and in considerable pain but, as far as I can tell, she hasn't actually broken anything," he commented quietly, as much to himself as to the anxious relatives. "The blood around her face has all come from her tongue, and not from a broken nose. She must have bitten into it as she landed. Both elbows and forearms are grazed, and have also been bleeding profusely.

"She's very lucky," concluded Dr Prince, addressing Ruth and John directly. "Her arms took the brunt of the fall, and there are no serious problems. Watch her carefully, and ring me immediately if she gets worse in the night. I'll pop in again tomorrow. But that hole up there must be filled in right away. I know you haven't finished the new staircase; but it could be your small daughter next time, with tragic results."

"It *will* be finished today," Ruth Goodchild assured him. She was the one in charge of *this* family. "Albert can see to this hole, while John finishes the stairs. They'll have to get what they need from John's workshop."

"Is that Austin's the builders?" asked the doctor. John nodded. "They're my patients too; nice family! John, could you get me some pillows? Emily's head needs supporting."

"We'll move her over to my place," continued Ruth. "She can have the bed in the sitting room."

As John put his foot on the first rung of the ladder, from above came a whimper and then a distressed little cry. Jimmy had not had his night feed.

"Let me have him," said Emily indistinctly, through her damaged and swollen tongue. John climbed up into the bedroom, and fetched two pillows, which he threw down to the doctor. Then he lifted the crying infant from the cot. Dr Prince stood on a stool, took him from John and handed him to his grandmother; Ruth had already propped Emily and the pillows up against the cupboard, ready for her to receive her baby son. Dr Prince sat with her as Jimmy guzzled contentedly at her breast. Meanwhile, her husband and mother-law were getting the bed ready next door and lighting the sitting room fire.

"Emily, can you remember what you were doing before all this happened?"

"No, I don't remember anything, Dr Prince," she said, struggling to pronounce the words clearly. "I'm scared of heights; I wouldn't go near that hole."

"John thinks you must've been sleep-walking. Have you ever walked in your sleep in the past?"

"Yes, I probably have. One night I woke up right on the edge of that hole; I've no idea how I got there."

"What did you do then?"

"I kept my eyes on the moon, and stepped back slowly. If I'd looked down, I'd've lost my balance and been over. Dr Prince, you don't have to wait any longer; I'm all right now."

"I insist on carrying you to your new bed, and see you safely tucked up before I leave. Your mother-in-law will have to clean you up though. If I may, I'll make myself a strong cup of tea."

"Help yourself, Doctor. There should be a biscuit tin there somewhere."

⁓

I woke to the pitter-patter of raindrops on the window beside my bed. My thoughts were confused: did my mother really fall down the hole or was it just a bad dream? I listened for the familiar sounds of morning. All was unnaturally quiet in the house. I couldn't hear Jimmy cooing or fretting in the big bedroom, nor any movement in the kitchen below. Where was everyone? Have they taken my mother away? What's going on? Have they all

11

forgotten about me?

Then I heard footsteps on the other side of the house.

"Maggie, are you awake yet?" came my grandmother's voice from behind the wrong door.

"Yes, Grandma," I answered fearfully. My grandmother doesn't come and get me up. Something's wrong; it wasn't a dream.

Grandma Goodchild came into the room, carrying a jug of warm water. She put it on the washstand and sat down on my bed. "Maggie, you will be staying with us for a few days," she said in crisp, matter-of-fact tones. "Your mother has had a nasty fall and she's in bed in our sitting room. Jimmy's cot is in there too. I'm going to wash and dress you now."

She poured the water into the basin on my washstand, and I tumbled out of bed. She pulled off my nightie and washed me thoroughly from top to toe. It wasn't the lick and a promise my mother often gave me. I knew Grandma wouldn't stand for any nonsense, so there was no sense in making a fuss, even if she was being a bit rough ... But how did I know that? Then I remembered something that had happened when I was little.

~~

We were living at Sonning Common and Grandma Goodchild had come to stay with *us*. She was too ill to look after herself and she was in bed in our downstairs bedroom ... Of course, that was why I'd always been afraid of her!

My mother had left the door ajar and I thought Grandma was asleep. I wanted to see what she looked like without her glasses, so I crept into the room to stare at her. I was standing up close, when she suddenly opened her eyes and glared at me furiously. I immediately backed away.

"What are *you* doing here, Maggie Goodchild?"

"Just looking, Grandma."

"Well don't then. Go away. I don't like little girls looking at me when I'm asleep." Her voice was harsh.

"Sorry, Grandma."

"I don't want you anywhere near me. So buzz off, do you hear? You're a naughty little girl; I don't *like* naughty little girls," she said quietly and with great venom.

12

I left the room, without a word, my heart pounding. It was the way she had said it. I knew that she found me irritating so, from then on, I had always tried to keep out of her way. My mother was careful to keep Grandma's door shut at all times. I didn't know it but my mother was having a hard time too.

My father's mother was a small woman with very strong features; she also had an iron will and was used to getting her own way; anyone who crossed her was asking for trouble, as my mother was quickly finding out.

"Emily, why does Maggie grizzle all the time?" Ruth Goodchild would ask my mother accusingly. "If she was *mine*, I would give her a good hiding. You're too soft with her!"

"She doesn't get so much attention now *you're* here. I have to leave her to her own devices, while I attend to *your* needs," answered my mother heatedly. "I don't know why you keep trying to tell me what to do in my own house."

"Your *own* house? It's not *your* house at all; it's *mine*," she said with an unpleasant smirk on her face.

"How's that? John had it built by Austin's, and he did a lot of the work himself, so *how* is it yours?"

"*I* put up most of the money. John's only got a small mortgage to pay off. Didn't he tell you?" she retorted sarcastically.

"That still doesn't give you the right to rule *our* household as well as your own. John's a big boy now."

"John respects his mother, and will do what I say."

"We'll see about that," answered my mother enigmatically.

"What do you mean by that remark?"

"I'm sure with your sharp mind, you can work it out. As far as I'm concerned, now you're on the mend, you've already outstayed your welcome. So when you're ready, I'll help you pack your things."

Grandma Goodchild seemed to regain her full health quite quickly after that acrimonious exchange. My mother could be stubborn, too, but she wondered apprehensively what her mother-in-law might say to John. If she told him about the quarrel, would he side with his mother, or his wife? Fortunately, Ruth Goodchild kept her own counsel.

13

When the day of departure came, my mother ordered a taxi for her and said, "Good riddance to bad rubbish," with a contented sigh, as we finally waved her off. I didn't know what she meant, but Mrs Cotton, our understanding next-door neighbour did. She was hovering by the hedge as the taxi bumped its way down the unmade-up road.

"You've had a tough time with that old biddy, haven't you Emily? You can relax now she's gone."

"My mother-in-law may well know how to make money, but she's no idea how to get anyone to like her. Respect her, yes, but *like* her, no, definitely not! Yet dear John worships the ground she walks on and wishes I were more like her."

"Never mind, she's gone now," soothed Ada Cotton. "Come and have a cup of tea. Maggie I've got some of those malted milk biscuits you like so much."

~~~

However, that was only the beginning of my mother's involvement in her mother-in-law's health problems. My grandmother's indifferent health was the reason my father finally decided to let out our new semi-bungalow in Newfield Road to Dr and Mrs Bourne, and now, a year or so later, we had to come to Crowsley to be near Grandma Goodchild.

Today, Grandma Goodchild was taking my mother's place, and doing the things that my mother usually did for me. I didn't like it one bit. But at least I still had my mother; she would soon be better. The hole would be filled in and the new stairs would be finished. Grandpa Goodchild had gone with my father to fetch the materials.

"Come on, Maggie," urged my grandmother. "Your porridge is ready. Your mother has already had hers."

Chapter 2

Counting the Buckets

My grandfather goes to the well. He lifts the heavy wooden lid and adjusts the bucket. It's fun to watch him draw the water. My grandmother's in bed with a cold, so I can count the buckets in peace. She doesn't want me around here; she shoes me away, yelling, "Buzz off, little Nosey Parker."

The bucket goes down; I wait for the splash. The sound of running water makes my heart beat faster. Grandfather pulls hard on the handle; I watch the coils of rope as they appear, one by one, on the roller. I hug myself with excitement, ready to shout, "Here's the bucket!" I try to count all its journeys; then I forget where I've got to.

It takes twenty bucketfuls to fill all our containers. I have no idea what all this effort is doing to my grandfather, nor why my grandmother yells at me the way she does.

It was an exceptionally warm afternoon for the end of April. My mother had spread out the thick tartan rug for us under the apple tree. Nineteen-month-old Jimmy was trying to build a wall with his bricks, and I lay on my back, gazing up at the tiny shafts of sunlight filtering through the pink and white blossom, thinking how delightful it all was.

Jimmy's little head was covered by a mass of golden curls. He was wearing his new blue rompers to match his deep blue eyes. Strangers always thought he was a girl and cooed, "Isn't she sweet?" My hair was dark brown and I had to wear it in two plaits. I hated my plaits; they made my scalp itch and I wanted to feel the wind in my hair. I was wearing my old yellow frock which was hurting me under my arms; it was far too tight. But, lying under the apple tree, watching the sunlight, I could pretend I had golden tresses, a gown made of apple blossom, and I was lying on a soft mossy bank or an enormous, green velvet cushion.

"Maggie, is Ann awake yet?" called my mother from the kitchen. She was still wearing her pink gingham overall, her long brown hair was coming adrift, and I thought she looked tired. I got up reluctantly from my dream world and tiptoed over to the pram. Why do grown-ups always ask you to do something else when you're enjoying yourself?

"No, Mumsie; she's asleep. Is it her teatime?"

"Nearly; I'd like to feed her first and then see to you and Jimmy."

Ann was eleven months younger than Jimmy; she was not a pretty baby and, when awake, she demanded everybody's attention and made far more noise than he did. I didn't want her to wake up yet and shatter our peace; but she did. No sooner had she opened her eyes than her whole body convulsed and she began to rock the pram with her screaming and kicking. My mother was used to Ann's impatience and had already heated her warm milk and put out her rusk. She quickly came outside to collect that squealing bundle of waving arms and legs from the pram. "Maggie, don't forget to watch Jimmy," was her parting shot.

Jimmy had lost interest in his wall; it was time for a run around the lawn. He was off before I realised he had gone, I was too busy daydreaming about going to school. Next week I would be five, and the summer term started three days after my fifth birthday. I was very excited; I would be a big girl at last, and be able to play with children of my own age.

Suddenly, I heard excited yells from the shrubbery, "Look! ... Look! ... Stick!" Jimmy emerged, clasping a long stick in his chubby little hands. Grandpa Goodchild had left the stick in the shrubbery by mistake; he wanted it as a support for the broad beans, but had forgotten to take it to the barn where he kept all his gardening things. Now Jimmy was trying to run with it. Oh no! He's going to trip over it or poke his eye out. I hate sticks; they hurt people.

"Give me stick, Jimmy," I commanded shakily as I ran towards him.

"No! No! No stick!" With that he rushed forward, brandishing his new toy. I backed away just in time. How can I relieve him of that stick without one of us getting hurt?

I tried to distract his attention by pretending there was something interesting in the nearby hedge. I foolishly turned my back to him and said, "Look, Jimmy. Come and see the hedge!" in a conspiratorial tone.

"Stick! Stick!" shouted Jimmy, as he ran up behind me. Any minute now, I'm going to be clobbered. Jimmy may be little, but that stick certainly isn't.

"Teatime," announced my mother from the kitchen window. "It's time to come in now." Jimmy dropped the stick immediately he heard the magic word 'tea', and ran to the back door. Thank goodness for that! I picked up the beastly thing and followed him into the house. I secretly put the stick in the corner beside the kitchen sink.

After tea, as my mother was bathing Jimmy in the sink, she caught sight of the stick for the first time. "Maggie, do you know where that stick came from? Did *you* bring it in?"

"Yes, Mumsie," I replied noncommittally. "It was in the shrubbery."

"What were you doing in the shrubbery? I thought you were playing on the lawn."

"I was running after Jimmy. We found it there."

"Your grandpa's getting very forgetful these days. I'm worried about him. He's always leaving things around. He can have it tomorrow. I'm *so* glad Jimmy didn't get hold of it."

My grandfather was a big, burly man with a kind, friendly face; his hair had been sandy before it turned white. He always wore his old clothes in the garden, but insisted on spending his money on a good, strong pair of boots. He refused to wear wellingtons unless it was actually pouring with rain or the soil was saturated.

Albert Goodchild was very proud of his garden. He had three-quarters of an acre of ground, with a fine lawn and flower beds at the front and, at the back and left side of the house, a large vegetable garden, as well as all manner of soft fruits and mature fruit trees. Only one small area on the far right had not been brought under cultivation and was left as a meadow, with grass and wild flowers. The house had been partially divided into two dwellings in the late 1920s, but the garden had always been Albert's domain.

"You can have the plot in the back corner, if you like," he said to my father not long after we moved in. "It needs clearing, of course, but it should be all right for growing some vegetables."

"Thank you, Father. I'm very grateful to you," said John Goodchild respectfully. Now, nearly two years later, the plot was still unused.

Every so often his father would ask, "Now John, when are you going to dig that ground and plant those vegetables?"

But he always received the same answer, "When Mr Austin can get another craftsman who knows as much about wood as I do, and I don't have to work such long hours."

When we came to Tudor Cottage, the Second World War was only two months old. By then, my father had been working as a carpenter and joiner at Austin's, a local building firm, for five or six years. Since the conflict began in earnest, many of his mates had been called up, and several had already gone to the front. This meant that he and the others who were left were working longer hours, including Saturdays. My father didn't complain, he was glad of the extra money, so the vegetable garden would have to wait.

Over the years, goaded on by his wife, Ruth, Albert had worked hard to keep the rest of the garden both attractive and productive. Ruth had always had an eye for profit and a talent for making money, and so she regularly sold off all produce which was surplus to family requirements at local markets or her own impromptu wayside stalls.

"Where are you off to today?" Albert would ask her before the war. He could see the old pram loaded up with vegetables, fruit and cut flowers, and knew she was not about to *give* them away.

"I'm going to Sonning Common, on the corner by Kirbys' Stores. I'll take a folding table and sell direct from the pram. The vegetables they offer never look fresh, and mine will be cheaper."

"Aren't you getting a bit too old for this sort of thing? This pram's jolly heavy. It's nearly three miles up and down those hills."

"You can't let good stuff go to waste when you can get five pounds for it," she retorted hotly.

"One day you'll go to meet your Maker, begging him to wait a bit while you sell your last pound of carrots."

Now it was wartime. In October 1939, the 'Dig of Victory' campaign had been launched, encouraging people to grow their own food. Many local people had taken up the challenge, so Ruth had fewer customers. Then her health took a tumble and her pram-pushing days were finally over. So, in 1941, the customers were coming to her. They arrived in ones and twos, having ridden along the country roads from Sonning Common or Harpsden on their sit-up-and-beg bicycles but Albert, who had a generous disposition and no head for figures, would gladly have *given* it all away. As it was, unbeknown to Ruth, he was keeping our family in fruit and vegetables for free.

Grandpa Goodchild enjoyed having children in the garden as long as they didn't interfere with his work or do any damage. He would let me watch him as he dug the soil, sowed his seeds, cut the hedges and pruned the fruit trees. Sometimes he would take me for a walk around his garden, telling me the names of some of the plants and answering my questions. The day after Jimmy found the bean stick in the shrubbery, we were looking at the spring flowers in the border near the front gate.

"What are these pink flowers called, Grandpa?" I asked as I stooped down to study them more closely.

"They're hyacinths."

"But they're only little. They're not *high*. Shouldn't they be called *lowa*cinths?"

Grandpa laughed; then he explained, "The first bit *hya-* doesn't mean 'high'; *hyacinth* is their Latin name. Some plants, like the bluebells that grow in that wood over there, have two names:

19

'bluebell' is their common name; their Latin name is *hyacinthoides non-scripta*, so bluebells belong to the same family as these hyacinths."

"Gosh, that's a long name! Grandpa, I didn't know flowers had families. Do animals have families too?"

"Yes, dogs and foxes belong to the same family."

"Grandpa, can we sing the song about the fox going off to his den-o. I still feel a *bit* sad that the grey goose is dead, though. Couldn't the fox eat grass instead?"

We sang the song all through, and there were several verses. All I can remember now is my favourite one:

'Old mother Slipper-slapper jumped out of bed,
and out of the window she popped her head.
"Run, John, run, the grey goose is gone,
and the fox is off to his den-o, den-o,
and the fox is off to his den-o."'

'Old Mother Slipper-slapper' is such a marvellous name for the old lady; I can just hear her slapping around in her slippers.

Grandma Goodchild was not only becoming increasingly frail in body but also progressively more crotchety in temperament, and very difficult to please. Quite apart from that, my mother was continuing to find the lack of electricity, proper sanitation and running water at Tudor Cottage a sore trial, with three young children to look after, and possibly a fourth already on the way. I didn't realise her true situation until I was very much older.

For me, it was exciting to watch Grandpa drawing the water up from the well but, if Grandma was in her kitchen or scullery, she would send me straight home again. "Buzz off home, Maggie Goodchild," she would shout, shooing me away as if I were a chicken.

"Why can't Maggie stay?" asked my grandfather. "She's not in *my* way and she likes to count the number of times the bucket goes down into the water."

"I don't want that child here, Albert; do you *hear*?"

Occasionally, Albert would be drawing the water while Ruth Goodchild was unwell in bed, cleaning the bedrooms or out on her bicycle; then he would come round to fetch me immediately.

"Do you want to count the buckets, Maggie?" he would ask with a twinkle in his eye.

"Yes *please*, Grandpa," I would answer gaily.

"We'll just check with your mother first, so she knows where you are."

Above the well was a beautifully tiled structure, built specifically to house the windlass, with its horizontal roller on supports and the heavy rope for lowering and raising the bucket wound around it. To the right was the pawl, a short pivoted catch which engaged with a toothed ratchet-wheel to prevent the rope going back the wrong way. The whole mechanism was controlled by a handle. When the well was not in use it was always covered by a heavy wooden lid. Albert's first job was to remove that heavy lid. When John was at home he would always give his father a hand, and the job would be done in half the time. However, my father would soon send me packing if I came to watch, just like his mother always did. Those two were so alike: they were both small in stature, neither of them liked parting with money and they couldn't seem to remember what it felt like to be a child. Maybe they had both been born as little grown-ups!

It was easy to operate the handle for winding down the rope and empty bucket; my grandfather sometimes let me do it for him. But it required a much greater effort to pull the heavy bucket up again when it was full to the brim with clear sparkling water. The drawn water was stored in large wooden water butts and metal drums, which were placed beside the well and outside the two separate kitchens. Our kitchen was on the opposite side of the house to the well, so my parents had to carry the water we needed round in buckets, from the main storage area by the well to our own containers.

After we had been at Tudor Cottage for four years or so, the well became contaminated in some way and the water was no longer safe to drink. This meant my father had to carry water from the cottage of our nearest neighbours, Mr and Mrs Hurst, two hundred yards down the lane, until we were connected up to the mains water supply sometime in the autumn of 1942 . But this did not happen in the lifetime of Grandma Goodchild.

Grandpa and Grandma were both very fond of rabbit pie. Grandpa had a gun which he used to shoot rabbits in the fields around the cottage. Many of them got into the garden and helped themselves to his cabbages and lettuces, so he felt quite justified in having some of them for his dinner. Grandma Goodchild used to skin and prepare the rabbits for the table herself.

One day I was walking round to her side of the house with a note from my mother. Grandma was in her little scullery, starting to prepare two dead rabbits. I looked on aghast, as I saw her ripping off their furry coats. I felt sick and upset.

"What are you doing here, little nosey-parker?"

"I've got a note for you from my mother, Grandma."

"Give it here."

"Oh! She wants to borrow my jam saucepan. Can you carry it?"

"I think so, Grandma."

She left the half-naked rabbits and washed her hands in an enamel bowl; she then went into her kitchen for the jam saucepan. She put it in my hands and I staggered home with the heavy object.

"How was Grandma?" asked my mother, as she took the pan from me.

"She called me 'little nosey-parker'."

"Oh did she! What was *she* doing that she didn't want you to see?"

"Taking the fur off a dead rabbit ... What will she do with the fur, Mumsie?"

"She may make a furry hat with it. But she's going to cook the meat for her dinner."

"Do *we* eat rabbits, Mumsie?"

"If we can get them. Grandpa sometimes gives us one. They taste a bit like chicken."

"How do you catch them?" I asked, but she decided not to tell me about the gun, nor about gin traps.

"Well, you have to chase them and put some salt on their tails."

For the rest of the day I went looking for rabbits all around the garden. In my pocket was a little bag of salt.

~

On Saturdays and Sundays my father would put me to bed and hear my prayers. When I was little he taught me to say:

'Gentle Jesus, meek and mild,
listen to a little child.

Pity my simplicity;
suffer me to come to Thee.'

I didn't really understand what I was saying. Daddy couldn't explain things like Mumsie did. He just got cross with me when I said it all wrong. My version of the last two lines was:

'Pity mice implicitly;
suffer them to come to Thee.'

I had no more idea what 'implicitly' meant than 'simplicity'; I just latched onto what I thought was the word 'mice'. I knew what mice were: mice scuffling in the attic, mice scuffling in the barn. Grandpa Goodchild set traps for them, but why was God so interested in mice? 'Suffer' was another word I didn't understand. I had learnt the text 'Suffer the children to come unto me, and forbid them not: for of such is the kingdom of God.' (Mark 10:14) at Sunday school. I understood 'forbid' because Daddy often said, "I forbid you to go into Grandpa's barn, do you *hear*?" It meant a good hiding if I disobeyed him. Perhaps he didn't want the traps to get *me* by mistake?

At five, I could still remember playing bedtime games with my father at 'Shalom', the house in Newfield Road, a year or so before Jimmy was born. At the time, he was decorating my bedroom and putting up a colourful nursery-rhyme frieze for me. As I was being put to bed, the steps were still standing nearby, and Daddy sat on the little seat at the top, looking down at me. He taught me some of the rhymes and we sang them together; then we played 'guess the missing words and lines'. I was quite quick at guessing, so he muddled them all up just to confuse me. He had Little Jack Horner pulling out Little Miss Muffet's spider instead of a plum, and The Grand Old Duke of York putting Humpty Dumpty together again. This is the only recollection I have of having fun with my father. Then, he was just like a big brother, laughing and giggling with me from his perch at the top of the steps.

He changed completely after we went to Tudor Cottage to live. Sadly, he lost his sense of fun and became much less approachable. Times were hard and he became hard. So, prayer times with my father became events to be endured, and got through as quickly and painlessly as possible. My unsaid prayer was always, "Please Jesus, help me get the words right tonight. May Daddy not be cross with me for *anything*."

Yet things were so different at first; once he called me his 'little ray of sunshine'. Because my mother's health was poor during the later months of her first pregnancy, and I was a premature baby, my father was exceptionally loving and attentive; he engaged a full-time nurse, a family friend, to help with the delivery and care for us both for a few weeks afterwards.

Apparently, during the first few days of my life, Nurse Payne was constantly playing games with me, trying to attract my attention. She would make sudden noises to my right and to my left, and wave her hands slowly over my face. I was born with deep purple eyes and she feared that I was blind. She was most relieved when I joined in these diagnostic games, and only then did she tell my parents of her unfounded suspicions. From that day forward, I expected *all* adults to play games with me, and couldn't understand why many of them didn't.

I don't think Grandma Goodchild had ever played games; she was far too serious for that. Though my other grandma, Grandma Nelson, did when I was still in the pram. My earliest memory of Grandma Nelson was 'Going ta-tas', or going out. I was about nine months old, sitting up in my pram, dressed to go out. We were in the narrow, dark hall of my grandparents' house in Uxbridge. I had a fluffy, pink cover over me, which had a cuddly black dog stitched into it. I loved playing with him and fondling his ears. Going to the shops was a great game, too, especially when all the ladies in the street peered in at me and said, "Isn't she a sweet little girl!" I would laugh and sing, clap my hands, and keep them entertained until Grandma said we must be on our way, as time was getting on.

When I was just under two years old, I remember staying at Grandma Nelson's house and playing a much more dangerous game. My father had left some razor blades loose on the dressing table, and my cot had been put right up against the dressing table because our room wasn't very big. After Sunday dinner, my mother had put me in the cot for an afternoon nap, but I wasn't tired so looked around for something to play with.

'What are these shiny things on the table here?' I thought to myself. 'I wonder if I can get at them. Yes, this one is just about within my reach. ... Got it! ... Oh dear! What is this red stuff on my fingers, on my cover and on my petticoat? I don't like it very much. ... My fingers are hurting. I'm going to cry.'

"What is it Maggie; why are you crying? ... My goodness!

Whatever have you done?" my mother cried. "Oh no! A razor blade. Maggie, where did you find it?"

"There." I pointed to the other one still on the dressing table.

Soon we were in the bathroom. My mother was gently washing my hands and bandaging the tips of all my fingers and both my thumbs.

"Look, Mumsie, dollies," The bleeding stopped and I made my ten dollies dance. She then dressed me in clean underwear and put my Sunday dress back on again. The soiled garments were put in a bowl to soak and I was carried downstairs to the sitting room.

"What's happened to Maggie's fingers?" asked my father suspiciously when he saw my dollies. I couldn't understand why he was so angry, and why my mother was almost in tears. Grandpa and Grandma were visibly uneasy. Everything was suddenly all wrong, and I felt a tight little knot of fear in the pit of my stomach.

"Where did you leave your razor blades?"

"In my shaving bag, of course."

"No, you didn't!" "You left them on the dressing table, right by Maggie's cot."

"I'm sure I did *not*."

"Then how is it that she has cuts on both thumbs and all her fingers?"

"That's your problem; you're her mother!"

My mother didn't reply. I sensed a disturbing tension in the dismal room. I didn't like the way my grandfather was looking at my father. I thought Grandpa Nelson was going to punch him on the nose for the way he had spoken to my mother. And, somehow, I realised that it was all my fault; if only I hadn't touched those shiny things on the dressing table. Was that the reason my father stopped calling me his 'little ray of sunshine'?

~~

On the Thursday before I was to start school, my mother woke me up early. "You must get up quickly today, Maggie; we're going to Reading on the bus."

"I'm still tired; I don't want to get up yet," I protested in a grizzly voice. "Will Jimmy and Ann be coming with us?"

"No dear; Mrs Hurst will look after them both while we're away."

"Not Grandma?"

"Mrs Hurst loves children, but hers are grown-up now, and she misses them. She says she will play with Jimmy while Ann has her morning nap. Jimmy and Ann will be happier with Mrs Hurst. Now we must hurry. We've a lot to do in Reading, so I want to catch the half-past-nine bus."

My mother poured some water into the bowl on the washstand. "I want you to wash your hands and face, and dress yourself. Then come down to the kitchen and I'll do your hair. Now, don't dawdle."

"No, Mumsie; I'll try to be quick." I replied, as she went down the attic stairs.

People only slept in the attic bedroom in the spring and summer when the weather was warmer. In the winter, it was far too cold at the top of the house. I had never slept in the quaint little bedroom before, with its sloping walls and narrow ceiling. Behind my bed was a locked door, which led into the boarded storage area beyond. What was in there I didn't know; but I had heard scuffling noises similar to the ones you could hear in Grandpa's barn – rats and mice, no doubt. "I hope they stay there," I told myself nervously as I put on my clothes. "I don't want them biting my toes."

The previous evening, I had got out of bed again as soon as my mother had said prayers with me, kissed me goodnight and gone back downstairs to the kitchen. I stood on the chair gazing out of the tiny window, instead of going to sleep. It was still light and there was so much to see outside; the lengthening shadows creeping across the fields, birds flying home to their nests, and the cows slowly wending their way back from the milking sheds at Mr Brooker's farm. Why do the shadows look like big flat jelly-monsters? How do birds know when it's bedtime? Do cows go to sleep sitting up? Will my teacher tell me the answers, when I go to school?

"Maggie, are you ready yet? You're not daydreaming again, are you?" called my mother from the big bedroom below.

"Yes, Mumsie."

During breakfast I was thinking of some other questions which had been troubling me: Why does Grandma Goodchild always shoo me away? Why does Grandpa Goodchild always do what *she* says? Why is Mumsie a teeny-weenie bit scared of Grandma Goodchild, and not my other grandma? Why can't Grandma Goodchild be *nice*? ... Why do grown-ups say one thing and mean something quite different? Maybe I could ask Mumsie while we're on the bus.

"Hurry up with your porridge, Maggie, or we'll miss the bus. I'm just going to take the babies down to Mrs Hurst's. While I'm gone, do what you have to do up the garden, and don't forget to put the lid on properly after you. We don't want any more trouble with the flies."

It was a long walk over the fields to the bus-stop. I didn't like hurrying as there was so much to see; the people working in the fields on Mr Brooker's farm, the bluebells making a big blue rug in the wood, some rabbits playing on the hillocks, and the cows grazing in the long meadow.

"You must keep walking, Maggie. We can look at everything when we come back. We *must* catch the next bus, we have a lot of things to buy for school next week."

"Do I have to have special clothes for school, Mumsie?"

"You need new shoes and a raincoat; and I ought to get you a school frock and cardigan. We'll see what we can find in Jackson's and the Co-op."

At last, puffing and panting, we reached the gate at the top of the second field. The first field was downhill, but the second had been a steep, uphill climb. After that we were on level ground. We joined the lane from Dunsden and Playhatch, crossed the road to Nettlebed, and walked up the lane to Kennylands Road. As we approached the bus-stop, the red Thames Valley bus was coming round the corner.

"Can we sit at the front, Mumsie? I want to see where we're going."

"Yes, I think the front seat's empty."

Once we were on the bus and the conductor had taken our fares, I thought about the questions I was going to ask my mother but, somehow, I couldn't find the right words. "Maybe Mumsie wants to forget about Grandma Goodchild," I said to myself, as I watched the road stretch out like a huge snake in front of me.

"Now, Maggie, we don't often go to Reading, especially just the two of us. So, if you're good, and we get the shopping done quickly, we'll go to Marks and Spencer's and have an ice-cream sundae. You'd like that, wouldn't you?"

"Yes, I like ice-cream, but *not* when I spill it."

"We'll sit at a table in the restaurant, so you won't spill it," smiled my mother.

We bought all my school things at Jackson's: a sturdy pair of black bar-shoes (I didn't want lace-ups in case the laces came undone), a navy raincoat which the shop assistant said I would grow into, a red gingham frock which would need to be taken up three inches, and a navy cardigan with sleeves which had to be rolled up at the cuffs. When the shop assistant had written out the bill, my mother opened her handbag to find her purse and her clothing-coupon book. The lady cut the right number of coupons from the book then placed them, with the money and the bill, into a special container, which she fed into a large cylindrical pipe on the wall behind her. There was a loud ping, which made me jump, as she sent it off to the cashier's office upstairs. We waited a few minutes then there was another ping, and a rattle, as the container came flying back with the change and the word 'paid' rubber-stamped on the bill. I found out sixty years later that this system was called a pneumatic system because it was operated by compressed air.

My mother had a few other shops she wanted to visit. One of them was Baylis's, where they had the same kind of containers for the money as at Jackson's, but, instead of the money going up a pipe, the shop assistants pulled a spring-loaded cord. This launched the cylindrical money containers onto special wires and sent them shooting noisily across these wires to the cashiers in the corner. This system was called a gravity system. Baylis's sold food items, not clothes. The customers bought all their provisions at one counter, and it was the shop assistants' job to walk around the store, collecting the various items on their customers' lists from the different shelves and displays. My mother bought some margarine and bacon. I was fascinated by the bacon slicer, but fearful that the man in the white overall might chop off one of his fingers by mistake.

Then, at last, it was time for Marks and Spencer's and the ice-cream sundae. I chose a peach melba and my mother had a banana split. My mother cut mine up for me with the spoon.

"Mumsie, why do they call it a 'Sunday' when it's Thursday?"

I asked with a mystified expression on my face.

" A *sundae* is a dish of ice-cream, with nuts, ordinary cream, and fruit on top. You don't write it like the 'Sunday' in 'Sunday school'."

"Will I learn to write it at school? Daddy showed me how to write my name. ... He says they will call me 'Margaret', not 'Maggie'."

"Only in the classroom. Your new friends will still call you Maggie."

Chapter 3

"Wake up, Maggie. It's time to get up," called my mother, as she climbed the attic stairs.

"I'm up already, *and* I've washed my hands and face."

"Here's your new frock. Let me help you on with it. I'll do your hair downstairs."

"Did you take the hem up, like you said?"

"Yes. It's still a bit long, though, but it'll have to do."

I was going to school at last; that magical place, where lively young teachers inspired their pupils and made sure that there was always something interesting for them to do. I was so excited that I had woken up while it was still dark.

My mother wasn't excited, though, she seemed a bit anxious. Perhaps she was going to miss me being at home to help her with things. Then I realised that we were *all* going to the school. Mrs

Hurst couldn't look after Jimmy and Ann, as she was catching the nine o'clock bus to Reading. Jimmy was delaying proceedings by complaining at being prepared for an outing so early in the morning.

"No, no, no!" he shouted. "Sleep. Want sleep."

"You're going in the pram, with Ann. Come on Jimmy; be a good boy," I coaxed.

"No! No-o! No-oo! No-oo. No-ooo." The shouts gradually turned into resigned little whimpers. I gave him a rusk to nibble.

Ann was taking a long time over her feed. In desperation, my mother took the bottle away from her, hurriedly changed her nappy and laid her down in the pram. She wrapped the bottle in a tea-towel and tucked it in between the covers. Then she dressed the disgruntled Jimmy. Finally, well after eight o'clock, the planned time of departure, they were both in the pram, Jimmy at the foot, propped up by cushions, and Ann fast asleep under the hood.

The three-mile trek from Crowsley to the village hall in Wood Lane, Sonning Common, where the infants' class met, was only over level ground for the first mile. For the rest it was a slow uphill climb, followed by a steep downhill slither where the pram tried to run away by itself, and uphill again to the school gate.

"I can't walk fast like you, Mumsie," I moaned. "My shoes are pinching me."

"You'll soon get used to them. You must keep up; we're going to be late."

The main school buildings were in Grove Road, but you had to be seven-and-a-half before you could go up to the Big School. The previous July we had been to see the headmaster, Mr Ford, in his dingy office opposite the classroom used by the Standard Seven pupils.

"Why are those big people in that room?" I queried as I gazed through the open door. "They should be at work."

"They'll be leaving school soon; then they will get jobs and go to work."

My mother knocked on the door marked 'Headmaster' and Mr Ford had come and ushered us inside. He was a small man with horn-rimmed glasses, a moustache and balding grey hair, dressed in a tired grey suit with an uninspiring grey tie. His secretary was also in the office, pounding away on a clattering typewriter. She was dark-haired and wore a crisp white blouse with a tartan skirt; she would have been pretty if it wasn't for the frosty, don't-disturb-me expression on her well-made-up face.

"We can't take your daughter until the term after her fifth birthday," Mr Ford had carefully explained. "We have so many infants that Mrs Claxton has over sixty children in the village hall. To keep numbers down, we take them in at five and move the bright ones up here when they are seven. It's the only way we can cope. We heard last week that we may be getting evacuees here at Sonning Common. I said, 'No,' unless they can provide teachers for them."

"So," my mother had concluded, "you can't take Maggie until the summer term."

"That's right; but we *can* put her name down now. Miss Brown, will you take the particulars?"

School began at nine o'clock. *We* didn't arrive until twenty past nine. "We're late, Maggie," sighed my mother.

"Mrs Claxton won't mind, Mumsie; she knows it's a long way, doesn't she?" I confidently predicted, but I had yet to meet my teacher.

Mrs Claxton had a reputation for being difficult, and my mother didn't want to start off on the wrong foot by upsetting her, especially the first day. She also knew that Mrs Claxton liked to pry into other people's lives and secrets, and wasn't above passing this information on to others.

In my dreams, teachers always smiled at me, so it hadn't even occurred to me that I might find Mrs Claxton rather intimidating. Mrs Claxton was neither young nor lively, but a short, stocky woman in her early 50s. Her steely grey hair was cropped very short, especially at the back where she had had it shaved like a man's. For most of the year she wore a knitted cardigan, checked blouse, and flannel skirt, all in unexciting shades of grey.

My mother parked the pram and its sleeping occupants beside the corrugated iron building, and we made for the front entrance.

As Mumsie gingerly opened the heavy wooden door, the hinges squeaked ominously, so she pushed me inside while she hastened to shut it as quietly as she could. I stared in disbelief at the scene in front of me, fixing my eyes on the endless rows of silent children, crouched awkwardly over their books and wedged into ill-fitting, double desks. No-one was moving but, as I stared, sixty bodies turned slightly, and sixty pairs of eyes looked up and stared blankly back at me. Behind them all, at the far end, was a large empty platform, instantly reminding me of a dark gaping hole.

"Get on with your work, children," came a strange voice from somewhere above me. It wasn't a friendly voice.

Then I saw its owner. There was Mrs Claxton, ensconced at her tall desk, several feet above contradiction. From this lofty throne, she was now glaring down at *us* as we approached her. I did *not* like what I saw. Her overall greyness and imposing girth, solidly perched above the ugly wooden desk, reminded me of an ancient tree trunk that had been killed by lightning.

Maybe, if I said something, she might smile at me? So I lifted my head up high and smiled innocently at this well-built matriarch, with her cold grey eyes and thin lips held firmly together in an expression of exasperation.

"I like this school. I want to be a teacher when I grow up," I confided cheerfully. This piece of information was not received at all well. What have I done? Why doesn't she smile back?

"What is the purpose of this interruption?" Mrs Claxton asked icily. "School started twenty minutes ago. Who is this insolent child? Doesn't she know when to keep her mouth shut?"

"Her name is Margaret Goodchild. She has just had her fifth birthday and Mr Ford said she was to start school today," answered my mother quietly. I was left pondering what 'insolent' meant. By the furious expression on Mrs Claxton's face, it must be something bad, but I had only intended to be friendly.

"Then why didn't you bring her at the right time?" she demanded accusingly. Her flat face was now becoming red and puckered like a squashed tomato, but I had the sense not to divulge my thoughts.

Just then, before my mother had any time to defend herself, the sound of crying echoed through the wall, right behind Mrs Claxton.

"Whatever is that dreadful noise?" she fumed.

Ann had woken up and wanted her bottle. She wanted it now, not in five minutes time. She began to rock the pram with her usual screaming and kicking routine, waking the more docile Jimmy. He let out a prolonged wail and didn't know when to stop. My poor mother was flustered and didn't know what to say. The noise from the pram was so pervasive that it was hard to concentrate on anything. Mrs Claxton's face was livid. She had had no babies of her own, and she had no patience with mothers who, in her opinion, had too many of them.

"Those are my babies out there," my mother stammered at length. "I'm leaving Maggie here. She has her lunch and I'll be back for her at three-thirty." With that, she fled, leaving me to the tender mercies of Fanny Claxton.

⟋

"You'd better come and sit down, Margaret, before you waste any more of my time. Sheila, will you show Margaret where to put her coat?"

"Yes, Mrs Claxton," answered Sheila Evans in a sing-song voice. I meekly followed the self-assured Sheila into the cloakroom, through a door to the left of the platform; she soon found me a peg on the bottom row, right in the corner. All the other pegs seemed to have names beside them.

"Mrs Claxton will put your name here later," announced Sheila. "We always come in and go out of *that* door," she continued, pointing to a second door at right angles to the one we had just passed through. The door led straight out of the cloakroom towards the place where, a few minutes earlier, the pram had been. "Mrs Claxton doesn't like people using the front door, except Mr Ford and the milkman."

"The milkman? What does *he* come to school for?"

"To bring our milk, silly!" I was beginning to dislike Miss Stuck-up Sheila already. "We have milk before we go out to play," she explained condescendingly. "Did you bring your mug?"

"No. We didn't know we had to have a mug."

"You'd better hurry now; Mrs Claxton's very strict."

When I re-emerged from the cloakroom, Mrs Claxton frowned and said in an unkind voice, "You took your time, Margaret

Goodchild. I hope you aren't going to be a nuisance." I didn't like the way she said the word 'nuisance'. "Now go and sit down over there," she said, dismissing me and indicating an empty place over by the front door, next to a boy wearing an ugly pair of wire-framed glasses. On the desk she had already placed a small piece of slate in a wooden frame and some coloured chalks. "You can draw a picture for me on that slate." So I looked around me and tried to draw some of the children sitting at their desks. I had to make them very small, though; I could have done with a bigger slate.

I had almost finished my picture when there was an almighty clatter outside. The sudden noise behind me made me jump. The door was then opened and a big, beefy man in a dark overall trundled into the room, with a large milk churn on a two-wheeled, metal trolley. He lifted the churn onto a low table in front of Mrs Claxton's towering desk. As he did so, a lady in an apron, with a headscarf over her straggly hair, suddenly appeared from another door directly opposite the cloakroom, to the right of the platform. She had come from a small kitchen, armed with a large metal tray, a blue and white striped jug, and a couple of measuring cups with long handles: one for a pint, and the other for a gill, just a quarter of a pint. The milkman departed with a silent wave of the hand to Mrs Claxton, and the headscarf lady came forward to open the churn. She carefully put the lid upside down on the table, and poured a pint of milk into the jug.

As she was taking the jug of milk to the kitchen, Mrs Claxton looked at the children in the row nearest the platform. Without a word, they dived under their desk lids, pulling out their mugs from the ledge underneath. They then lined up in front of the table, and Mrs Claxton started ladling out the milk, one gill per pupil. She was serving the third row of children when the headscarf lady returned with a steaming mug of coffee in her hand.

"Thank you, Mrs Larby, I'm ready for that," murmured Mrs Claxton gratefully. "You take over here. Oh! There's a new girl who hasn't brought a mug, could you fetch one for her?"

I was one of the last to go up to collect my milk. While I was drinking the refreshing liquid, the other children were hurrying out into the playground, Mrs Claxton was finishing her coffee, and Mrs Larby was loading the dirty mugs onto the tray. She then came over to me to collect the empty mug. "Please, where is the lavatory?" I whispered. "I want to go."

"It's round the back. If you come with me to the kitchen, I'll show you where to go," said Mrs Larby in a gentle voice. "You'll soon get used to school. My Alice started at the Big School today; she's seven. If you like, you can have *her* mug. It has a black pussy on it. Here it is," she said, taking it out of a cupboard.

"Thank you. I like pussies. How do I put my name on it?"

"If you tell me your name, I can write a label and tie it on the handle for you."

"It's Margaret Goodchild."

"When I've washed up the mugs, I'll put yours on the tray with the others, and you can collect it and put it in your desk. Now, I'll take you to the lavatory."

By the time I had done what I needed to do, Mrs Claxton was ringing the bell, signalling the end of playtime, and that kind Mrs Larby had disappeared. We all lined up and walked back into school, Mrs Claxton chivvying us along with words of admonition: "No talking, Billy White, do you hear me? Stop pushing, Andrew Baker, you little ruffian. Come along, Margaret Goodchild, stop wool-gathering, we haven't got all day!" I wondered what 'wool-gathering' meant, and if Mrs Claxton ever said nice things to children like, "That's a good picture, Margaret!"

Back in the classroom I found, to my dismay, that Mrs Claxton had taken my almost-finished masterpiece away already; so I couldn't finish it and she would never tell me what she thought of it. On the desk, in its place, was a tray of brightly-coloured beads and a string with a knot on the end. The other children sitting around me had similar trays on their desks, so I watched them to learn exactly what I had to do. They bent down, and untied bead strings, similar to mine, from the top of the iron legs at the front of their desks. They then began to make completely random patterns with the beads. I tried to make patterns in ones, twos, threes, fours, but soon ran out of beads of the right colours to continue the patterns much beyond six. I found out later that Mrs Claxton always put out the bead trays when she wanted to do something else, such as teach the older children, or add up the attendance register totals before Miss Brown, the school secretary, came to collect the registers on a Friday afternoon. She had two registers, one for the first year children and one for those who would be going up to the Big School the following year.

One Friday morning, a little later in the term, I sat down at my desk to discover that my bead string was missing. It was not hanging from its allotted place at the side of my desk. By then, I knew that this bead-stringing exercise was actually supposed to help us learn to count up to a hundred, but I couldn't do anything without a bead string, could I? So, I waited for the lunch hour and, while Mrs Claxton was talking to a visitor in the playground, I secretly crept into the classroom and pinched Jimmy Saunders' bead string. He hadn't tied it on very securely anyway! I quickly fastened it to my desk and tiptoed out again. Fortunately for me, no-one saw me.

However, safely hidden among the other children in the playground, I did know that I had broken the eighth Commandment: 'Thou shalt not steal'. I would confess my sin to God later, when I was in bed, after prayer time with my father. He wasn't perfect himself, so he didn't have to know about *all* my sins, only some of them. It's such a pity there's no commandment for parents which says, 'Thou shalt not lose thy temper, and beat thy children with a stick,' to go alongside the fifth commandment, 'Honour thy father and thy mother'. We, children, could honour our father; and our father could then throw away his stick.

That afternoon, right on cue, Jimmy Saunders put his hand up, as I knew he would. Mrs Claxton looked up from the registers, saying, "What is it, Jimmy?" in a much more pleasant voice than was her wont.

"Please Miss, my bead string's gone," announced Jimmy almost in tears. I held my breath. What was going to happen now? Could I be found out?

"Here, have this one," answered Mrs Claxton, holding out a brand new bead string, and the grateful boy went up to take it from her. Would she have treated *me* like that if he had taken *my* bead string? I didn't think so; Fanny Claxton definitely had her favourites, and I wasn't one of them. Come to think of it, who *had* taken my bead string in the first place?

I hadn't been at school many weeks before I realised that some games children played were neither pleasant nor fair. One afternoon, I was running around in the playground when I accidentally knocked Jean Crocker's arm. I said, "Sorry, Jean; I didn't mean to." But, Jean, being rather averse to pain in any form, immediately began to bleat like a stricken lamb. She was a well-known cry-baby and one of Fanny Claxton's special 'pets'. Mrs Claxton was friendly with Jean's mother, Julia Crocker, and so was Sheila Evans' mother, Gloria.

Sheila came straight over to see what was wrong with Jean, and to offer her assistance. She wasn't only a monitor, but also another of Fanny's pets. She enjoyed special privileges, one being the power to tell tales about other children with the guarantee that she would always be heard. Nasty Sheila would freely report what anyone said about another child, without first finding out whether the accusation was true or false. Unlike most of us, she wasn't a bit afraid of Mrs Claxton, nor of the retribution meted out to people who tell tales, as described in the rhyme:

'Tell tale tit, your tongue will be split.
And all the little puppy dogs shall have a little bit'.

Sheila rushed into school, rudely disturbing Mrs Claxton's tranquillity with the information that Margaret Goodchild had slapped Jean Crocker on the arm. Without coming out to the playground to check up on the story, the lazy, biased teacher told Sheila to bring me to her at once. As Sheila triumphantly dragged me into the building, I knew I was going to be smacked. I wasn't even given a chance to explain what had happened. Mrs Claxton simply rolled up my right sleeve and gave me six hard whacks on my bare arm, saying, "This is what happens, Margaret Goodchild, to naughty children who hurt others." She seemed to enjoy administering the corporal punishment. I was determined not to cry, though, not with Sheila Evans standing there to gloat over me. But I was convinced that it hurt ten times more than the knock I accidentally gave Jean Crocker. So much for the joys of playing with children of my own age!

My mother was finding the journey to school and back exhausting, especially on days when she had to bring Jimmy and Ann on one of the trips, and couldn't use her bicycle. By June, the doctor had confirmed that she was pregnant, and also that she was possibly carrying twins, though he was not absolutely sure he was hearing two heartbeats. She was worried about having more children to care for, especially as she knew John would have to join the forces in the next few months, even though he hadn't been graded 'A1' in his medical.

The doctor strongly advised my mother against trying to ride up the hills, as she had been doing. So, even with me on the back for most of the way, there were several times when we both had to get off and walk because of the gradient. Yet she was reluctant to make me do the journey on my own, and it wasn't just the distance. She didn't trust the Maloney boys to leave me alone.

The Maloneys, a wild Irish family, had recently moved into one of the newer houses in Crowsley. Two of the boys were pupils at Sonning Common Council School, one in Standard Two and the other in Standard Three (or Years Four and Five as they are called today). There were three older Maloneys who were casual labourers on local farms. Since the Maloneys' arrival, our neighbours scattered around the hamlet had had things stolen, and we had lost most of the rusty old metal objects that Grandpa Goodchild had been saving for scrap. They had been lying in a heap behind the barn, waiting to be collected by G.R. Jackson's of Chatham Street, Reading, who were loading up lorries with scrap metal for the war effort. Grandpa Goodchild once caught Patrick Maloney, the eldest, red-handed as he was trying to get through the barbed wire behind the barn. My mother was wise in not trusting those boys. Everyone knew they were up to no good.

I was also finding the school day exhausting, in spite of a half-hour's rest, heads down on our desks, at the beginning of afternoon school. I was becoming bored out of my mind with slates and bead strings. With sixty children in the class, Mrs Claxton just left us younger children to our play, while she concentrated on the older ones who would soon be moving up to the Big School. So, I was trying to follow the lessons the others were learning, even though the blackboard and teaching charts were so far away from my desk.

Mrs Claxton was teaching the alphabet in a different way to the way my father had taught me, by the sounds of the letters, rather than by their names. So it was, "a for apple, b for bat, c for cat ..." that everyone was chanting, but the sounds didn't work properly for the first *a* and *r* of my name *Margaret*: *ar* doesn't sound a bit like the a in **apple** followed by the r in **rat**, so I was confused.

On the way home one Tuesday afternoon, while we were pushing the bike up the hill towards the pond, my mother explained to me that the letter A had more than one sound: a in **apple** and **rat**, and a: in the beginning of my name *Mar-* and in the word *mar* meaning 'to spoil'.

"In *Mar-* the r doesn't have a sound at all," she continued. "But it does in the last part of your name; there, all the letters *g, a, r, e, t*, sound exactly as Mrs Claxton is teaching you."

"**G** for **goat**, a for **apple**, r for **rat**, **e** for **egg**, and **t** for **top**," I chanted happily. "*M-a-r-g-a-r-e-t* spells *Margaret*. Mumsie, I wish you were my teacher," I added wistfully.

"I wanted to be a teacher, and I passed the scholarship exam; but Grandpa Nelson couldn't pay the fees."

"What are fees?"

"Parents had to pay for their children to go to the grammar school, unless they were poor. We were poor, but my uncle George was rich; so the school board thought we were rich too. Your grandpa wouldn't do anything about it because I was only a girl. Uncle Ben didn't even *pass* the exam, but your grandpa paid for him to go to a good school, while I had to stay at the elementary school until I was fourteen."

"That wasn't fair," I protested.

"Anyway, when it came to the civil service exams I took after I left school, I did a lot better than the girls I knew who went up to the grammar school. So there you are! Let's get on the bike now." That was the last time I went home on the bike with my mother, at three-thirty.

The following morning, I woke up feeling very tired and could hardly keep my eyes open, so my mother came upstairs to help me get washed and dressed. While she took the babies down to Mrs Hurst's, I tried to eat my Sunnybisk, but I didn't feel hungry. When my mother came back, it was time to go to school. She helped me onto my little seat at the back of the bike, and we set off. I must have gone to sleep during the ride because I remembered nothing about the journey, not even walking up the steep bit after Blackmore Lane.

After dropping me off at the school gate, my mother planned to buy some groceries at Kirbys' Stores, which was right next to the village hall.

"Have you got the ration books, Mumsie?" I asked, as I waved goodbye.

"Of course, Maggie. I keep them in my handbag all the time."

There was a long queue outside Kirbys' that morning, and my mother had to wait in line for over an hour in the hot sun.

Meanwhile, I was sitting at my desk with a larger than usual piece of paper and a new box of wax crayons. A visitor was coming that afternoon, and Mrs Claxton wanted some bright new pictures for the wall. Normally, I would have been overjoyed at being allowed to draw a picture that would go up on the wall, but today I only wanted to sleep. "I must draw the picture," I kept saying to myself as I started to draw some children playing tag, a game where one child chases the rest of the group until he touches one of them; then that child does the chasing, and so on. I put the last child in her place at the edge of the paper and then dropped my head on top of it all as I fell into a deep sleep.

It was the milkman who first noticed me. That particular day, it was Mr King himself, the owner of the dairy, who delivered our school milk. He was a pleasant man and knew my parents, as he and his wife were friendly with Grandpa Goodchild, as well as being our milk supplier at Crowsley.

"Mrs Claxton, there's a little girl here who doesn't look too well. It's Maggie Goodchild, and I've just seen her mother going into Kirbys'. Shall I go and fetch her for you, before she cycles back to Crowsley?"

"How do you *know* Margaret's not well? She may just be being naughty," answered Mrs Claxton haughtily. "She's gone to sleep over her work, that's all," she continued, as she came over and prodded me roughly in the back. I opened my eyes, but didn't understand what was going on at all. Mrs Claxton's solid grey form was just a blur, as she removed my picture and the tin of crayons from the desk.

"That child's ill," persisted Mr King. "I'm going to look for her mother. I'm just off to Crowsley in the van, so I'll take them both with me."

"Just as you wish," answered Mrs Claxton noncommittally.

Mr King caught my mother as she was carrying the shopping to her bicycle, parked under the shop window. He carried her shopping to his van while she wheeled the bike, which fitted in neatly beside the crates of milk bottles. Then my mother came into school to collect me. Mrs Claxton watched our departure with frowning displeasure. I sat on a cushion, placed between my mother's seat and Mr King's, but I remembered little of what happened after that.

Dr Prince was called, and his diagnosis was 'nervous exhaustion'. "Just let her sleep. Don't bother to wake her up for meals. When she's slept it off, she'll feel better and may want to eat. But do make sure she has enough to drink. I'll come back again in two days' time."

I was wide awake when Dr Prince came again on the Friday afternoon. He smiled at me as he examined me thoroughly and prescribed a tonic. "Has she been having her cod liver oil and malt and her orange juice every day?" he asked.

"With three children, it isn't always easy to get to the clinic every fortnight, so we sometimes run out," my mother replied.

"In that case, I'll write you a note so that you can collect a month's supply at a time for the family. You should also be taking some for yourself, now you're pregnant. As for this little lady, let her do mornings only until the end of term. Then after the summer holidays, she can go back to school full-time. I'll write a note for her teacher. What's her teacher's name?"

"Mrs Claxton."

"Oh! Frances Claxton, or Smith, as she was when I first knew her. I don't know how she got the job teaching infants; she's not even a fully-qualified teacher. She did a few months at college and then gave up. But it's wartime and there aren't enough qualified staff to go around, more's the pity. I've heard many parents complain that she doesn't really understand the needs of small children."

"She hits us sometimes when we haven't done anything wrong," I chimed in.

"I think I've said enough," laughed the doctor. "I don't think there's much wrong with your daughter's intelligence. I'll have to be careful what I say in future."

Downstairs, he looked at my mother gravely. "I'm a bit worried about you, though. You're doing too much. I don't want you to miscarry. Isn't there someone else who could take Maggie to school for you?"

"No. There are some older boys, but I don't trust them. The whole family's causing trouble for us here in Crowsley."

"Could she manage the journey home on her own?"

"Yes, that's an idea; especially now she's only doing half days."

The following Monday I was going back to school, but I was coming home at twelve o'clock instead of three-thirty. I remembered that bit; what I didn't remember was that my mother had told me I would have to come home on my own. The Maloney boys would be no threat to me at that time of day; so as long as I watched out for cars, and there weren't many of those about anyway, I should be safe enough.

"Listen, Maggie, once more. Mumsie isn't coming for you today; you must come home on your own. You know the way, don't you?"

"Yes, I can remember it."

At twelve o'clock I left the school building with the children who were going to the Big School for school dinners with Mrs Larby and another lady. But I didn't go home. I had forgotten that my mother wasn't coming for me. So, I stood waiting outside the school gate.

Mr and Mrs King lived almost opposite the village hall. Mr King saw me standing there when he came home in his van at ten past twelve.

"Are you waiting for your mother, Maggie?"

"Yes, she's late today."

"Are you *sure* she's coming for you? It's not like her to be late." But I still didn't remember.

At half past twelve, Mr King came over the road and said, "You'd better come in and wait for your mother in our house. Mrs King will give you something to eat. Your parents don't have a telephone, do they?"

"No, but Mrs Hurst does; but I don't know the number."

"We'll look it up in the book."

Mrs King talked to Mrs Hurst, and Mrs Hurst walked up the lane to see my mother. As Mumsie wasn't expecting me until a quarter to one, she hadn't been worrying about my whereabouts; but she was very displeased with me when she heard about my forgetfulness, and the trouble it had caused to Mrs Hurst and the Kings.

"Tell her to hurry up and come home," she instructed Mrs

Hurst. "And please thank the Kings for me, for all their kindness. I'm so sorry for all the trouble this has been to you."

"It's no trouble at all. Now don't try to pay me for the telephone call," she insisted. "I won't take it, and, remember, I'm happy to have Jimmy and Ann anytime to give you a rest." Mrs Hurst's words, spoken cheerfully in her homely Oxfordshire accent, had a calming effect on my mother. "Don't be too hard on Maggie; she's probably still not quite herself after last week."

"You're probably right. She's not normally that forgetful; a bit of a dream sometimes, maybe."

Chapter 4

It was soon after I started on half days that the evacuees came to Sonning Common. Mrs Claxton was not happy when Mr Ford arrived one Friday morning to say that she would have another twenty-five children in her infants department the following week, and they would be coming with their own teacher.

"There isn't any room for them in here," she protested. "I have enough on my hands as it is, without taking on any Cockney brats and their inexperienced young teacher."

"You have no choice, Mrs Claxton. For your information, their teacher, Miss Barnes, is well-qualified with eight years of experience, and has excellent references." Fanny Claxton could not fail to detect his veiled reference to her own lack of paper qualifications. Her plain face reddened in anger and embarrassment.

"So, where do you propose to put this extra class?"

"They can use the stage; Mr Rogers will be bringing in some tables and chairs, a blackboard, and bookcases and shelves this afternoon. He'll also have to check out the lighting."

"What about books and art materials?"

"Let me see what you have in the store cupboard." He opened the cupboard, and surveyed the well-stocked shelves. "Yes, you've plenty of stock; let them have what they need from here for the time being." Mrs Claxton was not happy about sharing her resources.

I was disappointed that I wouldn't be there to see the new classroom being set up. I would miss all the furniture shifting from the removal van to the platform. Mrs Claxton took the easy way-out, giving everyone an extended playtime while Mr Rogers and his assistants carried out their disruptive activities.

The evacuee class assembled at the Big School on the following Monday morning so that Miss Brown could take all their particulars. Mr Ford then escorted Miss Barnes and her motley crew through the alleyway between Grove Road and Wood Lane, and introduced them to Mrs Claxton. By then it was almost ten o'clock.

Miss Shirley Barnes was young and beautiful, with curly blonde hair, laughing blue eyes, and a genuine concern for the children entrusted to her. She was also an excellent teacher and, unlike Mrs Claxton, well able to control her small class without resorting to threats or corporal punishment. She was not employed by the Oxfordshire County Council, but by the London Borough who had sent her to Sonning Common. She refused to be intimidated by the elderly matron and her dubious methods of controlling children.

"Cor, lucky things, fancy having a teacher like that," gasped Andrew Baker, within Mrs Claxton's hearing.

"You'd better watch your tongue, Andrew Baker, or you'll get a clip round the ear," spat Fanny Claxton.

Ridicule was another of the weapons Fanny used to subdue her charges. It was probably the one I feared the most. It was so unkind. During my first year with Mrs Claxton, I missed over six months of schooling through illness. When I returned to school in the summer of 1942, most of the evacuees had gone or they had been absorbed into the regular school population, and Shirley Barnes had returned to London. Mrs Claxton was in sole charge once more.

I had so much catching up to do; my father was in the army and my mother now had baby Gracie, so I had to do it on my own. I had never really learned to read Mrs Claxton's way; I hadn't got the hang of all the sounds. Today she was working on u for **umbrella**. She gave us all flash cards and we had to line up and read our own flash card to her, one by one. I had '**n u t** is **nut**' but I didn't recognise the **u** sound when it came in the middle of the word.

"Maggie Goodchild, you're the oldest girl in the class and you don't know that!" boomed Mrs Claxton. "Say '**n u t** is **nut**'; and then say it again."

"**N u t** says **nut, n u t** says **nut**," I chanted mechanically. How was this going to help me learn to read properly? I wasn't the oldest girl in the class. There were some who were nearly seven. "I hate you Fanny Claxton," I muttered under my breath.

Grandpa Goodchild liked poems and rhymes, all sorts of rhymes, including rhymes he had made up himself. We were walking by Mr Brooker's pond watching the ducks when he suddenly asked me, "Maggie, do you know any school rhymes yet?"

"Yes, I know some nursery rhymes and skipping rhymes; then there's 'Tell tale tit ... '"

"What about this one then?
'Dunce dunce double D
Can't say his A B C.... '"

"What comes next Grandpa?"

"I can't remember now. It's a long time since I was at school."

"*How* long, Grandpa?"

"Now let me see. ... I left school when I was twelve, so it must be sixty-one years."

"You must be very old now. ... Grandpa, what's a dunce?"

"Someone who can't learn his lessons properly. When *we* were at school, teachers were often quite cruel to children like that, and made them stand in the corner wearing a pointed paper cap on their heads with a large D on it. D for dunce."

"I know my ABC, Grandpa: A B C D E F G ... U V W X Y Z. But at school we give the letters different names: 'a for apple' and all that ...and 'n for nut'; 'n u t says nut', instead of 'N U T spells nut'. Mumsie calls what we learn at school 'phonics': 'Fanny's funny phonics'; that's a kind of rhyme, isn't it? They're all f sounds!"

"So they are," laughed my grandfather.

I had learnt that the word 'nut' had other meanings besides referring to the hazel nuts in the hedgerows that I liked to eat in the autumn. So I made up my own little rhyme about them:

'Fanny Claxton has a grey nut.
When she's cross she does her nut.
Fanny Claxton *is* a crazy nut —
Nutty Fanny Claxton.'

I sang it to my grandfather, and I sang it in the school playground as I marched or skipped. Other children were soon singing it too. It goes to 'Bobby Shaftoe'. We could sing it out loud now, since Sheila Evans had gone up to the Juniors. She was no longer around to tell on us.

~

One wet Saturday, my grandfather read me a hilarious story about some pigs from a book about farming. He had to explain some of the words to me first so that I could enjoy it too. It was called, 'The Charge of the Sow Brigade'. Sows are the mother pigs.

The Charge of the Sow Brigade
(A Pig-Keeper's Tale)

Once I had twelve sows and gilts, all in pig at the time. Now my sows were grazing over a wide area, some of them foraging about a furlong apart, just quietly munching and minding their own business.

We heard the baying of a pack of hounds in the lane. The local South Oxfordshire hunt was coming this way. So I went out to watch. Hounds came over the steep bank and into the field, trying to unravel the scent.

Boudicca, the rightful doyenne of my little herd, pricked up her ears and stood guard over the field, her eyes peeled. The other sows stopped their grazing and looked about too. Things were not as they should be. Strange sounds were in the air.

Like silly sheep, the rest of the pack started streaming after their comrades. Whimpering and howling, they dashed down the field parallel to the drove from which they came. This was too much for Boudicca. It was time to act.

Her first questioning grunts which had alerted the herd now changed to a savage, bloodcurdling shriek. Believe me, it was chilling in its fury and intensity. It was quickly taken up by all the other sows.

They began to close rapidly on their chieftainess. Ranged almost shoulder to shoulder, together they charged at the surprised intruders. I've never seen the like. That brigade of sows charged for nearly a hundred yards!

In spite of the scent, those fifty odd hounds went berserk, scrambling and scratching with utter humiliation through the brambles and holly bushes that topped the bank. Incredible! My own sows routing the local hunt!

June 1941

"John, come quick! I need your help," shouted Albert Goodchild, thumping on the kitchen window. It was seven o'clock on a Sunday morning, and the rest of the family were still upstairs; but Albert could see John at the sink and it looked as if he had just cut himself shaving.

"Hang on a bit, Father," responded John, grabbing the kitchen towel with his left hand and dabbing his bleeding chin. Finally, with his right hand, he managed to open the window. He was left-handed and that window was always stiff. "What's happened then?" asked John apprehensively.

"It's your mother. She's very poorly this morning," answered the distraught Albert. "She's not responding at all, and I don't know what to do with her."

John's heart missed a beat. He had been concerned about his mother for several days. She had somehow lost the will to keep going, even for Albert's sake. He followed his father in agonised silence.

Ruth Goodchild had been sleeping downstairs in the front room for the last three weeks. Today, she barely stirred as John walked in behind his father.

"How long has she been like this, Father?"

"Well, since yesterday. ... She didn't want anything to eat, just milk and water. ... She had some just before I turned in last night, but she left most of it. I had to finish it up myself. ... Then I found her like this, this morning."

"I'll go and fetch Dr Prince," said John quietly.

Dr Prince was out on another call when John Goodchild arrived on his doorstep half an hour later. His wife, Shirley, a peroxide blonde, in a shocking pink dressing gown, took the details and John returned homeward with a sad heart. He knew his mother was dying and believed that she would be going to a far better place, but he would miss her so much. She was the only one who really understood him.

"Oh goodness! I must let my brother David know immediately," he shouted to the wind, as the motorbike passed the Harpsden turn. "Perhaps, the Hursts would let me use their phone."

David Goodchild lived in Ruislip with his wife and five children, the youngest being unidentical twin girls who were two months older than me. David was the elder son and a big man like his father. He taught RE and Music in a Senior School in the Ruislip area, and was nicknamed 'Holy Joe'. Even before her final illness, David often came to see his mother at weekends. He slept peacefully in the little guest room at the front of the house, leaving the rest of his family to cope with the air-raids, and uncomfortable nights in their Anderson shelter without his fatherly presence. The guest room was dubbed 'Uncle David's room', and the bed was always made up with clean sheets ready for his next unannounced arrival.

Emily complained bitterly about these visits: "David comes ostensibly to check on his mother, but spends all his time with us, eating *our* meagre rations. He never thinks of bringing something with him when he comes; even his ration book would help." Emily often used long words like 'ostensibly'. She knew what they meant, but she was not sure that her husband did.

"Yes, I know, Emily, but he *is* my brother."

"But he's much better off than we are; and he's dreadfully greedy. We make the children eat the plain bread first, and then *he* scoffs the whole of our butter ration in one go. I'm sure Nellie doesn't let him get away with it at home. He wasn't even embarrassed that time I asked Maggie what she wanted and she piped up, 'I wanted *my* piece of brown bread and butter, but Uncle David's just eaten it.' He laughed as if it was a joke, and *you* felt obliged to scold her for impertinence. ... But really! It was *too* bad."

As John turned into the Crowsley lane, he was remembering these upsets over David's casual attitude to hospitality. He had to concede that David had always been a scrounger who blithely helped himself to other people's things, especially his brother's. "Oh dear! We're particularly short this weekend," he announced glumly to the cattle coming down the lane on the way to their pasture. "I'll have to see what Father can spare us from his cupboards, that's all."

David arrived just before tea.

"How was your journey?" asked Emily, knowing he would have something to complain about; he always did.

"Difficult," replied David. "You know, I had to wait for *three quarters of an hour* at Ealing Broadway, and then I just missed the bus out here, and had to wait another *half hour* at Reading Station for the next one. It simply isn't good enough!"

"There *is* a war on, you know!" retorted Emily.

David looked nonplussed for a second before adding, "But I'm here now, that's the main thing." Then his eyes brightened as he saw a pot of his dear mother's damson jam in the middle of the table, next to the rock cakes.

"I can see I'm st-still in time for tea," he stuttered with a self-conscious grimace. He had no idea why Emily found him insufferable.

On the dresser top, Emily had been cutting none-too-thin slices of bread and margarine; David hadn't seen those yet. There was no butter available this weekend.

"We'll go and see Mother first," suggested John quietly. "There's been little change during the day. She hasn't regained consciousness for more than a minute or two. The doctor came this morning and said it's only a matter of time. Her heart's very weak."

"Is it *just* her heart?"

"No, pneumonia's set in. She's been confined to bed for too long. Her lungs have become clogged up, she's too weak to cough up the infected stuff."

The two brothers walked silently into the sickroom. Their father was slumped in his favourite chair, snoring, and their mother was moaning amid the pillows. Outside, the evening shadows were slowly spreading across the front lawn. Albert woke up with a start, wondering how long his sons had been standing there, gazing down at him.

"Sorry! I think I must've dozed off," he spluttered. "How long have you been here, David?"

David pulled out the pocket watch his grandfather had given him. "I arrived about fifteen minutes ago, Father. I'm planning to stay the night. I'll just go upstairs with my case, if I may."

While David was upstairs, Ruth Goodchild slowly opened her eyes. She could dimly see her husband sitting in his armchair and her younger son on an upright chair at the foot of the bed. "How ... long ... have I ... been ... asleep?" she whispered slowly. Both men strained to catch her words.

"A long time," answered Albert. "All day, in fact. Would you like some milk and water, dear?"

"No, ... just ... cold ... water ... please," she articulated painfully, her throat parched. Albert fetched some water and held the glass to her thin dry lips. Most of it ran down her chin and onto her night-gown, but a few drops reached her aching throat. "That's all," she said with a little more vigour, just as David returned to the room.

"Oh Mother, you're awake?" smiled David, kneeling by the bed and taking her hand.

"David, will you do something for me?" she urged.

"Of course, Mother; what is it?"

"Say Psalm 23 for me."

David had a preacher's voice; it was rich and mellow. As he held her hand, he looked tenderly into her eyes and recited the Psalm just for her:

"'The LORD is my shepherd; I shall not want.

He maketh me to lie down in green pastures:

he leadeth me beside the still waters. ...'"

As he commenced the last verse, she gripped his hand more tightly:

"'Surely goodness and mercy shall follow me all the days of my life:

and I will dwell in the house of the LORD for ever.'"

"David, I'm going there now, to be with my Lord forever." As she said the word 'forever', she let go of his hand and closed her eyes with a contented smile on her world-weary face. David sat gazing at her for a few minutes before he realised exactly what had happened.

"That's it; Mother's gone," he said quietly. "'The LORD gave, and the LORD hath taken away; blessed be the name of the LORD.'"

"Then I'd better go and phone the doctor," said John briskly. "On the way out, I'll tell Emily what's happened. Then she can get the children settled before we have our tea." My father's way of coping with grief was to get on with what had to be done next. David's eyes lit up briefly at the word 'tea'. It was after six o'clock, and he had had an early lunch.

It wasn't until the following morning that my mother told me Grandma Goodchild had gone to be with Jesus, but I couldn't really imagine what happened when a person died. I'd seen dead animals, but they didn't have souls; they weren't like people who went to Heaven, were they? Did these people have their new bodies straightaway and simply fly up to Jesus with the clouds? I had no idea, then, about what happened to the old ones and my mother didn't think it the appropriate time to enlighten me. I didn't see the undertaker's vehicle arrive with the coffin, nor return to collect it for the funeral and, thankfully, I wasn't required to be present on that occasion. Mrs Hurst looked after all three of us while my parents went to the service at the Iron Room in Peppard, and then on to the interment at the cemetery attached to the Congregational Chapel in Blounts Court Road. I was nearly ten before I learnt the full truth about death and saw my first dead person, laid out on a bed with a sheet over him.

Jimmy and I were looking out of the kitchen window at Mrs Hurst's cottage as the mourners arrived at Tudor Cottage. There were so many aunts and uncles I had never seen before, all wearing black, and packed like sardines into a fleet of big black cars.

"Mrs Hurst, where are all those funny black people going?" I enquired.

"They're going to tea with Grandpa Goodchild, and your Mummy and Daddy. But *you're* having your tea here. I've got some animal biscuits, some doughnuts, and some cream buns for *our* tea."

"Oh goody! Goody-goody-goody!" Jimmy and I chorused in unison, jumping up and down on the red tiled floor. Ann woke up and started to yell. She wanted her rusk and warm milk.

"Maggie, can you feed Ann while I get our tea?"

"Yes, I know what to do, Mrs Hurst." Ann was really hungry and didn't spit any of the mush out as she often did, the mischievous little minx. "You're a good little girl today," I told her proudly. She gurgled and started to sing her own little tune at the top of her voice.

"She's a proper little song-bird, isn't she?" commented Mrs Hurst.

"A rather noisy one," I added.

Tea was such a jolly affair and we were all permitted to make our own contribution. Perhaps Mrs Hurst didn't know the saying that our parents and grandparents were fond of quoting at us: 'Children should be seen and not heard'. We were certainly being heard, and listened to with apparent delight!

Just as we were finishing our tea, Mr Hurst arrived home for his dinner. He had had a satisfying day at Shiplake tending his prize herd of Jersey cows, with their buff-coloured coats and big, soulful eyes. He was in a jovial and expansive frame of mind as he greeted his wife and gave her a quick peck on the cheek.

"What a merry party you're having here, Rita! It's just like the old days, when *our* kids were young." Then he turned to me and asked, with a twinkle in his eye, "So, what have *you* been doing this afternoon, Maggie?"

"Making pictures, and Jimmy's been playing with bricks."

"Let's see the pictures, then." I showed him my attempts at drawing Jimmy building a house.

"So this is Jimmy, is it?"

"Yes, can't you see his curls?" I answered, somewhat defensively.

One day, Jimmy would be losing those gorgeous golden curls and have a proper little-boy haircut. I remembered the large, framed photograph of Uncle David on Grandpa Goodchild's landing, which had been taken when he was two, or maybe three. The toddler had long ringlets and was dressed in a frock that looked something like one of my nighties. When I first saw the picture, I had mistaken him for a very pretty little girl! There was also a framed portrait of the whole family, taken a few years later. The boys both had reasonably short hair, but they wore clothes that were far too fancy, and light-coloured for a couple of *boys*. Grandma Goodchild looked quite attractive and sweet-tempered, with her fair hair softly framing her face. Grandpa stood straight and tall, beaming proudly into the lens of the camera.

"Here's your dinner, Ernie," called Rita Hurst. "I hope it's to your liking?"

"My dinners always are; and I'm certainly ready for this."

It seemed no time at all before our father was at the door to take us home. I had hardly heard the guests leave Tudor Cottage in their various vehicles; many to Reading to catch their trains; some to Sonning, Binfield Heath and Shiplake; and the rest to Sonning Common and Peppard. I was *far* too involved in what was going on inside Honeysuckle Cottage.

My father sat down briefly and told the Hursts about the funeral in his special Sunday voice. "There was a good turnout of local folk who came to pay their respects; the hall was packed out and some people were standing. The service was a triumphal affair, in spite of our sense of loss at her departure ...." My father wiped his eyes, and his voice faltered as he uttered the word 'departure'.

"Were there a lot of flowers?" asked Rita, quickly changing the subject. She wasn't used to the quaint old-fashioned language my father was using. The Hursts expected to hear it at the chapel, but not here in their own home. Rita was also embarrassed by his tears.

"No, just one family bouquet. ... Mother didn't want flowers. She wanted the money to go to the missionaries instead."

"Oh! I see," answered Ernie Hurst; but he couldn't really understand why someone would want a funeral without any flowers to brighten things up a bit.

"But there was one memorable thing about today's events," continued my father more brightly. "We all heard that, about the time my dear mother passed away, my cousin Eva gave birth to a beautiful baby girl; and she named her 'Ruth' after her grandmother." My father mopped his eyes again, and his faltering voice became a squeaky falsetto. "The Lord is so kind, ... he's taken one much loved person away, and ... and brought a dear little baby ... into the world ... to take her place, ... a precious, new, little life."

Late July 1941

I woke up with a start. "Whatever's that?" I asked my rag doll, Maisie, with the yellow pigtails. I could hear men's voices out in the fields and then a strange swishing sound. I jumped out of bed to see two men cutting the meadow grass with long curved blades on long handles. The men were scything the field in easy swinging movements, the grass falling at their feet as they worked. The hay-making was all behind that year after a very wet June and early July. Now it would soon be August, and Mr Brooker's men were making up for lost time. It promised to be a warm sunny day, just right for haymaking.

"Oh dear, I should be getting ready for school, not watching those two men," I told myself regretfully. "But why hasn't Mumsie come up to call me yet?" Then I remembered, there would be no more school until September. "Whoopee! No more Fanny Claxton for six whole weeks," I shouted, as I gleefully skipped around the tiny attic bedroom. I wanted to be out there with the men. I wouldn't get in their way; I'd just sit by the hedge and watch.

I heard my mother open the kitchen door, and I watched her walk across the grass to the clothes line with a bowl of clean clothes. She would be a few minutes hanging that lot on the line. My washing water was already in my basin, and my old yellow dress, now sleeveless, was lying on the chair with my undies; so why not wash and get dressed anyway?

"Mumsie, can I go and watch the men cut the grass?" I asked as I ate my Sunnybisk. "I won't get in their way."

"No darling, those scythes are very sharp and dangerous; you might get hurt."

"I just want to sit near the hedge, by the path."

"Promise me you won't walk out onto the field."

"I promise."

"All right then. I must see to Ann and Jimmy."

The men saw me as I sat down in the long grass. "Hello, young lady," called out the one whose name was Ed. "You mustn't walk out onto the field. These blades could cut your leg off."

"I'll stay right here. ... How long will it take to do the field?"

"Nearly all day," answered the one called Jeff. "The others will be here with the wagon soon. Then you can watch the loading."

As he was speaking, a horse-drawn wagon appeared around the corner of Mr Brooker's house and entered the field by the farm gate opposite. As it crossed the field towards us, I could see two men sitting in the wagon. One held the reins and the other was clasping two pitch forks in his large brown hands. These had long handles and two sharp prongs for lifting the grass and tossing it onto the wagon. The horse was brown with a white patch above the muzzle and white fetlocks, a large animal of eighteen hands or more. The hay wagon drew up right in front of me and the horse snorted, shaking his head from side to side and stamping his feet.

Apprehensively, I remembered a recent dream I had had about a horse. I was walking past Mr Brooker's farmyard towards the pond, and Jimmy was toddling along in front of me. An enormous cart-horse came by and stamped on Jimmy, and all that was left of him were two large footprints. It was only a dream, but I'd been wary of horses ever since.

"Have you brought the tea?" called Ed. "It must be time for a break."

"Yes. And Mrs B has packed us enough food to feed a horse ... pardon the joke, Alfred," laughed Pete as he dropped the reins, and jumped down from the wagon. His mate, Phil, handed him the pitchforks, and then picked up a large canvas bag from the front of the wagon. He also found a nosebag for Alfred. Soon the four men and their horse were all tucking into their snacks. I hadn't long had breakfast, but felt somewhat left out as I watched the men eat great hunks of brown bread and some cheese.

"Hey, darling, would you like a little something to eat?" asked Phil in a lilting Irish accent. "You can come and sit with us; we won't bite you. I could even tell you a little story if you like?"

"My mummy made me promise not to walk onto the field," I answered ruefully. "But I would like a story. What's it about?"

"How about 'the disappearing ducklings'? See we're not working now, so you're quite safe. There's a nice little cake here from Mrs Brooker."

I didn't know what to do. I was slightly in awe of those big beefy men; but I didn't want to upset them. Besides, Mrs Brooker made the most wonderful rock cakes, even better than Grandma Nelson's, and that was saying something! But how would my mother react if she found me out in the field? Would she tell Daddy that I'd disobeyed her?

"Are you coming, or shall I eat this nice little cake? Phil really does like telling farmyard stories," coaxed Ed.

"Does he?"

"Yes. He has his own little farm at home."

"No, don't eat the cake, I'm coming; I don't think Mumsie would mind me being here listening to a story while you're eating."

I sat down with them on a pile of cut grass which tickled the backs of my knees. The rock cake was scrumptious. It couldn't have been out of the oven all that long; it was still slightly warm.

The Disappearing Ducklings

Yesterday a brood of ducklings hatched out. Eight of them. They were a fluffy primrose-yellow; they looked so cute, arranged in a delightful cosy ring, much prettier than baby chicks. This morning all but two had disappeared. Six little ducklings had been spirited away. Or had a nasty animal come and gobbled them up while the mother duck was busy elsewhere?

The poor mother duck was not flapping her wings all over the place, but just bewildered and upset with herself. Had she been careless to lose them so soon? No. No. Those ducklings didn't stand a chance. The nasty animal that had gobbled them up was a cunning brown rat. Nothing anywhere is safe from a rat. It's a good swimmer, and can climb with ease; it gnaws through lead pipes, and runs along wires.

Newly-hatched ducklings are literally 'sitting ducks', helpless, defenceless, and there for the taking. How can a farmer adequately shield day-old, downy ducklings from a RAT!? Mount a guard on them twenty-four hours a day? Keep them in a rat-proof environment: somewhere safe where rats can't worm their way in or gnaw their way out; somewhere in his dreams?

"That's such a sad story. I didn't know rats were like *that*. What happened to the other two ducklings?"
"I shan't know until I get home tonight."

"Who's looking after them now?"

"My wife has them with her in the kitchen."

"Oh! I hope she won't step on them."

"She can't; they're on top of a chest of drawers. Now what's your name, Miss Chatterbox?" asked Phil.

"Maggie; but Mrs Claxton calls me 'Margaret' when I'm at school."

"Why aren't you at school today?" asked Jeff.

"Schools broke up on Friday, didn't they?" chimed in Pete. "My Mildred's in Standard Two now. She didn't like Mrs Claxton much. But she likes it in the Juniors. She didn't even want to break up for the holidays. ... Haven't *you* got anyone here to play with?"

"No, only Jimmy. He'll soon be two. Ann's still a baby, so she doesn't count!"

"Time's up," announced Ed, adjusting his cap. "Back to work, and Maggie must sit in the shade by the hedge. It's beginning to get quite hot out here."

I did as I was told. Jeff and Ed picked up their scythes and went back to the spot where they had left off, while Pete and Phil started to gather up the already drying hay with their forks and pitched it into the wagon. Alfred seemed to know exactly when he had to wait patiently and when he was required to move forward. All was so warm and peaceful in the meadow that I fell asleep until dinner-time.

~~

"A-a-a-r-r-g-h, ... h-e-l-p, somebody; I've just sliced my leg off," yelled Jeff. He had been daydreaming as he worked, and all the while the brutal afternoon sun was scorching his weather-beaten face. Now he was paying even more dearly for his lack of concentration.

Ed dropped his scythe and ran across to his mate. Jeff was lying amongst the grass he had been cutting, holding his injured leg aloft. Through his trouser leg, the wound was bleeding profusely.

"No, you haven't," pronounced Ed reassuringly, "but you've got a very deep cut." Then he called across to me. "Maggie, could you get your mother to come with a first aid box? Tell her, Jeff's cut himself with a scythe. Do hurry; he's losing a lot of blood."

As I ran, I started shouting, "Mumsie, Mumsie," at the top of my voice. I had to run right round the garden hedge and into the garden by the front gate.

My mother's hearing was acute and she realised immediately that there had been an accident. When I arrived, puffing and panting, at the back door, she was filling a small bucket with warm water. In a carrier bag by the door, she had placed cotton wool, bandages, antiseptic, a pair of scissors, old cloths and towels, and other things needed to cleanse and bind up a wound.

"I think there's a small gap in the hedge. So I'll carry the things over this way, Maggie," she explained. "You run back the long way, and ask someone to come to the hedge and get them. Then, if they need me, I'll come round too. Do you understand?"

"I think so, Mumsie."

There was no way either of us could crawl through that hedge; but the bucket of water and the carrier bag were soon in Ed's capable hands. He had been trained in first aid and soon staunched the blood flow and expertly dressed the wound. There was nothing left for Emily to do except collect the bucket and the bag, and all the soiled cloths for burning. Ed helped Jeff back to the farm, and Mr Brooker took him home in his estate car.

Young Bill, the new farm-hand who had just left school, came out with Ed and had his first lesson in how to use a scythe.

"This is much more fun than sluicing down the dairy," he confided cheerily.

"I wonder if you'll say that at eight o'clock tonight," suggested Ed.

"We're not working till *eight*, are we? What about my dinner?"

"You'll have to wait, won't you? Ever heard the saying, 'Make hay while the sun shines'? We work late at haymaking and harvest; make the most of the fine weather ... understand?"

"I suppose so."

Chapter 5

Mr Brooker was what country people called a 'gentleman farmer'; he owned the farm but had no idea how to do the actual work. He was a large, expensively-dressed individual who was regularly seen about his farm wearing plus-fours, a brown tweed suit having long wide men's knickerbockers, which were gathered up just below the knee. These short, baggy trousers were normally worn by the landed gentry or golfers, rather than small farmers. They were called plus-fours because the overhang at the knee required an extra four inches of material.

One Sunday afternoon we were all out for a walk and were just approaching the Hursts' cottage, when Mr Brooker shot past in front of us in his swanky 1940 Jaguar, kicking up a minor dust storm as he went.

"That man Brooker don't half give himself airs," commented Mr Hurst from his front garden. "Fancy buying something like that when there's a war on!"

"I should think that Jag's very heavy on petrol," answered my father mildly.

"'Course it is; he's got more money than sense, if you ask me. I ought to know; I used to work for him."

"Oh really! When was that?"

"Years ago; before I got this job in Shiplake with someone who's a proper farmer. ... Do you know, Old Brooker once asked a farm-hand to milk the heifers? They's the young cows that haven't yet had a calf."

"No, surely not," laughed my mother incredulously, gently rocking the pram to keep Jimmy and Ann quiet.

"I was there; I heard it all. It was Ed, who's been in charge of the haymaking. He was fairly new to the job then, so he coughed, and answered, very respectful like, 'Sorry Sir, I can't do that, there ain't no milk to be had from they heifers.'... I ask you!"

"Fancy someone who calls himself a farmer not understanding the connection between calving and milk production! Even *I* know that and I'm only a townie," added my mother.

"It's a wonder that Ed could keep a straight face," observed my father.

"Young Ed was rather in awe of the governor and his airs and graces. Now, his missus, she's kindness itself! You couldn't meet a nicer woman than Eileen Brooker; always asking after yer family, and wanting to know if you had any trouble like. When our Freda was ill with pneumonia, she gave us the money for the doctor's bills, and sent little gifts for Freda, to cheer her up when she was feeling low."

Jimmy suddenly interrupted the conversation with, "I want ducks! I want ducks!" Ann then relieved her boredom by lifting herself up in the pram and kicking Jimmy where it hurt most.

"Ann hurt willy," protested Jimmy, instantly retaliating by trying to punch her on the nose.

"Come on, children; stop it," I cried, grabbing Jimmy's hard little fists.

"Proper little mother, ain't she?" laughed Ernie Hurst. "She'll soon be big enough to push that pram all by herself."

"Yes, Maggie's nearly five-and-a half now," smiled my mother indulgently. "Anyway, we'd better go and see those ducks. It'll soon be teatime."

Late September 1941

It was cold in the attic bedroom, and there was a small cloud of condensation on the window. I did not want to get out of bed. My head hurt, my chest hurt, and I was shivering. I heard movement in the room below, so I knew it was time to wash and dress for school.

"Maggie, I'm late this morning," called my mother from the bottom of the attic stairs. "Be as quick as you can. I'm taking the babies to Mrs Hurst's now. Your breakfast is ready in the kitchen; but go easy with the milk. The milkman won't be here until after we've gone."

"Mumsie, I don't feel very well," I replied in a hoarse voice.

"You'll soon feel better when you're up and dressed," she assured me.

I tried to do as she said, but I didn't feel any better at all as I gingerly put my feet out onto the bedside mat. I thought I was going to faint and it was hard to breathe. I then started coughing, painful paroxysms of coughing, and I dropped down exhausted onto the mat. I came round to hear my mother calling anxiously from below.

"Maggie, where *are* you?" Oh dear! My mother was back already, and I was still lying on the bedroom floor.

"I'm up here; I can't get up," I answered weakly; but she didn't hear me. Then followed another fit of loud, choking, uncontrollable coughing. My mother could certainly hear that, even from the kitchen; she came upstairs immediately and was soon tucking me back into bed. She went downstairs to fill a hot-water bottle and placed it in the bed beside me. How lovely it was to have that comforting warmth!

"Maggie, I'll have to leave you for a few moments while I phone the doctor from Mrs Hurst's," she said, stroking my forehead. "You're not well enough to go to the surgery, so he'll have to come out here. Anyway, you might have something infectious."

"Mumsie, what's 'fectious?" I whispered hoarsely.

"Something nasty you might pass on to other people by coughing over them."

"Could I give it to Jimmy and Ann?"

"Yes, you could," she answered soberly. "We'll have to keep you up here by yourself."

Ten minutes later, my mother came back alone. Mrs Hurst was keeping Jimmy and Anne for the rest of the day.

Doctor Prince arrived at lunch time while I was finishing some bread and milk. I had always been slightly in awe of him, in spite of his kindly manner. As he was stomping up the carpetless attic stairs, I started coughing again; this time I definitely could *not* get my breath. Doctor Prince rushed in, picked me up from the bed, up-ended me and thumped my back hard. After such rough treatment, I could breathe again, but I also lost most of my bread and milk.

"Sorry, Maggie; I had to be cruel to be kind. It's important that you bring up that nasty stuff that's choking you." He very gently laid me back on the bed, and my mother made me comfortable. Then the two of them walked downstairs and left me to sleep.

—

"There's no doubt about it, Mrs Goodchild, your daughter has whooping-cough," announced the doctor when they reached the ground floor. "You will have to keep her away from other children."

"That's going to be difficult; I have two under-fives, they're with my neighbour down the lane at the moment and, as you can see, there's another on the way. I'm finding two flights of stairs a bit much now I'm so big. I'm exactly six months."

"You *are* rather big for six months. Sometime, you ought to come for a check up at the surgery. But for now, I can see you have your hands full. ... Is there anyone, a relative or close friend, who could look after Maggie for you until the worst is over and she's no longer infectious? It will be a few weeks before she gets over this completely. In the meantime, you wouldn't want the others to catch it, would you? Whooping-cough can cause serious problems for small babies. ... I forget, exactly how old are the other two?"

"Jimmy's just two, and Ann was a year old at the end of August."

"Hum ..." he paused and thought for a while. "Yes, try and find someone who can take Maggie for you. I don't think she'll be going back to school again until well after half-term."

"There's an older couple we know, at Amersham, who are rather fond of her. Maybe they'd be willing to help."

"Do they have a telephone?"

"I'm not sure; we've ever only communicated by post. ... They do have a car, so they must be reasonably well-off; they could be on the phone, but I don't know their number."

"You could ring the exchange and see if they can find out for you. The operator will know what to do, if you give her the address."

"Of course!" Emily exclaimed. "I used to be a telephonist myself before I married. I'm so out of touch, I'd completely forgotten the procedure. I'll ask Mrs Hurst if I can use the phone again when I go to collect the babies."

"Maggie should sleep for an hour or so. Why not hop in the car with me? It will save you a few yards. Do make sure Maggie has her cod liver oil and malt regularly. She needs to build up her strength."

~

"Are all the children in bed?" asked John as he arrived home from work that evening. It was seven o'clock; already the sun was low in the sky and the shadows creeping stealthily across the fields.

"Maggie's been there all day," announced Emily. "I had to get the doctor to her; she has whooping-cough. I must keep the other two away from her or they will catch it too. ... Dr Prince suggested I found someone else to have her until she's no longer a threat to Jimmy and Ann."

"That's a lot to ask of anyone," grumbled John. "Where could we find someone willing to do *that* for us? Ada Cotton's got that evacuee, Pauline, now, hasn't she? So she wouldn't want Maggie *there* with whooping-cough. No, we must shoulder our own burdens," said John with quiet finality.

"But in this case we can't, without putting Jimmy and Ann's health at risk," persisted Emily heatedly. "Young children can *die* of whooping-cough."

"We'll just have to trust God and soldier on," concluded John.

"No, we won't. I've already been on the telephone to Irene and Bert Long from Amersham. They're coming to collect Maggie tomorrow morning in their brand-new Morris."

"What were you doing contacting the Longs without consulting me first?"

"Following the doctor's orders, that's all," answered Emily defiantly. "Mrs Hurst was only too glad to let me use her telephone; *she* thought I was doing the right thing."

John stood there, glaring at her with a face like thunder. "It's of no interest to me *what* Rita Hurst thinks." Then, just as Emily was wondering what he would thunder at her next, his whole attitude suddenly changed. "I didn't know Bert was on the telephone," he mused.

"Nor did I for sure," said Emily in a more conciliatory tone. "But the operator was very helpful in obtaining their number for me. And Irene said 'yes' straight away. ... Said she would enjoy having a little girl in the house to keep her company."

"Oh well! We'd better let the arrangements stand then." Emily heaved a sigh of relief and served out their evening meal of cold meat and home-grown potatoes and carrots.

I didn't hear about these arrangements until the following morning. I woke up feeling so cold and miserable that I didn't even want to get out of bed to use my chamber pot, let alone get dressed or go anywhere. I hid my face under the covers when my mother told me I had to get up.

"Come on, Maggie," she coaxed. "You're going to stay with Auntie Irene and Uncle Bert in Amersham."

"Why?" I asked in bewilderment. "You told me I'd have to stay here until I'm better."

"I know; but if you stay here, Jimmy and Ann could still catch the whooping-cough."

"You said it would be all right if I stayed up here," I grizzled.

"But the doctor thought it would be better if you could stay with Auntie Irene."

I wasn't convinced by these arguments. Besides, I didn't know Auntie Irene and Uncle Bert all that well. So why *was* Mumsie sending me away? Was I *that* much of a nuisance?

Uncle Bert and Auntie Irene arrived about eleven o'clock. I was still feeling strange and the horrid coughing really hurt me. My mother had let me lie on the settee with a rug over me, while she got all my things ready.

"How is our little patient today? Any better?" asked Uncle Bert, smiling down at me. He had a jolly, easy-going manner, a round face, and warm, friendly eyes.

"I feel much better when you look at me like that," I laughed.

Auntie Irene had long blonde hair, which she wore in a roll at her neck. Her eyes were blue like Jimmy's; she was much more serious than Uncle Bert, but she seemed nice enough. So, maybe I would be happy with them after all, if I could manage to be good and not make a fuss.

The journey from Crowsley to Amersham took about two hours. The route was by slow country roads most of the way. We saw some bicycles and farm vehicles, but there were very few cars about; not smart ones like Uncle Bert's, anyway. Uncle Bert drove through Harpsden to Henley, then along by the River Thames. I couldn't see the river very well from my makeshift bed on the back seat; but I thought I could see a steamer in the distance, sailing downstream towards Hambleden Lock.

After Mill End, we were still following the river as it wound its way to Marlow, but I wasn't looking out for it anymore. I was feeling decidedly queasy.

"We'll soon be in Buckinghamshire, Maggie," Uncle Bert informed me. All the signposts had been removed after the fall of France in June 1940, but Uncle Bert knew exactly where he was going. "Now, we really are in Buckinghamshire," he called out cheerfully as we neared Marlow. "And we stay in Buckinghamshire all the way to Amersham."

At Marlow, we parked the car and went to the public lavatories. When I reached the cubicle, I started whooping and then I was violently sick, and Auntie Irene had to clean me up again afterwards. I felt wretched. I wasn't sure if Auntie Irene was cross with me, or not; all she said was, "*That's* better." When she had finished, my brown second-hand coat was more or less clean, but it still stank of vomit and so did the car. I did feel very much better afterwards, though, and soon took more notice of the countryside we were passing through as we made our way towards High Wycombe. We soon left the river behind and started to climb a steep hill up onto the Chilterns. The beech trees were all turning yellow and orange in the autumn sun.

"Why are the leaves not green any more, Uncle Bert?" I asked.

"Because they're going to die and drop off."

"Why can't they stay on for ever?"

"If they did, all the trees would die in the winter snow."

"Oh! ... Christmas trees don't; and *they* keep their leaves on."

"But what are their leaves like, Maggie?"

"Like needles, Uncle Bert."

"Exactly. The snow can't damage them, so the trees can keep their leaves all year round. They're called 'evergreens', and these beech trees are called 'deciduous' trees."

"Des-sid-yes ... des-sid-yus ..." I tried to say 'deciduous', but it didn't sound quite right.

"Des-sid-you-us," pronounced Uncle Bert very slowly.

"Des-sid-you-us," I mimicked.

"That's right; you've got it," encouraged Uncle Bert.

"I wish Mrs Claxton could explain things like you do!"

"Is she your teacher? Will you miss her?"

"No. She's horrid."

As we reached the top of the hill, I thought I might start coughing again so I kept quiet for a few minutes and took deep breaths. Then I realised I could kneel up on the seat and look back down on the valley, through the little window behind us. But we didn't stay on level ground for very long before we were descending another winding hill down towards High Wycombe.

"Uncle Bert, why do they call it *High* Wycombe when we have to go *down* this big hill to get to it?"

Uncle Bert laughed. "Perhaps it's because people don't know the difference between high and low. So, Maggie, you think it should be called *Low* Wycombe?"

"Yes, because we'll be starting to go up again soon, won't we?"

"Indeed we will."

As we crossed the High Street I could see a long straight hill ahead of us. "Do you like hills Uncle Bert?" I asked.

"Yes, Maggie; but my new car doesn't like *this* hill. It's called Amersham Hill; you'll see the station in a minute."

"Oh, yes! There's a train. It's just coming in. I can see the engine; it's puffing out lots of steam. ... Why doesn't your *car* engine puff out lots of steam, Uncle Bert?"

"It does when it gets too hot. It will be working very hard to get us to the top of this hill. If it gets too hot we'll have to open the bonnet and give it a rest."

"We made it!" I exclaimed as we eventually reached the top of Amersham Hill. "Do we have to stop?"

"Yes, we'll stop for a minute. You can get out and look at the view, while I check the engine." He opened the bonnet and I could see the engine steaming inside. Gradually the steam subsided and stopped its hissing.

"We can see a long way from up here, can't we? Are we nearly there, Uncle Bert?"

"It's not much further now."

"What's the name of your road?"

"You've got to guess. It has the name of a fruit in it."

I thought of all the trees in the garden at Tudor Cottage. "Is it apple tree? Pear tree? Damson tree...?

"Keep going," encouraged Auntie Irene. This was the first time she had spoken since we left Marlow. She had been secretly wondering how she was going to keep up with my endless questions when Bert wasn't around to field them all.

"Cherry tree. Is it cherry tree?" I asked excitedly.

"Yes. We live at number 22, Cherry Tree Road."

"Is it a big house?"

"You'll have to wait and see, won't you?" called Uncle Bert. "Time to board the bus again. First stop, Amersham."

Beech Trees in November

In the beech woods the trees are almost bare.
I scuffle through the carpets of dry leaves.
Purple in bud, luminous green in spring,
red gold in autumn, now discarded rags.

Things were not going well at Tudor Cottage. Jimmy and Ann did catch whooping-cough. Two days after I left home, they both started to make those awful choking noises and had to be slapped on the back before they could breathe again. They were very distressed and kept being sick. Dr Prince confirmed my mother's worst fears, but could do very little to ease the situation for her. The infection had to take its course, and the young victims must be kept as warm and comfortable as possible. Emily couldn't even risk leaving them long enough to let Rita Hurst know what was happening, and John refused point-blank to do so. He was still wittering on about shouldering their own burdens and not involving the neighbours.

After two days, Rita Hurst realised that something must be wrong at the house up the lane. She hadn't seen my mother pushing the pram past her cottage.

"I wonder, Tiddles, if those Goodchild babies haven't caught the whooping-cough after all." Tiddles, the old tabby cat, sidled up to Rita and started pawing at her apron as if he were being offered some food. He was most offended when Rita took her old tweed coat off the hook and got ready to go out. Fancy his missus going out with her pinny on!

She arrived at Tudor Cottage as both Jimmy and Ann simultaneously started to whoop. She could see what was going on through the kitchen window, so she walked straight in, unannounced, and made a beeline for Jimmy while Emily picked up Ann.

"Emily, you're exhausted," she said, as the two of them sat attending to the needs of their charges. Rita glanced around the cluttered kitchen. Ann's cot had been brought downstairs and placed in front of the warm stove. The pram stood under the back window, the autumn sunshine adding a little extra warmth and cheer. Jimmy was using the pram as a bed during the day. By the sink under the front window, Rita saw a bucketful of dirty nappies left to soak in the soapy water. When she had put Jimmy back in the pram, she would deal with those nappies and put them out on the line. "This is far too much for you to cope with in *your* condition. Let me stay and help you for a bit. Ernie won't need his dinner until seven-thirty; he's working late tonight."

"That's really kind. John has no idea what it's like coping with sick children, especially when they're not potty-trained. Jimmy's still very unreliable, even though he's two. I'm glad Maggie's being cared for, but I do miss her help at times like this."

"Have you heard any news yet?"

"Not yet. It's too soon."

"Do you want to phone your friends when we've put these two back to bed? I'll stay here if you'd like to use my telephone. Just go and let yourself in. The key's under the mat."

"Thanks. I'd like to talk to Irene; put my mind at rest."

While Emily went to talk to Irene Long, Rita dealt with the nappies, and then quietly bustled around the room, putting things to rights, as Jimmy and Ann settled down to sleep. Fifteen minutes later Emily returned. Rita couldn't help noticing that her ankles were badly swollen and that she was dragging her bulky frame wearily across the lawn towards the house. "The sooner that baby is born the better," she said to herself. "But how is she going to cope with an extra one ... or two? I do hope it's not two!"

"What's the news?" she asked aloud.

"Maggie seems to have settled in well. She's not coughing nearly so much, but Irene's doctor says she's still very weak and anaemic. There's no question of school for a while."

~

"Maggie, don't hang around in this draughty hall," scolded Irene Long. "Go and play by the fire. You *must* keep warm."

"Yes, Auntie Irene."

I was beginning to feel at home in the Longs' comfortable, modern detached house. As the weather became colder, the Longs lit more fires. I wasn't used to such luxury. Auntie Irene even lit the Valor oil stove in my cosy little bedroom, if she thought there was a draught coming through the window and I might catch a cold.

At Tudor Cottage, we sometimes had no heating at all if we were out of coal or paraffin oil. I often suffered from painful, itchy chilblains in the winter, but my father was not very sympathetic. He would say that children should be hardened against adversity, not mollycoddled. I should run around to get warm or, better still, go and sweep the floor and dust the furniture. My mother was convinced that my father didn't actually feel the cold like the rest of us did.

The Longs enjoyed their creature comforts. Not only did they have electric lights, but, also a very efficient dual hot water system comprising an independent domestic boiler and an electric immerser. They had a proper bathroom with hot and cold taps, a separate water-closet with a beautiful china bowl and pedestal to sit on, and an overhead cistern with a chain to flush the excrement away afterwards. When I sat on the throne, I kept comparing it to the smelly old pit-latrine at the top of the garden which we had to use at home. Sometimes I sat there so long that Auntie Irene had to tell me to hurry up; *she* wanted to use it!

Estate agents described their property as 'superior' and 'well-appointed'. There were gas points for a cooker and gas fires, and power points for a cooker, electric fires and various other modern appliances. The Longs chose a gas cooker, but they considered that the newly-available fixed or free-standing gas and electric fires weren't really safe, so they stuck to coal fires and used the paraffin heater in the bedrooms; they never left any of them burning unattended.

The only cold place in the whole house was the large, walk-in larder, leading off the kitchen. On the bottom shelf was kept my large jar of cod liver oil and malt. It was a four-sided jar and not easy for me to grab hold of with my small podgy fingers. So I left it well alone.

One evening, Auntie Irene was in a particular hurry. She was going out to a birthday party and was already running late. I tried to help her get ready, but all she said was, "Go away, you're flustering me," in an unexpectedly cross voice. So I went and sat in the dining room, on a little stool with a pretty, floral-patterned cover worked by Auntie Irene herself. I peered at the smoky fire through the well-fitting fireguard, and thought gloomily about how hungry I was. Tonight, I had to wait for my tea until Uncle Bert came home for his dinner.

"Maggie, do you think you could fetch the cod liver oil and malt jar from the larder, all by yourself, and bring it here?" Irene Long's tone had mysteriously softened, but my heart still sank. I was scared stiff I would drop that jar on the cold, hard floor.

"I'll try, Auntie Irene," I promised. The jar was unopened, and heavy as well as awkward to manage. I very carefully lifted it off the shelf, and was concentrating so hard on not dropping it, that I bumped my head on the door knob. Then I lost both my balance and my grip; the heavy jar smashed onto the concrete floor in a gooey mixture of malt and broken glass. I just managed to stop myself falling on top of it all.

Auntie Irene screamed, "Oh no! *Now* what am I going to do!"

"I'm sorry, Auntie Irene, I couldn't help it," I whimpered.

At that moment, Uncle Bert arrived on the scene. He always came round to the back door after putting the car in the garage. Finding us both in tears, he couldn't fail to notice the telltale mess on the kitchen floor, and quickly summed up the situation.

"Irene, you go and get ready or you'll be late for your party. I'll deal with this. I don't think we can salvage any of that malt as there are splinters of glass everywhere. Maggie should never have got that jar out for herself."

"I was in such a flurry that I asked her to," explained Irene, rushing upstairs. "Shirley will be here any minute."

"Then she'll have to wait, won't she?" answered Bert firmly.

He then turned to me with a serious expression on his face. "How did it happen, Maggie?"

After I had told him about the door knob, he looked hard at me, lifting my chin up and saying quietly, "Yes, you've got a bump coming up on your forehead. Does it hurt?"

"Yes, a little bit. ... I tried very hard not to drop it, Uncle Bert."

"I know you did. We'll get you some more tomorrow." He flashed me a sudden smile, saying, "And now we'll have our meal while I figure out the best way to clear up that sticky mess. We're eating here in the kitchen."

꙼

The Longs had a grown-up son called Brian who was a soldier. His photograph stood on the sideboard, next to the cut-glass fruit bowl they had received as a wedding present, twenty-five years previously. Brian looked very smart in his army uniform. He wore a cheery grin on his face, and had the same twinkly eyes as his father. I wanted to know all about him.

"Where *is* Brian, Auntie Irene?"

"He's with his regiment somewhere in North Africa, fighting the Italians."

"I thought we were fighting the Germans, not the Italians," I protested.

"The Italians are partners of the Germans."

"But where in North Africa, Auntie Irene?"

"We think it's Abyssinia."

"Where's that?"

"Look, Maggie, I've got work to do. Ask Uncle Bert when he comes home."

Uncle Bert explained that Italy, under Benito Mussolini, had invaded Abyssinia; and then on June 10th, 1940, Italy declared war on both Britain and France. So we were at war with the Italians, too. Italy controlled large parts of North and East Africa, and Italian soldiers were fighting us in both these areas. Uncle Bert showed me on a map where these places were.

The Longs usually had a letter from Brian every three weeks or so, though these letters were always censored and way out-of-date by the time they arrived on their door mat. The missives were read and re-read, and Irene would keep them in a special little box on her dressing table. The last one they had received was very short:

September 6th, 1941

Dear Mum and Dad,

Next weekend our regiment is being sent to North Africa and we have been given very little time to get organised. Please pray for me, I'm feeling rather apprehensive. I wish I had time to write a proper letter.

All my love,
Brian

When the Longs were at home, they listened in silence to all the daily news broadcasts on the wireless, from eight o'clock in the morning to nine o'clock at night. The Longs were especially happy when the news was good. Irene kept her own 'war diary' and, as well as her own day-to-day activities, she jotted down all the main happenings mentioned in the news. If she heard anything about Abyssinia or North Africa, she would write it down in her special notebook of prayers for Brian and his comrades. On Tuesday 18th November she wrote, 'The British forces are closing in on Gondar, the last Italian stronghold in Abyssinia.'

It was now early December, but the Longs hadn't heard anything from Brian for over six weeks. They were very concerned and, as the days passed, their anxiety became more and more apparent, even to me. Did they think that something bad must have happened to Brian? If they did, they certainly didn't want to talk about it in front of me.

All sorts of questions were buzzing around in my head, as I couldn't even imagine what a soldier's life would really be like. Soldiers were supposed to fight for their country against the enemy, but *how* did they do it? I suppose, by each soldier killing enemy soldiers, one by one. What if they didn't *want* to kill people? The Sixth Commandment says, 'Thou shalt *not* kill.' I had heard my father say that if *he* were called up, he would refuse to fight. He would be a CO, whatever that is? But my Uncle Ben joined up; he said it was his *duty* to serve his country. He was in the RAF Air Sea Rescue Service, saving the lives of men shot down over the sea. Grandpa Nelson had a photograph of Uncle Ben in his uniform standing on his bureau in the dining room. His air force hat was even smarter than Brian's army one.

The Saturday before Christmas 1941, I was awakened by someone pounding on the front door, immediately beneath the spot where I had been sleeping. Something about the urgency of that knocking made me afraid. I heard Uncle Bert walk slowly towards the door. I heard him draw back the bolts and turn the key in the latch. Then I heard him slowly open the door.

"Telegram," said the young man briskly. "I hope it isn't bad news." He didn't stop to witness Bert Long's response. They both knew what it might contain, without even opening it. It was from War Office Casualties in London and included the fateful words: *'Private Brian Long ... killed in action ... Gondar, Abyssinia ... 18th November 1941.'*

Christmas was not celebrated at the Long's home that year. Their friends, Tom and Rosa Kerswell, on hearing the tragic news, immediately invited the Longs over to Oxford to spend Christmas with them at Pine View, a draughty old house in Botley; and I was invited too. The Kerswells had a daughter, Clara, and a son, Robert, who were both home from their respective boarding schools. They were much older than I was and both spoke with plummy accents. They kept busy with their own pursuits and ignored me completely. But Auntie Irene and Uncle Bert found consolation with Tom and Rosa. The Kerswells could empathise with them completely; they had lost their eldest son at Flanders in May 1940.

Chapter 6

A Morning Serenade

The sun's rays were warm this spring morning, as I hid under the apple tree. Beneath the delicate pinks and whites, a pair of swallows flew straight towards me, settling down on the branches above.

They just sat there facing each other. I hoped something would happen before too long. Then the male began his serenade, a secret, low-pitched, twittering song. His whole range was only a few notes.

'Seeta, feeta, feetit, like drops of morning dew,
Seeta, feeta, feetit, I sing this song for you.
Seeta, feeta, feetit, my love for you is true.'

The female listened attentively; then she joined him in a tender duet.
    Then they cast themselves into the air, and with balletic precision they danced an awesome aerial pas de deux.

December was a cold, damp month and an anxious time for John and Emily at Tudor Cottage. Jimmy and Ann had survived the whooping-cough, and were now over the worst; but Emily's pregnancy had not been going well and she had finally been admitted to the maternity ward at Henley Hospital, a month before the due date. Dr Prince decided to have her hospitalised because her blood pressure was far too high. He feared that, if it was not brought down speedily, the result could be eclampsia; she would then suffer repeated convulsions, which could be fatal to both mother and foetuses. As it was, he wasn't happy about the condition of one of foetuses. The heartbeat was not as strong as it should be. He was glad, therefore, that she was now in the hands of a competent gynaecologist, a specialist who would also be on hand for the actual birth. Meanwhile, he had instructed the patient to rest and try not to worry.

"How *is* Emily?" called out Rita Hurst, as she stopped John outside her gate on his way back from the hospital. He had taken the day off work and followed the ambulance on his motorbike, waiting to see Emily settled in the ward before returning home. It had been a long day.

"They're dealing with her blood pressure and it's already starting to come down. But they're insisting on keeping her in hospital until after the birth. I don't know what I'm going to do with Jimmy and Ann. I can't keep lumbering *you* with them like this."

"Yes you can," smiled Rita Hurst. "What are neighbours for? I'll have them until you can make a more permanent arrangement for them. If you could bring me their night things and Ann's cot, we can manage. ... Oh! Maybe I should have some more day clothes, nappies, and some towels for them. Things don't dry so quickly in this weather, do they?"

To add to his general anxiety about his wife, John had just received his call-up papers. They couldn't have come at a worse time. He was expected to respond immediately, so he would have to go to Reading early the following morning. He had decided from the beginning that, if he *was* called up, his conscience wouldn't let him take up arms and fight. He also knew that, as a would-be conscientious objector, he would have to make a formal application and appear before the Conscientious Objector's Tribunal at Thorn Street to state his case. Coping with all this bureaucracy was *not* what he was good at; it would also take up valuable time when his family needed him most. It wasn't that he was seeking total exemption from military service; though it would be a relief if they *did* exempt him on compassionate grounds. He was prepared to work in Supplies or the Army Catering Corps, but not in a situation where he would actually be required to take life. Fortunately, it would be several weeks before his case would finally be heard.

~~~~

"The first problem is what to do about Jimmy and Ann." John coped better with problem-solving if he reasoned it all out aloud. "Rita Hurst has definitely hinted at a 'more permanent arrangement'. Could they stay with David and Nellie in Ruislip? I'll have to use Rita's phone and see what David and Nellie say. ... No, they've got five children of their own; but then, Nellie *is* a state registered nurse and midwife, so she would know what to do with sick children who are getting over whooping-cough. I'll go and ring her."

Nellie answered the phone and immediately agreed to take the toddlers. She was a small woman, but an excellent organiser and an expert at thinking on her feet. "Now, John, I will have to get someone to bring me over in their car. You can't manage them single-handed on the train, neither can I. ... I'm not able to do anything tomorrow. Let's say, ... I'll be over sometime on Saturday. Perhaps Mr Dawkins would be willing to help us. I'll ask him first."

"Thank you so much, Nellie, that's a real weight off my mind. Now I've only got Emily and the call-up papers to worry about."

"What about Maggie? Where's she going?"

"She's been at Amersham with the Longs for two months now. We sent her away hoping she wouldn't pass on the whooping-cough, but unfortunately she did."

"Are Jimmy and Ann still whooping?"

"Not really, but they do still have the odd coughing fit."

"I'll be able to deal with those, I am sure. ... I must go now and get a meal for David. He's been holding a School Concert this evening. He's especially pleased with his recorder group. It's quite a novelty, and they've been asked to perform on the wireless sometime next month. Recorders are all he thinks about these days! Must go; goodbye John. See you on Saturday."

Saturday came and Nellie Goodchild arrived in Peter Dawkins' 1936 Standard Ten at exactly eleven-thirty. Rita Hurst was at Tudor Cottage, helping John get Jimmy and Ann ready. Ann had a brief moment of truculence as Rita put her on the back seat of the car while Nellie got in beside her. Then Rita lifted Jimmy into the space on the other side of Nellie. Peter used the passenger seat for some of the bags and bundles, and Nellie clung on to the two toddlers, who were very soon lulled to sleep by the gentle purr of the engine.

Jimmy and Ann's coughing fits often kept the family awake at night. "Why do those babies keep coughing?" complained Rebekah, the Goodchild's eldest daughter aged eleven. She was highly-strung and a light sleeper. "I *must* get my sleep or I won't be able to study properly for my scholarship exam in two months' time."

"Try to ignore them; hide your head under the covers," soothed her mother. "They've been very ill with whooping-cough and it will take time for them to lose their coughs altogether."

"All right, I will try, Mother."

By day, Jimmy and Ann were restless, fretful infants, and couldn't understand why they had to live in these unfamiliar surroundings. Nellie found them more of a handful than she had anticipated; but it didn't take them long to realise who was boss in this large, well-organised household:

"Ann, will you stop that grizzling at once," scolded Auntie Nellie.

Ann turned up the volume and continued grizzling.

"All right, little Grizzleby, you can go up in your cot and grizzle where no-one can hear you."

"Jimmy, will you come here at once?"

"No," shouted Jimmy, running off in the opposite direction. He hid in the cupboard under the stairs, which had unwittingly been left open.

"All right, Jimmy Goodchild," pronounced Auntie Nellie, "I shall smack you for disobeying me." With that she put him across her knee and smacked his bottom twice. Jimmy howled at the indignity of it all, rather than the pain.

When they weren't at school, the four Goodchild girls: Rebekah, Rachel, Ruth, and Rhoda, grudgingly shared the roles of nursemaids between them. The two older girls, Rebekah and Rachel, were hoping to win places at the local grammar school and also had their homework to do. Rachel was due to sit her scholarship examinations the following year. The twins, Ruth and Rhoda, were nearly six; they would rather play with their dolls, which invariably remained wherever they had been placed, than care for two wriggly little human beings with minds of their own.

James Goodchild, the eldest by two full years, was in his second year at the grammar school and had already won a school prize. He stayed in his room for hours on end with his nose stuck into his textbooks, keeping aloof from anything remotely domestic. He was going to be an economist, and was determined to win a place at a good university, preferably Oxford or Cambridge.

~

Ten days early, Emily Goodchild went into labour on 23rd December. When she had given birth to Ann she only had a short labour, but this time things were different. Emily was very ill indeed and, for a while, it looked as if all three lives would be lost.

But Emily was a fighter and she also believed that God would help her; her Creator knew exactly what was going on inside her weary body, whereas the doctor could only guess at the problem. She could recite whole chunks of the Bible by heart and was not averse to quoting relevant portions back to the Almighty in her prayers. She started quoting Psalm 46 softly to herself as she lay there writhing in agony. When she got to verse five she said, "That's it, Father, that's the one I need right now!

'God is in the midst of her; she shall not be moved: God shall help her, and that right early.'

That's your promise to me, even if I *have* taken the text out of context. I believe that you're here and that you will help me give birth."

At last, the long labour was nearly over. The first head appeared and a few seconds later the tiny infant took her first breath and uttered a pathetic little cry.

"It's a girl," exclaimed the midwife. "She has a thick mop of black hair but her skin is very dry and yellow. She weighs less than four pounds, so we will have to put her in an incubator and watch her very carefully."

"She *will live*, won't she?" asked Emily apprehensively.

"We can't promise anything, but we'll do our utmost to make sure she has the best possible chance," answered the consultant, who had appeared on the scene without Emily ever realising he was there.

"The other one's coming very quickly," gasped the perturbed mother, and the second twin came away before she had had time to push.

There was a shocked silence in the delivery room. Outside Emily's range of vision, the midwife and consultant glanced at each other then looked away.

"Why isn't the baby crying? Why aren't you doing something?" demanded Emily with a catch in her voice, although in her heart, she already knew the answer. Things hadn't felt right with this one; something had gone seriously wrong. This one would definitely *not* live; it was probably stillborn.

"Mrs Goodchild, we think it best that you don't see this one," announced the consultant. "You can hold your daughter briefly, before we put her in the incubator. Here she is."

Emily gazed at the little yellow scrap in her arms, holding her close and cooing endearments into her shell-like ears. "God keep you safe my little darling; I'm going to call you 'Grace'."

"We must put her in the incubator now, and you need to rest, Mrs Goodchild. Will your husband be coming in later?"

"I expect so," replied Emily faintly, and she fell into an exhausted sleep.

⌒

John Goodchild had many talents and abilities but understanding the workings of the maternal mind was not one of them; nor was the wisdom to know when to keep his private opinions to himself. John wasn't a family man at heart; he would have been happy with just one child, son or daughter, then he could have said that, at least, he had fulfilled his duty to his wife. Three children were more than he had bargained for, and now he was entering the maternity ward expecting to find two more little Goodchilds waiting to greet him.

The ward sister called John into her office before he could reach the crowded ward. "You *are* Mr Goodchild? ... I'm sorry, Mr Goodchild, I have some bad news for you," announced Sister Fox, solemnly. 'Oh no! I've lost Emily; what shall I do with all these children?' John thought to himself, panicking. "One of the twins didn't survive. She was malformed and very weak. She only lived for a few minutes, and we didn't try to resuscitate her. ... I'm very sorry."

"How's Emily?"

"She's had a tough time, and we want to keep her in for another week so that she can get her strength back."

"What about the living baby?"

"She's jaundiced and underweight, but she's holding her own at the moment. She's in an incubator, but we've had her out for her first feed. Would you like to see her? Your wife is calling her 'Grace'."

"Can I see my wife first?"

"Of course, she's in bed sixteen. But don't stay too long, she's quite fragile at the moment."

John strode off down the ward, looking for bed sixteen. What did she mean by 'fragile'? he wondered. Then he saw her, lying there, propped up by a pile of pillows. She smiled wanly, leaving him to speak first.

"Hello, Emily? How are you now? Sister says you're a bit fragile."

Emily looked up at him with large, soulful eyes. "I've lost one of my babies," she sobbed. "They wouldn't even let me say goodbye."

"Sister said she was malformed, a freak, so it was a good thing you *didn't* see her," said John, with brutal frankness.

"She was still a little person, and I gave birth to her. Don't you see? I *have* to grieve for her."

"I don't see why you're so upset. You've got *four* other children; can't you be satisfied with *them*?"

"The Good Shepherd had *ninety-nine* sheep, but he still grieved for the *one* he'd lost. He grieved for it so much that he went after it, before the wolf could get at it."

"Emily, you're being irrational. What you've just said doesn't make any sense. The baby died because something was wrong with it; it wasn't properly formed. It wasn't even a *proper* baby." As her uttered the word 'proper' there was a contemptuous harshness in his voice; it rose in decibels as well as in pitch.

"You don't have to humiliate me in public," answered Emily in a dejected little whisper. "Our baby was ... is ... still a living soul. I wonder if I'll recognise her in Heaven? ... I'll call her 'Faith' ..."

"... That's a point! I must get down to the registry office. Do I have to register *both* births, I wonder. I suppose so ..." Emily didn't answer. He had completely ignored her grief, and she felt as if he were stabbing her where it hurt most.

John was now taken up with the logistics of how he could get down to Henley between nine o'clock and five-thirty on a weekday, without losing too much time from work. After considerable deliberation, he stood up abruptly and addressed his distraught wife. "I must go now," he said gruffly. "Sister said she would take me to see baby Grace." With that he was gone. It was some consolation to Emily that he was willing to call her baby 'Grace'.

As she was drifting off to sleep she thought about some words in Isaiah 49, verse fifteen:

'Can a mother forget her sucking child, that she should not have compassion on the son of her womb? Yea, they may forget, yet will I not forget thee.'

"I won't forget little Faith and God will take care of all three of us: Faith, Grace and Emily."

January 1942

Now back at home with her four children, Emily was gradually establishing some sort of domestic routine, and Rita Hurst was helping out with the grocery shopping until she was well enough to venture into Sonning Common by herself. Emily was now less distressed at losing baby Faith. "It's all for the best," she told herself repeatedly. "I have my work cut out caring for those you *have* given me, Lord."

But for several days now, she had been particularly concerned for the safety of her brother, Ben. News from him was scarce at the best of times, and he had had very little home leave in recent months. She had been praying for him every time his picture came into her mind. "Lord, please protect Ben. I know he's in real danger right now." Was he operating over the Channel, the Irish Sea or the Atlantic? She had no idea. The Air Sea Rescue Service was there to save lives wherever servicemen and women were in danger of drowning. What about enemy attacks on shipping convoys? Were they involved there too? She wished she knew more about what Ben actually did.

Then, on the 30th of January, a telegram arrived from her father in Uxbridge: '*Ben reported missing, presumed dead. No details.*' "That's it. Ben has died for his country, and Beryl's a widow. Poor Mum and Dad! What must they be feeling?"

April 1942

Sunshine on a birthday makes the occasion extra special. My sixth birthday was on the last Saturday of April. The weather was glorious, like a day in high summer. The birds were singing their little hearts out, and the shadows were dancing a pavane under the apple tree, as zephyrs played through the leaves and blossoms.

"Mumsie, I like being back home again with you, Jimmy and Ann, and Gracie," I confided as I put my arms around my mother's waist. We were washing up after dinner and I was already thinking about my birthday tea. My mother was washing the utensils and I was wiping them very carefully and then stacking them on the kitchen table.

"But you *were* happy with Auntie Irene and Uncle Bert, weren't you?" she asked.

"Yes, they were very kind, but I did get bored sometimes. I wanted to go to school like the other children. ... And it wasn't the same after they knew that Brian was dead. They looked so sad; I was afraid to talk about him. I didn't want to make them cry again. ... Mumsie, will something like that happen to Daddy? He's in the army now, isn't he?"

"No, darling, Daddy's not fighting the Germans; he's helping to send food to our British soldiers who are doing the fighting."

"Where *is* our Daddy then?"

"He's in Buxton, and Buxton's in England."

"How far is it?"

"It must be about a hundred miles away, I should think."

"When will he be coming home again?"

"He doesn't know; but he will be given some leave so that he can come and see us, perhaps before Christmas."

"That's a long time! Will he be wearing his uniform?"

"Yes, he'll have to wear it all the time he's in the army."

"What will it say on his sleeve, Mumsie?"

"NCC — that stands for Non-Combatant Corps; 'Non-Combatant' just means 'not fighting'."

"So none of the men he's with are fighting Germans or Italians?"

"That's right; and many of the men in his unit love Jesus, like Daddy does."

"Will he remember what we all look like when he comes home? Gracie will be sitting up by then, won't she?"

"She might even be walking, if she goes on getting stronger ..."

"... and drinks up all her milk," I added.

"Gracie's got a bad tummy, she can't help being sick. Dr Prince hopes that she will get better as she gets older."

"So do I. Then I can take her out in the pram."

"Listen! ... I can hear Jimmy and Ann waking up from their nap. If I put Ann in the playpen with her toys, outside on the rug, you can play games with Jimmy and I can make your birthday cake."

"Will there be six candles on it?"

"Wait and see. I haven't even started it yet, so I need to get a move on, don't I?"

"Yes, it's nearly three o'clock already."

I wasn't looking forward to seeing Mrs Claxton again. Somehow I had hoped I would be in another class when I came back from Amersham. But I hadn't been to school for over six months and I wouldn't be ready to go into a higher class. Irene Long had been expecting me to go home after Christmas, so she hadn't enrolled me at the school down the road, even though I was well enough to be with other children again and had been begging her to let me go.

No-one, not even Dr Prince, realised that it would take another three months for my mother to recover from the trauma associated with Grace's birth and the stress of coping with a very sick baby. Then my father having to go off to Buxton at the beginning of March added to her difficulties in so many ways, especially as she had to queue up at the Post Office each week to collect her money before she could shop or pay the bills. But, in other ways, things were easier. She was free to make her own decisions now for the first time since her marriage in June 1935, and Ernie and Rita Hurst were only down the lane if she ran into insurmountable problems.

We children finally came back together as a family at the beginning of April. I came home first so that I would be able to help my mother with Jimmy and Ann. They had both grown and Ann was running around all over the place. She needed the playpen to restrain her or she would be out of the gate and across the fields in no time.

~

Fanny Claxton was *not* happy to see me turn up at school after the Easter holidays, nor was she exactly civil to my mother. As she spoke, an unpleasant sneer flitted over her face, and I wished I was tall enough to punch her on the nose.

"Where *has* Margaret been since the end of September?"

"I sent a letter to Mr Ford explaining about the whooping-cough and I also told him that she was going to stay with friends in Amersham, and why."

"So what school did she attend in Amersham then?"

"She hasn't been to school; the Longs didn't expect her to stay with them beyond Christmas, and then I was taken ill ..."

As she said this, Mrs Claxton glanced at her knowingly, thinking, "You were 'taken ill', were you? That's not what *we* heard ..."

"... so she stayed on till the beginning of April. ..." continued my mother lamely. "They didn't think she could be enrolled once the new term had started."

"Poppycock!" exploded Fanny. "It's a wonder the school attendance officer didn't catch sight of her. ... What do you expect me to do with her *now*? Give her individual attention? If you think that, you've got another think coming, Mrs Goodchild. She will

87

just have to sit with the five-year-olds and catch up as best she can."

"Can't you give her some homework to do? I can make sure she does it."

"Mrs Goodchild, just look around you. I have sixty plus children in this classroom. Why should I give *your* daughter preferential treatment? I have more important things to do. Goodbye, Mrs Goodchild; you've wasted enough of my time as it is."

My mother departed without another word, completely baffled by this unsympathetic and hostile reception. Mrs Claxton sat me down in exactly the same position I had occupied when I started school the previous year, over by the front door. Dickie Wheeler, the boy in the wire-framed glasses, was now in one of the blocks near Mrs Claxton's desk, and my new deskmate was a sad little boy called Alan Field. He was just five years old and I soon discovered that he was living in a world of his own and had no idea what was going on around him. I felt so miserable that I wanted to cry. However was I going to catch up from *this* position?

⇒

April 1941

Albert Goodchild was a simple-minded and generous man who took everything that was said to him at face value and regarded all his acquaintances as personal friends. Consequently he shared some of his secrets with the wrong people, without realising that he was providing them with juicy information for their gossiping tongues. Not long before Ruth died, he had had a distressing encounter with Frances Claxton when she came to buy some potatoes.

Mrs Claxton had been buying fruit and vegetables from the Goodchilds for years, ever since she first arrived in Sonning Common with her new husband. Clarence Claxton had been wounded in the First World War and was now a semi-invalid, unable to work or support himself. Frances was happy to be the bread-winner and wear the trousers in return for the enhanced status immediately afforded to her by a sight of her wedding ring. She was secretly delighted when she discovered, by persistent probing, that she had something in common with the highly-

88

respected Ruth Goodchild. They both exercised power over their menfolk at a time when society still refused to grant women equal status with men.

"Your wife is a very thrifty woman, isn't she Mr Goodchild?"

"Yes, she certainly is; I've so much to be thankful for in Ruth," enthused the innocent Albert.

"How did you two meet, Mr Goodchild?" Here, Fanny just about managed a faint smile.

"It's rather a long story," hedged Albert.

"I heard somewhere that you'd been married before, is that true?"

"No, not exactly," answered Albert, beginning to feel uncomfortable.

"But you *were* engaged to someone else before Ruth, weren't you?"

"Yes, but we changed our minds," Albert blustered.

"You mean, *you* changed your mind."

"Mrs Claxton, what do *you* know about my personal affairs?"

"An old lady I know, named Ivy Harding, told me she once sued you for breach of promise," gloated Frances Claxton. She enjoyed making people squirm, especially inadequate men and timid children.

"How do *you* know Ivy?"

"She's an acquaintance of my husband. ... She told me that you wouldn't, or *couldn't*, pay up. So Ruth bailed you out, didn't she?"

"What if she did? Why are you raking all this up now?"

"I'm interested in people's lives, I suppose. ... Is that why you married her?"

"I must terminate this most upsetting conversation. My wife's ill in bed and I must get her some tea. You needn't come back for any more fruit or vegetables. And I'd be grateful if you didn't repeat our conversation to anyone else."

But, of course she did, and Julia Crocker and Gloria Evans were only too happy to spread the gossip abroad, and make a laughing-stock of the gentle Albert.

May 1942

Now it was Emily's turn to suffer from the cruel tongue of Mrs Claxton. She had no idea that malicious rumours about her had been spreading like wildfire through Sonning Common and its environs. No-one knew where these originated, but Julia Crocker and Gloria Evans certainly had something to do with passing them on. The unfounded stories concerned Emily's relationship with Reg King.

People had heard that John had been called up and was no longer at home, so Mrs Claxton knew that much. She also knew that Mr King was the Goodchilds' milkman and remembered that, the previous year, Reg King had taken Emily and Maggie home in his van, after Maggie had collapsed at her desk. "*Collapse*, my foot, she was just asleep!" Frances Claxton had muttered to herself. "... Um, Reg King and Emily Goodchild? There probably *is* something going on there. Well, Joan King's no oil painting and looks years older than her husband. Nothing going on there anymore; whereas Emily Goodchild, *if* she could afford the right clothes, would be quite a catch, especially with her husband safely out of the way. This has the makings of a nice little scandal, especially as those concerned are church people who think they're so good and saintly, and consider the rest of society as dirty, rotten sinners. It would be so satisfying to see them fall off their self-erected pedestals, wouldn't it?"

Emily suddenly found people eyeing her up and down when she went into the Post Office to collect her money, or entered Kirbys' Stores to obtain her weekly rations. She then observed them averting their eyes and whispering together in impromptu huddles. Others glanced in her direction and pointedly moved away as she approached. Why were these village people shunning her in this obvious way? Had someone been tittle-tattling? She would make it her business to find out who started it and what it was they were saying about her. Emily had excellent hearing and this auditory acuity was already serving her well in bringing up her children; now she would use it again to catch the scandalmongers.

Emily stood in line at Kirbys', apparently deep in thought and totally oblivious to her surroundings, but secretly picking out individual voices and listening in to various conversations going on around her. It would be a long wait; it always was now so many things were rationed: meat, eggs, bacon, butter and margarine, sugar, preserves and dried fruit, to name but a few.

She heard various polite routines about the weather and the

progress of the war. A well-spoken gentlemen was telling his neighbour about 'the biggest air raid of the war', in which we sent a thousand bombers to Germany. The target was apparently Cologne, and only forty-four were lost. Next, a coarse female voice gave a penetrating account of the behaviour of Aunt Ethel's irritable bowel — ugh, it was revolting! And then, from way back in the queue, she heard someone mention her own name.

"You know Emily Goodchild ..."

"Who's she?"

"She lives out at Crowsley with four kids. Her husband's just gone into the army. ... You know what, she's having an affair with Reg King, the milkman."

"Who told you that, Pauline?"

"Frances Claxton."

"Who did *she* get it from?"

"Gloria Evans."

"Do you believe *everything* Gloria Evans says? Because I don't. She's just a troublemaker. Reg King is a good, upright Christian who goes to church every Sunday."

"But that doesn't stop him having a lady love, does it?"

"If you're not careful, you'll be had up for slander, Pauline."

"Too right you will, if I find out who you are," said Emily to herself. "I'll be writing all this down. ... Thank goodness, I've still got a good memory."

Emily had always been on good terms with the Kirbys. Mrs Kirby was a friendly, dark-haired woman, who knew most people in the Sonning Common area. She wasn't just Doug Kirby's dependent but a full partner in the business. That's why she was known to take offence when people wrote 'Kirby's' rather than 'Kirbys'' with the apostrophe after the 's' when referring to their business, especially as the sign over the shop front read 'D & J Kirby Family Grocers'.

"As I get my rations, I'll ask *her* who that loud-mouthed Pauline is," decided Emily. "The cheek of it! Standing there and, quite literally, talking about me behind my back."

"Hello, Emily? How are things with you?" asked Joyce Kirby with a smile.

"Not too bad, all things considered." Then she dropped her voice and leaned over the counter. "You don't happen to know who that woman is at the back of this queue — Pauline somebody?"

"That's Pauline Brown. She lives in one of the new council houses on the corner of Blackmore Lane. A bit of a gossip, is that one!"

"You don't happen to know the number, do you?"

"No, but it's the one right on the end as you turn into the lane. There's a 'Beware of the Dog' notice on her gate."

"Thanks!"

"She hasn't been talking about *you*, has she?" Emily nodded. "Look, you come through into the house. I'll get Doug to carry on here for a bit."

"Doug, could you oblige?" She called out to her husband, who was somewhere at the back of the premises. "I need to talk to Mrs Goodchild."

"Sure, I've just finished stacking the new stock in the store." He hurried into the shop and took his wife's place behind the counter. "What can I do for you, Mrs Bowers?"

"So, tell me all about it, now we're on our own," encouraged Joyce Kirby in the privacy of their small sitting room.

"She was telling falsehoods about me just now, right here in your shop. I want to put a little note through her letterbox, warning her that what she said about me is slanderous; and if she doesn't stop it, I'll take the matter further."

"Was it about you and Reg King?"

"Yes. So *you've* heard it too. The Kings have been good to us, and I would hate them to be upset by unfounded rumours. I'm sure Joan would know it's all a pack of lies, but it might spoil a good friendship, even so."

"The person you want to get on to is Frances Claxton."

"Not *her* again. She spread something about my in-laws, just before my mother-in-law died. It happened to be true, but it was something they'd wanted to keep to themselves. Poor Albert, it just added to his grief."

"Don't worry, I'll talk to the Kings. Trust me, I'll be very diplomatic. They may even have heard the rumours and are hoping they don't reach you at Crowsley. ... Anyway, it might be a good idea to stop Pauline in her tracks. Here's a pen and some paper. Will you make it anonymous?"

"I don't think so! It might bring her to her senses if I threaten to take legal action against her. Thank you so much for your help. With any luck, I'll get this in her letterbox before she gets home."

"If you give me your list and ration books, I'll fetch your things, and you can make yourself some tea. Do you know how to use an electric kettle?"

"Yes, my mother has one. Thank you."

Emily's note was terse and uncompromising:

> *Dear Pauline,*
> *Are you aware that slander is a punishable offence? If you carry on spreading untrue stories about me, I shall take you to court.*
> *Emily Goodchild*

The next day Reg knocked on Emily's door as he delivered the milk. He came straight to the point. "About those filthy rumours, forget them! We all know the truth, don't we? Joan says, 'Call in for a cup of tea or coffee when you next come to the shops.'"

"Thank you, Reg. It's great to have friends like you. Tell Joan I would really enjoy that. ... If it wasn't for the Hursts, I would be very lonely out here."

"How's your father-in-law doing?"

"He's still a bit lost, poor man. He's very forgetful, especially about leaving lamps burning, and he's *always* forgetting to observe the blackout. I have to check up on him all the time. My mother-in-law kept him in line but, now he's on his own, he's not coping at all well; he's rather a liability."

"I'm sorry to hear that. ... But then, your mother-in-law was a very remarkable woman, even if she wasn't all that easy to get along with."

"Yes, she was certainly good for poor Albert."

Chapter 7

Real angels wear trousers. They look like people we know, so we can trust them and feel safe. God looks down through the clouds with his clear-view binoculars. He sees big trouble and sends help fast!

June 1942

The story of the supposed liaison between Emily and Reg King died a natural death, but not before the scandalmongers had found something else about Emily to take its place. The last slice of Goodchild gossip from the mouth of Frances Claxton was the most unpalatable of all and, though only partially true, its substance had lasting repercussions for their family relationships. People were now saying, somewhat belatedly, that Emily had tried to get rid of her twins and that's why one had died at birth and the surviving twin was so delicate.

"So much for the Church and its teaching on the sanctity of human life!" pontificated Mrs Claxton. "Hypocrites, the lot of them! They tell us how we should live our lives, and then they do just what they like themselves. That's church people for you, C of E or Non-conformists. ... Yet, these particular Non-conformists are the worst of all; they actually believe they're the only ones who *are* right, and then brazenly try to get rid of their unwanted babies. I ask you!"

Emily did nothing at all to counter this story; no threatening communication was put through Fanny Claxton's door. Mrs Claxton was a dangerous enemy; Emily didn't have the energy to fight her and, as no-one else but herself was implicated, she simply responded by crying herself to sleep for many miserable nights. At least, John wasn't there to make matters worse. If blame was to be apportioned in the case, then John was the bigger sinner. He was the one who had panicked, not her.

June 1941

"A fourth pregnancy, no it can't be!" was John's initial response to the unwelcome news. "We've only been together the once. You told me it was the safe time, and that you wouldn't conceive, so how *can* you be pregnant?"

"I must have got my arithmetic wrong or be super-fertile, or something ..."

"Emily, I can't *feed* any more mouths," he shouted. "We ca*nnot* have any more children, do you hear?"

"I didn't become pregnant on my own."

"No, but you misled me."

"Not deliberately."

"You're irresponsible. Every time we come together, you fall for a baby. You'll have to stop it somehow. Talk to Nellie, she's a nurse!"

"No, I won't. It's wrong to take a little life once it's started," sobbed Emily.

"You'll have to; it's not a living soul till it's born."

"Yes, it is. What about Psalm a hundred and thirty-nine where it says, '... thou hast covered me in my mother's womb. ... My substance was not hid from thee, when I was made in secret. ... Thine eyes did see my substance, yet being imperfect.'? Then in Psalm fifty-one, David says, 'Behold, I was shapen in iniquity; and in sin did my mother conceive me.' These texts suggest that he became a living person at conception."

"In Psalm fifty-one, the Psalmist was talking about his sin, not about when he became a living soul, person, or what have you. What is more, it strongly suggests that conception itself is sinful if you don't want to have a baby. ... So, Emily, we can't have this child. You *must* write to Nellie for advice. I'll see what you've written before you send it." With that, he walked out of the back door towards the outside toilet. Emily knew he would sit up there for some time.

Emily reluctantly wrote to Nellie, and John posted the letter himself, on his way to work the following Monday. Within the week, Emily received the following reply:

> *21st June, 1941*
> *Dear Emily,*
>
> *Thank you for your letter. I don't know that I can be of any help to you now that this baby is already on the way. Anyway, I am happy to share my experience with you, as it may be helpful in preventing further pregnancies in the future.*
>
> *Once the twins were born, I decided that I couldn't go on bearing children. David fervently believes that God only sends us the children He wills for us, whereas I believe He expects us to use our common sense in the matter. David still wants us to share the same bed and for me to meet his emotional and physical needs as, and when, they occur. (He thinks nothing of waking me up in the middle of the night and then chiding me for my lack of enthusiasm for the whole messy business!) He doesn't worry his head about possible outcomes — he enjoys his moment of ecstasy and then goes off to sleep without a care in the world. So, I went along to my doctor and discussed the whole matter of birth control with him.*
>
> *David would not agree for us to use any of the commonly used methods — sheaths, caps, pessaries, etc. — and your*

John wouldn't either, so we have to take something immediately after the event. I have been going to a herbalist for a concoction of pennyroyal (Mentha pulegium) and taking it the morning after. Pennyroyal is used for stomach cramps and lots of other things, so tell the herbalist what you need it for and he will make it up for you and prescribe the correct dosage.

You don't say in your letter how long you have been pregnant, but I would not advise an abortion. Things don't always go well and most family doctors are unwilling to do them unless the mother's life is seriously at risk. Village women who take the law into their own hands with knitting needles and crochet hooks often do themselves irreparable damage, so don't do anything silly. I don't think pennyroyal will be effective so long after conception. You could ask your herbalist, but I'm not sure what he would say. Maybe you should talk to your family doctor first as he knows your medical history.

I must finish this and put it in the post before I get the evening meal.

Yours affectionately,
Nellie

On the Friday morning, Emily sat reading and re-reading the letter. It was reassuring to receive such a sensible message from her sister-in-law. Even Nellie wasn't in favour of abortion once the foetus had started to develop. Would that be enough to change John's attitude and make him see sense?

Unfortunately, when John read the letter that evening, he failed to grasp the full import of Nellie's reply.

"Fancy telling us all that about their private life! I thought Nellie had a bit more delicacy than that! She gives us no help at all on the real problem."

"Yes, she does. She says she wouldn't advise an abortion and you are asking me to get rid of this baby — that's abortion!"

"Can't you take a double dose of that herb she talks about?"

"That might do me harm in other ways. I suppose I ought to see Dr Prince and check it out with him before we do anything."

"No, we don't want other people knowing our business. You go to the herbalist in Reading. It's in Union Street, isn't it?"

"Yes, I know the place," snapped Emily. "That's where I get my Dandelion Coffee."

"Well, go into Reading tomorrow. I'll mind the children; there's no overtime this weekend."

The following morning, Emily trudged across the fields and caught the number seven bus. Her heart was heavy and her troubled mind working overtime. John was asking her to do something wrong. Yet in Ephesians chapter five of her Bible, wives are commanded to be subject 'to their own husbands in every thing'; it's even written as two words, meaning every single little thing. But what if their husbands try to make them do things which they both know are morally wrong? Would Scripture still condemn her for following the dictates of her *own* conscience? Could she stand up to John's rages, if she dared to disobey him? What if he actually resorted to physical violence and laid into *her* in the way he laid into his children when they exasperated him? She didn't want to lose the baby *that* way.

The herbalist, Joshua Rigby, was a wizened little man with frizzy grey hair, but he certainly knew his herbs. As Emily discussed her dilemma he wrinkled his brow in concentration. When he finally spoke, his utterances were considered and enunciated very clearly and precisely.

"Pennyroyal has been known to cause women to abort their foetuses," he deliberated, "but I don't know what else it might do to you without a doctor on hand to assist you. Have you been to your family doctor about your problem?"

"No, my husband won't let me. He's afraid of people finding out about our affairs."

"Surely you can trust your own doctor's discretion and confidentiality, can't you?"

"Of course we can. But there are always gossips in a rural community and sometimes private information *does* get into the wrong hands."

"I wouldn't take any risks, if I were you. The body is a very complicated machine. If you tamper with its workings in one area, you will affect the way it works elsewhere. I'm happy to sell you the pennyroyal. It has many beneficial properties; if you suffer from stomach cramps, or delayed menstruation, for example. But as a reliable method of bringing about an abortion, I have serious doubts."

"Thank you for being so honest with me; I can't go home without it, anyway. Have you any literature on its recognised uses?"

"Yes, I have a helpful little pamphlet here, with useful information about the herb itself, how to use it, and the doses you need to take in each case. I sell it already made up like this, or you can buy the dried herbs for you to boil up yourself."

"I'll take the bottle."

"That will be a shilling, please. Thank you for your custom."

On the way home Emily read the little pamphlet all through. It was immediately obvious that Joshua Rigby was no writer. She wished she could edit his pamphlets for him. But despite the spelling mistakes and his cumbersome grammatical constructions, she felt she understood exactly what pennyroyal could be used for and why she shouldn't use it to try to abort her unborn child.

~

John seemed flustered as Emily walked through the kitchen door. Ann was sitting up in the high-chair, beating a frantic tattoo with her fists on the tray in front of her. Jimmy was lying on the floor grizzling that he wanted something to eat, and I was trying to pick up some mess under the kitchen table with a dustpan and brush which were far too big for me.

"Can't you see you've left some behind?" he scolded angrily. I dissolved into tears.

"These children have been very trying while you've been away. I hope your visit to the herbalist has been worthwhile."

"We'll talk about it later, after we've had our meal. It will be the last of the cold meat and I'll mash up some Pom; that will be quicker than scraping the new potatoes."

After lunch, all three children were put to bed and John and Emily sat down at the kitchen table. Emily knew there would be ructions and hoped the children upstairs would soon fall asleep.

"So what did he say? Do you know what to do now?"

"Yes. I must not use the pennyroyal for trying to abort my baby. He doesn't know what other damage it might do to me if I did what you suggested. He gave me this leaflet all about the herb. He also said I ought to go and talk to my doctor." At the word 'doctor,' John bristled.

"I forbid you to go to Dr Prince about it. We will keep this to ourselves, do you hear?"

"Then you must know that what you're asking me to do is both wrong and very risky. I don't want to take the consequences."

"Wrong or not, we made a mistake which we must put right. You've *got* to get rid of it." As he said this, he got up from his seat and stood over Emily. There was anger and menace in his eyes as well as fear. "Where's the bottle?"

"In my bag."

"Go and get it *now*."

Emily knew what was coming. He would stand over her and make her take the wretched stuff. She couldn't even remember what the dose was for re-starting her monthly cycle. She held the bottle in her hand and hastily tried to read the label. She thought it said 'one tablespoonful' but the print was rather uneven. John snatched the bottle out of her hand and, not even bothering to study the instructions, he yelled at her to fetch a tablespoon. Then he clumsily emptied some of the dark liquid into the spoon.

"Open your mouth, Emily. You've got to take it."

She meekly opened her mouth, and offered up a despairing SOS to her Creator. John poured two whole tablespoonfuls down her throat. It tasted innocuous enough, but only time would tell what its long-term effects on her inside would be. In the short-term it appeared to have no effect whatsoever. The baby was safe for now, and John said no more about getting rid of it.

Three months later Emily knew that there were *two* foetuses in her womb. Her pregnancy was not going well and John was obliged to let her seek medical advice. He was no longer panicking solely about the extra mouths he would have to feed but about what would happen if he were to lose Emily. Her blood-pressure was rising dangerously and John was behaving, at times, like a demented idiot. What had he done to her, forcing that herbal concoction down her throat?

May 1942

Now, almost a year later, thanks to Frances Claxton and company, Emily had to confront the whole unhappy episode all over again. She cried for the lost baby. She cried over her lost health, convinced that the pennyroyal had, in fact, upset her inside in the way Joshua Rigby had said it might. She cried over her relationship with her husband. John was truly sorry for the way he had treated her, but he couldn't love her in the way she longed to be loved. His letters from Buxton were so dry and formal, never a hint about how he was really feeling as he adjusted to his new environment. His enquiries about the children always concerned their conduct, never their emotional or spiritual needs. Perhaps Maggie could write him a letter, all by herself. It would help her catch up with her reading and writing, too.

"Can I really write a letter to Daddy? Would he like it?"

"I'm sure he would. Here's some paper."

"Thank you, Mumsie."

Maggie worked hard on her letter. She wanted to do it all by herself, though there were many words she didn't really know how to spell, and some of her lower case letters landed up the wrong way round. It was strange, she had no problem writing the upper case letters correctly.

> Monday
> Dear Dabby,
> How are you? Do you like it in the army? Do you have enuff to eat?
> I am going to qlay with Pat. She has a qarty on Fribay. She will de seven. She goez to the dig scool in Grove Roab. I am still in Mrs Claxton's class dut I have a reebing dook now.
> I must go to deb now. It is eit a'clock.
> Goobnite, Dabby,
> love from
> Margaret Goobchilb

Emily smiled at the reversed B's, P's and D's, and other misspellings; but she left them all just as Maggie had written them, expecting that John would smile at them too. Maggie's letter would no doubt cheer him up.

Imagine her dismay when, the following week, she received an irate letter from her husband, deploring Maggie's lamentable lack of progress with her writing. Hadn't he tried to teach the child to write, even before she went to school? Where did she get those dreadful spellings from? He told Emily that Maggie should be made to read aloud from one of her Sunday school books before she went to bed each night. And he wanted her to have learnt the twenty-third Psalm before he came home on leave.

My mother didn't tell me what my father had said about my letter. I hoped he would send me a letter back, but he didn't.

"Did Daddy like my letter?"

"Of course he did, darling. He's busy; that's why he didn't write back. But he wants me to help you with your reading and writing. You missed such a lot of school while you were in Amersham."

"Yes, and Mrs Claxton's made me sit with the five-year-olds so I can't always hear what she's teaching the big ones up the other end."

"Well, Mumsie will try to help you at home. So when you write a letter to Daddy, we'll look at it together and go over any mistakes. Then you can send him a perfect letter with no mistakes. Would you like that?"

"Yes, I would."

"I'll help you with your reading, too."

"But Mrs Claxton won't let me bring my reading book home, will she?"

"She might if I ask her nicely. If not, we can read some of your prizes together."

"They're much harder than my reading book."

"You'll see. You'll be able to read some of them by the time you're seven."

Lessons with my mother were great fun; and when she was too busy to teach me, she always gave me something interesting to do. Sometimes it was a picture to draw and write about, and other times she gave me some spellings to learn.

Mrs Claxton refused to allow me to bring my reading book home. So I learnt to read from much more exciting books. My mother gave me various strategies for learning new words and 'Fanny's funny phonics' was only one of them. Suddenly learning became enjoyable, and even my father noted, with some surprise, that my letters were improving. Then he started to write letters to me.

The summer after my sixth birthday, I was pushing Jimmy and Ann around the Triangle on most days that I wasn't at school. The hamlet of Crowsley looked something like a triangle from an aerial photograph or road map. On the short side up to Brookers' Farm, the lane was at right angles to the road running between Peppard and Shiplake Row. At the farm it turned an almost right angle, and then most of the dwellings were on the long, slightly bent side of the triangle, which rejoined the Shiplake Road near the main gates of Crowsley Park. Our lane led off the long side at the edge of Brookers' farm and turned into a footpath at Tudor Cottage. There were no dwellings on the Shiplake Road, which made the third side of the triangle, apart from the Crowsley Park mansion and workers' cottages, which were not visible from the gates.

My mother now had her hands full with baby Gracie. Gracie was a sickly baby and took up a lot of my mother's time. She still had difficulty feeding, and was very small for her age. In her cot, she looked like a china doll, with her big blue eyes, long lashes, and a mop of dark wavy brown hair. She was always so quiet and still.

I always enjoyed taking Jimmy and Ann for a ride in the pram, until one afternoon I encountered Ryan and Sean Maloney by the pond, throwing stones at the ducks. They were both several years older than I was.

"Don't do that; you'll hurt the ducks!" I scolded.

"And what will *you* do about it? ... What've you got in your pram? Oh little'uns! Perhaps they'd like a swim in the duck pond too; what d'yer think?" Ryan Maloney was a nasty piece of work, and I was alarmed by the menacing tone in his voice.

"Don't you touch the children!" I stormed angrily.

"Hark at her: 'Don't touch the children, don't touch the children,'" they both chanted derisively. "Who are *you*? Little Holy Mother? ... Let's tip the pram in the pond! Go on, let's!" hissed Sean, the older of the two, right into my left ear. Then the two of them tried to wrench the handle of the pram out of my hands. Ann and Jimmy both shrieked in terror.

At that moment Ed and Jeff, who I remembered from the haymaking, appeared from the farmyard, standing with arms akimbo, and looking as if they were spoiling for a fight. "You get away from that pram, or you'll have the two of us to reckon with," thundered Ed. The Maloney boys backed away, and then took off at high speed down the lane towards the Shiplake Road.

The next time I met up with Ryan and Sean Maloney it was a Saturday morning and I was wheeling the pram along the Shiplake Road, midway between the two Crowsley turnings. This time, there was no-one else in sight, let alone within earshot. I was completely on my own, and I knew it.

"Oh! here's Little Holy Mother and her little'uns," called out Sean in mock surprise.

"Sean, can you see anyone else about?" answered Ryan, moving his head from side to side.

"No, there's only us; very convenient. Let's tip those little'uns in the ditch," threatened Sean. "See, Ryan, there's muddy water in that ditch. Let's put them *all* in the ditch. Time to get our own back!"

"You're in our power this time, little girl," continued Ryan, thoroughly enjoying himself. "This is a lonely road, isn't it? So you'd better start saying your prayers. Not that it'll do you any good; we're *much* stronger than you are!"

"No, you're *not*," I answered tremulously. "God is stronger than you are."

"But, God's not here, sunshine, is he?" sneered Sean. "He doesn't care a damn about you lot; he can't even *see* you through those clouds up there."

"Oh yes he can," I answered, suddenly emboldened. If I can keep them talking, God *might* send someone to help me.

"Come on, Sean; let's get it over with," snarled Ryan derisively. The two young thugs grabbed the pram handle and pushed me viciously into the middle of the road. Jimmy and Ann started screaming in fright, poor little things. As I was scrambling to my feet, around the corner came Mr King, the milkman, in his van. He slammed on his brakes and drew up in front of me. At first, I didn't realise it *was* Mr King; there was a younger man in the van with him.

"Hey, what d'yer think you bullies are up to?" bellowed Reg King angrily. "Leave those children alone, d'yer hear me?"

The two Maloneys smirked at him insolently. "We're in charge here; this is none of your business, Mister."

At this, both men got out of the van. "It *is* my business," responded Mr King coldly. "I know those children and you're nothing to do with them. We will report what we have seen to the police, won't we, Jerry?"

"Yes, I know exactly who you two are," added the red-headed Jerry, an off-duty policeman whose father happened to be Henry Knolls, the local Chief Constable. "You Maloneys are already in trouble with the law, aren't you?" With that the two ruffians ran off, clambering through the barbed wire fence and into a field of grazing cattle. I wished there had been a herd of bulls in that field; but there were only the cows quietly minding their own business.

"Shall I help you lift the pram into the back, Reg?" asked Jerry. "I'll stay back here with the babies in the pram, and the little girl can have my seat."

"Are you all right, Maggie?" asked Mr King kindly.

"I am now *you're* here. I did ask God to send someone. Those horrid boys were going to put us all in the ditch."

"They won't be bothering you again; we'll see to that. But, maybe, you'd better stay in your own garden for the time being."

However, that was not the last I would see of Sean and Ryan Maloney. It was a good thing that I didn't know then what they were really capable of, or I would have been far too afraid ever to walk the lanes again on my own.

May 1942

The Grange was the only property of any size in Crowsley, apart from the mansion in Crowsley Park. It was the home of Sir Gerald and Lady Elizabeth Peel and had its own private drive leading off the Triangle, about three hundred yards beyond the ramshackle semi-detached house occupied by the Maloney family, if you were walking there from Tudor Cottage. To visit the Grange was like entering a different world; the elegant 18th century house was set in parkland, surrounded by formal gardens and immaculate farm buildings. By comparison, Mr Brooker's farmyard was little more than a grubby postage stamp.

I arrived home from school one day to find Lady Elizabeth sitting at our kitchen table drinking tea with my mother.

"Maggie, this is Lady Elizabeth Peel; come and say 'hello'," announced Mumsie as I entered the room.

"Hello, Lady Elizabeth Peel."

"Nice to meet you Maggie. Just call me 'Lady Elizabeth'."

"Nice to meet you, too, Lady Elizabeth."

"Maggie, I've been telling your mother about a Brownie pack I'm starting at the Grange on Saturday mornings, and I wondered if you would like to come? ... Unfortunately, there are no other girls from Crowsley apart from my daughter, Stephanie; but you'll soon get to know them all. There's Jane, Belinda, Penny, Andrea, Felicity and, of course, Stephanie. They're all a little older than you, and go to a different kind of school, but they're nice, friendly girls."

Before I could answer, my mother thought of a snag.

"Oh dear! Lady Elizabeth, I've just remembered something. My husband won't agree to it; he's already told me he doesn't want Maggie to join any of the uniformed organisations, like Brownies or Guides."

"That's a pity! Anyhow, we will be a very small pack, with only six or seven girls. ... Actually, I hadn't even thought about putting them in uniform. Would that make a difference?"

"Yes, it would. It's the *uniform* he objects to, not the activities. ... It's ironic though; he's wearing a uniform himself now, much against his will, I may add," chuckled my mother. "He's stationed at Buxton, in the Army Catering Corps."

"So he doesn't object to serving his country, then?"

"No, it's just that he, personally, feels it is wrong for *him* to take a life."

"That's understandable. I'm involved with the Red Cross, and our work is to *support* our boys. We *save* life, even enemy lives, rather than destroy it. ... So, Maggie, would you like to join our Brownie pack?"

"Yes, please, Lady Elizabeth," I answered, even though I was very much in awe of this grand lady, with her fine clothes and posh voice. She did have a kind face, though; maybe I'd soon get used to her and her classy ways. But what about the other girls? Would they look down on me?

Brownies started the following Saturday. All six girls; Jane,

Belinda, Penny, Andrea, Felicity, and Stephanie, were bigger than me and spoke with a plum in their mouth, like Lady Elizabeth. They each attended the PNEU School in Peppard: this means Parents' National Educational Union; the parents had to pay school fees as well as for the girls' attractive, green and grey school uniforms. I began to feel rather envious of these privileged young ladies as the weeks went by. They wore smart clothes, even on a Saturday, and they always seemed to know what to say. Brownie uniforms would have made us all *look* the same, but they wouldn't have done anything for my social standing or for my lack of confidence in the presence of my superiors.

"Let's start with some knitting," announced Lady Elizabeth on that first day, after she had introduced me to everyone. She gave each of us a ball of brightly-coloured wool and a pair of size nine needles. Felicity made a face. Andrea stated that she didn't know how to knit, and Stephanie looked at her mother with an unspoken question in her eyes. What has knitting got to do with Brownies?

"We are going to knit squares to make blankets for the war effort."

"Can't we just buy them?" suggested Stephanie.

"No, we can't. Ladies everywhere are knitting things like pullovers, scarves, balaclava helmets, mittens, socks, and gloves ... for the civil defence workers, to keep them warm and comfortable. But it's easier for us to knit blankets for the Red Cross as they don't require any shaping. It's all straight knitting. I'm going to knit some squares, too. It's very important for us *all* to do something for the war effort."

"How many stitches do we have to cast on?" I asked timidly.

"Twenty-four."

"Do I knit it all in plain, or in plain and purl?"

"All plain; we call it garter stitch. Then we get a blanket that is the same on both sides."

I liked knitting, and I was glad that I could just get on with it by myself. Most of those other girls needed Lady Elizabeth to start theirs off for them and sort out their mistakes, and dropped stitches as they went along.

"How many rows do you want?" I asked her half-an-hour later.

"Let me see. Well done! You've almost got your square,

Maggie. Just another three rows will do it. Do you know how to cast off?"

"Yes, Lady Elizabeth."

My finished square was a beautiful cherry red. Lady Elizabeth showed it to everyone else. I felt so proud that I could do something more quickly than those older girls. Later I went walking home with three more balls of wool; blue, yellow and green, and the pair of knitting needles, wrapped up in a brown paper bag.

Our second activity was more difficult. It was a game called 'Chinese Whispers', although Lady Elizabeth just called it 'Messages'. She explained it like this:

"You are going to spread yourselves all round the outside of the house, leaving a big gap between you and the next person. ... Stephanie, I'm going to whisper something into your ear. When you have heard it *twice*, you are going to run and pass what you think you have heard on to Felicity. Felicity will pass what she has heard on to Andrea, and so on, right round the house until the message finally gets round to Maggie. ... Then we'll all come together on the front porch and Maggie will tell us what she thinks she has heard. ... You will all be surprised how much the message has been changed as it has gone around the house."

Lady Elizabeth's message was: "You must run and hide. Then wait for the all-clear."

I heard and reported the following: "You have won a ride. Ben's late; it's a tall deer."

This makes no sense at all as a coherent message; but then Penny *was* giggling rather a lot when she whispered it into my ear. We all laughed when everyone repeated what they thought they had heard, and we could soon see how it came to be changed so much. We played three more games, starting with a different person each time, but the results got worse instead of better. Finally, Lady Elizabeth told us about a message that was apparently sent over the wireless by some officer in the army.

The message sent out was: "I'm going to advance. Send reinforcements."

What was heard at the other end was: "I'm going to a dance. Send three and four pence."

It made perfect sense, but when Lady Elizabeth explained the original message to us, we wondered how the battalion fared without the extra soldiers they needed.

As the weeks went by, I began to look forward to Brownies. Every week we did something new, and I learned a lot from the other girls, too. They seemed to do such exciting things at *their* school, studying subjects like French and Latin, as well as 'The Three Rs': Reading, Writing and Arithmetic. Lady Elizabeth was such a lovely person and I couldn't believe at first that she wasn't just being kind – that she really *did* want me there in her Brownie pack.

Chapter 8

30th July, 1942

There was an air of edgy anticipation in the Maloney household. Nobody said anything out loud. But the menfolk were definitely up to something, something big if it actually came off. What if it didn't? Only Bridget Maloney, the long-suffering skivvy in this male-dominated family of misfits, ever worried about consequences. None of the others cared a fig about what *she* thought of their criminal goings-on. They had all been on the wrong side of the law; even the younger boys had been caught shoplifting and engaging in other kinds of petty crime. Tonight they were planning to carry out a burglary at the Grange.

Sir Gerald and Lady Elizabeth Peel had lots nice things in that grand house of theirs. The Maloneys didn't see why they shouldn't relieve them of some of these desirables. There would be plenty of people who'd be glad to get their greedy mitts on the loot. It was their big chance to make a killing, as long as they were vigilant and didn't bungle the whole operation.

"Bridget, go to bed early tonight, d'yer hear?" instructed Bob Maloney. "Don't you dare wait up for us. We've all got business to do."

"You're not taking Sean and Ryan," protested Bridget.

"Oh yes, I bloody well am. They're our look-outs; we need them to get through small spaces."

"No, Bob; they're too young. I don't want them getting caught."

"They won't be, if they bloody well do as they're told. Now shut up woman, or I'll box your ears!"

"There'll be a scene if you do, Bob Maloney. ... Now, come on, where're yer all going, Bob?"

"We're not telling. If something goes wrong, you know nothing, right? You can't grass on us to the coppers."

～

"Cor, it ain't half cold out here," complained Ryan. "How a'we s'pposed to find our way in *there* without a light?"

"Let's go round the back first," suggested Sean. "Mrs Perkins could've left sommat open. ... Yes, here's the kitchen."

Just then, from the direction of Woodley aerodrome, where the Phillips and Powis aircraft factory designed and tested the new Miles Magister and Miles Master pilot training planes for the RAF, a searchlight suddenly lit up the sky and moved its beam in their direction. For a few seconds they could see all the back windows of the house very clearly.

"Look! ... There. *That* little room! The window's open a crack. ... Thank you, Jerry!" whistled Ryan, something he'd heard grown-ups say in irony, after an air-raid.

"You get in there, Ryan. You're the littlest. I'll fetch the others and you open the back door for us."

Now, in the distance, they could distinctly hear the drone of enemy aircraft; but neither boy had time to pay any attention to it. Sean headed for the ancient yew tree where he knew Bob, Patrick, Rory and Shamus were hiding. The thick boughs, with their millions of thin, sharp leaves, had hidden them all completely. However, there was sufficient illumination from the searchlight for them to see Sean rushing towards them.

"There's a little window by the kitchen. Ryan's trying to climb in. Let's make for the back door."

As they all crept towards the house another searchlight lit up. "Dammit!" hissed Patrick. "This'll wake his Lordship."

As he was speaking, the enemy planes had apparently been spotted, for faraway gunfire started up from the anti-aircraft batteries, no doubt bringing down at least some of the bombers. Crowsley was too far out into the country for any air-raid sirens to have been heard, but the searchlights were still playing across the sky. The raids were not actually intended for the Reading area at all, but for Coventry, Birmingham and other important towns in the Midlands. News of the damage done in these raids appeared in the daily newspapers two days later. Fortunately, the devastation was nothing like the massive raid on Coventry in November 1940, when the city's 14th century cathedral was destroyed and more than a thousand people were either killed or seriously injured.

~~~

So far, so good. ... Ryan had successfully eased himself through the pantry window, and was standing at the back door waiting for the others.

"Right; you two boys, hang around down here. ... Pat and Rory, you make a start on *this* side of the house," rasped Bob, indicating a location vaguely to the front and left of the kitchen area. "Go for anything you think will sell. You *have* got yer torches and sacks? ... Good. ... Shamus and me, we'll see if we can find some of her Ladyship's jewellery. Let's hope she's got her own room!" That was something he hadn't been able to find out in advance.

~~~

Lady Elizabeth Peel did not have her own bedroom. She shared a king-sized bed with Sir Gerald, her husband of fifteen years, and Sir Gerald was a light sleeper. The searchlights had disturbed him, and he felt uneasy. He sat up in bed listening intently. He could just hear the thrum of distant bombers. But something else was amiss, right here in the house. Intruders ... there were intruders moving around downstairs. He couldn't exactly hear them, but he could sense their presence, even smell them. He switched on his bedside lamp, and felt under the bed for his shotgun. Then he put on his black velvet dressing-gown and matching slippers, and strode out of the room on to the landing. He was a tall, handsome man with an imposing presence, even without the gun.

Bob Maloney was creeping stealthily towards the staircase. From below, he watched aghast as the door of the master bedroom opened and the first thing he saw was the glint of Sir Gerald's gun. Shamus saw it too. Sir Gerald normally used it as a sporting gun for shooting wild duck, game or rabbit; but he found it very useful for scaring off would-be trespassers and thieves. Both men were hidden behind the banisters as he switched on the landing light. Then he began to descend the magnificent staircase, eyes peeled and shotgun at the ready. There was nothing for it. They would have to scarper.

"Hey, there! What do you think you're doing in my house?" bellowed Sir Gerald from the third stair down. Bob and Shamus didn't stop to enlighten him. The kitchen door was still unlocked; they'd collect the boys on the way out. In an attempt to chase after them, Sir Gerald missed his footing, sliding over a bulge in the carpet caused by a loose stair-rod. He pitched forward and landed head-first on the highly-polished wooden floor below.

~~

Patrick and Rory were in the large sitting room at the front of the house, stuffing their sacks with clocks, delicate vases, and other attractive little knick-knacks. They heard a movement on the stairs and then Sir Gerald's voice, and two pairs of feet scuttling away in the direction of the kitchen. They also heard the ominous thud as Sir Gerald's heavy frame hit the floor. Damn! They'd been discovered already. If they were going to get away with the loot without being seen, they'd have to clamber out through the window. Bugger the bloke who'd just fallen down the stairs! He wasn't *their* responsibility.

Rory held the sacks, while Patrick opened the large sash window and then jumped out on to the flower bed below. He took the two sacks from his brother and then ran off with them towards the yew tree. Rory hurried after him, leaving the window open behind him. There was no way of shutting the damn thing from the outside.

Meeting up under the camouflage of the sturdy yew, the Maloneys waited anxiously for any signs of movement from the house. They saw none, so after five minutes they all sped off across the grass towards the farm buildings. They then found a gap in the hedge and scurried home across the fields. There were still searchlight beams in the sky, and they could just hear the distant roar of yet more aircraft. Their sole concern was to arrive home before anyone saw them. Once they were clear of the Grange and they realised that it was now about two o'clock in the morning, they began to relax. They thought it highly unlikely that anyone would catch a glimpse of them now. But they were wrong.

Ernie Hurst was cycling home from Shiplake. He had been called out to attend to a sick heifer, and he and the Vet had worked for over an hour on her, before they were both satisfied that she was out of danger and could safely be left.

As he was passing the turn to the Grange, Ernie looked out over the fields towards the Thames Valley near Mapledurham, and across to Aldermaston. The skies were now lit up in that direction. Obviously, more enemy activity was expected from another quarter. Suddenly, his attention was diverted by the appearance of a little huddle of silhouetted figures in the foreground to the left of him. Four adults and two youngsters, by the look of it. They had probably come from the Grange and were making tracks for one of the nearby houses. They seemed to be in rather a hurry. This looked suspicious. The Maloneys ... Oh no! What have *they* been doing at the Grange? He ought to report them to the police. Hastily switching off his dynamo, he cycled the rest of the way without lights.

Once home, Ernie immediately dialled 999 and asked for the police. When he got through to the officer on duty, he came straight to the point.

"I'm Ernie Hurst of Honeysuckle Cottage, Crowsley, reporting something suspicious ..."

"Yes. Okay, Sir. Let's have the details."

"A group of men and boys have just left the Grange in Crowsley. I saw them crossing the fields between the Grange and the new houses. ... I think they're the Maloneys, and that they've been up to something. Two of them seemed to be carrying sacks. They could've committed a serious crime. ... "

The officer yawned, and then remarked inquiringly, "You're out late, Sir."

"Yes, I was called out to a sick heifer. The farm's in Shiplake."

"Do you know where these ... er ... Maloneys live?"

"Yes, Officer. They live in the second of the new houses as you come up the lane from the Shiplake end; you know, near the park gates?"

"Yes, I know it, and I'm pretty sure we'll recognise the house. ... I'll send someone out to investigate. Thanks for your help, Sir. Goodnight, or what's left of it."

"Goodnight to you, Officer."

Lady Elizabeth Peel continued to sleep soundly for several minutes after the accident, despite her husband's angry words, the commotion made by the escaping Maloneys, and his headlong tumble down the stairs. When she finally awoke, she instantly sensed that something was wrong; the pink glow from the bedside lamp, the empty space beside her where her husband should have been sleeping ... where had he gone? ... His dressing-gown was not on its peg, the bedroom door was ajar, and the landing light was on. ... Where *was* he? Everything seemed so quiet. ... No, was that a moan? A plaintive murmur coming from the bottom of the stairs?

She jumped out of bed in a cold sweat; grabbed her pink silk dressing-gown, and made for the stairs. Then, for several seconds, she stood transfixed at the top of staircase. ... There he was, sprawled out across the floor not far from the bottom step, face down and lying so still. She knew instinctively by the way he was lying that he had fallen onto his head. Why, oh why, hadn't she woken up as soon as it happened? Numb with shock, she silently moved down the stairs. She came to the third tread. The carpet was loose and the rod had come adrift. She could see at once why he had lost his balance. Misty-eyed, she knelt down and carefully felt for a pulse. Yes, he *was* alive but barely conscious. What if he'd broken his neck in the fall? Why was he out of bed in the first place? ... Oh God, why did this have to happen to Gerald? ... Why now? What had been going on while she slept?

"I must ring for an ambulance," she told herself calmly. "It'll take nearly an hour to get here from Henley, but it can't be helped; he needs an orthopaedic specialist, that's for sure. I'll have to call Mrs Perkins and see if she will come in to sit with Stephanie while I follow the ambulance."

~~~

"Mummy, I'm frightened. Has a bomb dropped somewhere near here?" Nine-year-old Stephanie appeared on the landing, shivering in her flannelette nightie, her long, blonde hair strewn across her face. She ran into her parents' elegant bedroom, beautifully furnished in pastel shades of pink, green and cream, expecting to find them both in bed. "Where *are* you, Mummy?" she cried out in alarm.

Instead of her parents, she found Mrs Perkins sitting in her mother's comfortable armchair, fast asleep and her mouth wide open. The book she had been reading had fallen on to the carpet in front of her. The words on the cover were, 'Gone with the Wind'.

"Sorry, Stephanie; I must've gone off to sleep," spluttered the kindly housekeeper, recovering her wits. "Your daddy's been taken to the hospital; he fell down the stairs. Your mother's followed the ambulance in the car. I don't know when she will be back. ... Now, darling, what is it? Did you have a bad dream?"

"I heard noises; lots of different noises. I thought the Jerries were dropping bombs or something."

"Not here, darling."

"How *did* my daddy fall down the stairs?"

"We don't know that yet, Stephanie love. ... It's nearly four o'clock, and *you* must get some more sleep. Would you like me to do you another hot water bottle?"

"Yes please, Mrs Perkins. ... I still feel a little bit scared. And now I want to know about Daddy."

"We won't know anything until Mummy gets back in the morning."

The hot-water bottle had a soft fluffy cover around it. By the time Mrs Perkins had tucked it back down in the bed beside her, Stephanie was almost asleep.

The news from the hospital was definitely not good. Just a loose piece of carpet and yet such terrible consequences! Alice Perkins had only to glance at Lady Elizabeth's face to realise that the situation was grave.

"How is he, your Ladyship?" she murmured.

"As well as can be expected. He's broken his neck and will never walk again."

"Oh, no! ... I should've noticed that loose stair-rod. It's *all* my fault!"

"No it isn't. It's no one's fault. It was an *accident*. ... They're sending him to Stoke Mandeville, so that he can learn how to cope with life as a quadriplegic."

"What's that?" cried Alice Perkins.

"He is paralysed from the neck down. He won't be able to use his arms or his legs, and his only way of getting about from now on will be in a wheelchair. The rehabilitation programme will take several months, so he probably won't be back home with us here much before Christmas."

"Oh dear! I am *so* sorry, your Ladyship. ... Anyhow, I've found out why Sir Gerald was out of bed. You've had burglars. Several things are missing from the sitting room and I found one of the windows wide open. Look, I've made a list of what's missing: there's your grandfather's carriage clock, your pretty Wedgwood vases, and many of your cut-glass animals and birds from Austria..."

"Don't worry. I'm not that bothered; they're only *things*. It's Gerald I'm worried about. How will he cope, stuck in a wheelchair for the rest of his life? He's always been so active."

"Shall I phone the police?"

"Yes, I suppose we ought to."

At ten o'clock in the morning, the Maloney household was in ferment. They couldn't decide what to do. Patrick and Rory thought they'd got away with it, and that no-one could possibly link *them* with the thefts at the Grange. Bob and Shamus were not so sure. Bridget had already been packed off to Reading on the first bus, with clear instructions as to where she should try to sell the first sack of loot, and Sean and Ryan were still asleep in their beds. Now the remaining adults were quarrelling among themselves.

"Dad, don't forget we've been caught by the police before; they'll think of us immediately, bloody bastards. They'd love to put us away," argued Rory. "They may even find our fingerprints on summat."

"Nah, we didn't touch nothing. We didn't have the time," answered Shamus.

"But *we* did, in the sitting room. We opened some drawers ... as well as picking up what was lying around," acknowledged Patrick.

"Go and bury the second bloody sack in the back garden, Pat ... just in case they come and try to search this place."

Patrick had only just buried the sack and its contents when a police car drew up outside the gate. So he continued digging the plot, hoping to fool the coppers. There were two of them.

"Hi! We're looking for Bob Maloney. Is he at home?" inquired the one called Jerry. He was Constable Jerry Knolls, whose father was Henry Knolls, the Chief Constable.

"Who?" answered Patrick, playing for time.

"Bob Maloney. ... Who are you?"

"Me? I'm the gardener." Jerry was suspicious, but Patrick appeared to ignore them and went on with his digging.

His companion, Bruce Holmes, was the sergeant carrying the search warrant. He knocked loudly on the back door, shouting, "Open up; police." But there was no response from those inside. Bob, Rory and Shamus had hidden themselves up in the loft as soon as they heard the police car approaching, and the door was locked and bolted.

"Come on Jerry, let's go round the front." But they were not prepared for what happened next.

Ryan and Sean had woken up while the policemen were talking to Patrick. They wondered where in the house their father was hiding; but they knew that he would expect them to try to and get rid of the bloody coppers before they had time to search the place. "Wouldn't it be fun to hit a policeman?" suggested Ryan. "Where are those rounders bats we pinched from school?"

"Under the stairs."

They quickly found the bats, unlocked the front door, and mounted the two stools conveniently placed beside the door, in front of the clothes rack. As Bruce turned the handle and walked in, closely followed by Jerry, both policemen were instantly clobbered around the face with the rounders bats.

"No, boys. Put those sticks down," commanded Bruce, as soon as he could catch his breath. His nose was bleeding and Jerry had a very painful jaw, but neither man was willing to let these unruly youngsters get the better of him.

"We don't like coppers. None of us do," answered Sean, lifting the stick to give Bruce another battering. But Jerry managed to overturn both stools with a single kick, and the two boys were disarmed, landing in an ignominious heap on the floor.

"Let's have the handcuffs, Sergeant. These two need to be taught a lesson."

⌒

Back at the Grange, the forensic team were busy collecting evidence. First, they put a layer of special dust on both the window frame where Ryan entered the house and the one where Patrick and Rory made their exit. As expected, they were able to see the greasy fingerprints of all three intruders very clearly. The second procedure was to carefully transfer these fingerprints onto special paper for identification purposes. Patrick and Rory had not only left theirs on the various drawers they had opened, but also on other surfaces around the sitting room as they had hastily removed each stolen item, piece by piece. Bob and Shamus had inadvertently left their fingerprints on the banisters as they had watched Sir Gerald emerge from the bedroom with his gun, and Sean's were found on the kitchen table. It was almost by chance that the team found Bob's and Shamus's fingerprints on the banisters. They had been wondering who had been at the bottom of the stairs just before Sir Gerald's accident, and decided to check the bottom few banisters. The fingerprinting was slow, painstaking work, but very satisfying when it produced results.

⌒

While the fingerprinting was in progress, Detective Inspector Andrews was also at the Grange, interviewing Lady Elizabeth Peel. He was a lively little man, almost retiring age, with a mop of silver grey hair. He wore a heavy brown overcoat, a couple of sizes too big for him, which he carefully removed before beginning the interview.

"I am very sad to hear of your husband's tragic accident, your Ladyship. Are you sure it *was* an accident?"

"I'm sorry, Inspector, I can't tell you anything about the intruders and their behaviour while they were in this house, as I slept through it all. But, looking at the loose carpet and broken stair-rod, I'm pretty sure that *they* were the cause of his fall, not any kind of foul play. ... My housekeeper, Alice Perkins, has made this list of everything that has been taken from the sitting room, if you'd like to see it."

The Inspector studied the list carefully. "Some of these items must be quite valuable."

"Yes, I should think that, altogether, the stolen items must be worth over five hundred pounds. But I'd rather lose *them* than have my husband in a wheel chair for the rest of his life!"

"Of course. It's a bad business, your Ladyship. ... That reminds me, I must pay a call on the Maloney household before I leave Crowsley. They're your neighbours just down the road. Do you know anything about them?"

"No, not really, though I may have seen them in the lane. ... Would you like some coffee before you leave, Inspector?"

"Yes, please. Black with two sugars."

"I'll just go and tell Alice ..." As she returned to her armchair, Lady Elizabeth struggled desperately to steer her thoughts away from the accident. So she thought of a question *she* wanted to ask him. "Inspector, do you find there is more crime now that we are experiencing shortages of various kinds?"

"Not overall, I don't think. In Reading, though, we're certainly meeting cases of food hoarding, which has recently been made a punishable offence. We now have a Food Executive Officer whose job is specifically to prevent the hoarding of food," chuckled D I Andrews. "One food inspector went to the home of a Mrs Elsie Carter in Caversham and found, hidden under the stairs, seventy pounds of preserves of various kinds, nearly two hundred tins of fish, eighty odd tins of milk, another eighty odd tins of meat, and a hundred tins of fruit."

"Goodness, was she running a guesthouse?"

"No, there were only the two of them. She'd bought it all wholesale from Kingham's before the rationing began."

"Whatever was she thinking of?"

"She said she was only doing what Government pamphlets told her to do and pleaded her innocence. *She* hadn't breached any rationing orders. ... Anyway, what with the fines and other costs, she was given a month to pay a sum of nearly fifty pounds. ... Then there's the profiteers. Old Jonesy, in St Mary's Butts, sold razor blades above the controlled price, so they fined him the colossal sum of three hundred and seventy-seven pounds. If he didn't cough up he'd face three months in jail!"

"What about crimes like theft and burglary?"

"No more than usual. Though, you'll laugh at this one. Out Wantage way, a vicar living alone in a very large vicarage came home late one night to find a tramp fast asleep on his sitting-room carpet. He could see how he'd got in; but nothing whatsoever was taken. The tramp looked so comfortable he let him stay there for the night. ... Just one more, then I really *must* go. This isn't about a crime; it's about a stray bomb that fell on a local country house; the Chronicle didn't say where. Anyway, the family was at dinner, when a bomb came through the roof. It fell straight through one of the bedrooms, landed in the sitting room and embedded itself in the grand piano. They had to get someone to defuse it. The paper noted particularly that it was a *German* piano, and deserved to be ruined!" At this, Lady Elizabeth even managed a wry smile.

$\backsim$

Inspector Andrews arrived at the Maloneys' house a few minutes after Ryan and Sean had been handcuffed. His beady eyes noticed Bruce's bleeding nose and Jerry's swollen jaw. He also saw the rounders bats lying on the floor, the stools standing by the clothes rack, and the two handcuffed boys sulking in the corner.

"Did these little ruffians hit you with those bats?"

"They did, and we're teaching them a lesson."

There was a creaking of boards up in the loft, and the boys instinctively looked up to the trapdoor on the landing.

"I think we'll find the others up there, Sir," said Bruce.

"And the one digging outside is also one of them," continued

Jerry. "I wouldn't be surprised if he wasn't trying to hide some of the stolen goods."

"Let's take them all down to the station. We've got two cars," answered the Inspector.

Bridget was picked up later and charged with receiving and selling stolen goods. The whole family were given custodial sentences, and the boys were sent to an approved school for young offenders for three years. Everyone in the hamlet was glad to see the back of them for a while. But we all knew that they would be back.

~

"Mumsie, I'm so bored. I do miss school and Brownies," I complained, as I watched the rain bucketing down outside. And the school holidays had only just begun.

"September will soon be here, Maggie. You'll see. You can give Lady Elizabeth a nice surprise when she sees how much knitting you've done."

"The others are good at knitting too now. They've *all* caught me up. ... We've nearly got enough squares for four blankets. Lady Elizabeth hasn't had time to sew them all together yet."

Our last session of Brownies was held on Saturday, 25th July. Lady Elizabeth informed us all that there would be no more Brownies until September, but she gave us plenty of wool to go on knitting the squares for the blankets. I enjoyed the knitting but I knew I was going to miss everyone. Even though I had never been to their homes, Jane, Belinda, Penny, Andrea, and Felicity had become my friends. How could I ever have thought that they were stuck up? And Stephanie said she would invite me round to the Grange for tea sometime in the holidays. I hoped so much that it would be soon. But in early August, a boy I had never seen before came to the kitchen door with a letter for my mother; she opened it immediately, and I could tell from her expression that something was wrong.

The Grange, Crowsley
4th August, 1942
Dear Mrs Goodchild,

It is with great sadness and regret that I have to inform you that I will not be restarting the Brownie Pack at the beginning of September as promised.

You may have already heard about my husband's accident on the night of 30th July, which has resulted in quadriplegia. The only part of his body he can move now is his head. He is being treated at Stoke Mandeville Hospital and will be there for some months as he learns to adjust to life in a wheelchair.

For this reason, Stephanie and I will be spending the weekends at Stoke Mandeville so that we can be with Gerald as much as possible. He is very depressed about what has happened to him and needs all the support he can get. We must be there for him.

Tell Maggie to go on making the squares. I will come and collect them in due course. Once we have established a settled routine, Stephanie and I can always work on the blankets while we sit and talk to Gerald.

Yours sincerely,
Elizabeth Peel

My mother, Emily, had been into Reading on Saturday, the first of August and had seen the placards outside the newspaper shops announcing: LOCAL LANDOWNER PARALYSED IN FALL. She even went into the newsagent's in Friar Street and glanced at the front page of the Chronicle, but failed to see the name of the victim. She was horrified now that she realised the victim had been Sir Gerald.

"What's wrong, Mumsie? Is it bad news?"

"Yes, Maggie, it is. ... Lady Elizabeth's husband has had a nasty accident. He will be in hospital for a very long time. The hospital is far away from here, so Lady Elizabeth and Stephanie will be going to stay near the hospital every weekend. There won't be any more Brownies, Maggie."

I started to cry. I cried for myself, not Sir Gerald. No tea at the Grange now. I wouldn't be seeing my new friends ever again. I couldn't imagine how Stephanie and Lady Elizabeth would be feeling, in the way my mother could.

"Why can't he be at a hospital in Reading or Henley?"

"Stoke Mandeville is a special hospital for people who can't use their arms and legs any more. Sir Gerald won't be able to walk now. He will have to learn how to get about in a special chair, and do things without his hands."

"How did he get like that?"

"He fell down the stairs and broke his neck. ... But Lady Elizabeth wants you to carry on with the knitting. She says she will come round to collect it and still make up the blankets for the Red Cross. She can do that as she sits and talks to Sir Gerald."

"Will the other girls keep on doing their knitting too?"

"Yes, I'm sure they will. I expect their mothers had a letter like mine, too."

Chapter 9

September 1943

Today was the beginning of the new school year and, at last, I was finally going up to the Big School. What is more, I could now read books other than my set readers and I could write a letter to my father that didn't need to be corrected by my mother; I had my own Thorndike Dictionary and I was learning how to use it. My mother had found it in William Smith's second-hand book shop in London Street, one day when we went to Reading.

Fanny Claxton hadn't been at all interested in my out-of-school achievements. However, she had to agree that I was always word-perfect when it was my turn to read to her but that was, on average, only twice a week. I was now on Book Four which included stories like 'The Three Billy Goats Gruff', 'Little Red Riding Hood', and 'Jack and the Beanstalk'. Some of them were rather scary, even though I knew everything would be all right in the end. Would I still be on the same book in my new class?

As we finished breakfast, it was a quarter to eight. Jimmy, Ann and Gracie were still upstairs in their beds, so I was surprised when I saw my mother putting on her raincoat and getting out the shopping bags.

"You don't *have* to take me to school, Mumsie; I do know the way."

"I want to see Mr Ford, and make arrangements for your school dinners. And it would be nice to see your new teacher. I also need to get some things at Kirbys'; we're nearly out of sugar. Mrs Hurst will coming up here to mind the others while I'm out."

"We *are* going on the bike, aren't we?"

"Of course; it's much easier carrying things on the bike, and very much quicker."

"I like the bike, especially when we're going downhill. I can feel the wind in my face and we seem to be going faster."

"Here's Mrs Hurst now."

"Everything all right, Emily?" called Rita Hurst as she opened the kitchen door.

"I think so. ... I'm afraid the little ones are still asleep upstairs," continued Emily apologetically. "I've put their clothes out for them. There's some hot water in the kettle. Will you see to them upstairs?"

"Yes, I think it will be easier that way. Have you a bucket for the nappies?"

"It's upstairs already. I'm sorry that you have to carry all the hot water up yourself."

"That's no bother. ... But you could get me some bacon if they have any at Kirbys'? Here's my ration book, just in case."

"Joyce said they were expecting some in when I spoke to her last week. I still find the shortages a troublesome nuisance."

"Don't we all!"

When we arrived at the school gates, there were many people

hovering around, even though it was only a quarter to nine. Over by the door to the Senior School some girls were skipping, two girls turning the rope, and the third girl in the middle doing the skipping. As she skipped, the turners chanted:

'Rat-a-tat-tat, who is that?
Only grandma's pussy-cat.
What do you want?
A pint of milk.
Where's your money?
In my pocket.
Where's your pocket?
I forgot it.
O you silly pussy-cat.'

They had just got to 'Where's your money?' for the second time when the skipper trod on the rope. Then they all changed places and started again. Would I ever be able to skip like that?

I stood watching the skippers enviously, as my mother parked the bike by one of the Sycamore trees which stood behind the railings in a long line of seven. As we walked towards the door labelled 'Junior Entrance', I could still see them out of the corner of my eye.

"I know where my classroom is," I exclaimed excitedly. "We came up to see our new teacher just before the holidays. Her name is Mrs Morrison. The classroom is only little, but the desks at the back are so big that I couldn't put my feet on the floor. ... At the Big School, we start at ten to nine, not nine o'clock."

"You can't go in yet, you'll have to wait for the bell."

Just as my mother said that, Miss Brown, Mr Ford's secretary, rang the bell and out into the forecourt came all the Junior School teachers. Mr Ford walked out of the Senior Entrance and then stood right in front of us all with some lists in his hands.

"Good morning, everybody. We will go into school one class at a time. We will start with the new children in Standard One. You are in Mrs Morrison's class; Mrs Morrison will show you where to hang your coats and take you into the classroom right at the far end of the Junior corridor. Parents, you may go in with your child, if you wish." He then proceeded to read out forty-seven names. Most of the boys and girls whose names he called had been with me in Mrs Claxton's class, but three of them were completely new to Sonning Common Council School. Mrs Morrison smiled at each one of us as we walked towards her. As my surname began with G, I was number twelve on the list and we all filed into school one after the other. In the cloakroom, Mrs Morrison had already labelled our pegs. I was one of the shortest in the class, so I was very relieved to find that my peg was on the bottom row, not the top one.

"Who handles the dinner money?" asked my mother in everyone's hearing.

"We will collect it in the classroom," answered Mrs Morrison, addressing us all. "If you give your child two shillings every Monday, she will bring it to me when I call her name on the dinner register. Today, parents can come into the classroom too as everything is new, and we haven't made out the dinner register yet."

I made for a seat right in front of Mrs Morrison's desk. Soon she had all the children sitting down in the desks, with one spare seat at the back, and the parents standing along the back wall. "It looks as if we have one hundred per cent attendance this morning," she said brightly. "We'll sort out the dinner money first and then you parents can get on and do your shopping." Mrs Morrison collected the money and wrote a careful list as she went along. When she had finished, the parents quietly disappeared.

Mrs Morrison marked the attendance register, starting to learn all our names, and then read us a story about Jesus welcoming the children, from 'The Children's Bible'. Mrs Morrison asked us questions about the story afterwards. It was more like a conversation about the story than the interrogations we used to suffer from Mrs Claxton. When someone gave the wrong answer, she simply smiled and explained that bit of the story to us all again. She absolutely encouraged us to make our own comments about the story; then everyone had to pay attention to the particular child who was doing the talking.

Mrs Morrison was so different from Mrs Claxton. We soon realised that she genuinely enjoyed being with children, and that we would have nothing to fear from her if we behaved ourselves and did our best. She was about my mother's age, and her son, David, was also in the class. She had fair hair and was taller and slimmer than my mother. Behind her glasses, I saw friendly grey eyes and I soon felt quite sure that I would be happy in her class.

As we finished talking about the story, Miss Brown came into the room to collect the dinner money and Mrs Morrison's list of names.

"I'll be writing up the dinner registers this morning and I'll be bringing them back, and collecting the attendance registers, before two o'clock this afternoon."

"Thank you, Miss Brown. I hope you can read my writing!"

"Don't worry; I'll be back if I can't."

The next lesson was Arithmetic. That seemed an awfully long name for counting and tables and sums. In the Infants School we had done little more than learn everything parrot fashion, without really thinking about what we were saying, or understanding the concepts behind our utterances. Mrs Morrison intended to remedy these deficiencies. Instead of making us mechanically chant our two times table, she had us counting real children in the classroom.

"Margaret Goodchild," she called, and I raised my hand. "I want you to count all the children in your block. If it helps, you can count out loud." I was in block two.

I counted all the children and there were eleven; one in each seat. "There are eleven, Mrs Morrison."

"I can see twelve; there is one you have forgotten." I looked at the children behind me and then at Jean Crocker, who was sharing my double desk.

"There really *are* eleven, Mrs Morrison."

Then she touched me on the shoulder. "Who is this little girl? Shouldn't she be included too?"

"Oh silly me! I forgot to count myself."

"How many desks are there in this block?"

"Six."

"And how many children in each desk?"

"Two."

Mrs Morrison wrote on the blackboard **6x2=12**. She then asked Jimmy Saunders, who was sitting in block one, to count the children in the first two blocks.

"Twenty-three, Miss."

"Who have you forgotten to include? He's wearing a green jersey."

"That's me, Miss." Mrs Morrison wrote **12x2=24**. Then, little by little, the whole table was built up and written down on the left-hand side of the blackboard, by counting the rows of children in those first two blocks. This was a fun way to learn our tables and I was quite disappointed when it was time to have our milk and go out to play.

In the juniors, our milk came in special third-of-a-pint bottles. These were placed in crates standing outside every classroom door. At the appropriate time, we each had to collect a bottle from the crate. In the top of each bottle was a cardboard disk with a small circle punched in it. When this was removed, our teacher inserted a straw, and we all sat at our desks drinking our milk.

Mrs Morrison not only enabled me to grasp the concepts behind the learning of tables and the doing of simple sums, she also taught me how to sew and awakened within me an interest in music. Her elder son, Michael, had been having piano lessons since he was four. Now, although he was only eleven, Miss Yapp, his piano teacher, was urging his mother to let him try for a junior scholarship to the Royal Academy of Music, in London. One afternoon, Mrs Morrison arranged for him to come and play one of his pieces to us on the piano in our classroom.

"Now, children did you enjoy that?"

"Yes, Mrs Morrison."

"What did it remind you of? Use your imaginations."

I put my hand up immediately. "A wasp trying to get at the jam," I blurted out eagerly. The other children laughed at me and I felt confused. It sounded exactly like a wasp buzzing about a jam pot.

"Well done, Maggie, you've got the right idea. The piece is called 'The flight of the bumblebee' by Rimsky-Korsakov. Bumblebees and wasps are similar in many ways. ... Now, Michael, will you play it again for us, while we make our fingers fly like bumblebees?"

As I listened, I made my fingers buzz and bumble about in time with the music. Normally I would be frightened of wasps and bumblebees, but this bee music was magic; I was a large, hairy bee flitting from flower to flower, and then up and away towards the clouds.

The music lesson was over far too quickly, and Michael Morrison made his way back to the Standard Four classroom. He did come back to play for us again later in the term but, in January 1944, he began his studies at the Royal Academy of Music. From then on, his general education was arranged around his music. He was being trained for a career as a concert pianist or a professional accompanist for singers and solo performers.

"Mumsie, can I learn to play the piano like Michael Morrison?" I asked when I arrived home that evening.

"We will have to wait until Daddy comes home on leave. I know he wants you to learn to play, but lessons cost a lot of money and you would have to practise every day. ... Michael Morrison is a very gifted boy, so you can't expect to play like him; but one day you might play well enough to play the harmonium for Sunday school."

"Like Auntie Frances does?"

"That's right."

"Mrs Morrison plays the hymns at assembly. We have assembly every morning with Standard Two. They come into our classroom."

"What hymns do you sing?"

"'All things bright and beautiful' and 'Fair waved the golden corn'; we're learning them for harvest."

"Are you going to have a special harvest assembly?"

"Yes; a real farmer is coming to talk to us and Standard Two, but it's not Mr Brooker."

The farmer who came was called Mr Barnicot; he said he spoke 'proper Cornish' but actually lived and farmed at Rotherfield Greys, on the way to Henley. He brought a two-wheeled plough into the classroom; some of the big boys had to put half our desks into the corridor to make room for it, and lots of us sat on the floor.

"Sorry, children, I couldn't bring Dobbin and Bobby with me. They're the horses that pull my plough. But I've brought a big picture of them to show you later."

"Why *didn't* you bring them, Sir?" asked silly Willy Watson.

"Would you like to be trampled on? ... Of course you

131

wouldn't. I've come to tell you about this here plough, and you're going to learn the names of all these bits and pieces. See these bits here; what do they look like?" I put my hand up. "Yes; little girl in the front."

"Funny-shaped coat hangers. But what are the chains for?"

"The trace chains connect the *whippletrees* – that's what they are – to the horses. Let's have the two biggest lads to be the horses. Come and hold these chains over your shoulders like this. Yes, they hang down quite low."

"Willy and Douglas," answered Miss Aldridge. The two boys played their parts well.

"The *whippletrees'* job is to distribute the load evenly between these two horses. Now, see this section at the front of the *whippletree*? That's called the *pommeltree*. You say it."

"*Pommeltree*."

"See this chain which runs back to the *hake*? The *hake* is here on the side of the neck and the chain runs through it and on to the bridle or muzzle. Here we *do* need my picture because of the special shape of the horses' heads. Unlike boys, horses have long necks and long faces, don't they?"

"Yes, I'm glad I don't have a long face," said Jean Crocker.

"The ploughman controls the plough by these *stilts* or handles. What do you think this long piece of wood running from front to back might do? Yes; the boy by the window."

"Keep the plough from tipping over?" answered Jimmy Saunders, hesitantly.

"Well done. It's called the *beam* and it's the mainstay of the whole implement. Now can you all see this iron piece here at the bottom of the beam?"

"Yes Mr Barnicot."

"That's the iron knife called a *coulter*, which cuts straight down into the soil, separating the new furrow from the unploughed land. And this triangular piece of iron here; see how sharp the edge is? That is called the *share* and it cuts this way, horizontally, separating the furrow slice from the soil below. Now see this bit immediately behind the *share*, with the twist in it? That's called the *mouldboard* or *breast*, and it turns the furrow slice over. Just *two* more pieces to show you and then we're done. See this plate here? That's called the *landside plate*. It slides against the newly cut face of the furrow to stop any loose soil or stones from getting into the body of the plough. That's this part here."

"I didn't know a plough could have a body," said Eileen Crowle.

"It's a good name for it, because *this* is the bit that does all the work! Now, last of all, the *slade*; this slides along the bottom of the furrow and helps to keep the plough steady."

"What a lot to remember!" sighed David Morrison.

"Don't worry, children," answered Mrs Morrison. "I've written all the words down and Mr Barnicot has let us keep the picture to put on the classroom wall. Let's give him a clap for telling us so many interesting things."

Later in the term, Mrs Morrison taught us the hymn:
'I was made a Christian when my name was given,
one of God's dear children and an heir of Heaven.'

My parents didn't approve of that one at all! I wrote it out in my next letter to my father. His response was not what I had expected:

> *October 26th 1943*
> *Dear Maggie,*
> *Thank you for your letter, but I was rather disturbed to find that you are being taught erroneous hymns. You were* NOT *made a Christian when your name was given, Maggie. You won't become a Christian until you trust in the Lord Jesus for yourself. Some church people believe in Infant Baptism but we don't. So I don't want you to sing that hymn again because it is* NOT *true. Ask your dear Mother to explain all this to you if you don't understand what I am saying here.*
> *I was pleased to hear about your progress in reading, writing, and arithmetic, and of your interest in music.*
> *Your loving Father,*
> *J. Goodchild*

Mumsie, what do 'disturbed' and 'erroneous' mean?"

"Let me see the letter."

"I see. ... Daddy isn't happy about that new hymn you've been learning; so he's disturbed about it. He isn't happy because what you've been singing isn't true — it's erroneous."

"I didn't think Mrs Morrison told lies."

"She doesn't; it's just that she believes something that we think is wrong."

"What is 'infant baptism'?"

"Well, babies are taken to Peppard Church for a special service called a 'Christening' where their names are read out and the vicar dips his finger in a big bowl of water, called a 'font', and makes a wet cross on the babies' foreheads. That's what Mrs Morrison's hymn is all about. So some people believe that the Christening really does make babies Christians; that is what we believe is wrong. But others at Peppard Church, like Daddy's friend, Mr Bussie the organist, believe that, as the parents and family friends promise to teach the babies about Jesus while they're growing up, they will be helping them to make the decision for themselves when they are old enough to understand what they're doing."

"Is that like Daddy says here about trusting Jesus for yourself?"

"Yes, it is."

We sang the hymn at the very next assembly and I completely forgot that my father had said I shouldn't sing it. It had such an easy tune, and I liked the sound of my own voice. Did the biblical injunction: 'Children obey your parents' in fact apply to singing hymns disapproved of by your parents? Mrs Morrison would think I was being naughty if I refused to join in. Parents weren't always right, were they?

＿＿

At the beginning of December, we started making paper lanterns to decorate the classroom for Christmas. We also started rehearsals for the Nativity play. Mrs Morrison chose me to play Mary. I didn't have to say anything, but simply sit there trying to look sweet and gentle. Jimmy Saunders was Joseph. His hair was almost black; all he needed was a black beard and moustache to make him look like a man. But why does Joseph always look such an *old* man in pictures and on Christmas cards? My mother said that he was older than Mary; and that Mary was probably only about fifteen, not much older than the girls in Standard Seven. I'm so glad Jimmy Saunders doesn't look like Grandpa Goodchild!

I wondered *where* we were going to perform the play. Wouldn't it be fun to do it on the big stage in the village hall?

"No, Maggie, we're not going to do our play in the village hall; just here, in the classroom. We'll push back the desks and Standard Two can come in and watch. It will probably be in our last assembly before we break up for Christmas."

At first I was disappointed; but then ... wouldn't it be a bit scary up there in front of everybody, upon that high platform?

Mrs Morrison borrowed some dressing-up clothes from a lady at Peppard Church. I was given a long blue frock to wear that completely covered my feet; but it didn't matter as I didn't have to walk very far, and we were not going to re-enact the donkey ride from Nazareth to Bethlehem, nor the flight into Egypt.

"Mrs Morrison, why aren't we doing the flight into Egypt; that's also in the story ... and King Herod killing all those babies?"

"No, Maggie, I think it will be quite enough to have the scene at the inn, and then the shepherds and wise men coming to the stable."

"Mrs Morrison, the wise men didn't come to the stable. It says, 'And when they were come into the *house*, they saw the young child and Mary his mother ...'"

"I know it does, but for *our* play, we have to make it very simple. We've only got this space up here by my desk."

I had the distinct impression that Mrs Morrison was finding me rather tiresome. Maybe if I didn't shut up, she'd choose another Mary.

Over the blue frock, I wore a long white veil which covered my hair, and was fastened at each side of my head with a hair grip to stop it slipping off. Somehow I didn't think the real Mary had plaits under her headgear. Would my mother let me have my hair loose that day? No, she'd be cross about the tangles afterwards, wouldn't she?

Andrew Baker, Billy White, and David Morrison were the shepherds and a dainty little girl called Jill Bradley was the Angel of the Lord. She was a platinum blonde and had a very fair complexion. I wanted to inform Mrs Morrison that angels were like men with wings, not little girls in white nighties; but Andrew and Billy were tossing a toy lamb about at the time, so I kept my mouth shut.

"Andrew and Billy if you can't behave, you won't be in the

135

play. Now crouch down as if you were afraid, and put your hands over your eyes, to shield them from the bright light."

"There ain't no bright light, Miss," replied Andrew, flatly.

"When you act in a play you have to *pretend*. ... Jill is an angel surrounded by the glory of the Lord, which is a wonderful light shining down on you. ... That's better; now I know that you're afraid of the light. David Morrison, you crouch down too."

David thought this play-acting was rather silly; he wasn't imaginative like his older brother. He wanted to be a bank manager when he grew up.

The shepherds were wearing old flannel dressing gowns and a piece of cloth held around their heads with an elasticated headband. They each had a shepherd's crook made out of wire and covered in papier mâché. Michael Morrison had made those, and also Jill's wire halo, which was covered in tinsel to represent a holy glow.

"Careful with that crook, Billy; you nearly tripped Jill up."

Jill's nightie was a new one made by her mother for her elder sister, Eileen. The collar and cuffs were edged in pillow-lace worked by her grandmother. Everyone agreed that Jill looked truly angelic.

Derek Adams, Colin Atkins and Graham Nash were the three kings. Mrs Morrison had chosen them because they were the tallest boys in the class and looked the most kinglike.

"Stand up proud and tall, Graham. Remember you are a king, and you are carrying a bar of pure gold." As Mrs Morrison said the word 'gold', Graham's cardboard crown, covered in gold paper, tumbled off his head.

"Put your crown on more firmly so that it rests on your ears. ... Yes, that's better. Now all three of you walk very slowly from the corner behind the piano until you reach this chalk mark; then kneel down reverently facing Maggie and Jimmy. ... Good. Now we must practise the carols. None of you up front must say or sing anything out loud. You just do the actions. The story will be told through the words of the carols. So, scene one. ... Mary and Joseph stand over here by the corridor and Brian Berry, you are the innkeeper; you stand by the blackboard. Mary and Joseph walk towards the innkeeper and pretend to ask him for a room. That's it. ... Brian you shake your head. Not like that or it will fall off! ... That's better. Good. You show them to the stable; and now we'll sing:

'Little Jesus sweetly sleep.
Do not stir.
We will lend a coat of fur.
We will rock you, rock you, rock you.
We will serve you all we can,
Darling, darling, little man.'

"Maggie, just rock the baby very gently. Now, shepherds, huddle in your field and we will sing, 'While shepherds watched their flocks by night'. Jill, be ready to come on stage as we sing about the angel of the Lord. Then, as we sing verses 2, 3 and 4, you hold up your hands and pretend to speak to the shepherds."

"Mrs Morrison, where's the shining throng?" asked Jean Crocker.

"You are; those of you who will be sitting out here in the front will be the angels singing."

"Can *we* be dressed up too?" asked Eileen Dixon.

"We haven't got enough dressing-up clothes, but you can all have some tinsel in your hair. Would that do?"

"Yes, I suppose so," replied Eileen.

"I want Miss Aldridge to say, 'What a lovely choir of angels'."

On the day of the Nativity play, all the desks were pushed back as far as they would go. Mrs Aldridge's class squeezed themselves into them and Mrs Aldridge, Mrs Morrison and the headmaster sat in chairs alongside. The tinsel-headed choir were in their best clothes, sitting on mats in front of the desks, and the mime artists performed their moving tableau in the space that was left at the front.

There were just two things that went wrong: Graham Nash lost his crown as he bowed down before the baby Jesus, but was quick-witted enough to pick it up and pretend to lay it at Mary's feet; and naughty Alan Beaton sang the alternative version to the beginning of 'While shepherds watched ... ' in a husky stage-whisper that everyone could hear:

'While shepherds washed their socks that night,
all seated round the tub,
a bar of Sunlight soap came down,
and they began to scrub.'

There were a few titters, but most people either gave him a cold stare or ignored him completely. He then looked rather silly.

I felt sad as we packed up for the Christmas holidays. I knew

I was going to miss Mrs Morrison and all my friends in Standard One.

"Don't forget your lanterns, Maggie. You'll be able to hang them on your Christmas tree, won't you?" said Mrs Morrison with a kindly smile.

⌐⌐

The Christmas holidays, 1943, were a disaster; everything seemed to go wrong. They started with a snowstorm on Saturday the 18th December, and there were deep drifts in the gardens and lanes around Crowsley; we all had to stay indoors. My mother couldn't collect her allowance and buy groceries and the milkman and the baker couldn't get their vans beyond the main road, so we had to go without. We were also running short of coal; we had to manage with the oil stove until it was time for Mumsie to cook our midday meal. Then, after dinner, she put us all to bed for the afternoon, thinking we would be able to keep reasonably warm under our blankets.

Grandpa Goodchild was in bed with influenza; my mother had him to look after as well as the four of us. Fortunately, he had more food in the house than we did, so she was able to borrow milk and bread from his larder. The milk had frozen and popped its top and the bread was stale, but they were ideal for a bread and milk tea.

It wasn't until the Monday that the snow began to thaw. Then it was wet and slushy everywhere and my mother had to walk to Sonning Common in her wellington boots to collect her money, buy the things we needed and order some more sacks of coal. That day she had used all the coal that was left in the coal shed to light the kitchen range for us; she was afraid that if she left us with the oil stove, one of us might bump into it and start a fire. I was responsible for looking after the others, as Mrs Hurst had gone to visit her sister and wouldn't be back until after Christmas. I just hoped Gracie wouldn't fill her nappy, but she did.

"Oh Gracie! How could you? ... I'll have to do you on the rug; I can't lay you across my knee like Mumsie does. ... Stop wriggling, or we'll make a mess on the rug."

I cleaned her up reasonably well, and did the best I could with the clean nappy. It was hard to get the pin in just right; but thank goodness she wasn't a boy, or I might have done him an injury with it.

⌐⌐

My mother had only been gone half-an-hour when a taxi drew up at the gate. It was Jimmy who spotted it first.

"Maggie, there's a car out there. Come and look."

I went to the window and saw the taxi driver helping someone out of the seat in the back. He looked like a little old man and he had a walking stick. Then the taxi driver took out a case and some bags, and opened the gate for the man, who was finding it hard to walk, even with his stick.

"Who's that?" asked Ann, jumping up at the window.

"*I* don't know. ... *No*, it can't be," I gasped. "Yes, it is; ... it's *Daddy*. The army's made him ill. He's not wearing his uniform, and he can't walk properly. ... What have they done to him?"

I quickly found my wellingtons and ran out to meet my father. By then the taxi driver had turned his vehicle round and was already passing Honeysuckle Cottage and turning left towards Mr Brooker's farm.

"Daddy, you've come home. Mumsie's gone to Sonning Common; we're on our own and Grandpa isn't well; he's in bed." The words came tumbling out in such a rush that I don't think my father understood anything that I had been saying to him.

"Maggie, can you manage this case for me? ... Thank you, dear; that's better! ... They've sent me home because my legs are bad," he panted. "They're so bad that I can hardly walk; it hurts so much. ... Kind people helped me get on and off the train, and I had to get a taxi all the way from Reading Station. ... I couldn't lift my foot high enough to get on the bus and ride as far as Swan's Garage, and get a taxi from there. ... The conductor was so impatient and no-one would help me."

"How nasty of them! ... Where's your uniform, Daddy? Mumsie said you'd be wearing it when you came home on leave."

"I've left the army for good. They've discharged me as unfit for active service. I've spent the last three weeks in hospital."

"Poor Daddy!"

It took my father ten agonising minutes to hobble from the front gate to the kitchen door, and through the kitchen into the sitting room.

Chapter 10

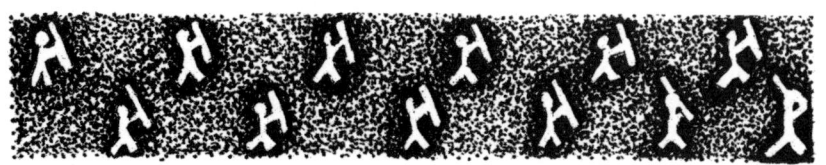

On a newly-painted blackboard,

serried ranks of silent, chalk-white soldiers march towards me.

Without even a flicker of an eye-lid, they approach from the left,

always from the left,

moving mechanically, mindlessly, with relentless precision.

Six abreast, the rows keep coming, passing straight through me,

filling my mind with a nameless terror.

There is no way of stopping them;

no way of turning off the soundless projector

hiden in the wall behind me.

I wake myself up, sit bolt upright against the wobbly headboard;

but they are still there, advancing, ever advancing.

When Emily arrived home with her two heavy bags of shopping, John was lying on the settee in the sitting room fast asleep. I had been able to make him a cup of tea before the fire went out, but now the whole house felt cold and damp. Gracie was sleeping fitfully in her cot, and Jimmy and Ann were playing discontentedly with their bricks on the cold tiled floor. Emily was shivering as she took her coat off by the back door.

"Oh dear, Maggie, has the fire gone out already?"

"Yes, Mumsie; and Daddy's come home from the army. He's asleep in the sitting room. He's got bad legs and can't walk properly."

Emily was dismayed when she heard this bombshell. The timing of John's arrival couldn't have been worse. Emily felt sure that she had caught the influenza from her father-in-law; there was no more coal on either side of the house, and the earliest the coalman could promise a delivery would be Wednesday morning. How was she to care for a sick husband under these circumstances? If only Rita Hurst had been at home she could have phoned the doctor and Rita would have given her a hand with the invalids.

"There's nothing for it," she said at last. "Maggie, you'll have to take a note to Mrs Brooker for me." She saw the fear in my eyes.

"I'm sorry, Maggie. But we need help, or we'll *all* be ill. ... You're thinking of Rover, aren't you?" I nodded.

Rover was the large mastiff the Brookers kept as a guard dog. Emily knew that Maggie had good reason to be frightened of Rover. He was big and boisterous, and had knocked her down in the lane when she was only four.

"I'm scared of Rover, Mumsie. Will he be locked up somewhere? ..."

"I'm sure he will," replied Emily reassuringly.

I walked gingerly up to Eileen Brooker's solid oak front door and knocked hesitantly. The attractive brass knocker, shaped like a lion's head, was way above her head. No-one came to the door. Then I knocked a little louder and hurt my knuckles on the hard wood. I heard Rover stirring in the passage. He was soon wide awake and came bounding up to the front door, barking ferociously. He rammed his muzzle into the letterbox, lifted the flap with his nose and bared his teeth at her through the gap, growling menacingly. I cried out in terror.

"Quiet Rover, what's all this noise about? There's nobody there," scolded Mr Brooker from the end of the passage.

"Yes, there is," I shouted through the letterbox. "It's Maggie Goodchild with a note for Mrs Brooker."

"Wait there." Then to the dog, he said, "*You're* coming into the dining room with me, for now." I heard Rover padding up the passage, and the sound of the dining room door closing behind him."

"You'd better come in, young lady," invited Mr Brooker, towering above me in the hallway. "My wife's here in the kitchen."

"Hello Maggie, you look frozen. Come and sit by the fire while I read your mother's note. ... Oh dear, your poor mother *is* having a hard time of it! Look, you stay where you are. Let me give you some hot milk; would you like that?"

"Yes please, Mrs Brooker."

The milk was creamy and comforting, and I soon felt much better about everything. But outside the wind was getting up, and Mrs Brooker thought it would be snowing again before too long. She put on her warm tweed coat and a thick scarf.

"Maggie, I'm going out to find Ed. You know Ed, don't you?"

"Yes, Mrs Brooker; I've seen him working in the hay field."

"He's going to get some logs for your fire, while I get some milk from the dairy and a few other things your mother might like." With that, she opened the kitchen door and walked off down the path, crossing the lane into the farmyard beyond. As I sat looking around the large kitchen, smelling deliciously of freshly-baked bread, a tabby kitten appeared from behind the kitchen table. He immediately jumped up onto my lap and purred contentedly. I stroked his soft furry body and decided that I liked cats.

When Eileen Brooker came back, to my surprise, she had nothing at all in her hands. The milk, cream, cheese, apples and root vegetables she had selected for Emily were being packed into a small cart, along with enough logs to last the family until after Christmas.

"I'll just telephone Dr Prince for your mother. She wants him to visit your father."

Dr Prince was at his house and took the call personally. "Yes, Mrs Brooker, tell Mrs Goodchild I'll be at Crowsley about five o'clock, after I've made a couple of visits in Sonning Common."

Eileen Brooker wrote this down on a piece of paper and gave it to me to put in my pocket. "Do give this to your mother as soon as you get home."

"Yes, Mrs Brooker."

"Were you surprised, Maggie, to see your father this morning?"

"Yes. But he didn't look like my daddy at all! He's ... he's ... so old and ill."

"He'll be much better when we've got the house warm again and the doctor has given him some medicine. ... Now take *this*." She then handed me a loaf of bread, still warm from the oven, wrapped around with a clean tea-cloth. "I'll have the tea-cloth back when you've finished with it; there's no hurry."

"Thank you Mrs Brooker."

A few minutes later, I left Brooker's farm in style, perched up with Ed at the front of the cart, right by Alfred's tail. Mrs Brooker had wrapped a thick tartan rug around me; and behind us, the cart was piled high with the logs and other good things. Unfortunately, it was too big to go through the gate at Tudor Cottage.

"Maggie, do you have a wheelbarrow we could put these things into?" asked Ed.

"There's one in Grandpa's barn."

"Can you show me where it is?"

I opened the barn door and the wheelbarrow was standing right in front of us. Ed started piling the food items into the barrow, and then wheeled them across the grass towards Emily's kitchen. Emily saw them coming.

"Mrs Brooker sends these things with her compliments," announced Ed. "Where would you like me to put them?"

"On the kitchen table would be fine. Do thank her for her generosity."

"She's given us this lovely loaf, too," I added, placing the bread on the table. "And here's the note about the doctor; he's coming at five o'clock."

"Now the logs; shall I bring some straight in and get this fire going for you?"

"Yes please, Ed. The rest can be piled up under the lean-to. ... Ed, could you do me another favour? My husband can't walk up the stairs at the moment; could you help me bring the single bed down from upstairs, before you go?"

"Certainly. Let me light the fire, stack the rest of the logs for you, and then we'll fetch the bed." Having done as good as he said, Ed departed.

The bed they brought downstairs was my bed, and I later found myself sleeping with my mother. Emily *had* caught influenza; her head hurt and she coughed and sneezed every time she woke up from a fitful sleep. She was also prone to bronchitis, which sometimes turned to pneumonia. The immediate prospect was grim.

There were no Christmas celebrations at Tudor Cottage that year. My lanterns did not hang from a Christmas tree, but stood on the back window sill in the kitchen. The magic word 'presents' was never mentioned once. The postman brought a few Christmas cards, and I was allowed to arrange these on the top of the piano and on the mantelpiece in the sitting room where my father slept. Christmas 1943 was described in the local newspaper as 'the austerity Christmas', so we weren't the only family going without; but this knowledge made none of us feel any better about it. Although we had no more snowstorms, flurries of snow kept coming and going, and the weather remained decidedly raw.

We all caught influenza, one after the other. Grandpa Goodchild was over the worst when my mother went down with it, so, he kept the fires burning for us. (Miraculously, the coalman *did* deliver our coal on the Wednesday before Christmas, as promised.) As my mother appeared to be getting over the influenza, I caught it; and as I began to feel a little better, my mother came down with bronchitis, which soon turned to pneumonia. At this point, my father caught influenza, and so did Jimmy, Ann and Gracie. The three little ones were miserable and grizzled most of the time they were awake. As I was getting better, I had to look after them, while my father tried to look after himself. We all spent a lot of time in bed and existed on a diet of bread and milk, dried egg, and the fruit and vegetables supplied by Mrs Brooker. Dr Prince made regular visits and kept us topped up with cough mixture and aspirins, plus penicillin for my mother and morphine for my father.

It was while I was still sleeping with my mother that the nightmares began. I don't ever remember having recurring nightmares before those Christmas holidays at the tail-end of 1943. When they started, I had no idea what they were or where they came from, only that something new and terrifying was happening to me at night and I suddenly became afraid of the dark.

In one nightmare, everything was pitch black and row upon row of German soldiers in white uniforms marched towards me; I was petrified of those silent, ghostly Jerries. In the other, I was alone in the desert and enemy bombers appeared from nowhere. They filled the air with an explosion of decibels and the hideous machines began falling from the sky. But, to my relief, the ear-splitting noises would cease abruptly as I willed myself to wake up; whereas the chalky images kept on appearing for many minutes after I had awakened, and resumed their unflagging procession the moment I returned to sleep.

In the light of morning, the bedroom invariably looked just like it always had. It seemed weird to be sleeping with my mother, though. I was used to my own little bed, in the attic in summer, and the little room next door in the winter. Would my father have to sleep in the sitting room for ever?

As the days grew warmer, my father's sciatica and rheumatic problems did improve considerably, until he was actually able to climb the stairs without too much discomfort. But the return to my own bed made no difference to the night-terrors. Night after night, they persisted for a period of two years or more, and I could never bring myself to tell anyone about them. They were too upsetting to bring out into the open.

How could I tell my parents that their eldest daughter had gone mad and was possessed by some unseen power that made her keep dreaming about such horrible things? Nobody must ever know. At all costs, I had to keep my awful secrets to myself or something much worse would befall me. During the daytime, I would pretend I was someone else. I would be happy and sing; I'd try to be good and make people like me. I wouldn't look in the mirror; I'd pretend I had golden curls like Jimmy used to have and that I had a pretty face.

During the war years, my parents, Emily and John, had no wireless set and took no daily papers; though, with her excellent eyesight, Emily was skilful at reading other people's newspapers over their shoulders, if they gave her half a chance. She had no scruples about picking up discarded papers either, even when she saw them in litter bins. Emily was frustrated by John's insistence that, as citizens of Heaven, they should keep themselves separate from the affairs of this wicked world; so she listened in to other people's conversations and asked questions, making it her business to find out what was going on, both locally and nationally.

On the tenth of February 1943, my mother was looking out of the kitchen window at the back of the house when she saw a single, low-flying aircraft away in the distance. I was at home with a cold that afternoon, and I went outside with her to get a better view.

"That's not one of ours, Maggie; that's a Jerry and he's lost. I bet he's going to unload his bombs on Reading, before flying back to Germany."

I couldn't see the enemy bomber very well, it was too low in the sky, but my mother could. We were too far away, and the wind was in the wrong direction for us to hear any sound from that plane.

"Yes, Maggie, Reading's getting it. I think I can see the bombs, oh dear!"

My mother's desire to find out exactly what had happened in Reading was insatiable; she had to find a pretext to go to town and see it all for herself. Two days later she was devouring the local paper, viewing the damage at St Laurence's Church and the Town Hall, and picking her way through the rubble in Minster Street. Apparently, the single low-flying Dornier bomber had swept over the centre of the town, machine-gunning the streets and dropping bombs. The main headline read:

'HIT AND RUN RAID ON TOWN.
DEPARTMENTAL STORE AND OFFICES DAMAGED'

Subheadings included:

'Machine-gunned the streets',

'Direct hit on a British restaurant' and

'Like a little soldier', telling the story of Clarence Brown aged seven, who was buried in debris near the department store. This little boy was hauled out by soldiers saying, "I'm all right;" and immediately went on to show his rescuers where two women were buried. These women were rescued, together with a young girl. "The boy was just like a little soldier," said one of his rescuers. "He showed no fright of any kind when adults around him seemed stupefied."

My mother read the whole account, and was surprised that, for security reasons, it didn't, in fact, name the town as Reading. It wasn't until very much later that any indication of the scale of casualties was given to the general public. The official figures were: 41 killed, 49 seriously injured and 104 slightly injured.

As she finished reading the story of Clarence Brown, a man in uniform came up behind her and spoke very quietly into her left ear. "This is not the true account of why those bombs fell on Reading. They want us to believe that the plane was lost. It wasn't; the pilot just missed his target."

"How do you know?"

"By a little careful map-reading and an elementary knowledge of trigonometry. He was out to bomb the railway line somewhere near Sonning Cutting, at the junction between the Great Western and the Southern Railways. If he had succeeded, he would have effectively sabotaged our whole railway system and permanently disrupted communications. I've been looking at a detailed ordinance map of where the six bombs fell, all in a straight line. That straight line should have been across the railway and not the town at all."

By the time I was taken into Reading by my mother, most of the general clearing up had been done. I was horrified at the sight of the damaged buildings, but I saw nothing so horrendous that it would give me nightmares.

Children at school who went to the flicks, as we called the cinema, saw all the newsreels and were consequently much more familiar with the sounds and sights of war than I was. They would sometimes tell exaggerated stories of what they had seen; but these tales didn't upset me, they were too infantile and crude.

I was definitely squeamish about blood, though, and the gory details of accidents and operations. When we were told about the French Revolution in Standard Two, Miss Aldridge had to pick me off the floor after she had regaled us with the details of an execution by guillotine. But my nightmares were not about blood; they seemed to be totally divorced from all the happenings of my everyday life. That's what made them so scary.

~~

The bleak Christmas of 1943 was superseded, at last, by a joyous Easter. John Goodchild's legs were much better and he was now back at work in his old job at Austin's. Emily had recovered from the pneumonia, Albert Goodchild was pottering about in his beloved garden once more, and everyone at Tudor Cottage felt much more energetic and optimistic in the warm spring sunshine.

The sitting room, although somewhat shabby, was now a comfortable place for entertaining the occasional visitor and enjoying music together as a family. However, Frank Riley, the new piano tuner, was not at all happy about the state of the piano when he came to tune it. It was patently obvious to him that it had not been tuned properly, if at all, for at least three years.

Frank was an unprepossessing man of uncertain age, whose clothes were loud and whose over-brylcreemed hair was parted severely down the middle. Emily considered him a pompous little squirt, with his self-conscious smile and squeaky little voice.

"Mrs Goodchild, you *must* let me tune this instrument every six months. It will take several visits before I can restore it to the proper pitch. We've *really* let things go, haven't we?" he simpered.

"*We've* had rather more important things to worry about than an out-of-tune piano," retorted Emily.

"Who plays, you or your husband?" continued Frank, abruptly changing the subject. He hadn't the slightest interest in other people's problems.

"We both do when we have the time to enjoy it, and now our daughter has started lessons."

Who's her teacher?"

"Miss Yapp; she's a funny old stick, but she seems to know what she's doing."

"That Michael Morrison winning the scholarship was a real feather in her cap, wasn't it? Let's hope *your* daughter can make a go of it too!"

"There's no reason why she shouldn't," snapped Emily. Anyone would think from his irritatingly condescending manner, that he was a concert pianist instead of a second-rate tuner!

My first piano lesson was quite a shock. Miss Yapp was nothing like the lovely Mrs Morrison. She looked old enough to be her mother, with her wrinkled face, horn-rimmed spectacles, and straggly grey hair drawn back into an untidy bun. She was quite friendly and encouraging that first time, and I soon learned the names of the white notes: C, D, E, F, G, A, B, C.

"Miss Yapp, why do we start at C, and not A?"

"We are learning the key of C major first because that is the easiest; it has no black notes. From bottom C to top C is called an octave."

"An octave... When do we learn the names of the black notes?"

"When you know all the white notes and can play the scale up and down again with both hands."

When I went back for my second lesson, I could play the scale with each hand separately; but when I tried to play them together, the left hand wanted to follow the right, instead of keeping up with it.

"That's because you're right-handed," explained Miss Yapp. "We have to train this little hand to keep up."

Ouch! She scratched me with her nails when she grabbed my left hand. I know she didn't mean to, but it still hurt.

But when Miss Yapp was cross, I'm sure she deliberately dug her sharp finger-nails into you as she plonked your fingers angrily onto the right keys. Her nails reminded me of corrugated iron with their ugly ridges. Did my two grandmothers ever have nails like that? I didn't think so.

Piano lessons could sometimes be rather daunting, and it had nothing to do with the amount of practice you had done prior to the lesson. On some occasions, Miss Yapp didn't seem to know what she was doing and looked rather wild. Then you were afraid of what she might do next and kept very quiet. Once I heard Mrs

Kirby say to my mother that Miss Yapp went to the 'wrong church'.

"Mumsie, does she go to Peppard Church? Is that the *wrong* church?"

Both women laughed hilariously, but I didn't see the joke.

"Not Peppard Church but the Hare and Hounds," spluttered Joyce Kirby.

"But *that's* not a church — it's a-a-a ... "

May 1944

David Goodchild arrived unexpectedly late one Friday afternoon. He had his little case with him. Emily was unaware that he had come through the gate and round the path by the well, on Albert's side of the house. He knocked at the sitting room door, instead of crossing the grass and making for the kitchen door as most people did.

"Someone's knocking at the front door," I yelled. "I think it's Uncle David."

"Oh no!" groaned Emily. "I thought we were going to have a nice family weekend by ourselves. ... Hello David, have you come to see your father?"

"Not specifically. I've come to see you *all*. I understand my brother is now back at work. That's *really* good news!"

"He still gets very tired, and likes to flop once he's home in the evenings."

David marched into the sitting room humming a little tune, totally oblivious to Emily's muted welcome. Jimmy watched his uncle as he opened the case and took out some butter and sugar for my mother. Nellie had insisted that he did not arrive at Tudor Cottage without bringing something towards his keep, as he had often done in the past.

"Mumsie, Uncle David has his pyjamas in his case; I saw them."

"So, he expects to spend the whole weekend with us, I suppose," grumbled my mother under her breath.

"Is he going to play the piano?" asked Jimmy.

"He might," answered my mother, thinking distractedly about

how she was going stretch her meagre food supply to feed her greedy brother-in-law. She was just about able to manage her own family affairs now, but the pneumonia had certainly taken its toll, physically and emotionally, and entertaining the eccentric David was invariably draining.

David asked for a cup of tea and then walked over to the piano and saw my 'Smallwood's Tutor' sitting on the music rest.

"Is Maggie having lessons?"

"Yes, she's just started this term with Miss Yapp in Sonning Common."

"I don't think much of Smallwood; I prefer to write my own material for *my* pupils. ... Let's hear you play something, Maggie."

I thought I'd bore him with scales, and then he might play some of his own music. As he sat drinking his tea, C, G, and D major; then F, B flat and E flat, both hands together, were executed with reasonable precision, if not aplomb.

"Let's hear one of your pieces, Maggie. This one's called 'Raindrops', can you play it yet?"

"It's my new piece."

I began hesitantly reading the notes and playing the composition at half the speed it was meant to be played; it sounded more like a funeral march than raindrops falling softly on the path.

"Maggie, let me show you how it should go. ... See, it's very light and delicate. You don't hold the notes down; you let them bounce up again. We call it 'staccato'."

"Miss Yapp calls them 'pips'."

"She's probably thinking of the time signal before the news on the wireless."

"We haven't got a wireless, Uncle David."

After tea, while my mother was putting the little ones to bed and I was finishing the washing up, my father lit the sitting-room fire. Although it was spring, the evenings could still be chilly; he didn't want his older brother complaining of the cold. I liked fires. It was fun to watch the changing shapes and patterns made by the flames, and see their cheery reflections on the wall. Even though it was still light outside, the sitting room was already shadowy.

As my mother came down the stairs, my father lit the Tilley lamp and placed it on the small table by the piano. I covered my ears when the lamp started hissing, as the pressure built up to supply the burner with fuel; I was always relieved when my father pumped it and the hissing finally stopped.

"Mumsie, will you sing 'Love's Old Sweet Song'?" I asked immediately as she entered the room. "I like the bit about the flickering shadows. It's one of my favourites."

Emily saw David make a face. She decided to sing it anyway; why not indulge in a little Victorian nostalgia to please Maggie? There would be time enough for the highbrow stuff later. John quickly found the sheet of music and prepared to accompany her. Soon the sweet voice was singing the only words I knew off by heart:

"'Just a song at twilight when the lights are low,
and the flickering shadows softly come and go.
Though the heart be weary, sad the day and long,
still to us at twilight comes love's old song —
comes love's old sweet song.'"

"Emily, that song suits your voice, even if it is sentimental nonsense," admitted David. "What else have you got?"

"Here's 'The Rosary'", announced John. "That's a pretty little ditty."

"Isn't it about Catholicism?" queried David.

"It's a love song, from the novel called 'The Rosary', by Florence Barclay," responded Emily. "It's a story about a gifted artist who goes blind and eventually marries the woman who looks after him. ... Florence Barclays' novels all seem to be about older women who marry men several years their junior!"

"Surely, you don't have time to read *novels*, Emily?"

"Yes, David; we all need some relaxation; mine is reading. I'm not clever with my hands like my mother."

The song was a sad one, full of yearning, which came out in the music and in the way my mother sang it ... just as if, deep down, she was sad too. There were three verses:

'The hours I spent with thee, dear heart,
are as a string of pearls to me;
I count them over, every one apart,
my rosary, — my rosary.

'Each hour a pearl, each pearl a prayer,
to still a heart in absence wrung;
I tell each bead unto the end, and there,
a cross is hung — a cross is hung!

'O memories that bless and burn!
O barren gain and bitter loss!
I kiss each bead, and strive at last to learn
to kiss the cross — to kiss the cross.'

I didn't understand the sentiments being expressed; but I caught the mood and kept on repeating the phrase, 'each pearl a prayer', under my breath, pondering its meaning. Then there was something about a cross and somebody called 'Dearheart' ... or was it 'dear heart' or 'sweetheart'? I knew that 'sweetheart' meant 'boyfriend'. Had my mother had a boyfriend she once loved very much, and then something bad had happened?

The next song was Liddle's 'Abide with me', my father's favourite. "That's better," said David, approvingly, when he saw the title.

"Would you like to play it, David? Then I can listen. These words have a special meaning for me."

As David played and Emily sang the first verse, John's eyes filled with tears. Liddle's version had a haunting melody line, which matched the poignancy of the words:

'Abide with me, fast falls the eventide;
the darkness deepens, Lord with me abide;
when other helpers fail and comforts flee,
help of the helpless, O abide with me.'

Those words had consoled him as he lay, alone, feverish and in terrible pain in that draughty military hospital. The next three verses had also had relevance to his desperate situation, and then came the last verse:

'Reveal Thyself before my closing eyes,
shine through the gloom, and point me to the skies;
Heaven's morning breaks, and earth's vain shadows flee —
in life, in death, O Lord, abide with me.'

Yes, he had really thought he was going to die. He had wanted to see his Lord, and he had done so, fleetingly, before the vision faded and he had found himself back again in his narrow hospital bed. ... So it had only been a dream, after all! ... But something had changed, though; he no longer had that ache in his chest and his legs were definitely less painful.

I had no idea what my father was thinking about, but I saw his tears. Music always did something to you as you listened to it.

As I carried my candle up to the bedroom, Uncle David started playing some of his own music. My bed was directly above the piano so I could still hear it through the floorboards. It was church music by Bach, Beethoven and Hadyn and was much more involved than the simple songs my mother had sung, but I kept listening until I finally dropped off to sleep. Downstairs, my father soon dried his eyes and entered into the technicalities of his brother's performance without even a whiff of envy. There was no denying that David was much more than a competent music teacher; he was an accomplished musician in his own right.

Chapter 11

The sky is a lurid yellow, streaked with fiery red clouds,
like a sunrise without a sight of the sun.
I am alone, and naked, in an uninhabitable hell,
the eerie silence charged with a nameless dread.
Noisy black shapes appear over the horizon;
enemy bombers with elongated wings and multiple engines
bear down on me with a screech, and a roar.
I cover my ears; I cover my eyes; but my screams echo unheard.
Guns blaze, bombs explode,
and the hideous machines fall out of the sky,
but I am still here.
The whole scene, like a loop of magnetic tape
replays itself ad infinitum in Technicolour and ear-splitting
sound.

"Children, I've had *enough* of all your noise," screamed Emily Goodchild hysterically from the kitchen window. "Go up to your beds at once, without any tea."

"That's not fair," answered Ann, glaring at her mother defiantly from the middle of the lawn. "We're not being naughty, not now anyway."

"I was only playing aeroplanes," added Jimmy wistfully, slowly putting his arms down by his sides.

Little Gracie murmured to herself, "Mumsie always cross; Mumsie always cross," and promptly burst into tears.

I stood there feeling that, somehow, this was all my fault; I had failed in my role as 'little mother' yet again, had I? This wasn't the first time our mother had packed us all off to bed without any tea. Surely we weren't making *that* much noise. As spring merged into summer, she seemed to be gradually falling apart. Could something really bad be happening to her? That was such a scary thought; where did it come from? I hastily pushed it to the back of my mind. Life without Mumsie here would be absolutely awful; so I determined to do exactly as she said without arguing.

"Maggie, you *will* make sure the others are tucked up properly, won't you?" she instructed me in a calmer voice. "I need to rest, I'm not very well."

"Yes, Mumsie, of course I will. I hope you soon feel better," I answered quietly.

It was only ten to five. The clock in the sitting room said nearly a quarter *past* five, as we walked by it on our way to the stairs. The silly thing kept gaining, so we had to work out what the real time was. My father usually waited to put it right until it was exactly half an hour fast; it would have to gain another six minutes before he would do that again, maybe in two or three weeks' time. But, in the meantime, the calculations involved were doing wonders for my mental arithmetic.

As it was a bright day, none of us wanted to go to bed, and sleep was out of the question. To begin with, we were all feeling hungry and there was nothing to eat upstairs; it's hard to go to sleep on an empty stomach. Outside, the sun was still smiling on the fields, and the evening shadows were barely visible. Later they would come out of hiding and march stealthily across the landscape.

Jimmy was starting school in September. He had lost his golden curls and was dressed in second-hand grey school trousers. Today he had been making the most of his present freedom, running around all over the place, pretending to be a bus, a motorbike, or an aeroplane, and now he felt he had been cheated of his precious playtime.

Ann was four next week, and her favourite game was crashing into Jimmy when he least expected it, but he had taken it in good heart. She was the sharpest of the four of us, and also by far the most energetic. When she was a little older, she would always be telling people, "My name is Ann Goodchild; I came in a hurry, and I've been in a hurry ever since." She had been born in the ambulance, arriving before the paramedics could get our mother to the maternity ward at Henley Hospital; and she was very proud of being so proactive in the birth process. Now we were upstairs, she wanted to do a dance on our parents' bed.

Gracie would be three at Christmas, and she had been toddling around the lawn, singing to herself like a chirpy little robin in her red smock. Sometimes she went exploring if we didn't keep an eye on her; she had already been to visit Rita Hurst down the lane and climbed up a ladder behind my father while he was picking cherries; but today she had stayed on the lawn all the time.

Thinking my own thoughts, I had been idly watching the younger ones at play. I wasn't allowed to ride my bicycle in case I knocked one of them over. The previous week, while I was still getting the hang of keeping the bike upright, I was coming up the slope, swaying from side to side, and Jimmy wouldn't get out of the way. So I stopped dead in front of him, the bike toppled sideways and I fell on top of him. Jimmy squealed and made a great fuss but, for once, my parents blamed him, not me. Today, nothing remotely like that had happened. None of us had been quarrelling or screeching. In fact, we had all been perfectly happy together.

"Look, children," I said suddenly, after I had been struck by what I thought was a brilliant idea. "If we get undressed quickly, we can all sit on the big bed and I'll read you a story."

"Goody, goody," enthused Ann. "I want to hear Red Riding Hood and the Wolf."

"I'm going to gobble you all up," shouted Jimmy from his own little bedroom.

"Shush! Mumsie will hear us," I remonstrated, as I helped Gracie off with her clothes in the adjoining bedroom.

The 'big bed' was a three-quarter-sized bed which Ann and Gracie shared; Gracie slept at the head and Ann at the bottom. It was located in a small curtained-off area in my parents' large bedroom, which had windows facing both the front and the back garden. The Little Red Riding Hood book was on the small bookcase by the bed. There was also a copy of 'Goldilocks and the Three Bears'.

Although I was now eight and going up into Standard Two in September, I wasn't very confident when it came to reading aloud; but the three youngsters didn't seem to mind. Their interest was certainly engaged.

"Once upon a time there was a little girl. People called her Little Red Riding Hood," I began.

"That's a silly name for a girl," protested Jimmy.

"If you listen to the next bit you'll know why people called her that. 'She was given that name because she wore a red cloak ...'"

"Let me see the picture," demanded Ann; so we looked at the picture of the little girl in her red cloak with its red hood.

"Why is it a 'riding' hood?" asked Jimmy. "She's not riding a bike. She's walking along the road."

"I'm not really sure. Perhaps men who rode horses had ones like that. Let's get on with the story."

⁓

Downstairs, Emily was lying dejectedly on the settee in the sitting room. Her head ached, her thoughts were all mixed up, and her tummy muscles were as tight as a drum. She felt she was sinking into an enormous black hole and there was no way out. ... She drifted into an uneasy doze.

When she woke up, she immediately thought of her children, and a terrifying wave of guilt suddenly swept over her. She'd sent them to bed without their tea simply because she couldn't cope with their clamouring, and she hadn't even tried to summon up the energy to get it for them. "What a neglectful mother I am," she said aloud, despairingly. "I love them dearly, but I'm going crazy.

What must they think of me? Maggie, there, with her big reproachful eyes ..."

This was followed by another breaker, which came crashing down over her defenceless head. "What will happen when John comes home? What's the time? Six-thirty already. It's Friday, and in an hour, he'll come in with his pay packet, and demand to see exactly how I've spent last week's money, before he gives me any more. I've forgotten completely where most of it's gone, and I've lost the paper I wrote it all down on. Did I put it in the bin by mistake? If that's so, it's been reduced to ashes. ... Why is John so hard? He'll never believe I really lost it. He'll just tell me I'm a deceitful woman, and I'm not telling the truth. Why can't he say, just once, 'It doesn't matter, love; let's forget it.' But no! Every farthing has to be accounted for, before we can go to bed." As she finished speaking, she buried her face in her hands, and shed silent tears of anguish.

Then Emily heard a scraping noise in the room above. It was Jimmy dragging his potty over the floorboards. "The children are still awake, I wonder how they are?" She was thinking aloud all the time these days, when she was alone; sometimes her ramblings were coherent and sometimes they were not. Now they spurred her into decisive action. "I must take those poor children some bread and milk. They must be thirsty as well as hungry, poor lambs."

She put margarine and sugar on four slices of bread, cut it all up into small squares, and half-filled four cereal bowls. Then she boiled the milk and poured it over the bread, and as she did so, the margarine melted and made little golden circles in the milk, and the bread became soft and easy for us to get down.

~

We all heard our mother coming up the stairs carrying the tray; we guessed what would be on it. The little ones immediately sat up in their beds, and I ran swiftly down the attic stairs to make sure the bedroom doors were still open. She carefully balanced the large wooden tray on the top of the chest of drawers, and handed out the steaming bowls, saying,

"Be careful you don't spill it; I've left your pinnies downstairs."

The milk was warm and creamy, with a light skin on the top. I sat on the big bed by Gracie and fed her like a baby, as she was becoming very sleepy. Slowly she sucked on the spoon, every now and then; I consumed my own bowlful in between her erratically-timed mouthfuls. Mumsie was propping Ann up at the bottom of the bed, and we could hear Jimmy slurping contentedly next door.

"Children, I'm sorry you didn't have your tea at the proper time," said our mother with a look of contrition. "I'm feeling a bit stronger now; I thought the bread and milk might help you all to go to sleep."

"Yes it will; Gracie's nearly asleep already," I answered.

"I want potty," announced Ann, crawling hurriedly out of bed.

"So do I," chorused Jimmy from the other room.

Soon, we were all tucked up in our beds once more but, up in the attic, I couldn't get to sleep; the disturbing thought I had had earlier came back to haunt me. What if Mumsie went away and never came back?

I sat up in bed, listening to the gentle sounds of evening, the quiet mooing of the cows, and the cries of birds returning to their roosts. Then I heard the putter of my father's motorbike in the distance, and soon the noisy machine was popping away right beneath my bedroom window. He often rode it across the grass, to save going all round the house by the path. But, tonight, it seemed to me like an omen of disaster, which filled me with foreboding.

I dreaded Friday nights. My parents often quarrelled over money. I could never hear what was actually being said two floors below me, but I knew instinctively what was going on. The voices raised in anger, the thump of fists on the kitchen table, and the harsh sounds of clattering pots and pans, could all be felt throughout the fabric of our part of the old house. Occasionally, I picked up something worse, and I hid under the covers. Was *he* hitting her? Or did *she* throw something at him? ... What would happen tonight, with my mother in the disturbed state she was in?

John Goodchild was in a bad mood. He had not received his overtime pay.

"You'll have to wait till next week," Miss Timms, the flighty little cashier had said, in her maddening, take-it-or-leave-it tone of voice.

"That's all right for you; but you haven't got six mouths to feed, have you? I've earned the money; why *can't* I have it?" he had protested angrily.

"There was no time to get it all ready for this week. No-one has had their overtime money today. Now will you *go*, you're holding up the line! We all want to get home tonight, don't we, chaps?" she added, smirking knowingly at the young fellows behind John in the queue. John was still smarting from her rudeness as he made his way to the kitchen door.

Inside, Emily was doing her best to pull herself together. She had tidied herself up, as well as the kitchen. The table was laid, the cold mutton neatly arranged on the plates, and the potatoes were cooking on the range. Perhaps, everything would be different this Friday. Then she saw the stern expression on John's face.

"Hello dear! Did you have a good day, today?" she asked, sweetly. It was always better to get her word in first, rather than wait for him to launch into the familiar tirade against her, or the people at work. Whatever the original object of his displeasure, her turn would surely come in the end. But, sometimes, just sometimes, a soft word of hers *was* able to turn away his wrath; though not tonight.

"It *was* a reasonable day, until I collected my pay-packet. That impertinent Miss Timms didn't have my overtime money ready, and she made fun of me in front of the younger men. I hope you've still got some of last week's housekeeping money in your purse, because you're going to need it. You can only have twenty-five shillings tonight."

Emily was devastated. What was she going to do now?

"Are those potatoes ready yet?" he asked brusquely, nodding at the steaming saucepan.

"No; they need another five or ten minutes."

"Well, then, we'll have our little talk before we eat. Have you got your list of expenses ready for me to see?" he asked in a quiet, menacing voice.

"No, I haven't; I seem to have lost it," answered Emily, beginning to tremble.

"Don't you give me that one again! I want a truthful account of all your expenditure, do you hear? Or you don't get *any* of what's in this pay-packet." He raised his voice, and waved the envelope in the air, as he uttered the word 'pay-packet'. Then he flung it on the table with a thud, as the coins landed on the hard wood.

Emily flinched, and began hesitantly, "There was the joint from the butcher, three large loaves from the baker, then the milk. ... I didn't go to Kirbys' at all this week, nor to Reading. ... "

"How *much*? How *much*? You crazy woman. I don't want to know *where* you shopped, or the details of *what* you bought, but just what you've *spent* on all the wretched items." John was dangerously angry now; to him 'wretched' was a swear word, and a sign that his temper was about to boil over, like the potatoes on the range.

Emily was feeling desperate. She knew things were going wrong in her head, as well as her marriage. If John wasn't careful, she would do something dreadful. Once John's temper was roused, he had no idea how to press the escape button and avert such a calamity.

"Are you going to tell me, or shall I box your ears, like I do Maggie when she defies me?"

"If you do," she screamed, "you'll live to regret it, John Goodchild!" His answer was to slap her hard across the mouth, muttering insults. Emily fell back and hit her head against the larder door. She quickly recovered from the shock, went over to the stove, and picked up the pan of potatoes, which had already boiled dry. She swiftly removed the lid and threw the pan and its contents straight at John. Then she grabbed the pay-packet and ran out of the back door shouting, "Enjoy your dinner, you bully!"

While John experienced a nasty bang on the head from the upturned saucepan, and fielded the overheated potatoes, Emily ran for the gate, out into the lane, across the fields, towards the bus-stop in Kennylands Road. She had no idea of the time and prayed that John wouldn't catch up with her before the Reading bus arrived to whisk her away. This wasn't the first time she had thrown something at him, and it wouldn't be the last. It was the only sure way of stopping his rages.

John wasn't seriously hurt. Fortunately, as all the boiling water had evaporated, his only wounds were the relatively small, burned and dented areas of scalp where the saucepan had caught him, and a few sore places on his face and neck from the overheated potatoes. All these could be soothed by the application of a little Vaseline.

John's quick temper subsided as swiftly as it had arisen. He had an unusual way of recovering his inner equilibrium after upsets of this nature. He found that if he put his physical world to rights, his emotions would eventually follow suit. So, when he had picked himself up, he carefully washed the cooling potatoes which were still whole under the tap, and put them on one of the plates. The saucepan he left to soak in the sink, and the smashed potatoes he gave to the cats, Purdy and Gormy, who were semi-wild and lived in the hedge where they were born. They would eat anything. The meat from Emily's plate he put in the larder, with the rest of the joint, under its wire cover. He would eat that tomorrow.

While John sat down to eat, he thought ruefully about his sudden change of circumstances. He knew exactly where Emily was going. She had run home to mother once before, after only two months of marriage. But this was the first time she had run away and left the children. He couldn't run after her now and leave the children on their own in the house, could he? But what was he going to do for money until he received his next pay-packet? .. Horrors, what was he going to do with Ann and Gracie, while the other two were at school? He didn't even know when term started or anything about the children's routine, apart from family prayers. That was Emily's province, not his. Had he been too hasty with her over her casual attitude to money?

Up in the attic, I knew my worst fears had been realised. I heard the angry voices and the bang of the saucepan on the tiled floor, then the sound of my mother's feet as she ran under my window towards the gate. I stood on the chair by the window to see her scurrying across the footpath, behind the hedge, and then out onto the open field. She was leaving us, just like that; and she didn't even look back once.

All was ominously quiet downstairs. Had she killed my father? ... Then I heard muffled sounds. Was he picking himself up? ... He was running water. Now he was opening the back door and calling the cats. He's not going after Mumsie; he's just letting her go and he's eating what's left of his dinner. He doesn't even *care* that she's gone.

I cried myself to sleep and then came the nightmares.

It was after 9.30 pm when Emily arrived at Uxbridge Station. The ticket collector looked at her suspiciously as he took her ticket. She had no luggage and she looked a wild, dishevelled mess. Anyway, it wasn't *his* job to sort out undesirables; that was the job of the police. He was relieved when he saw Emily walking purposefully away in the Cowley direction. Perhaps something unfortunate had happened to her, and she wasn't the kind of woman he had thought she was.

At Number 34 Victoria Road, Alex and Ella Nelson had already locked up and were getting ready for bed.

"Who's that ringing our doorbell at this hour?" said Ella crossly. "Go and see who it is, Alex." Alex limped towards the front door. He had been born without proper feet: the doctors had done their best for him, but he walked with his feet turned inwards, swinging his left leg and putting most of his weight on the right.

"It's Emily," he called, as he caught a glimpse of her reflection through the coloured glass.

"You'd better let her in then, hadn't you? Mark my words, there's been trouble again. Ever since they've had that Gracie, there's been nothing but trouble!"

Ella Nelson was a plain little woman, and something of a harridan, with her sharp tongue and forbidding appearance.

"Whatever's happened, Emily?" gasped the gentle Alex, concern written all over his face. "You look awful!"

Alex couldn't believe the state Emily was in. She had a cut lip and had obviously suffered a blow to the back of her head, judging by the congealed blood in her hair. Since leaving Crowsley she had made no attempt to tidy herself up and had deliberately avoided any contact with fellow passengers.

"I'm sick in the head; I had to get away," she answered in a strained little voice as she walked into the narrow passage.

"Where are your things?" asked Ella in surprise.

"I didn't bring any; I just picked up the pay-packet and ran."

As she uttered the word 'ran' she suddenly lost consciousness, falling to the floor with a thud. Then her whole body began making sudden uncontrollable movements. She seemed to be having a fit, and the jerky motions grew faster and faster.

"Ring Doctor Reade, Alex. I don't know what to do with her," shrieked Ella in desperation. "No, wait, get me a spoon quickly. She mustn't swallow her tongue."

Alex returned with a dessert spoon. Ella knelt down as best she could in the confined space, opened Emily's mouth and placed the bowl of the spoon over her tongue. Meanwhile, Alex went over to his desk in the dining room and picked up the telephone. Doctor Reade lived five minutes' walk away, in the only detached house in Lawn Road.

"Doctor, could you come quickly, my daughter's having convulsions. ... It's Alex Nelson, 34 Victoria Road."

"I'll just get my bag. Be with you in a minute."

"He's on his way," announced Alex. "I thought Emily had outgrown the epilepsy."

"So did I. Perhaps this is something else. Didn't she say she was sick in the head?"

The violence of the convulsions was gradually lessening, and the worst was over by the time the doctor actually saw Emily. However, his expression was grave. He shone a torch into her eyes and checked her pulse.

"Has Emily ever suffered from epilepsy?

"She did as a child," replied Alex. "But we thought that was in the past."

"I'm getting very little response; I'm not a hundred per cent sure it is epilepsy. The convulsions could be hysterical in origin. She really needs to go to hospital. How did she get in this state?"

"She arrived like this, just before ten. She's travelled here from Reading, without any luggage and, before she passed out, she said she was sick in the head and had to get away," answered Ella.

"Have you a pillow for her head? ... I'm going to call an ambulance. We'll have to take her to St. Bernard's; she needs a psychiatric hospital."

"You're not taking her *there*?" St Bernard's is for crazy people," shouted Ella. "Emily's not a nutter ... she's ... she's *ill*!"

"I know; and we need to find out exactly what is going on. And St Bernard's is the best place to get an accurate assessment. It has a very good reputation. But even after she's discharged, she may need nursing care and supervision. If it's what we popularly call a 'nervous breakdown', it may take a few months for her to get over it. Will you be able to look after her?"

"Of *course* we will," answered Alex.

The next day, he sent the following telegram to John:

<u>10.40 a.m.</u>　　　　<u>Uxbridge, Middlesex</u>　　　　<u>20 words</u>
Emily arrived safely, but taken ill on arrival. Being treated at St Bernard's Hospital, Hanwell. No visiting yet.

Alex Nelson

Lower Farm, in Cholsey, was managed by Harald Nielsen. Harald was Danish and his wife, Freda, a local girl. They had six children: Mary, Dorothy, Raymond, Sheila, Elizabeth and Phyllis, and they were all in their teens. The four eldest were employed on the farm and the two youngest were still at school. Elizabeth and Phyllis disliked farm work and wanted to work in an office when they grew up. No dirty hands and wellington boots for *them*, thank you very much!

The Nielsens readily agreed to take Jimmy and Ann when they heard of John Goodchild's plight. He had met them at the Wallingford Easter Monday Conference the previous year.

That rather grand title was given to a tea meeting organised in a large meeting room in Wallingford, for various small congregations worshipping in the locality. These earnest folk had separated themselves from all the established Christian denominations, and had become known collectively, for the last hundred years, by the nickname of 'Plymouth Brethren'.

The Nielsen family had all been at the Easter Monday

Conference, and John happened to sit opposite Harald and Freda at the long trestle table set up along one side of the meeting room. Over sandwiches and cakes, Harald and Freda talked about the farm and about their little Gospel Hall in Cholsey.

"John, do you ever go out preaching?" asked Harald.

"Yes, I do; but mostly I'm at the Iron Room in Peppard."

"Would you be willing to take our Gospel Service one Sunday evening?"

"I'd be glad to."

Since then, John had been over to Cholsey on three or four occasions. The last time he went, Freda's parting words were, "Sometime, you must let your children come over to see us at the farm."

Now, the Monday after Emily had run away, Freda and her daughter Mary were taking Jimmy and Ann away to the farm for several months.

"I want to go to school with Maggie," sobbed Jimmy as they drove away in the old Austin Seven.

—

"Come on, you two, stop dawdling," chided Freda, the first Monday morning in September. "We don't want to be late."

"I want to go to school, too," grumbled Ann, stomping her feet. "I can do everything *he* can do; it's not fair!"

As the trio arrived at the school gate, the children were already filing in from the playground. Ann looked around her and was surprised that there weren't more children about.

"It's only a little school; there'd be lots of room for me."

"Ann, you're only four; you can't go to school until you're five," explained Freda, rapidly running out of patience.

"No-one will know, will they? We could be twins."

The headmaster, Mike Cole, was an energetic redhead in his early thirties. He was standing in the corridor helping the children sort themselves out, as it was the beginning of a new school year. Mr Cole not only had eyes in the back of his head; he also had excellent hearing.

"Good morning Mrs Nielsen. Where did you get these two from?"

"Jimmy and Ann Goodchild are staying with us for a while.

Their mother is very unwell. ... I won't say any more now in front of the children."

"So, Ann, what makes you so keen to start school?"

"Jimmy's coming to school, and we do everything together, don't we Jimmy?"

Jimmy nodded, and thought to himself, "Yes, we do; but no prizes for guessing who's boss."

"When will you be five, Ann?" continued Mr Cole.

"August the 26th, 1945, and Jimmy is five on September the 8th, 1944. I'll be five before he's six!"

"Mrs Nielsen, if you like, I can take them both off your hands?"

"What about Ann's lunch? I've only brought enough for Jimmy."

"We can arrange something, don't you worry. We'll see how Ann gets on today. If she's as bright as I think she is, she's definitely ready for school."

⁓

Eight days after Emily had left Tudor Cottage, Nellie Goodchild arrived on the Saturday morning to fetch Gracie, in Peter Dawkins' 1936 Standard Ten. Gracie hardly knew Nellie, and was certainly not going to get into that car if she could help it. She wanted Auntie Rita to look after her. Rita Hurst had been at Tudor Cottage helping John to get her ready, and together the two women finally coaxed the truculent toddler into the back seat beside Nellie. I looked on in tears wondering how it would be without the others. Would I have to behave like a grown-up all the time from now on?

⁓

Gracie took a long time to settle down with the Ruislip Goodchilds. She felt miserable, and completely abandoned by her family. Ann and Jimmy had each other, but she had no-one. Also, she knew that she was going to be sick, not once, but many times. On the journey, she barely lasted out to Maidenhead before she was throwing up all over her aunt's best coat.

"John could at least have warned me this might happen,"

Nellie thought to herself as she fished a nappy out of the carrier bag at her feet. At least she was well prepared at the tail end!

⌒⌒

One Wednesday afternoon Gracie was particularly unhappy. Her aunt was booked to speak at a women's meeting in Pinner, and cousin Rebekah was off school recovering from a cold. She didn't like Rebekah; Rebekah was spiteful and sneaky.

"Now, Rebekah, don't forget to watch Gracie all the time. She can climb up onto the table; so don't leave pencils, compasses or scissors lying about, whatever you do."

"No, Mother, I won't."

Rebekah had a geography project to finish, and she was determined to get it done that afternoon, Gracie or no Gracie. It wasn't very often that she had the dining table all to herself. So, if that tiresome youngster so much as grizzled, she would dump her in her cot without a word or pang of conscience.

Gracie was sitting on her rug quietly playing with her bricks, when Rebekah suddenly realised she needed to go upstairs in a hurry.

"Oh no, the curse! I'm two days early, that's not fair," grumbled the fourteen-year-old. "I'm certainly not having that pesky *child* watching me!"

Furtively, she glanced across at Gracie, who appeared to be engrossed in her building plans.

"There's nothing for it; I'll just have to chance it. If I have to struggle upstairs with *her*, that'll only make matters worse."

Gracie was *not* thinking about bricks; she had been watching Rebekah using those scissors. She wanted to play with the shiny things too.

Her actions now matched her thought processes exactly. Get up onto the chair and reach across the table; there, I've got them. Now throw them onto the rug, and get down carefully and quietly. Rebekah mustn't know. ... Now what shall I cut? I don't like this hair all round my face. ...

⌒⌒

The twins, Ruth and Rhoda, came out of school early. They wanted to do their piano practice before their sister Rachel came home.

They had a duet to learn. As they walked in the back door, they heard a strange snipping sound coming from the dining room.

"Oh Gracie! What *have* you done? Where's Rebekah?" cried Ruth.

"Upstairs. ... Look scissors!"

"Rebekah, where *are* you? Look what Gracie's done! She's only cut her hair," shouted Rhoda from the bottom of the stairs.

"Oh no! I had to go to the lavatory. *Now* what are we going to do?" Rebekah didn't know whether to laugh or cry. Gracie had cut her curly locks across her forehead and down one side of her face, narrowly missing her left ear lobe. She looked so comical. But what would Mother say?

"Shall we cut it so that it's the same all over?" suggested the practical Ruth.

"No, Father said that we should *never* cut our hair, it would displease God," answered Rebekah.

"But Gracie's only a baby, so that doesn't count," objected Ruth.

"I wish I could cut *my* plaits off," sighed Rhoda. "I hate them. My hair's so thin and straggly, it looks so silly."

"Let's clear this mess up and start getting the tea," said Ruth. Mother will be here about five o'clock, won't she?" As she said that, Rachel came in the back door.

"Whatever's going on here?"

Nellie Goodchild was only cross with Rebekah for a few seconds. She quickly understood her eldest daughter's embarrassing predicament.

"You'll get used to managing it in time. You'll see. ... Ruth, you want to be a hairdresser. See if you can make this hair look the same all over."

Chapter 12

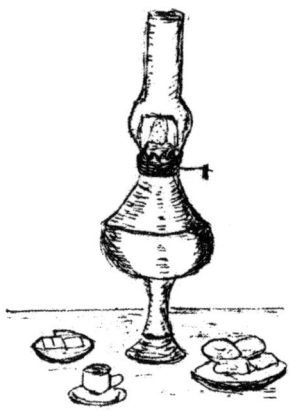

The days were closing in once we were into September and my father had to show me how to light the Aladdin lamp. I watched him fill it up with paraffin oil. Next he took off the glass and put it down on the kitchen table. Then he turned up the wick just a little.

"Now, Maggie, I want you to open this box of matches. ... Take one out, and strike it on the side of the box like this. ... Hold it up, not down, or you'll burn your fingers. ... Now take the match to the wick. If it flares, you need to turn the wick down a little bit. ... That's it! Now, watch me put the glass on. You hold it at the bottom, like this. You have to get it level and turn it round to the right. You must be quick because the glass gets hot very quickly. I'm going to turn it off again. Now I want you to do it."

I was afraid of that oil lamp. I couldn't get it right and I was far too slow. In the end my father got very cross with me. I wanted to cry, but I knew that would be disastrous. I didn't want a good hiding. I'd rather burn my fingers than make him *that* cross. After at least ten attempts, I was finally able to get that glass on properly.

"Now, Maggie, I want you to put the lamp on tomorrow

evening as soon as it gets too dark to see what you're doing. I will be working until seven o'clock, or even later some nights. Do your practice while it's still light, and any schoolwork you've been given. Then lay the table for tea. I'll get my dinner when I come home. Now, do you understand all that?"

"Yes, Daddy."

The first week all went well, and I had no problems with the lamp, and I was so relieved. Perhaps I was becoming a bit too cocksure. The following Monday, everything went wrong. I could *not* get that glass level. Then everything became far too hot. The wick flared and the flames came through the top of the glass. The knob was so hot that I couldn't get hold of it to turn the lamp off. I didn't know what to do! I ran out of the house, slamming the back door behind me. I ran and ran until I arrived at the Hursts'.

"Please come, there's a fire," I cried as Ernie Hurst came to the door. "I couldn't get the glass on properly and now the table's on fire."

"Rita, come and look after Maggie, there's a fire at Tudor Cottage."

I'd never seen Ernie Hurst run like that before. What would he find? I was frightened that the whole house would go up in flames. Grandpa Goodchild wasn't there any more to stop it; he was in a hospital for old people in Henley.

"Maggie, I didn't know you were still there. I thought you'd gone to your friends at Amersham. I'd no idea. Come and sit here in the warm."

"Thank you, Mrs Hurst. ... I didn't light the lamp properly, and everything got too hot. Now there's a fire and Daddy will be very cross with me. ... He showed me how to do it, but tonight everything went wrong."

"Now, don't cry. It's not your fault. You weren't doing anything naughty, were you?"

"No, but I didn't get it right, and I should have done."

"It's eight o'clock. Hasn't your daddy come home yet?"

"No. He works late to earn more money."

"Have you had any tea?"

"No, I lay the table and Daddy sees to the food when he comes in. I sometimes cut the bread for him; I have tea and he has dinner."

"Right, I'm going to get you something to eat, and you're going to stay here with me for now."

"But Daddy will be cross if I'm not there when he comes home."

"No he won't. Ernie will tell him what's happened."

After my tea, I fell asleep on the Hursts' comfortable sofa. They always called it a sofa, not a settee.

~

Ernie had put out the fire by the time my father arrived at Tudor Cottage. There was very little damage other than a scorched tablecloth and a mark on the ceiling above the lamp. The lamp was still functional. There was a hole in the mantle and a crack in the glass but, fortunately, my fears were unfounded. It hadn't been a real fire, and the house was still intact. My father walked down the lane with Ernie, and I woke up to the sound of their voices.

"John, please let Maggie stay with us until you get home. She shouldn't be alone all that time at her age. She's only eight, isn't she?"

"Yes, she's eight-and-a-half." My father cleared his throat, and then he went on. "That's very kind of you, Ernie. It's her music practice that's the real problem, and she also helps me with the meal."

"She can practise here. We can get the piano tuned, can't we Rita? It'd be nice to hear the old joanna again."

"Yes, let Maggie come here and have her tea with us. Then you've only yourself to think of when you come home. ... Though it wouldn't be any more trouble to get something for *you* while I'm cooking for Ernie. If you got here between half past seven and eight, you could both eat together. How about it?"

"Thank you very much, Mrs Hurst; but you must let me pay you."

"All right; but you must call me Rita, not Mrs Hurst. ... How's Emily, now?"

"She's no longer in hospital, but it's going to be a long time before she comes home again."

~

173

'The Iron Room' was the name given to the meeting place of the local Christian Brethren Assembly in Peppard. It was a plain, corrugated iron building, of the type often used for non-conformist chapels and village halls in country areas in the 1930s and 40s. In those days, the Christian Brethren did not use the word 'church', either for themselves or their building, nor did they consider themselves to be one of the many Christian denominations. They used the term 'Assemblies' (with a capital 'A') to refer to their own gatherings and the label 'the denominations' to denote the rest of Christendom. They took St. Paul's, 'Come out from among them, and be ye separate', to imply separation from other Christian groups, as well as from unbelievers and evil doers.

This uninspiring place of worship had been erected on a narrow plot of land, along the quiet stretch of road between Gravel Hill and Peppard Common. It was tightly squeezed between the high fences belonging to two imposing and desirable dwellings. The local population could, therefore, be forgiven for their total ignorance of what went on there, even if they did occasionally spot a small band of worshippers, all dressed up in their Sunday best, solemnly entering the building.

By the gate to the Iron Room was a notice board, listing the times of the various services in fine copperplate lettering:

The Lord's Day

9.45 am	Sunday School
11.00 am	The Lord's Supper
6.30 pm	Gospel Meeting

Weekdays
Tuesday 7.30 pm Prayer & Ministry
Wednesday 3.00 pm Women's Meeting

No female member of the regular congregation was allowed in without a suitable head covering over her long hair, 'suitable' being interpreted as a proper hat with a brim. Any female outsider who might find herself in the women's meeting or gospel meeting without a head covering was 'kindly requested' to bring one if she came again, but her inquisitiveness would seldom be followed by a further visit.

My parents first took me to the Iron Room in the summer of 1936 when I was a month old. My pram was placed in the small classroom behind the meeting room during the Lord's Supper, or communion service. The Brethren didn't believe in infant baptism, nor did they formally dedicate young children. So my parents prayed over me privately at home and then, without any ceremony, started to bring me with them on Sunday mornings. In those early months I usually slept peacefully throughout the proceedings.

The meeting room itself had a bare wooden floor with a wine-coloured carpet down the middle. The walls were painted cream and adorned with framed Bible verses from the King James Version, carefully transcribed in ornate lettering; the curtains at the windows matched the carpet. At the far end was a platform with a lectern for the speaker, who was invariably male, except in the women's meetings. For the Lord's Supper, the chairs were arranged in a square around the table bearing the bread and wine. The whole service was conducted completely extemporaneously, 'brothers' jumping up to pray, read from the Bible, or give a short exhortation as they felt led, often punctuated by long periods of silence. The 'sisters' kept quiet except when hymns were being sung, always *a cappella*.

When I was four, I wanted to know why no-one played the harmonium at this particular service. "The Lord wants to hear our voices, not the wooden brother in the corner," explained Grandpa Goodchild, but his answer didn't make a lot of sense to me. My father played the harmonium at the Gospel Meeting; surely the Lord could still hear our voices at that meeting, too? Mine was quite loud, anyway, and God definitely wasn't deaf, I reasoned. I picked up the words of hymns quickly, if not very accurately. One hymn we used to sing was called 'Rescue the perishing'. I used to sing 'rescue the perishers'; to Grandpa the 'perishers' were naughty boys, so my version seemed equally valid. Perhaps they needed rescuing from *him*; if he ever caught them, that is.

Occasionally local lads would play ball games in the narrow space between the building and the high fence to the right of it. These games often resulted in a broken window or two. It was my grandfather's responsibility to deal with broken windows. He hated the job. "Wretched little perishers, I'd like to wring their ruddy little necks," he would explode, as he arrived at ten-thirty to open up the hall for the celebration of the Lord's Supper. Half an hour later, he would be holding forth in prayer, using very different language. "Lord, Thou dost see us here gathered before Thee; may we know that Thou art with us..." It was as if I had two different grandpas rolled into one; or was it three?

When I was about seven, Grandpa used to take Jimmy, Ann and myself for walks around the Triangle to give my mother a break. As we walked, my grandfather would make up rhymes which he set to hymn tunes. They were always about rabbits, foxes and farm animals, which talked and did the same sort of things that human beings do. They weren't naughty like some school rhymes, but when I was in the Iron Room at the Lord's Supper and my father started a familiar hymn tune, Grandpa's rhyme set to that particular tune immediately came to mind. Jimmy and Ann didn't yet know the difference between a hymn and a rhyme, so instead of singing, 'Hark! my soul; it is the Lord,' to the tune 'St Bees', they sang, 'Farmer Brooker took his gun' at the tops of their voices. While the 'brothers' frowned in displeasure, some of the younger 'sisters' were giggling behind their copies of 'Hymns of Light and Love'.

⌁

At Sunday school, we sang lots of shorter songs called 'choruses'. Here, I was not the only one to sing the wrong words. One favourite was, 'I will make you fishers of men'; but we all sang lustily, 'I will make you vicious old men' and, amazingly, none of the teachers ever seemed to notice the irreverent substitution.

My favourite Sunday school hymn was, 'There is a happy land, far, far away'. I often thought about Heaven and imagined what it would be like, especially when I was trying to get to sleep. But, one Sunday, when I was about six, I heard Willie Watson sing some very rude words:

'There is a happy land, far, far away,
where little piggies run, three times a day.
Oh! how they squeal and run,
when they hear the butcher come;
three slices off their bums, three times a day.'

'Bum' was a forbidden word; at home we had to use the word 'bottom' if we ever mentioned that particular part of our anatomies. Whenever I thought or dreamt about Heaven, I pictured angels bathed in an unearthly white light, and imagined other beautiful beings gracefully floating around as if there were no such thing as gravity. These were people who had just died, enjoying themselves in their brand new bodies. There's always wonderful music; but never any dirty pigs in *my* heaven!

The highlight of the Sunday school year was the Christmas party. A few weeks before the party date, new children would suddenly turn up at Sunday school; but they would generally stop coming as soon as the Christmas holidays were over and the new school term had begun.

The party began at three o'clock and, before tea, we watched a magic lantern show, a projected set of painted glass slides shown one at a time, rather like a film strip, telling an exciting story. A special favourite was John Bunyan's 'Pilgrim's Progress'. Some of the characters had very strange names such as Mr Malice, Mr Liar, Mr Nogood and Mr Facing-Bothways. The weirdest was Mr Facing-Bothways. He was like an owl: owls can turn their necks right round so they can look behind them. At the end, the slide projector was very hot; but my father always finished the afternoon with some fascinating moving slides which made patterns like a kaleidoscope.

After tea we played games, but when the balloons came out, I ran away and hid in the vestibule behind the front door. I had keen hearing, and a genuine fear of loud noises. As soon as the balloon races were over I reappeared and joined in the party again. My parents were too busy organising the games to notice my peculiar behaviour.

Another highlight of the Sunday School year was the summer 'treat'. We often had games and sports on Peppard Common followed by tea outside the Iron Room, seated at trestle tables which extended the whole length of the building, set up between the side wall and the fence a few feet away. After the sandwiches, we had sugar doughnuts with a hole in the middle and drank cups of milky tea or lemonade.

The River

Once or twice, we were taken in a charabanc to Caversham for a steamer trip on the River Thames, instead of going to the common for games. My first trip, at the age of five, from Caversham Bridge to Goring Lock was a mixed experience.

The sun smiled down on the forty of us from a cloudless blue sky. I was one of the youngest. My mother had dressed me in my favourite blue frock, with its pretty smocked bodice, and my new straw hat. This had pink flowers around the crown.

"Why are you all dressed up like *that*?" scolded Penny Stradling. "You'll get dirty." Practical Penny was two years older than I was and quite a madam.

"I'm a fairy princess."

"No, you're not, Maggie Goodchild. You're just a stuck-up little prig. Why did your mum doll you up like that? You look silly!"

"No I don't! *You* look scruffy!"

All the other children were dressed in their everyday clothes. Suddenly, I realised that I stood out like a sore thumb, and pretending to be a fairy princess no longer bolstered my ego.

We sat on the top deck at the back of the Salter's Steamer, where there was no canopy. We drifted leisurely past open meadows and grazing cattle to our left, with elegant mansions peeping out from steep wooded hillsides to our right. I sat very still, listening to the shouts of people in small boats having fun. Some rowed energetically and others were being powered along by temperamental outboard motors spluttering behind them. Children splashed excitedly in the shallows; swans honked at any human who ventured too close to their private bank; and the occasional heron stood motionless, like a cardboard cut-out, in the middle of a reed bed. I saw it all as if through a window.

"We're having *much* more fun than you are, Maggie

Goodchild", shouted Susan Summerfield. "*We're* back here watching the waves."

"What waves?"

"The ones the boat leaves behind, silly!"

"Oh!" was all I could say. At that point I had neither seen nor heard of that kind of wave.

As we neared Mapledurham Lock, I was rudely jolted out of my detachment by a long, piercing blast on the steamer's horn, warning the lock-keeper that we were approaching. "What's *that*?" I screamed hysterically, knocking off my hat, as I stuck my fingers into my ears.

"*Now*, what's happened to the fairy princess?" shouted Jill Nash from the back of the boat. I could hear both of them laughing at me.

"We're only going into the lock," came the soothing voice of Auntie Frances, my favourite teacher. "Let's go down below, and then you can see the water rising as we get ready to go out the other end."

"Will we hear that awful noise again? ... I don't *like* it!" I whimpered.

"You will, when we get to Whitchurch, and then again when we get to Goring. Just twice more, that's all."

"Why is it so *loud*?" I demanded.

"The lock-keeper may be having his afternoon nap, and the captain has to wake him up," suggested Frances.

"He shouldn't *be* asleep, it's not bedtime," I retorted crossly.

"Come on. ... Look! The gates are opening, let's go and see what's going on."

Four years later I was staying with my grandparents in Uxbridge when Grandma Nelson suddenly announced one Friday teatime, "It's an early night for you, Maggie. Tomorrow we're going on an outing."

"Where are we going, Grandma?" I asked excitedly.

"On the river," announced Grandma, flatly. "Grandpa likes the river, so we're sailing from Hampton Court to Windsor."

"How many locks are we going through?" I asked, suddenly remembering the horn and my ever-present fear of loud noises.

"I've no idea! You'll have to count them, won't you? We shall be on the steamer for four hours and we'll be taking our lunch and tea with us." It was clear from her monotonous tone of voice that Grandma didn't really like the river, but I did, if only I could find a way to silence that blasted horn!

We caught the Hampton Court bus at the bus station. It was a fine sunny day and we were wearing our straw hats, but carrying our waterproofs with us 'just in case' ... This was one of Grandma's favourite expressions but she invariably left us to fill in the specific eventuality for ourselves. On this occasion there wasn't even a hint of rain. "If it isn't already raining, do macs and brollies actually charm the rain away?" I wondered, as I yanked the cumbersome brolly bag up onto my shoulder.

We arrived at Hampton Court in plenty of time to buy the tickets and make ourselves comfortable before boarding the steamer. "The toilet! ... of course! ... *That's* where I'll hide, as we come to each lock," I decided. "There, no-one will see me blocking my ears up, not even Grandma."

Grandpa chose seats on the top deck where he could catch both the sun and rare glimpses of famous landmarks. The river was wider here than at Caversham and the whole landscape far more open. We were soon passing under Hampton Bridge and it wasn't long before we could see Molesey Lock in the distance.

"Grandma, I want to go to the toilet," I whispered, urgently, as we drew nearer to Molesey.

"*Already*?" interjected Grandma.

"Yes, but there's no need for *you* to come. I know where it is."

"All right, but don't make yourself a nuisance," she cautioned.

There were seven more locks between Molesey and Windsor: Sunbury; Shepperton; Chertsey; Penton Hook, Laleham; Bell Weir, Egham; Old Windsor; and Romney Lock, Eton. At the approach to each lock, I hid in the ladies' toilet (mercifully, always vacant) and then stayed below, waiting expectantly for the gates to open and close again behind us. Then the lock-keeper would walk unhurriedly past the onlookers, up to the other end of the lock to open the sluices in the gates ahead of us. Down in the saloon, I was exhilarated by the force of the water swirling and crashing around us, as the vessel was jerkily lifted up to the next level. The flight of steps below the path was submerged in a matter of seconds.

When we started moving forward, I quietly returned to my grandparents. Grandpa and Grandma found the delays at the locks irksome and were always in a better humour once we were underway again.

"You took your time down there, didn't you?" commented Grandma, irritably, after one of my longer absences. "I hope you didn't get in anyone's way?"

"No, Grandma. They didn't even see me," I added, sweetly.

"Now we can eat our sandwiches, if you say grace, Maggie. Grandpa is waiting."

I wanted to sing, not mutter, so I sang at the top of my voice:

"Thank you for the world so sweet;
Thank you for the food we eat;
Thank you for the birds that sing;
Thank you, God, for *everything*.
　　　　　Amen."

⌒

Uncle Brian and the Children's Mission

Uncle Brian was a children's evangelist who came to stay with us the summer after my mother finally returned home from Uxbridge. She was still rather frail and had hoped that Mr and Mrs Lunn would have hosted him, especially as they had a car and proper modern sanitation, and were also reasonably well-off. The children's mission was Gladys Lunn's idea in the first place. "She's always full of good ideas as long as *she* doesn't have to implement any of them herself," grumbled my mother, as she heard the unwelcome news.

"Brian Hepworth should stay with us as *we* are the ones who are inviting him to run the mission," Percy Lunn had announced at the planning meeting.

"No dear!" interrupted Gladys. "Shiplake is too far away from Sonning Common and Peppard. He needs to be on the spot if he's going to visit the schools and meet the children's parents ... and follow them up properly. The Goodchilds are only *three* miles away. They're the obvious choice."

"We have no car. All we could offer him would be the use of my father's bicycle. Besides, Emily isn't really up to entertaining yet," protested my father, gravely.

"Ah! But a little outside company would do Emily no end of good. Deal with her depression in no time!" So the children's mission at the Iron Room took place as Gladys had planned and Brian Hepworth slept in Uncle David's room.

Uncle Brian was a rotund little man with silver hair who loved his food as much as Uncle David did — even riding around on Grandpa Goodchild's old bone-shaker did nothing to reduce his

182

girth! He had a wife but she didn't accompany him on his missions.

"Daddy, why doesn't Uncle Brian bring his wife with him?" I puzzled.

"She has to look after the house while he's away."

"... and the children, and the animals, I s'pose."

"The children have all grown up, but Auntie Agatha isn't well enough to come with him."

"She must miss him!"

"Yes, but he's the Lord's servant, and sacrifice is part and parcel of serving God."

"What's 'sacrifice', Daddy?"

"Something special you give up for the Lord's sake," answered my mother quickly. She knew that if she left my father to answer the question we would be there all night.

~~~

The mission took place during the first two weeks of July. Uncle Brian arrived on the Saturday, and took Sunday school on the Sunday as the first day of the mission. He had drawn some pictures to show us. Some were a bit weird, even though they were supposed to explain his talk. He couldn't draw as well as my father could!

His first picture was a snake on a pole. It was a bronze snake, not a real one. The Children of Israel (most of them were grown-up, but that's what the Bible called them!) were fed up with walking. They'd walked all the way from Egypt and were going a very long way round to get to the land of Canaan, which God said he would give them. So they said to God, "Why have you brought us here to die in the desert? There's no bread or water, and the food you *have* given us is horrible." But God was angry with them and sent some snakes to bite them. Lots of them died. So they went to Moses and said they were sorry and Moses prayed for them. God told Moses to make a snake and put it on a pole. The people who looked at the bronze snake lived and those that didn't died. But that wasn't fair, as some people had already died before Moses even made the snake! (Uncle Brian didn't say that, but it's true!)

The next pictures were the weird ones. Uncle Brian had drawn four snakes on four poles, and wrote a different message on each one. On the black one he wrote: 'SEPARATED BY SIN'; on the red one: 'PUT AWAY SIN'; on the yellow one: 'SAVED FROM SIN'; and on the white one: 'FREE FROM SIN'. He told us that the Children of Israel sinned when they grumbled at God. We have sinned too; we don't have to look at a bronze snake but at Jesus on the cross. I understood that bit very well, but I couldn't understand what the four coloured snakes had to do with it and what the words written on them were supposed to mean.

If we wanted to earn an extra point and get an extra hole punched in our special invitation cards, Uncle Brian said we could do our own drawings of the four snakes, but we had to get all the words right for it to count. I thought *that* would be easy, but I forgot about the drawing until late Sunday afternoon. By then I wasn't too sure what was on the red snake: was it 'put under sin' or 'put from sin'? Neither seemed right. I couldn't remember the correct word in the middle, so opted finally for 'under'. I did my drawing extra carefully hoping I would be marked on my artistic efforts rather than my factual accuracy. But I was wrong. I didn't get that extra hole — only one for attendance. Also, when he asked us questions, Uncle Brian ignored my raised hand and always chose someone else. That was because my father was one of the leaders!

On Sunday, Uncle Brian had given us all extra invitation cards to pass on to our school friends. At lunch time on Monday he was standing outside the school, near the school gate, ready to hand out more invitations to the children going home for lunch. I saw him through the window at the bottom of the junior corridor. No teachers seemed to be about so I ran out to greet Uncle Brian.

"Margaret Goodchild, where do you think *you're* going?" It was Fanny Claxton's voice behind me, her class of infants now occupied the end classroom by the front door. "Come here at once. You know you're not allowed out in the lunch hour. You can sit here in my room while I see what that man is doing hanging around the gate."

"It's Unc ..."

"Be quiet; I didn't ask *you* to speak!"

"Interfering old cow," I muttered under my breath. It was a good thing she didn't hear me, or she would have boxed my ears for my insolence. As it was, I wondered if I would miss my lunch altogether. The bell could ring anytime in the next ten minutes.

~~

"May I ask you what are you doing, Sir, hanging round the school gate? Show me those cards you are handing out! I am always *very* suspicious when I see middle-aged men like you hanging around young children."

"They are invitation cards to the children's mission we are holding at the Iron Room for the next two weeks, starting this evening." Brian Hepworth began to redden around the collar when he realised exactly what she was insinuating.

"Are you running this mission all by yourself?"

"Of course not! A group of local people are organising the meetings and all I do is stand up front and give the talks."

"I would like to see some of these people before I give you permission to distribute invitation cards outside *my* school. I really ought to confiscate them."

"No, you can't do that. I'll bring Mr Goodchild and Miss Russell with me when I come back at four o'clock."

~~

Mrs Claxton returned to her classroom well pleased with her handling of the encounter. "He actually thought I was the headmistress," she smirked to herself. "Mr Ford needn't know anything about it." Then she remembered me. "Margaret Goodchild, go and get your dinner, if they still have any left." I didn't enjoy the cold mince, potatoes and cabbage, but at least I didn't go hungry.

At four o'clock, Fanny Claxton was nowhere to be seen. Grandpa Goodchild and Auntie Frances were at the gate with Uncle Brian; the juniors all seemed to be taking the invitation cards and some even promised to come.

"Don't *lose* your cards; you will need them for your points when you come tonight. Your points go towards a prize at the end of the mission."

185

When Grandpa Goodchild saw me he said, "Maggie, if you wait a few minutes, I'll take you home on the bike. Uncle Brian is going to tea with Mr and Mrs Russell and Auntie Frances, so *I* will be riding the bike till tonight."

"I want to go to the children's mission, too. But it starts at six o'clock, doesn't it?"

"I'll get you back on time."

"Let Maggie come to tea as well," suggested Auntie Frances. "Then she won't get too tired. I know Mum and Dad won't mind."

I was a little afraid of Mrs Russell, but it was better than having to hurry or missing the meeting altogether. Mr Russell was kind like Grandpa Goodchild and he often teased me about my long plaits. He didn't make up stories and rhymes, but he liked telling jokes and laughing at them himself. Today he gave me a riddle, as we stood watching the people go by in Grove Road.

"Maggie, do you know what's black and white and read all over?"

"A white umbrella with a black handle, and red spots."

"No. Try again."

"A red umbrella, with a black handle and white spots?"

"It's not an umbrella."

"Is it a white frock with red and black spots?"

"No, it's nothing to wear."

"Is it a ball or a balloon?"

"Nope."

"Is it a flag?"

"No. Don't you give up yet?"

"Not yet. Is it a window with a black and white frame in a red brick wall?"

"Nope. Shall I tell you?

"Okay."

"It's a newspaper!"

"That's not *red*?"

"Yes, it is. Lots of people read a newspaper like the 'News Chronicle'. It's *read* all over, from cover to cover."

"Oh! That's not *fair*. I wasn't thinking of *that* kind of 'read'! That kind of 'read' and the colour 'red' sound exactly the same. So, how would I know which one you meant unless you wrote it down?"

"That's why it's a good riddle – it makes you think. ... All right! Here's something else. 'Why did the chicken cross the road?'"

"It had lost its chicks."

"Maybe; but that's not the answer."

"It wanted to go back to the farmyard."

"Could be; but that's not the answer."

"It just wanted to."

"To do what ...?"

" to cross the road, of course – to get to the other side."

"You've got it! Well done! The chicken crossed the road *because it wanted to get to the other side.*"

While we had our tea the grown-ups did all the talking, especially Uncle Brian. He could talk and eat at the same time. Mumsie told us it was rude to talk with your mouth full. Maybe, he didn't know that! Anyway, most of what he said was over my head and about people I'd never even heard of. I couldn't ask him about them because I had been taught to keep quiet whenever grown-ups were talking. Also, to wait to be asked if I wanted something more to eat. If it had been left to Uncle Brian, I would have gone hungry that meal. Fortunately, Auntie Frances was looking after me and made sure I had some homemade cake, as well as bread, butter and jam.

Mrs Russell didn't say a lot, but she looked across at me from time to time. I don't think she liked children, but Mr Russell and Auntie Frances did.

~

About forty-five children arrived at the Iron Room before six o'clock. Some were from Sunday school, but many had never been to the Iron Room before. One boy, Godfrey, went to a private school and arrived in his smart brown cap and blazer, with gold braid and school badge worked in gold thread. He had a posh voice and answered more questions than anyone else, so he went home with four points punched on his card that first day. Grandpa and my father punched the holes, but they wouldn't let *me* answer if others still had their hands up.

Auntie Frances played the harmonium for the choruses. Uncle Brian taught us a new one:

"Climb, climb up Sunshine Mountain;
heavenly breezes blow.
Climb, climb up Sunshine Mountain;
faces all aglow.
Turn, turn your back on doubting;
look into the skies.
Climb, climb up Sunshine Mountain;
you and I."

He told us that God was in Heaven and he wanted us to be there too one day; but he didn't tell us where Sunshine Mountain was, nor why we had to climb it. According to my mother, it meant that God wanted us to believe in him and try to please him every day, 'living in the sunshine of his love'.

My heart sank. If I couldn't please my parents for just *one* day without being told off, how could I ever please God? My parents weren't even perfect themselves, but God was, so I'd been told. I could *never* please a god like that, however hard I tried! So, for the duration of the mission, I was miserable inside. Not much sunshine there; more like being in a cold, iron dungeon.

Not being allowed to answer questions until everyone else had had a go really rankled. I couldn't get as many points as most of the other children; so at the end of the mission when I came to collect *my* prize there was only one book left, 'Little Margery', a book I had been given as a Sunday school prize when I was five. There she was again, with her blond hair and bright red dress, sitting like a pudding in a basket chair which was much too small for her!

"Daddy, I've already got this one," I explained.

"That's all that's left. You can read it again, *can't* you?"

"Yes, but I've still got the *other* one."

"All right. It can go to someone else at the next prize giving."

So I had nothing! Everyone had a prize except me. Couldn't he have changed it for something else, or did he *really* think I was different from every other child in Peppard?

Chapter 13

A One-sided Conversation with a Hedgehog

I call you Mr Prickly Pointer because of your hard prickly spines.
I touched you once when I was little and you made my finger bleed.
Your pointer is your little pointed face with a knob for your nose.

I know just what you looked like when you were a newborn baby.
Your spines were soft and white and you couldn't prick anybody
then. Now you can erect your spines at will, just when you want to.

You enjoy your nightly saucer of bread and milk that I put out for you...

Once I saw Mrs Prickly Pointer and your four little babies by the
back door.

They looked so cute with milky faces. Their spines weren't quite
hard yet.

You are my garden friend, taking away the slugs, and snails, and
horrid insects. But why do you eat some of my other friends, like

the frogs and toads? Why can't you just take away the real pests who are nobody's friends?

You can roll yourself into a tight little ball at the onset of danger. But why can't you keep out of the way of motor cars and lorries? Can't you hear them coming, or see their bright lights when it's dark?

Why did people call you urchin or hedgepig? Hedgehog sounds so much nicer! Why do they say you suck milk from cows when your mouth is so much smaller than a cow's teat? Can you really carry away apples and pears on your spines?

September 1945

Emily had been very relieved when the children's mission was finally over and Brian Hepworth had returned home to spend time with his wife before launching out on a similar mission in Cholsey, hosted by Harald and Freda Nielsen.

"Well, Emily, that was a good time we had with Brian Hepworth, wasn't it?" commented John. "It's a pity that *you* weren't able to get out to any of the meetings."

"It was all I could do to keep things going here, John. I still feel absolutely exhausted! Brian's a nice enough man, but not very imaginative. He made such a lot of extra work, and often the children suffered as a result. I don't know what I would have done without Rita Hurst."

"I was hoping that you'd get *her* to come with you to the meetings for adults. They were very poorly attended, hardly any outsiders in to hear the Gospel."

"How could I do that without leaving the children on their own? Maggie's too young for that kind of responsibility – especially now there are rumours that the Maloneys are coming back! I would have thought the Lunns could have given us a lift some evenings or helped to entertain Brian."

"Did you ask them?"

"How could I without using Rita's phone? You saw them most evenings, why didn't *you*? ... Anyway, I really would have thought that Gladys could have mucked in too. This whole mission was her idea in the first place, but she didn't even come near us the whole time Brian was here, and she had to pass the *end of the lane!*"

"The Lunns are busy people, Emily."

Emily was too weary to continue the discussion. "None so blind as those who *won't* see," she mumbled under her breath. Already she was fearful she would have another breakdown if she wasn't careful. And John hadn't even seen the warning signs. As it was, she had a sore chest and was finding it hard to breathe.

Less than two months later, Jimmy and Ann were packed off to Cholsey again and Gracie was reunited with their cousins at Ruislip. Jimmy and Ann were the first to go. This time they knew what to expect, and clambered into the old Austin Seven with the minimum of fuss.

"Will we see the ducks again, Auntie Freda?"

"Yes, you will, Jimmy. We've got lots more than when you came last time. We've also got some turkeys."

"I don't like turkeys," said Ann. "Last time I saw one up close, it tried to push me over."

"Maybe you got *too* close and frightened him."

Gracie left less than an hour later. She did not leave so happily.

"I want to stay with Maggie. *She* put me to bed."

"No she can't," answered Nellie Goodchild in her no-nonsense voice. "Maggie has to go to school and do her music practice. She'll have no time to look after *you*. Now stop pouting and sit still on that seat."

"I'm so sorry to put you to all this trouble once again, Nellie," mumbled John.

"It will be easier this time, now she's a bit older."

I felt miserable once they had all gone and wanted to cry, but thought better of it when I saw my father's face. The following day Grandpa Nelson came with family friends to fetch my mother while I was at school. I came home to an empty house. The key was under the mat, and on the table I found this note:

Wednesday, 10.30 am
Dear Maggie,
Grandpa Nelson has just come with Mr and Mrs Mutter to
take your mother to Uxbridge. I am now going to work and

*shall leave Austin's about 7 o'clock, and see to my meal when
I get home. Please do the washing up, tidy the kitchen and cut
some bread and marge for your own tea. I'll be having some
Pom and corned beef. We'll eat together when I come.*
Your loving Father, J. Goodchild.

I spent another lonely autumn with the cats, Purdy and
Gormy, and a host of imaginary playmates. The Hursts had family
concerns of their own and Auntie Rita was hardly ever at home.
Her new granddaughter, Elaine, was born prematurely and
needed round the clock care and attention.

Christmas 1945

I had been dreading the Christmas holidays and was scared about
being left alone all day while my father was at work. We broke up
on the Friday before Christmas and my father was working right
up to Christmas Day the following Friday. On weekdays, he was
leaving home at half past seven in the morning and would not be
back until half past seven at night, a whole twelve hours. In the
winter he hardly saw the house in daylight!

"Don't you go bothering Mrs Hurst, Maggie! She's got enough
problems of her own. I want you to sweep the kitchen floor and
dust the furniture, after you've washed up the breakfast things.
You can also make the beds, and sweep and dust the bedrooms.
Oh! And you can brush down the stairs, using the dustpan and
brush. You know how to get rid of the fluffs, don't you?"

"Yes, Daddy," I answered, glumly, as he put on his outdoor
things and carefully placed his sandwiches in his haversack next
to the thermos flask.

"This afternoon, you can do your practice. Don't forget your exam
is coming up after Christmas. Your scales need a *lot* more work!"

"Yes, Daddy." Then he was gone.

I hated housework. My father always found out if I had swept
the dust under the mat, or tipped it in the coal scuttle. My pretend
friends Jenny and Jill wouldn't lend a hand. And it never worked
if I pretended to be one of *them*. It didn't help me do a better job
or make the clock go faster.

Just after nine, I was startled by a loud knock on the kitchen door.

"Postman – here's a letter for you."

"Hello. I'm coming!"

"Are you here on your own?"

"Yes."

"I saw your Dad on his motorbike up by Austin's."

"My Mum's at Gran's and the little ones have been taken away. Jimmy and Ann are at Wallingford ..."

"This letter's from Wallingford. See the postmark."

"I hope they're not ill, or anything ... "

"Anyway, do make sure you give this to your Dad, won't you? I'm going on to Binfield Heath now."

I kept thinking about that letter all day but dared not try to open it. Besides, I didn't find grown-up writing very easy to read, except my mother's. When I thought about her I started to cry. "How long is she going to be away *this* time? ... I've got to be brave. Come on, Jenny and Jill, let's get started upstairs."

My father was in no hurry to open the letter. He didn't realise the agonies I had been going through all day.

"We'll have our meal straight away. You must be hungry." He washed his hands, boiled some water on the paraffin stove and mixed up the unappetising potato powder, then opened the tin of corned beef.

"Do you ever get tired of corned beef and Pom, Daddy?"

"No, Maggie. It fills you up; that's the main thing."

I thought that school dinners were better than the food *he* was eating. At least we had some variety and always had a second vegetable, even if it was only mashed swede.

All the time we were silently munching, I was worrying about that letter and my bread and jam tasted like cardboard. (My father called it 'bread and scrape' – scrape it on and then scrape it off again! He was really stingy with the jam.) Something awful must have happened! People don't bother to write letters unless there is bad news, do they?

"Maggie, you clear the table while I see what Mrs Nielsen has to say."

I held my breath and watched my father's face as he read. It didn't *look* like bad news. In fact, he seemed to be relieved and even smiled to himself as he folded the letter neatly and put it back in the envelope.

"Maggie, this letter has taken four days to get here. The Nielsens want you to go to the farm and spend Christmas with them. How would you like that?"

"When can I go?"

"Tomorrow. Uncle Raymond is coming for you in the farm van and you will be staying with them until the New Year. By then your mother should be over the pneumonia and back here with us again."

"I didn't know pneumonia lasted *that* long!"

"She's had other things wrong as well as the pneumonia."

"What things, Daddy?"

"Never you mind! It's none of your business," he answered angrily. I couldn't understand why my question had suddenly made him so cross. Had he been nasty to her and that had made her ill again? I never found out. All I remember is how tired she had been when Uncle Brian was with us.

~~~

I was happy at Lower Farm with the Nielsens. Everyone worked very hard but they were a cheerful, jolly family and laughed a lot. When I arrived, Jimmy and Ann both tried to talk to me at once.

"We have a grandfather living here now, and he *loves* children," shouted Jimmy.

"Jimmy and I have given our hearts to Jesus," said Ann.

"How did you do that?"

"I love Sunday school, and specially the children's meetings," added Jimmy, butting in and ignoring my question. "We get to stay up late and we sing lots of new choruses. Uncle Raymond plays the fiddle and Auntie Dorothy plays the 'cordion."

"It's an *accordion*," corrected Ann.

"I sleep with Auntie Elizabeth in the little room, and you will sleep in the big bed with Auntie Phyllis and Ann," continued Jimmy, pretending he hadn't heard Ann's intervention. "Oh! Sometimes the Italians come to Sunday tea, with the officer who looks after them. Then they come with us to the meeting. They've taught us to say, **'Come state? Benio grazia!'**"

194

"What does that mean?"

"How are you? Very well, thank you!" chipped in Ann. (Thirty years later I was learning Italian myself and discovered that it wasn't **benio** but **bene**.)

"What are Italians doing in Cholsey?"

"Uncle Raymond says they're prisoners of war, and they live in the camp over there somewhere."

"What, over that hill? Do they work on the farm?"

"Only on the big ones, not ours," answered Uncle Raymond, coming in to warm his hands by the fire. "They won't be coming to tea again till after Christmas, but you might see them if you're around till New Year."

When Christmas Day finally came, I wondered whether there would be any presents. Ann and I woke up at the same time, and we both had the same idea. Auntie Phyllis was already downstairs and we could hear sounds of activity coming from the kitchen, so we scrambled to the bottom of the bed and felt around for lumpy objects tucked into the bedclothes.

"There's a box in the middle here," exclaimed Ann. "Look it's got my name on it!"

"I think I can feel a pencil case and a colouring book," I replied. "Are we allowed to open them?"

"Course we are," shouted Jimmy from the next room. "I've got some dominoes. Look! They're in this wooden box." He opened the bedroom door, leaving a trail of coloured paper all over the tiny bedroom.

"I've got a puzzle with lots of pretty colours to make patterns with," enthused Ann.

"My present is just what I thought it was – some pencil crayons and a colouring book about gardens. It says, 'To Maggie, with love from Grandfather.' We mustn't forget to say 'thank you' to him."

Christmas dinner was a lively affair and Ann decided she liked turkey meat, even if she didn't like live turkeys. Auntie Sheila had made some crackers out of cardboard and crepe paper. Each one contained a slip of paper with a command to complete a certain task satisfactorily before being allowed to have some Christmas pudding:

Grandfather had to quote his favourite Bible verse; he chose Hebrews 13 verse 8: "Jesus Christ the same yesterday, and today, and for ever." Auntie Freda told a funny story about a dog who thought he was a cat, but couldn't say 'miaow'. And I had to sing my favourite Christmas carol, 'Away in a manger'.

Jimmy had to say a nursery rhyme; he chose 'Humpty Dumpty' and made us all laugh as he fell over himself trying to do all the actions. Ann had to say the alphabet backwards, and then asked us if we would like to hear her count from a hundred backwards as well. Auntie Sheila replied, "Not now, Ann; we would like our Christmas pudding *hot*, not cold."

Then Uncle Raymond recited a silly poem about a hen and a cow:
"The hen it is a noble beast
but a cow is more forlorner;
standing lonely in a field
wi' one leg at each corner."

I piped up with, "There's no such word as *forlorner*! It should just be 'forlorn'. And a hen is a *fowl* not a beast. And neither does a cow have corners. It's not a *table*."

"Maggie, it's here in this poem. And MacAnon, whoever he is, got a special 'poetic licence' to write 'forlorner' and 'corner'."

"Come on, that's enough," interposed Uncle Harald. "We've all earned our Christmas pudding; so let's get started."

The afternoon was rather an anticlimax. After we had all helped with the washing up, we went to the sitting room and, one by one, the grown-ups fell asleep. Jimmy was grumpy because no-one wanted to play dominoes with him, and Ann curled up on the hearth rug and fell asleep like a contented kitten, complete with purr. Eventually, Jimmy fell asleep on the rug too.

I was left alone with my thoughts. They were not happy ones. Why was I such a bad person? I tried so hard to be good. Grandfather certainly wouldn't have given me that present if he had *really* known what I was like! At home, I was always being punished for something or other. Once, and *only* once, I stole some sugar, but many times I told little white lies to get myself out of trouble, and I did like answering my mother back *so much*. (Is that one of the reasons she kept going away?) But I could never do that to my father; the consequences were too awful to think about! Whatever I did, I was *never, ever* good enough for him! So, if I wasn't good enough for my father who had a bad temper, how could I *ever* be good enough for Jesus, and go to Heaven with him? Now Ann and Jimmy were saying that *they* had given their hearts to Jesus and would be going to Heaven; so why can't *I* go too?

I was still worrying about being too bad to go to Heaven when Uncle Harald woke up with a snort. "Are you the only one awake, Maggie?"

"Not now. I think Jimmy will soon be awake too – he's just wriggled."

"What we want now is a nice cup of tea. I'll go and put the kettle on."

Soon everyone was awake and talking about the next meal – Christmas cake, mince pies, and real farmhouse butter and cheese with our bread. "Raymond, once we've all emptied our teacups, will you play 'Happy Families' with the children while the rest of us get our Christmas supper ready?"

"Certainly, Mum. 'Happy families' will be fun, won't it Maggie?"

"Do you have 'Mr Bun, the Baker'?"

"Oh, yes, and Mrs Bun, Miss Bun and Master Bun."

"Is Jimmy Master Goodchild?"

*

After supper, we went back into the sitting room to sing Christmas carols, hymns and choruses, accompanied by the violin and the accordion. We each chose our favourites, and the grown-ups told us why they had chosen theirs. Auntie Mary chose the children's hymn, 'Jesus loves me', which I had learned at Sunday school.

"I've chosen this hymn because it reminds me of the day I gave my heart to Jesus. I had been a bit of a tearaway and was always getting into scrapes. Mum and Dad can tell you all about what I got up to. At the time it seemed such fun but I always felt so bad afterwards. The second verse says:

'Jesus loves me! He who died
Heaven's gate to open wide.
He will wash away my sin;
let his little child come in.'

And I thought, 'Does that mean me? Will he wash away *my* sin?' So I asked him to, and he did. That was fifteen years ago now. I especially like the last verse:

'Jesus loves me! He will stay
close beside me all the way.
Then his little child will take
up to heaven, for his dear sake.'"

The last two lines she had sung were a little different from the words I had learned, which were:

'If I love him when I die,
he will take me home on high.'

But they meant more or less the same thing. I wanted Jesus to take all my sins away too. "How do I ask him?" That's what I wanted to know.

Auntie Sheila had no idea what I had been thinking but she then chose the chorus:

'Into my heart, into my heart,
come into my heart, Lord Jesus.
Come in today, come in to stay;
come into *my* heart, Lord Jesus.'

As we all sang it together I thought to myself, "If I say those words to Jesus and really mean them, will Jesus hear me? Will he come into my heart too?" There was only one way to find out. So as soon as the singsong was over, and Uncle Harald had closed in prayer, I hurried up to the bedroom and knelt down by the bed. I said those words to Jesus, clearly but quietly, so no-one else could possibly hear; but I really meant them. Then I undressed and went to bed. I didn't remember any more until the following morning, when I woke with a haunting, heavenly melody still sounding in my ears.

"I wonder what's wrong with Maggie?" mused Phyllis,

realising Maggie wasn't there in the kitchen for her bedtime drink. "I'll go and check on her; she's been a bit peaky all day."

The room was in darkness, apart from a glow from the oil lamp on the landing. Maggie was fast asleep in her usual place in the middle of the bed, with her clothes neatly folded in their place at her feet. She seemed more relaxed than she had been since her arrival, and wore a faint smile on her lips.

"She's fast asleep. I think she may have something important to tell us in the morning. Ann and Jimmy, you must be 'specially quiet; we don't want you to wake Maggie up. She needs her sleep."

On New Year's Eve, very early in the morning, Grandfather went to be with Jesus. We children woke up to a very quiet farmhouse. Everyone was downstairs tiptoeing about, and we knew that something serious had happened. As the three of us cuddled up in the big bed, we heard a car door bang and someone ring the front door bell and then voices in the hall.

"Thank you for coming so promptly, Doctor," said Auntie Freda, as she showed their family doctor to Grandfather's room. It sounded as if the whole family were clambering up the stairs and crowding into the bedroom. We heard nothing more until the doctor had finished his examination.

"I should take the death certificate to Wallingford today as soon as you can."

"I'll see to that," answered Uncle Raymond.

At breakfast everyone was rather subdued, but not really sad for Grandfather as he had gone to Heaven. Auntie Freda mopped her eyes a few times though. Then she turned to talk to us.

"I expect you children have guessed what has happened."

"Grandfather has died," I answered in a wavering voice. "He has gone to Heaven, hasn't he? We didn't know he was ill."

"He wasn't really ill but just very old and tired, and God said, 'It's time for you to come and stay with me in my house for ever.' Would you like to see him and say goodbye?"

In the bedroom, the curtains were drawn and Grandfather was covered in a clean white sheet. We crept up to the bed as Auntie Freda turned back the sheet. Grandfather lay there so still and pale against the white sheets.

"This isn't really Grandfather; it's just his empty body that we will be burying when we have the funeral service after you've gone home. We are sad to lose him, but he will be so much better off where he is."

"Grandma Goodchild is in Heaven. Perhaps Grandfather will see her there," said Ann.

February 1946

Botheration! The Maloneys are back. I thought they'd been sent away for good; so what are they doing here, walking towards Blackmore Lane? They've only been away for three years; what punishment is that? They'll do more bad things, I know they will. They mustn't see me; I'll hide behind this tree until I've watched them turn into Blackmore Lane.

There's nothing for it, I'll just have to go to school the long way round. I'll probably be late; but I'd rather be told off by Old Locky than thrown into the stinging nettles by Sean and Ryan Maloney. They'll both be in the seniors now, so they won't be sharing *our* playground, thank goodness!

I set off at a cracking pace, but it was much harder to walk quickly, going uphill. In Blackmore Lane the slopes are much gentler. Wretched Maloneys! Why did they have to come back so soon? I huffed and puffed as I struggled to keep going, and nearly jumped out of my skin when I heard the sound of a horn behind me. It was Ed from the farm.

"Morning, young lady. You're all hot and bothered; are you late for school?"

"I've got to go the long way because those horrid Maloneys are back. They've gone down Blackmore Lane, and I didn't want them to see me."

"Hop in; I'm going up Grove Road. I'll take you to the school gate."

I gratefully climbed into Mr Brooker's van and sank into the passenger seat. The seat was a bit worn and I could feel the springs through the cover, but I was safe ... for now, anyway.

"Thanks, Ed. ... I'll have to be careful tonight, though, won't I?"

"Don't you come out earlier than the seniors?"

"Only a little bit ... and the Maloneys will soon catch me up. They've got longer legs. P'raps I should come back this way again; hang around until they've gone, to be on the safe side."

"Sorry, Maggie. I won't be on the road this evening. I've got things to do in the yard."

During the school day, I forgot all about Sean and Ryan. We had to write a composition about the place where we lived and then draw pictures to illustrate our home. I wrote about my attic bedroom and the view through the window, playing in Grandpa Goodchild's barn on a rainy day, and how lovely the woods were when the weather was fine. I drew Tudor Cottage, Grandpa's barn and the bluebell woods, under each separate piece of writing. This was much more fun than doing sums where there was only one right answer, and I sometimes got the wrong one.

In the afternoon, Mr Lockyer put the best work up on the back wall of the classroom. Mine went up first, though I had to read the composition out loud before he would do it. I still didn't like reading aloud; I was frightened I'd say it all wrong or people would laugh at me. But I got through it somehow. Pat Coombes was last. She was the best reader in the class. Pat went to elocution lessons because she wanted to be an actress when she grew up; so she liked reading up front and we always enjoyed listening.

The school bell rang and the spell was broken. Would I be able to dodge the Maloneys? My tummy began to tie itself into knots. I hung around the school until Mr Parkes, the caretaker, literally shooed me out of the building.

"Haven't you got a home to go to?" he grumbled.

"Yes. But there's no-one in it."

"You can't stay here all night; so go home, or I'll report you to the Headmaster."

My father wouldn't be home until half past seven, my mother was still at Uxbridge, and Jimmy and Ann had stayed at Cholsey. I had cried when Uncle Raymond brought me home on my own on New Year's Day and there was only my father to welcome me. And now I had the Maloneys to worry about. Would there be someone to save me this time if they *did* see me?

I dawdled home along Blounts Court Road, past the house where the Laval family lived. They came from Alderney just before the invasion in 1940, and were French-speaking. They spoke English with a funny accent and took some time to settle down at Sonning Common Council School. Their house was the last house in Blounts Court Road. There were no more houses until the other side of Crowsley.

The Maloneys were hanging around by the Harpsden turn, sitting on the grass under the very tree I had hidden behind that morning. I didn't see them until it was too late. But then what could I do? I had to get home.

"Look who's here, Sean," mocked Ryan.

"We've got her now, haven't we?" agreed Sean. "There are two of us, and no interfering adults anywhere around. Let's see what she has in her knickers, shall we?"

"No!" I screamed. "Don't be dirty. That's rude!" I know I shouldn't have said it. I should have kept very quiet and thought about the angels instead. ... It was the way he said 'knickers', with that ugly smirk of his. He doesn't like me one little bit. ... He's going to hurt me and Ryan's going to let him. Are they *both* going to hurt me?

Before I knew what was happening, Sean grabbed me round the waist and Ryan pulled my hair and pushed me face down into the grass. Then he sat on me, pinning my arms to the ground. His body was heavy and his pressure on my arms was excruciating.

What were they going to do next? "Daddy come home now, ple-e-ea-se." I whispered desperately.

"We'll have had what we're wanting long before *he* comes home. ... Get on with it, Sean. I'm getting impatient; I want my turn too, remember."

"I can't get at her; you're in the way. Get off her."

"No, I rather like it. It's like riding a horse, sitting up here."

With that he dug his knees under my armpits and squeezed himself even tighter, all around me, in and out, in and out. It hurt. But I knew if I squealed, or so much as whimpered, he would dig his knees in ever tighter.

Then he put his face down and started nibbling my ear. That hurt too. Then my neck. He pulled my hair and started biting my neck in time with his squeezing. Something was happening inside his trousers, and his squeezing and biting got even more frenzied. I began to feel sick.

"You dirty, rotten swine, Ryan. You're having it off with her up there."

Ryan ignored him. He started grunting like a pig and I blacked out.

My father came home early that evening. There was no overtime. Ryan and Sean both heard the motorbike as soon as it rounded the bend by the Lavals' house.

"That's her dad coming. We'd better scarper," urged Sean, still miffed at his brother's behaviour. "He won't see her lying there; let's just make ourselves scarce. She's *his* problem, not ours."

The two Maloneys hurried off towards Crowsley as I was coming round. I heard the motorbike and staggered to my feet. My ribs hurt and so did my hands and arms, and the horrid bites all over my neck. But I had to get to the road or my father wouldn't see me. Then I'd be here all night.

"Maggie, what *are* you doing here? Look at the state of you!"

I struggled to clamber up onto the pillion seat and found it hard to cling on tight. I felt so dizzy. I knew that I would be in trouble when I got home, but a good hiding couldn't be worse than what Ryan just did to me. ... Did Ryan do it to me because he hated me or because he liked hurting people? Why did God let him do it when I loved Jesus? Was I still a bad person, after all? ... As we passed the Maloneys, they acted as if nothing had happened.

"Good ev'ning, Guv," they called, respectfully, as we passed.

Mrs Hurst was waiting for us as we approached Honeysuckle Cottage. She obviously wanted to talk to my father and waved us down. Judging by her expression it was something serious she had to tell him.

"Could you come in a minute, there's something I ought to tell you. It's best that Maggie doesn't hear it though. ... She can sit in the kitchen and have some milk and a biscuit."

As I was trying to dismount, I lost my balance completely and fell into Mrs Hurst's arms. I don't remember what happened next.

"Maggie's been hurt, look at her! Where did she get all these marks on her neck? They look like dog bites. And somebody's been pulling her hair. Here's a whole chunk of it on her cardigan. ... I bet it's those Maloneys."

"Oh! We just passed them on the road. They wished me good evening."

"They're evil. It's about them I wanted to tell you. Let me lay Maggie down on my settee. She's out for the count. ... Poor little lamb, I think we should get the doctor to her right away to see what else they've done to her. Let me ring him now."

"He's coming right away. So, while the kettle boils for our tea, I'll tell you about Ryan and Sean Maloney. They are vicious and cruel. Do you know the Marshalls in Kennylands Road?"

"No. I don't think so."

"Well, they've got a daughter, Dawn, who's not quite right. She has a cleft palate and can't talk properly. The Maloneys got hold of her and raped her. Both of them. Her mother found her lying in a pool of blood in a field near their house. The poor lamb had to go to hospital and be stitched up. She was so frightened and upset by the whole thing that it was only yesterday that she was able to tell her mother anything about it. It happened two weeks ago, at least. ... I was hoping to warn you before they got to Maggie."

"I find it hard to believe that school boys could do such dreadful things. What an evil world we live in! Could they have done *that* to Maggie, too?"

"Let's hope not! But that's why we need Dr Prince. Maggie's not safe here with those two around!"

"I really don't know what to do now. Maggie couldn't stay at Cholsey indefinitely. They haven't got the room, and she needs to be at her own school to prepare for the scholarship exams coming up next year. Also, she's got her music exam next week."

"Haven't you got any relatives or friends living locally who could help? I would offer myself, but baby Elaine really isn't thriving, and Jean still needs me on a regular basis. … What about your cousins in Reade's Lane?"

"What Edith and Ted, Eva's parents? We haven't been in contact with them for ages, and I certainly haven't visited them since my mother's funeral. Goodness that's nearly *five* years ago now! Baby Ruth will soon be going to school. Somehow we've just been taken up with our own concerns, with Emily so up and down."

"Why not try them and see? They can only say no."

"I wonder if they're on the phone. They might be; they're in better circumstances than we are."

"Let me look. E. Goodchild – Reade's Lane – here we are: Kidmore End 3751. I'm assuming 'Ted' stands for 'Edward'."

"Ted always hated the name Edward, funny fellow!"

"You talk to them while I make us this cup of tea. Dr Prince will be glad of one too when he arrives."

Chapter 14

Auntie Edie and Uncle Ted were a bit like Auntie Irene and Uncle Bert at Amersham, except they were older. Uncle Ted was good fun, and when he laughed he screwed up his eyes so that they looked like two little dots hiding in a mass of creases.

"Maggie, if you keep saying 'well' you're going to fall into it."

"Do I keep saying 'well'?"

"Yes, you do."

"*Well*, I don't mean to."

"There you go again. There's another one. You'll get wet feet if you're not careful."

"Wet feet? … Oh! I get it! You're thinking about Grandpa's well. *Well*, that's no good any more. … Oh dear! I've done it again, haven't I?"

"I'll give you a thruppenny bit if you can go a whole day without starting a sentence with 'well'." I didn't get my thruppenny bit until the following Friday.

Auntie Edie was kind but she didn't like washing my long hair, especially after Nitty Nora found head lice in it! 'Nitty Nora the flea explorer' was what we called the school nurse, and she inspected our heads twice a term. Her usual verdict on the state of my hair was, "Needs shampooing". But this time, she made me stand by the wall while the rest of the class were searched too. Out of our class of forty-eight children, thirteen of us ended up standing by the wall and the headmaster, Mr Ford, was called in to talk to us.

"You children have nits in your hair and if we don't do something about it straightaway, the whole school will be infested."

"You mean we've got fleas, Sir?" asked Billy White.

"Not exactly. But fleas have laid their eggs in your hair, as they've jumped from one head to another. We'll never find out who started it, but you've all got to take a nit-comb home with you and some special shampoo to help kill off these head lice eggs – 'head louse', plural 'head *lice*', is the proper name for this type of flea. We will also be sending you home with a letter, telling your parents what they must do about it, especially how to use the shampoo and comb."

It was such a palaver, and Auntie Edie certainly didn't enjoy washing my hair twice a week and combing it through with the nit-comb every evening before I went to bed. "I can't understand, Maggie, why your father won't let us cut all this hair to make this job a bit easier. It's bad enough getting it plaited everyday."

"He says it's in the Bible that women should have long hair. When I told him I was only a little girl, he boxed my ears. I'd love to have short hair like everyone else. My hair is so heavy, and sometimes it really pulls my scalp if it's plaited too tight."

"Yes, it's so thick that it's hard to get the tangles out, let alone the nits!"

Some weekends I went back to Tudor Cottage if my father had no Saturday work, but most of the time I stayed in Sonning Common. On Sundays, Auntie Edie and Uncle Ted went to the little Baptist chapel at the bottom of Grove Road, but my father wanted me to go to all the Sunday meetings at the Iron Room. I was always glad when it rained, because then I could go to the chapel with Auntie and Uncle. It wasn't nearly so far to walk there and the services were much livelier. I wondered why we had 'meetings' at the Iron Room and they had 'services' at the chapel. Auntie and Uncle had no idea, and it wasn't very smart to ask my father. He didn't like me asking questions; he told me it was insolence. But how do you find anything out if you're not allowed to ask questions?

April 1946

For my tenth birthday I was given a special birthday treat, a two-week holiday at Uxbridge with Grandma and Grandpa Nelson. It was a treat because Grandma didn't expect me to help with the housework. She wanted me out of the house as much as possible, so I could spend all my time at the children's playground (which we called the 'Rec', short for 'Recreation Ground'), just across the River Frays from Grandma's back garden. My mother, Jimmy, Ann and Gracie had now returned to Crowsley, and Doctor Prince thought that I needed a change of scene as I kept catching every cold that was going around.

As I was sitting in the slow train to Paddington waiting on platform nine at Reading Station (which stopped at nearly every station, including Slough where I intended to alight) I remembered the first time I had made the journey to Uxbridge all on my own. It was early August 1945, and I had stayed on the train until we arrived at West Drayton. The Uxbridge train was already in the bay waiting for me and my fellow passengers. A sprightly elderly gentleman had helped me negotiate the steep steps on and off both trains, and also carried my case for me.

"You're rather young to be travelling all on your own. How old are you? Six or seven?"

"I'm nearly nine-and-a-half," I protested. "But I *am* the smallest in my class."

"You're the same age as my grandson, Christopher. He's the tallest in *his* class."

"I go to Sonning Common Council School. Which school does Christopher go to?"

"Leighton Park School. It's in the Shinfield Road, in Reading."

"I haven't heard of that one."

"It's a boarding school, but Christopher is a day boy. He comes home again each evening. Are you going to stay with your grandparents?"

"Yes, they live in Victoria Road."

"I'm visiting my daughter. She lives in the Greenway, opposite the senior school. ... Here we are, Uxbridge already. It doesn't take long, does it? Will you be able to find your own way from here?"

"Yes. But I think I can see Grandpa at the barrier. Yes, he's there! I can see him waving."

"Will you introduce me to him?"

"Grandpa, this kind man has been helping me. His name is..."

"... Robert Sherwood retired GP. Aren't you the shoe repairer, with the shop on the corner of Cowley Road and Rockingham Road?"

"That's right! It's a good situation. Plenty to see through the window and lots of people coming in off the street with little jobs for me – as well as all my regulars – so it's very good for trade."

Grandpa and Doctor Sherwood had then gone on to talk about VE Day, celebrated on May the 8th, and the end of the war in Europe. But they hadn't sounded half as excited about it as our teachers at school had been when it was first announced. We had even had our own school victory party! After that, they had quickly moved on to discuss what was then still going on in Japan and whether the Americans should have dropped those atom bombs. But much of the talk had been above my head – something about mushroom-clouds, burns and radiation sickness – it had all sounded so horrible that it made me feel sick.

"How long do you think the Japs are going to hold out?" my grandfather had asked.

"I think news of their surrender is imminent. There's no way they can carry on fighting after Hiroshima and Nagasaki."

"Let's hope you're right! Thank you so much for taking care of Maggie for us. Good day to you, Sir."

By the time Grandpa and I had arrived at 34 Victoria Road, it was almost dinner-time and Grandma Nelson had been much more animated than usual. "Alex, there was a man on the wireless this morning saying that things in Japan are so bad that Emperor Hirohito has no option but to surrender. We can expect to hear that the war is over any time now."

The following day, August the 14th, had been declared VJ Day and World War II was finally over. Victoria Road had had its own street party to celebrate victory with trestle tables down the middle of the road; all the children in their best clothes, flags flying everywhere and everybody dancing the hokey-cokey around the tables once all the food had been consumed. I had danced around too in the white muslin dress Grandma had made me for Sundays. It had a sash and little yellow flowers worked into the muslin. Grandma and Grandpa had dressed up and joined in the fun as well and I had been allowed to stay up until ten o'clock that night.

As I was reminiscing, I had just got to the part where we did the hokey-cokey, when the guard blew his whistle and we started to steam out of the station. "I mustn't forget to get off at Slough this time, because there's no train from West Drayton to Uxbridge mid-morning, so I have to catch the 458 bus from Slough to Uxbridge and get off at the Post Office in Windsor Street," I told myself as, even as a ten-year-old, I was rather forgetful. I lived in a dream-world when left to my own devices.

After dinner, Grandma suggested I had a lie down on my bed in the little back bedroom, while they had a snooze in their armchairs downstairs. I had no intention of spending the afternoon sleeping, so I stood looking impatiently out of the window at the Fassnidge Memorial Ground. I could see the mown grass, footpaths and flower-beds, but not the swings and roundabouts in the play area, nor the bowling green and tennis courts, because they were behind a thick privet hedge.

"Time for work, Alex. The clock says a quarter to two."

"Time and tide wait for no man," grumbled my sleepy grandfather. I heard him get up from his chair and make his way to the outside toilet. I suddenly thought that, if I hurried, I could walk with him for a little way; maybe he would come with me as far as Rockingham Bridge and go the long way back to his workshop.

Awl, Thread and Toecaps

Your hands are rough hands, a shoe-repairer's hands, a common cobbler's hands. In your cluttered little shop, set on a corner where four roads meet, you view the world and work at your trade.

Your hands are calloused hands with blackened finger-nails and palms made greasy from cobbler's wax. I watch you, feet on treadle, hands to needle, renewing the stitching on someone's old boot. Or, my school shoes on the last, tapping in brads to heels and toe tips, to give the scuffed lace-ups new life.

At five-thirty precisely, you down tools, remove your leather apron, and wash your hands in the green bowl. When you get home, she'll make you scrub them, and change your clothes before you have your tea. You're the master in your shop, and at church; a ten-year-old granddaughter can see who runs the home. We're friends, you and me! I'm for the scrub at half past eight.

"Maggie, mind you come back home when the hooter goes at half past five."

"Yes, Grandma."

The Bell Punch Ticket Works not far away, in the Colne Valley, employed about two thousand workers and you could hear the hooter all over Uxbridge, at eight-thirty in the morning for clocking on and five-thirty in the evening for clocking off. Grandpa said you could time your watch by it. You also knew when it was one o'clock and two o'clock and when the workers had their tea breaks.

"Now Maggie, don't forget to stay in the Rec and play with the other children. We don't want you wandering off into town all by yourself and talking to strangers."

"No, Grandpa, I won't."

There were quite a few other children on the swings. Some I remembered from last year, like the twins, Janet and Jean, but they didn't remember me. Also, in the playground, there was a man with white hair and glasses, wearing what looked like a long black frock coming down to his ankles. It reminded me of the way the Rector of Peppard Church was dressed when I had gone to evensong with Ada Cotton; though he didn't wear the loose white garment over his black frock that the Rector had worn. I wondered what he was doing there dressed like that and why he was talking to some of the girls. Perhaps he was an evangelist like Uncle Brian, and was inviting them to a children's meeting at St Margaret's Church. But when I went over to the group, he wasn't talking about anything in particular, just asking them their names.

"Hello. I haven't seen *you* here before. What's your name?"

"Maggie Goodchild. I have come to stay with my grandma for two weeks. I live near Reading in Berkshire. Have you heard of Sonning Common and Crowsley?"

"No, I can't say that I have. I've heard of Reading and Huntley and Palmer's biscuits."

I wanted to ask him why he was dressed like that, but thought he would think I was being rude. As I was trying to see how many buttons he had on his attire, he answered my unspoken question.

"I see you are looking at my cassock and dog collar, Maggie. I wear these clothes because I'm a minister at the Church of St John the Baptist, in Hillingdon."

"So you have come a long way to talk to us. Do you take Sunday school classes and children's meetings?"

"Yes, sometimes I do. I also go into schools and help the children with their schoolwork, especially before they take their scholarship exams when they are eleven."

"I have to take the scholarship exam next year. I don't think I'll pass, Mr Lockyer doesn't give us hard enough work to do. He teaches Standard Three and Standard Four together in the same classroom."

"You don't look old enough to be in Standard Four."

"I'm ten, and I have to take the exam just before my eleventh birthday. My father doesn't think they teach us properly at Sonning Common Council School. I don't know many long words and my spelling's not very good."

"Spell 'arithmetic' for me."

"A-R-I-T-H-M-A-T-I-C."

"One mistake; it's not M-A-T-I-C but M-*E*-T-I-C."

"A-R-I-T-H-M-E-T-I-C."

"Now spell 'headmaster'."

"H-E-A-D-M-A-S-T-E-R."

"Well done!"

"But I only know it because I've read it so many times on Mr Ford's office door."

"Let me see if I have an old envelope in my pocket." I was fascinated as he put his hand through a slit in his cassock and fished out a crumpled envelope from his trouser pocket. "Yes, this'll do. I'll write twenty words for you to learn. If you come back tomorrow afternoon, I'll test you on them. Then I'll give you another twenty to learn. I'll be here about half past two. I must go now as I have to visit an old lady."

"Where does she live?"

"Quite near the church. Goodbye Maggie."

When he had gone, I put the envelope in my pocket and had a go on the swings. Many of the children began to drift off, and then a new group of slightly younger children arrived with their mothers and there was more competition for the swings, so I tried the sliding chute for the very first time. I had seen older children careering down it at breakneck speed and tumbling off at the bottom: so I decided that I would sit bolt upright, and then I might slide down a little more slowly. I also tried to control my speed by keeping my hands on the sides, but ended up with friction burns on my palms.

After many goes, I managed to perfect my descent. I was beginning to wonder what the time was when the hooter went and I nearly jumped out of my skin. It felt as if the sound was coming from directly behind my head and it made my ears hurt. I hurried back towards Grandma's and, as I got to Rockingham Bridge, I could see the Bell Punch workers coming towards me, three or four abreast, taking up the whole of the pavement. So I scuttled over the bridge and into Lawn Road, as the hordes of employees continued up Rockingham Road towards the High Street and their transport home.

While Grandma was making the tea, and Grandpa had his head in the 'News Chronicle', I had a quick look at the words I had to learn. Some of them I hadn't even seen before. "What's a 'catastrophe, C-AT-A-S-T-R-O-P-H-E', Grandpa?" (Only I had pronounced it as '<u>ca</u>tastrof'.)

"Do you mean '<u>ca</u>tastrofi'?"

"Oh, is that how you say it?"

"When something goes very wrong, or there's a bad fire or lots of people get killed."

"Where did you get that filthy envelope from, Maggie?" asked Grandma as she came into the dining room with the teapot.

"A minister in a cassock and dog collar was at the Rec. He gave me some spellings to learn."

"Why?"

"He was telling us that he goes into schools and helps the children who are going to take the scholarship exam. And I told him I was taking it next year, and that I didn't think I'd pass because there were lots of words I didn't know how to spell. So he gave me these to learn."

"Oh, did he? And couldn't he find a clean piece of paper to write them on?"

"That's all he had in his pocket."

"You'd better go and wash your hands at the sink before you eat your tea."

Grandma said no more about the spellings and I copied them out carefully into the back page of an old Receipt book of Grandpa's. (Once he had filled in all the Receipt slips and given them to the customers, he didn't bother to keep the book of carbon copies. He kept all his accounts in a ledger, a large account book where he wrote down everyday how much he had spent on materials and how much his customers had paid him for his work.)

"Maggie, if you write each word three or four times across the page, that will help you remember them. Then, when you think you know them, I can test you."

"This is a bit like writing lines, but much more interesting."

By bedtime, I had mastered nearly all the words, and, after we had had prayers, Grandpa suddenly asked me what time I was seeing the minister and what his name was.

"I don't know his name, Grandpa. He just said he was a

minister at St John's Church, Hillingdon, and he'd be in the Rec at about half past two."

"I think I'll come with you tomorrow. We'll both go to the workshop at a quarter to two and then I'll come round to meet him with you at half past two."

━━

When Grandpa and I arrived at the Rec just after half past two the following day, the minister was already there, talking to a little girl with curly hair and her mother. I couldn't help seeing him frown when he looked up and noticed that I wasn't alone. His greeting wasn't quite as friendly as yesterday's.

"Hello Maggie. Have you brought your granddad with you this time?" Before I could say anything, Grandpa answered for me.

"I just wanted to see who had been helping my granddaughter with her spelling. She couldn't tell me your name, only that you were a minister of the Gospel."

"That's right; the Reverend Earnest Priestley, retired vicar, and now helping out at St John's, Hillingdon, as an honorary minister and parish worker."

"It's a wonder you have any time left to help children with their spelling?"

"I've taken an interest in helping children with their schoolwork for many years now – especially coaching them for the scholarship and common entrance exams. I don't charge anyone for it; it's all voluntary work. It's always such a shame when a bright child loses out because of poor teaching or just because the father isn't wealthy." As he said that, I remembered what Mumsie had said about why *she* didn't get a place at a grammar school, but Grandpa didn't bat an eyelid.

"Anyway, I must get back to the shop. Myself, I'm not all that bothered about secondary education for women, but I know Maggie's parents think differently and want her to go to Henley Grammar School, so thank you for what you are doing. She has written out all the spellings you gave her yesterday in her book, and has been learning them. Now, I've told Maggie to stay here and not wander out of this area, and come home when the hooter goes at 5.30."

"Your grandfather's a fusspot, isn't he? I don't know *where* he thought I was going to take you. Mind you, it *is* getting a bit crowded here. I'm sure he won't mind if we go and sit in the shade over there. I can see an empty seat."

I felt a bit uneasy, as it was obvious that the Reverend Earnest Priestley and my grandfather didn't like each other very much. Yesterday, when he was just the man in a frock, he seemed much nicer. I was slightly afraid of the Reverend Priestley and I didn't know why. Fortunately, he was pleased with my spellings and wrote another twenty words straight into my book. He read these to me and explained what they meant, and then put them into sentences for me. After a while I began to relax, perhaps I had only imagined that underneath he wasn't really very nice.

Soon it was almost time for me to go back to Crowsley. It was my very last session with the Reverend Priestley. Before we even started on the spellings, he wanted to talk to me about other things, including when he would be seeing me again.

"It's like this, Maggie. You have been doing very well with your spellings, but there are other things you need to be able to do if you are going to pass the scholarship exam; things like understanding what words mean and how to use them in sentences, how to decipher simple codes and other kinds of puzzles, and understand a passage you've been asked to read and answer questions on it – we call that comprehension. Then, in arithmetic, there're all the different kinds of sums: addition, subtraction, multiplication, and division, and problems on them that you have to solve. You have to understand how to measure different lengths in feet and inches; how to weight things in pounds and ounces, and capacity where you have to fill containers in pints and quarts or gills. Do you know what a 'gill' is?"

"It's a quarter of a pint. It's how much milk we used to have in our mugs in the infants' school."

"Good. If you give me your mother's full name and address, I can send her some English and arithmetic papers from previous scholarship exams for you to work on. When you have done them all, I can then visit you at home and go through them with you. Would you like that?"

"Yes, please. My mother's name and address is:

Mrs. J. Goodchild,
Tudor Cottage,
Crowsley,
Nr. Reading,
Berkshire."

"Now, we will run through the last twenty words, and when we've finished, we will take a nature walk together right round this park and see if you can name the trees and plants we shall be passing. The first paper you will be given is a kind of intelligence test, and they will be testing how much you understand about the world around you. So we will be talking together about what we see, and I shall be asking you some questions as well."

The walk started well, and the Reverend Priestley showed me how to identify the different trees by their leaf patterns and their general shape. But when we got to the flower beds, he wanted me to bend down and look right into their faces. When he bent down too, he came very close to me and almost knocked me off balance. I certainly didn't want him to see my navy school knickers! (The senior girls at school called them 'passion killers' but I had no idea why.) Then he seemed to be breathing down my neck and I was instantly reminded of what Ryan Maloney had done to me. Would *he* bite my neck too?

"I must get up. I'm not comfortable down here," I panted, struggling to my feet in panic.

"Whatever's the matter? Don't you *want* to know the names of the parts of a flower – petal, stamen, pistil, stigma, style, ovary?" He glared at me angrily. "I didn't think you were a silly, empty-headed, ungrateful little girl like the rest of them. I really thought you *wanted* to learn. It seems I have been wasting my time."

"No, you haven't wasted your time. I'm sorry. I was frightened I wouldn't be able to get up again, that's all." By this time, other people were walking by the flower beds and turned to look in our direction. This made the Reverend Priestley even angrier.

"Now all these people think I have hurt you or something."

"You haven't hurt me but, when I get right down, my knees feel weak and I get scared." I said this loud enough for everyone to hear, and his anger evaporated as if by magic. He was then as nice as pie as he walked me back to the play area.

"Now, Maggie. When I get the papers, I will send them to your mother with a little note of explanation. When you have done

217

them, I expect her to invite me to your home, so that we can go over them together."

"I'll tell her about you and the walk, and show her the spellings, as soon as I get home. Then she will be expecting the papers."

The papers came as promised a few weeks later, and I started on them as soon as I had had my tea. I was allowed to work on a little table in the big bedroom by the window overlooking the back garden. At first I needed some help in understanding what I had to do; and often I had no idea what the answers to the questions were supposed to be. So, the first evening, I just flipped through the papers and wrote what I could in the spaces provided.

I started on the English paper. A few of the questions were really easy, like completing proverbs. This was a matching exercise, so even if you didn't actually know all the proverbs, or understand the meanings of some of them, you could still guess what the answers might be. If you do it wrong, you just get rubbish, for example:

A rolling stone **gathers no moss.** ✓
A rolling stone **is not gold.** x
A stitch in time **saves nine.** ✓
A stitch in time **gathers no moss.** x
All that glitters **is not gold.** ✓
All that glitters **saves nine.** x

But I did ask Mumsie to explain what the proverbs meant, in case the question asked us to say what they meant in the actual exam.

I had much more trouble with the arithmetic paper, especially when they wrote the numbers in a row across the page instead of in a column under one another, or wrote the numbers in words rather than figures. For example: '14 + 119 + 2150 = 2283' or 'Add together fourteen, one hundred and nineteen, and two thousand, one hundred and fifty.' Sometimes, we had to write the answer in words too: 'The answer is two thousand, two hundred and eighty three.' It was so much easier to read:

218

14+
119
2150
2283

You can see what you're doing and are less likely to make a mistake.

⌇

It was almost Whitsun before I had finished the two papers. Mumsie had taught me most of the things I didn't know, but there were still a few places where we weren't quite sure what we were being asked to do.

"It's a pity there isn't a syllabus or list of requirement that we could get hold of from our local education authorities," sighed my mother. "Things have changed a lot since *I* took the exam. Anyway, we're ready for the Reverend Priestley's visit tomorrow." She had arranged for him to come on the Tuesday of half-term.

"Will he be working with me up here in the bedroom, Mumsie?"

"No, you'll be using the kitchen table. *I* want to hear what is going on too."

"Is that so you can help me again afterwards?"

She nodded, but didn't say any more. She was expecting him to arrive on the eleven o'clock bus from Reading.

"Do you want me to go to the Bird-in-Hand to meet him?"

"No, Maggie. I've sent him the directions and he will find his own way across the fields."

"When Daddy's army friends came, we went to meet *them*."

"That's enough, Maggie."

⌇

Whit Tuesday was a beautiful sunny day and the Rev. Earnest Priestley enjoyed his walk across the fields, but he would have enjoyed it a whole lot more if Maggie had come to the bus stop to meet him. Why didn't she come? He thought he had finally won *her* confidence, but he wasn't quite sure of her mother's attitude to him. The letter in his pocket was non-committal, brief and to the point, and expressed no gratitude to him for his efforts to advance her daughter's education. Hopefully, he would be able to win over the mother too, once they had actually met face-to-face. After all, hadn't he invested a lot of his own time and money in engineering this rendezvous with little Maggie Goodchild?

The Reverend Priestley chose to wear his best suit and his dog collar, so that he should look the part of a serious man of God. Maggie would be expecting to see him in the cumbersome cassock, but *that* would have been most inconvenient and uncomfortable on a warm day like this.

As he reached the top of the second field, he could see the chimneys of Tudor Cottage over to his right. He continued along the path until he came to the hedge, then stopped and peered between the branches to get a better view, muttering to himself, "It seems quite a big place, so they must have enough space to give us a room to ourselves; that is really important to the success of this particular enterprise."

"Maggie, I want you to go up to the attic bedroom and look out for the Reverend Priestley. Give me a shout when you see him."

"Then can I run and meet him?"

"No, Maggie. I want you to stay up there until I call you. There are a few things I want to say to him first."

"Why can't I? He'll think I don't want to see him."

"No he won't. I'll make sure of that."

"Mumsie, he's coming now. I can see him. But he's not wearing his cassock."

"It's probably too hot for that today. Are you sure it's him?"

"Yes, he's just stopped behind the hedge. Maybe he's trying to look at the house. Now he's walking on again."

"You stay where you are and I'll go to the gate to meet him."

I couldn't see the front of the house from the attic bedroom window, and the gate was too far away for me to hear what they were saying. But, after less than ten minutes, I heard my mother open the kitchen door and come in alone. I looked out over the fields and there was the Reverend Priestley hurrying away up the path. He was by the wood and would soon be out of sight. What had gone wrong? He wasn't going to look at my work after all!

Mumsie came up the attic stairs and sat down on the bed.

"Why has he gone? I haven't even talked to him yet."

"He didn't want to work with you in the kitchen, so I told him that if he wasn't prepared to work with you there, there was nowhere else."

"But couldn't he've worked with me on the little table in the big bedroom?"

"No, Maggie. I needed to see what was going on and he was insisting on having you all to himself somewhere else, so I gave him the money for his train fare and he left immediately. Maggie, he wasn't a very nice man."

"Would he have got cross with me?"

"Yes, he probably would." I remembered the scene by the flower beds and said no more.

∿

In my disappointment, I cried myself to sleep that night. I thought that the Reverend Priestley's hasty exit would mean the end of any hopes I had cherished about going to the grammar school and training to be a teacher. I knew that there were lots more things I needed to learn if I was ever going to pass that exam, but I was not going to get that chance in Standard Four. When our class got too big, lucky Pat Stratton and Stephen Miles got sent up to Standard Five in the senior school. Mr Lockyer said it was because they were the two oldest in the class. That wasn't true. Pat Stratton was a month *younger* than I was! They were sent up because they were the two children most likely to pass the scholarship. Their new teacher, Miss Watkins, took us for music and she was brilliant. She encouraged us to learn and made our lessons exciting so that we would want to do well. Old Locky was more interested in art and craft than in English and arithmetic. He didn't mark our exercise books very regularly and so we didn't always find out what we were doing wrong. How could we correct our mistakes if we didn't even know that we had made them?

"Maggie, you look rather down in the dumps today, what's wrong?" My mother's question took me by surprise. I hadn't realised that my desperation showed in my face. "Are you still thinking about the scholarship? If so, don't give up yet. Neither

221

you nor Jimmy is doing as well as I would like you to be. Jimmy is wetting the bed again and doesn't want to go to school, and you aren't sleeping properly at night, are you?"

"No, Mumsie. I'm having bad dreams again. Not about enemy soldiers and bombing raids, but about being in a class where no-one wants to do any work. The other children are bigger and stronger than me and the teacher lets them do what they like, so I can't get on with my work."

"Well, I have written a letter to a lady doctor I've heard about who helps children like you and Jimmy. I want her to take a look at you both and suggest what I can do to help you get over what is bothering you. I shall tell her about the scholarship too and your ambition to be a teacher."

"When are we going to see her?"

"It won't be for a week or two. We haven't yet made a proper appointment, so you'll have to be patient."

Chapter 15

May 1946

Jimmy and Ann did *not* like the long walk to school and back. They grumbled and fussed all the way to school and all the way home again.

"Why do we have to walk all this way?" grizzled Ann. "There ought to be a bus."

"You had to walk to school at Cholsey, didn't you?"

"But that wasn't as far as this. It was only *one* mile, and there weren't any hills."

"Sometimes we went in the van," chimed in Jimmy. "And once we went in the trap with Uncle Raymond. But the horse didn't like all the people, and kept stopping before we got to the school. Silly old Dobbin, Uncle Raymond had to hit him with the reins to make him go on again."

On the way home, they kept dawdling and messing about and invariably *I* was the one who got into trouble if we didn't arrive home before five o'clock. Why were they giving me such a hard time? ... It was some consolation that the Maloneys were no longer around to bother us, but I was fed up with the pair of them and wanted to bang their little heads together.

The previous summer, back at Crowsley after their *first* stay in Cholsey, they didn't make a fuss about the long walk between Crowsley and Sonning Common, and they were a year younger then. When, at first, Mrs Claxton refused to have Ann in her class because she hadn't had her fifth birthday, Ann protested that *she* could cope with school just as well as Jimmy and I could. She could walk three miles and back, and she could also read 'Book One', and count to one hundred! Mr Ford intervened after he had read Ann's report from the school at Cholsey, which my mother had brought with her. Mumsie came to school with the three of us that first week, and then we were on our own. I'd had no trouble with either of them, but, this time, things were different. And my father didn't understand my problem at all.

"Maggie, if you want to be a teacher when you grow up then you'd better get some practice on these two."

"Daddy, that's not fair! I'm only three or four years older than they are."

"You can still make them do as they're told."

"How can I when *I'm* not allowed to smack them?"

"Any more of that backchat and *you'll* be the one who gets smacked!"

I smarted from the injustice of it all. If I acted like a grown-up and somehow managed to make those little horrors obey me without smacking them; then that was good. I'd be in the clear. But if I failed to win them round, then it would be *my* fault we were all late home and I would get smacked. And I would definitely be smacked if *I* smacked *them* to make them hurry up and they told on me. I didn't enjoy being piggy in the middle all the time, two strict parents on one side and two uncooperative little siblings on the other. I couldn't bribe them to make them behave. I had *nothing* to bribe them with. We didn't get pocket money like some children did! When I *did* receive any money for my birthday, my parents immediately took it away for safe keeping. They said it would go into my savings account, but I had never been shown my account book.

Ann was the troublemaker. She got everyone into trouble, especially poor Jimmy. She made my father laugh at her saucy ways and had fewer smacks than all the rest of us put together. The devious little minx! I would have loved to wipe that insufferable grin off her face once and for all! But I didn't dare. I wouldn't be able to sit down for a week if I laid into *her* – Daddy's pesky little pet!

But the cunning little whatsit had never been Grandpa Goodchild's little pet, though. Oh no! Especially when she was little and pulled up all his radishes before they were ready to eat and trampled all over his lettuces. I was at school that day so, thankfully, it had nothing to do with me. Grandpa spanked her little bottom really hard, and carried her across his shoulder back to Mumsie. She put her to bed without any tea. Grandpa told me all about it one day when I was helping him with some weeding.

"You know, Maggie, you've never been naughty like that little sister of yours, always trying to interfere with my garden. Whenever my back was turned, there she was, up to mischief again."

"She's always getting *me* into trouble. I'm supposed to stop her doing naughty things, but I'm not even allowed to touch her. If I do, I get punished instead of her. So, she gets away with it."

"The trouble is, she doesn't have enough to keep her occupied here at home. She'll be better when she goes to school."

"Fanny Claxton will smack her. Then she'll know it!"

Now it was May 1946 and Ann knew all about Fanny Claxton's smacks but was totally unfazed by them. Unlike most pupils, Ann was not afraid of Mrs Claxton. She regarded her as an opponent whom she was determined to outsmart, and she didn't care in the least if she was smacked for her pains. Mrs Claxton's hand only stung her arm for a few minutes anyway, and it was worth the discomfort just to watch the funny faces Mrs Claxton pulled while she did it. Ann couldn't twist her round her little finger as she could her father, but she could always stand her ground in a skirmish.

"Ann Goodchild, stop staring around the room. Get on with your reading."

"I've already finished the book."

"Then read it again."

"I have read it twice already."

"All right, little madam, you can come out here and read it to the rest of the class then." So she did, both loudly and clearly.

"I didn't make any mistakes, did I?"

"Here's a harder book for you. See what you can do with that one!"

"Yes, Mrs Claxton. Thank you, Mrs Claxton." The rest of the class tittered at her audacity.

But Jimmy was genuinely afraid of Mrs Claxton, and she knew it. He was always getting into trouble for something or other, however hard he tried to be good and do his work properly. His apparent timidity irritated her and she was often cruel and spiteful to him in class.

"Jimmy Goodchild, you are a year older than your sister and yet she can read much better than you can. Aren't you ashamed of yourself?"

"Yes, Mrs Claxton."

"When are you going to pull your socks up and make an effort? … I'm talking to you, Jimmy Goodchild. Answer me!"

"Yes, Mrs Claxton."

"When, Jimmy? *When*?"

"I'm trying, Mrs Claxton."

"But not hard enough, you lazy boy! All you're doing is trying my patience. And I won't stand for it, do you hear?"

Jimmy's answer was to burst into tears, and the other boys made his life a misery in the playground by calling him a sissy and a booby. That's why he sometimes wet his pants at school. He also started wetting the bed again and had to sleep with a plastic draw-sheet under him every night, thanks to Fanny Claxton's bullying.

～

I told Grandpa Goodchild about Ann's tussles with Mrs Claxton one Saturday after the summer term began. I also told him about how horrid she was to Jimmy.

"I'm amazed that the woman is still around. She must be retirement age by now. Was it only last year that she tried to stop us handing out those invitation cards to Brian Hepworth's children's meetings?"

"Yes Grandpa, it was. ... Now Fanny Claxton's up at the big school too, she has to do what Mr Ford says. But when she's on dinner duty, we all have to watch out. If she catches us walking out of school or going into the cloakroom to fetch a hanky, she makes us sit in one of her little desks for the rest of the lunch hour. They're uncomfortable enough for me, and I'm only little. How the big boys manage to get into them, I don't know!"

Since Ruth's death in June 1941, Albert Goodchild had become increasingly absent-minded and accident-prone. Throughout the war, he could never quite understand about the importance of observing the blackout, even out there in the country away from the towns. He couldn't seem to appreciate that just a glimmer of candlelight at a single window might inadvertently help enemy bombers flying overhead. (At least, that was what Reading Council's Air Raid Precautions Committee was telling everyone!) This carelessness was a big headache for Emily, especially while John was in the army and she was solely responsible for the safety of the household.

As time went by, there were other, more intimate, problems Emily had to confront when she did his washing for him. She regularly put stained or soiled garments in a bucket to soak before she could wash them with the rest of the laundry. Why couldn't he do this for himself at the time of the 'accident'? He was worse than a baby in nappies, and much more infuriating! At least Jimmy had always told her immediately when *he'd* had that kind of accident.

Then, Albert was always losing things like keys, collar-studs and cufflinks, and time after time he needed Emily's help with his collar and cuffs when he was putting on his Sunday best for a Sunday meeting. He repeatedly cut himself shaving and came round to her with a bloody towel wrapped around his face, begging her to staunch the flow and cover the cuts with sticking plaster. In the autumn of 1944, he spent a few weeks in Henley

Hospital because of an accident with his cut-throat razor, where he severed an artery and lost so much blood that he became dangerously anaemic. When people asked her how many children she had, Emily felt like saying, "I have five children, and the oldest and most difficult of the five is in his seventies."

In the summer of 1946, Albert had a more serious accident and spent many weeks in Henley Hospital. All he did was trip on a rug and fall over the coal scuttle, but he fell awkwardly and tore some ligaments and badly dislocated his left ankle. They put him in the geriatric ward at Townlands Hospital because of his incontinence and growing senility. He hated it in that ward because few of the other patients could carry on a sensible conversation with him, and he became increasingly depressed.

"Why can't these people talk to me?" he grumbled to the nurse dressing his ankle.

"Some have had strokes; others are very deaf and can't hear what you're saying; and several are in the last stages of dementia and hardly know where they are."

His ankle took a long time to mend and, for the first month, he was unable to get out of bed, so John tried to visit him on Saturday or Sunday afternoons. Then he decided that Maggie should learn to ride her bicycle on the open road and get used to dealing with traffic, so that she could accompany him to the hospital. In preparation for the five and a half mile ride into Henley, he ordered her to ride eight times round the Triangle without stopping, which would be about six miles. But the Triangle was all on the level, and that did not adequately prepare her for Devil's Hill and the steep decent into Harpsden Bottom, followed by the narrow lane into Harpsden, then along Harpsden Road into the busy Reading Road and the volume of traffic to be encountered in Henley town centre. She rode in front of him and he shouted instructions to her as they went along.

"Use your brakes, Maggie. You're going too fast. You'll come off if you're not careful. Can't you see how steep this hill is?"

"Yes, Daddy, but there's so much to think about all at once."

"You've ridden down a hill before."

"There aren't any hills in the Triangle. I've never been down here before, not even in a car."

"Well, just watch what you're doing and keep your eyes on the road."

"Yes, Daddy."

This method of cycle training worked well on the outward journey and, miraculously, once they were in Henley all the traffic lights they passed happened to be green. John hadn't warned her about observing traffic lights; she was keeping her eyes glued to the road immediately in front of her and hadn't even seen them.

Maggie hated it at the hospital. The smell of disinfectant and carbolic soap made her feel sick. A prominently displayed notice outside the geriatric ward read:

Children below the age of twelve are not allowed on the wards. They must remain in the corridor and not make themselves a nuisance. Hospitals are not suitable places for young children.

"Maggie and I have cycled all the way from Crowsley and this is the first time she has cycled so far," explained John to the sister on duty. "She really needs to take a rest before we have to go back again. Can she have a chair to sit on in the corridor, please?"

"How old is Maggie?"

"She's ten."

"Your father is over there in the corner. She can sit over there with you, if she keeps quiet."

"Thank you, Sister."

The chair wasn't very comfortable, but Maggie could rest her head on the wall behind. Albert was glad to see his younger son, as he had a long list of complaints to get off his chest. Maggie had heard only the first three before she dosed off.

She awoke to discover that she needed to go to the lavatory. "Daddy, I need to do a wee-wee."

"Go and ask that nurse over by the door."

"Yes, Daddy."

"Please Nurse, where is the lavatory?"

"There are some lavatories over there, but they're meant for the female patients, not visitors."

"I think I'm going to wet my knickers."

"You'd better use one then. But don't hang around in there or I'll be in hot water for letting you go."

There were four cubicles in that small room, and each one had its own door. But the female patients didn't seem to know how to close them. Maggie was terrified when she encountered three bony old crones with white faces, wispy white hair, no teeth in their gums, and wearing long white nightgowns, perched silently on three white pedestals. Their nightgowns were open at the back and they wore no slippers on their feet! Were they ghosts, skeletons, white witches or hags from hell? She didn't recognise that these apparitions were only very old ladies. She wanted to scream. Their faces were blank, and they ignored her completely as they remained just where they were without making a sound. Maggie entered the vacant cubicle and locked the door. She was almost too afraid to pull the chain in case they came out of their trance and screeched at her, or pulled at her hair or frock. She had read too many stories about wicked witches, malevolent spirits, and other scary beings.

"What in the world have you been doing in there?" grumbled John. "It's time for us to go and you haven't even said 'Hello' to Grandpa yet!"

"Hello, Grandpa, does your ankle still hurt?"

"Not as much as it did. But I can't really walk on it without hanging on to something."

"I hope you come home soon. I miss you."

"Come on; give us a kiss."

The journey home was much more daunting. Maggie knew she would have to ride *up* Devil's Hill and had no idea how she was going to manage it. But, first, she had to get through Henley town centre. As before, her father rode behind her. This time he didn't shout out instructions. He was going to test her road sense and she fell at the first hurdle – the traffic lights on the corner of Market Place and Bell Street. She was so busy watching the road that she didn't see the red light. Even if she *had* seen it, its significance may not have registered. In the 1940s there were no traffic lights in Sonning Common. In Reading, red lights meant that pedestrians could cross the road. Here, in Henley, she was no longer a pedestrian, but she was too busy coping with the bike to make that mental switch.

Cycling along Duke Street, she had almost reached the Reading Road before realising that her father wasn't following her.

"What has happened to Daddy? Why isn't he following me?" She dismounted and waited anxiously until she saw him riding towards her.

"What happened to you, Daddy?"

"Maggie, why didn't you wait at the traffic lights for the red light to go green?"

"I didn't see it. I was watching the road. ... I thought you'd been knocked off your bike."

"It's a wonder that *you* weren't knocked off your bike by traffic coming out of Bell Street!" (There was no one-way system in those days.) "Anyway, we must get home."

Maggie was relieved to find that even her father couldn't ride *up* Devil's Hill. But pushing their bikes up the long incline from Harpsden Bottom took up too much valuable time, and John had only enough time to gulp down a cup of warm tea before having to set off again for the Gospel meeting at the Iron Room. It was his turn to preach and he wished he had had more time to go over his sermon again before having to stand up in front of his modest congregation and deliver it.

"Maggie had better go to bed with the others tonight, instead of coming out again with me," was his parting suggestion. Maggie heaved a contented sigh and all four young Goodchilds were fast asleep in their beds by seven-thirty.

Emily expected John to be in a bad mood when he arrived home again about a quarter past eight. The dwindling numbers at the Iron Room were a constant source of discouragement, and having to preach the Gospel to the already converted often seemed a thankless task. But then, one day, unannounced, a stranger *might* walk through that open front door!

When John reached the Iron Room, he was just in time to see a short man in a smart suit walk into the building. He thought he was dreaming. But no, the Fowles family had a new lodger, and there he was, sitting in the row next to their daughter, Marian. Marian was twenty something and rather plain and dowdy. At first, John thought that the smart newcomer was her 'intended', but then remembered that Mrs Fowles took in lodgers. For the whole service, John focused his attention on the visitor. His sermon was delivered with more animation and conviction than usual, and he made quite sure that he explained everything he had to say as clearly as possible. There was no way of knowing whether the stranger felt he was being targeted; he just sat there impassively with his eyes fixed on John the whole time he was speaking.

"That was a word from the Lord, John," commented Percy Lunn afterwards, as John stepped off the platform.

"Would you mind locking up for me tonight, Percy? Maggie and I went to see Father this afternoon, and I had to come straight up here after a quick cup of tea. I'm really exhausted."

"Certainly! See you on Tuesday, God willing."

Meanwhile, Dot Fowles was busily introducing Jock Findlay to the rest of the congregation. "Jock's proper name is John, but everyone calls him Jock. He's from Aberdeen."

"I've got a position in Wellsteed's, managing the soft furnishing department. I've been there a week."

"What made you leave Aberdeen?" asked Frances Russell.

"Job prospects are better down here, and so are wages."

"You're very welcome," cooed Gladys Lunn. "We're only a small company, but you will find everyone is friendly and you'll soon feel at home. We have a weeknight meeting on Tuesdays at seven-thirty. On Sundays, our morning meeting, 'the Lord's Supper', is at eleven o'clock, after the Sunday school." The way she talked about this 'morning meeting' made Jock think it must be special in some way, probably Communion, but *he* was more interested in the Sunday school.

"Do you have a big Sunday school?"

"Not really – about twenty regulars and another twenty or so who turn up before treats and outings and then leave again after a few weeks. Are you interested in helping us?" Jock didn't quite know what to say to that, and mumbled something about having lots of nieces and nephews.

"I take it there is no *Mrs* Findlay?"

"No, I'm still a bachelor."

Emily was surprised to hear John ride up to the lean-to before eight o'clock. She hadn't finished getting the meal ready, but at least there was a kettle of boiling water for his tea.

"You're early. Weren't there many out tonight?"

"Not many, but Mrs Fowles brought her new lodger so I had someone to preach to. He didn't take his eyes off me the whole time. Where he stands, I don't know, but *him* just being there made it all worthwhile."

"The meal's almost ready, so here's some tea to be going on with."

"Did the children go to bed without any nonsense?"

"Yes, they were all asleep by seven-thirty. Maggie could hardly keep her eyes open."

"I won't take her again for a while. She's not up to it yet. She went right through a red light. Didn't even see it!"

"Did you remind her about the traffic lights beforehand?"

"Of course not! She's seen traffic lights before."

"But only as a pedestrian, not a road user."

John felt it wise to leave the discussion there and they both sat silently enjoying their wartime luxury, a tin of pink salmon.

Albert was expected to be discharged from Townlands Hospital in the late autumn but it soon became apparent that he wouldn't be able to manage on his own, even with his son and daughter-in-law living next door. The Sunday evening before he was due to be discharged, John and Emily were again seated at the kitchen table silently consuming their dishes of pink salmon.

Both were thinking about Albert Goodchild; John was facing his father's senility head-on, and wishing that the Lord would be merciful and take him before he got any worse, while Emily was wondering how she would cope now he was coming home.

"Your father will certainly need a lot of looking after when he comes home tomorrow. I'm not sure I'll be able to give him all the attention he really needs."

"He's still so confused and distressed. I didn't think for one minute that the doctors at Henley would even contemplate sending him back here in *that* state. I've seriously been thinking of asking the Lord to end his misery and take him *right* home – as soon as possible."

"I agree that that would be the very best outcome."

"Yes, we've got to be realistic. One of us should go and talk this over with Dr Prince and see what *he* suggests. Maybe a district nurse could come and dress his foot and help us look after him?"

"I'll try and do something first thing tomorrow morning. I'll phone the hospital first to find out what time we are to expect him."

"David hasn't been over for a while – we'd better warn him that Father is deteriorating."

"Then there's the whole matter of selling this place after your father has gone."

"David's the elder son so I suppose he'll have to take care of all that, and then we shall have to give the Bournes sufficient notice so that they can find somewhere else to live. It's going to be a real upheaval after all this time."

"But life would be so much easier for all of us if we moved back to Sonning Common."

Albert Goodchild was not discharged as expected the following day. Almost overnight, he had picked up an infection which rapidly went to his lungs. Now he was seriously ill and fighting for every breath. Emily was given this sobering report from the ward sister; so instead of phoning Dr Prince, she rang Austin's and asked if she could get an urgent message to her husband.

"John, your father's not coming home after all. He's gone down with pneumonia and he's very poorly. Shall I ring Nellie?"

"Yes, then she can let David know at school. But I don't think he'll be able to get away just like that. I'll see if I can get time off to go to Henley straight away. It's times like this when I wish I still had my motorbike. It's a pity I had to sell it."

"So, shall I see you back home for the evening meal at the usual time?"

"I hope so."

*

During the day, Albert's breathing improved and he was taken off the danger list. David Goodchild didn't arrive at Tudor Cottage until the following weekend. Surprisingly, a letter from him, addressed to John, had been delivered later on that Monday morning. All afternoon Emily had been itching to open it, even though it hadn't been addressed to her. As soon as John walked through the kitchen door, Emily approached him with it.

"John, there's a letter here from David. It could be important!"

"Can't it wait until I've had a bite to eat? David will know all about Father by now."

"No. I might have to go back to Rita's to make another phonecall if it's important. You read the letter while I dish up the food."

John opened the letter, carefully splitting the envelope with his dinner knife. He had no difficulty in reading his brother's elegant, copperplate handwriting:

29th June, 1946
Dear John,

Nellie and I have been very concerned about Father's declining health, even though we haven't been in touch lately. So, I would like to come over for a visit next weekend if that is convenient to you and Emily. Is there a bicycle I could use so that the two of us could go over to Henley and see him together?

I have also been thinking that we brothers ought to spend some time together discussing Father's funeral and settling his affairs, especially the sale of Tudor Cottage. I am assuming that you and Emily want to return to your own house in Sonning Common. (?)

I have taken the liberty of broaching the subject with a brother in our Assembly, who is an estate agent. He advises that we sell the house as it is, and not try to do it up in any way. He says that well-off city people might be interested in it as a weekend cottage or a couple who are interested in older properties might enjoy the challenge of restoring it to its former glory.

I know for a fact that, behind the stove in Father's little sitting room, there is an ingle-nook, complete with the original beams. And of course, you know that the original ceilings have all been lowered with plasterboard to make the place warmer. In the right hands, Tudor Cottage could be made to look very attractive indeed. Sadly, we don't have the time or money to do the job and see it for ourselves.

That reminds me, I want to bring my pastels with me to sketch some of the outside features of Tudor Cottage before it is too late. All I have now is the big picture of the well, which I did while I was at college. I expect you remember it. It hangs in our hall near the front door.

I hope to be with you about 9 pm on Friday evening. Please let me know if this is <u>not</u> convenient, otherwise I will see you then.

Your loving brother,
David

"That's good, David is already thinking about disposing of this place once Father's gone."

"I hope he hasn't got any harebrained ideas about trying to do it up first?"

"No, quite the opposite. But I think he will be very sad to let it go when the time comes. He's talking about doing some more of his pastel drawings before it's sold."

"I like the one he did of the well. I wish he'd do one for us!"

"Anyway, he wants to come over and see Father next weekend and bring his pastels with him. He expects to arrive about nine on Friday evening, and only wants us to contact him if it's not convenient. … But I'd still like you to go and ring him at the Hursts while I eat my meal. That will put his mind at rest about Father's pneumonia."

"I'll probably find myself talking to Nellie again. David's hardly ever at home!"

David Goodchild was used to riding a bicycle and so had no difficulty with his father's old bike. But he, like Maggie, was not used to country roads. He had completely forgotten how to cope with narrow lanes and steep hills, and the perils of rounding a bend and almost colliding with a farm tractor, or a herd of cows making their way from the field to the milking parlour. David nearly came off the bike a couple of times on the way to Henley, but John resisted the urge to shout instructions to his elder brother.

Once at the hospital, David's presence made a profound difference to Albert's state of mind. Now almost over the acute stage of the pneumonia crisis, he was back to being confused and sad. But one glimpse of David and his depression lifted like the morning mist at a sight of the sun, and for the whole visit he remained alert and positive. The two brothers were able to talk to him about what he wanted included in his funeral service, whether or not he had made a will, and how he wanted them to dispose of his things after he had gone.

"I have been thinking about all of these things in my clearer moments, but I get so confused sometimes. I haven't actually made a will but now you're both here I can tell you what's in my mind. Somewhere in my locker drawer there's a writing pad."

John got up from his chair and searched around in the cluttered little drawer. "That'll do nicely," said David. "I will write down your wishes and then, when we have thrashed it all out to everyone's satisfaction, we will all sign it and I'll write today's date. Then I can go to our family solicitor to make out any necessary documents. ... We'll start with the funeral."

"I want a bright, happy funeral service. Ever since your mother died I've wanted to go and join her, so I don't want you to weep for me. I want you to be glad. I must have hymn 432, 'Forever with the Lord!' Then there's that other joyful one; how does it start? You know the one that says:

'He and I in that bright glory,
one deep joy we'll share.
Mine to be forever with him –
his that I am there.'"

"We'll find it, Father. Don't you worry! Any preferences for Scripture readings?"

"I must have Psalm 23, but if you want one from the New Testament as well, you choose it. ... I think that hymn I want starts, 'Who is this that comes to meet me on the desert road? ...' but it may not be in 'Hymns of Light and Love'."

"Now, Father, what about your will?"

"David, can you arrange for the sale of Tudor Cottage?"

"I have my estate agent friend in Ruislip, but we ought to advertise it in the Reading area as well."

"When we let Shalom to the Bournes, we used Nicholas, a long-established firm. We could go and see them as they know us already. What do you think, David?"

"Yes, do that."

"Once the house is sold, I want you to split the proceeds between you fifty-fifty. John and Emily have been keeping an eye on me for nearly seven years now; so, David, I hope you are happy about that?"

"Of course, Father."

"As far as everything else is concerned, make your own arrangements. There's nothing of any real value, and I expect a lot of the stuff will have to be got rid of. Make a bonfire or something."

"Don't worry, Father, we will clear it all out properly."

The three men had been so preoccupied that they hadn't

realised visiting time was almost over. David was surprised to see the ward sister pick up the bell.

"Let's pray together briefly before we go and leave you, Father."

David was not known for expressing himself in the minimum of words, but this time he judged it perfectly.

"Heavenly Father, thou hast heard our conversation, and we commit ourselves into thy hands. Be very near to our dear father, and watch over him here in this hospital bed. We trust thee to take him to thyself when the right time comes. May he not suffer any further pain and misery.

"Now a beautiful prayer by Cardinal Newman:

'O Lord, support us all the day long of this troublous life, until the shades lengthen and the evening comes, and the busy world is hushed, the fever of life is over, and our work is done. Then Lord, in thy mercy, grant us safe lodging, a holy rest and peace at the last; through Jesus Christ our Lord, who lives and reigns with thee, one God for ever, Amen.'"

"Weren't we going to sign that paper, David?" asked John, suddenly remembering what they had previously decided to do.

"Of course, I'd almost forgotten. Father, you write your signature here at the top. Now I'll write mine."

As John started to write his signature, he was startled by the bell and spoilt his signature with an uncharacteristic squiggle. Sister took the bell to the other end of the ward, and John's second attempt was satisfactory.

"Didn't you two hear the bell? Visiting time is over and we have work to do now."

"Sorry Sister, but we all needed to sign this piece of paper. Can we please talk to you for a minute on the way out?"

"Yes, if you don't mind coming to my office."

"Sister, what is *your* opinion on our father's condition? He has told us that he wants to die and go to that better place."

"He's no longer critically ill but he is definitely getting weaker and his heart beat is a little irregular. Do you want us to call you if he deteriorates any further?"

"No. We have said our goodbyes and committed him into the Lord's hands," answered David.

"Even though I'm fairly local, it would be difficult to keep taking time off work," answered John. "If I hear nothing further from you, I'll be back again next weekend."

The two brothers took their time walking up Devil's Hill. "David, that prayer you recited, how did you find it? I didn't know you were into set prayers."

"I came across several beautiful prayers while I was at college. I often use them when my own thoughts dry up. They are such a comfort, and I can concentrate on the Lord as I mouth the familiar words. I want Father to experience that 'safe lodging', 'holy rest', and 'peace at the last'."

Albert died in his sleep during the night, and the funeral took place as he had planned as soon as it could be arranged. A large company gathered at the Iron Room to celebrate his life, instead of mourning his passing. It was decided that none of the grandchildren should attend the funeral, not even David's teenagers.

"All the children should be at school. Their education is important. All mine have exams of one kind or another and your Maggie has the scholarship coming up soon, just like our twins," was David's conclusion, and John agreed. Weeping grandchildren might spoil the celebration Albert had requested.

Chapter 16

August 1944

A small group of German prisoners of war arrived unexpectedly at the Iron Room one sunny Sunday evening. Percy Lunn was preaching and John Goodchild was welcoming people at the door, while Maggie was helping with the hymnbooks. The officer in charge who drove the truck was a Christian and had very much wanted his men to meet some Christian families.

"I do hope you are happy to receive us. We all come from the camp out beyond Gallowstree Common. All the men are German but they understand some English and have been doing farm work locally for the last two weeks. They came with me tonight at their own request."

"You're all very welcome here, Officer. I'm afraid we are only a small company of the Lord's people, but we *are* about to hold a simple Gospel service which finishes about 7.30."

"I've heard about you through a family in Cholsey, the Nielsens. They have befriended some Italian prisoners and regularly invite them to their home."

"Yes, the Nielsens looked after our children when my wife was ill. They are very hospitable people. … Come and sit down everyone. I must go to the organ and get ready to play the hymns." They all smiled at Maggie as she handed each of them a copy of Sankey's 'Sacred Songs and Solos'.

Percy Lunn had chosen some well-known gospel hymns: 'Rock of ages, cleft for me' by A M Toplady; 'Guide me, O Thou great Jehovah' by William Williams; 'What a friend we have in Jesus' by Joseph Scriven; and 'The Lord's my Shepherd' by Francis Rous. The Germans were soon singing along with everyone else, and several of them had very good voices. When it came to the Bible reading, Luke 15: 13-31, Percy was very careful to read the chosen passage slowly and clearly. He also remembered to speak more slowly when he came to the sermon. From time to time there was quite a bit of interpreting going on within the group, but everyone was paying attention.

At the end of the service, Gladys Lunn invited them all to stay for a cup of tea. "I am sorry that we only have powdered milk but we do have some sugar and also some biscuits left over from the women's meeting." Frances Russell busied herself making sure everyone had something to eat and drink. Then the young men introduced themselves to the locals, who had great fun trying to pronounce the German names correctly: Klaus, Fritz, Hans, Heinrich, Johan, Josef, Reinhard, Rudolf, and Wilhelm. Finally they each wrote their names for us on a sheet of paper.

When Maggie saw the list she plucked up the courage to ask, "Why does the 'j' in Johan sound like a 'y' and the 'w' in 'Wilhelm' sound like a 'v'?"

"That's the way we say it in German," answered Fritz. "Maybe one day I teach you some German?" After this, Fritz fished in his pocket for his mouth organ and began to play a lively tune, and then they all started singing together in German.

241

"I like that. What do the words mean?"

"It's a children's song, like nursery rhyme, about a farmer and all the animals. I sing it for *you*. Did you hear the sounds the animals made?"

"Yes, but *our* cows say 'moo' and our sheep 'baa', yours were different."

"Of course, they're *German* cows! Now we'll sing you a German hymn."

As they started singing, John recognised the tune as '*Ein' Feste Burg*'. There were four verses. "Is that hymn by Martin Luther?"

"Yes, words *and* music."

"It has been translated into English as 'A mighty fortress is our God, a bulwark never failing.' Here it is – number 2 in our hymn book. I don't expect we have time now to sing it for you in English."

"No. We'll have to be on our way. I need to get everyone back to their billets by ten o'clock, or we won't be allowed out another time."

"We've enjoyed having you with us. Goodnight and safe journey."

~

The Germans came to the Iron Room for two years on and off. They visited Tudor Cottage and made a big fuss of Jimmy, Ann and Gracie. They also visited the Lunns in Shiplake, the Fowles in Blackmore Lane and the Russells in Grove Road. In 1946, after the war was over and they were finally released, they came to say goodbye. Addresses were exchanged and Fritz promised to send all the little Goodchilds a German mouth organ each.

"It's not a mouth organ, it's a harmonica," insisted Ann.

"They're just two different names for the same thing," explained Emily. "The best mouth organs are made in Germany by a firm called 'Hohner'. Isn't that right, Fritz?"

"Yes, I always choose Hohner. They make other musical instruments, too, even pianos."

"I don't want you to go," said Maggie.

"My Mummy wants me home," explained Fritz. "She hasn't seen me for four years and we're missing each other. I won't forget the mouth organs – they will remind you all of me. I won't be able to send them immediately when I get home. But maybe they will come for Christmas."

<hr/>

July 1946

"Mumsie, the postman is coming," called Jimmy from the little window at the bottom of the attic stairs. "He's got a letter in his hand."

"Thank you, Jimmy." Emily had been waiting for a letter from a lady doctor who specialised in children's psychological problems, but had heard nothing for several weeks. As she walked out to meet the postman, she really hoped that this was it at last.

"Just the one, Mrs Goodchild. I hope it's the one you've been waiting for."

"Yes, I think it is. It's got the right post mark. I was beginning to think that *my* letter had got lost or that the recipient had gone away for a long holiday."

"You'd be surprised how few letters actually do get lost. Even during the war we managed to keep everything going pretty well, all things considered."

Emily opened the letter and this is what it said:

Dear Mrs Goodchild,

Thank you for your letter. Please forgive the delay as I have been out of the country for nearly a fortnight at a medical conference in Switzerland on traumas in childhood and their effect on mental health.

I would be happy to see your two children, Margaret and James, in my surgery in Chain Street at 2 pm on Tuesday 24th July. It is held in a large grey building almost opposite St. Mary's churchyard. You will see all the brass plates as you approach the front door. I am on the first floor. Turn left at the top of the stairs, and it is the second door on your right.

I hope this will be convenient. I am only in Reading one day a week so all appointments are on a Tuesday.

Yours faithfully,
J. Adamson

Emily was a little perturbed that no fee had been mentioned, and she really had no idea what to expect. Her family doctor had a special rate for families on low incomes, but she had no experience of consulting specialists who worked independently. However, she need not have worried.

The first thing Dr Adamson said, once the three of them were seated in front of her on that Tuesday afternoon was, "Now, Mrs Goodchild, I don't want you to worry about my fee. This consultation is free and I think we will be able to help you without any further cost to you, other than bus fares. But, first of all, I want to talk to the children individually. Jimmy, tell me about school. Why don't you like going to school? Is it your teacher that upsets you or some of the children?"

"I sometimes get into trouble because I can't do my work properly. Mrs Claxton tells the whole class about it. That makes me cry. Then the other boys laugh and call me names when I go out to play."

"So your teacher doesn't help you with your lessons?"

"No, she says she hasn't got the time to bother with me. She just makes fun of me."

"That's not very kind! Why hasn't she got the time to bother with you?"

"Because there are too many other children in the class."

"Does she help any of *them*?"

"Yes, those who are her special pets."

"Is Ann one of her pets?"

"No, but Ann already knows how to read and write properly. She's clever."

"Does *she* ever try to help you?"

"No, she's too busy with her own work. She's in the top block and I'm in the third block."

"Do you get upset about wetting yourself?"

"Yes, because I can't help it. And ... and Mrs Claxton doesn't always let me go when I want to and I can't hold it."

"I see. ... Now, Maggie, do you know why you get nightmares?"

"No, not really. I suppose it's because I get afraid of things."

"Here, let me see your arm. Has someone been biting you?"

"No."

"How did that bite mark get there then?"

"I get very cross with myself sometimes, and then I bite my arm."

"Why do you get cross with yourself?"

"Lots of reasons. I hate these heavy plaits; I hate being shorter than all the others in my class. Some girls make fun of the clothes I wear and they say I smell; and I want to pass the scholarship and go to the grammar school so that I can be a teacher, but I can't because I'm not learning the right things."

"Why aren't you learning the right things?"

"Because Mr Lockyer doesn't think any of us will pass anyway."

"Why's that?"

"Those he thinks will pass have gone up to Standard Five in the seniors."

"And you haven't?"

"No. He said it was because of age, but Pat Stratton is a month younger than me and *she* went up."

"Oh dear! We'll have to do something about this, won't we? When *are* the scholarship exams?"

"Next February," answered Emily.

"So we have a little time to do something about this. First, we need to find out exactly what these children's IQs are. We don't want to give Maggie false hopes or expect either of them to do more than they are capable of achieving. In the past I have referred children to the University Psychology Department in London Road. The department regularly needs children for the students to work with, but they are on vacation until October. As well as the IQ tests, the department runs a play group where children's actual behaviour can be monitored over a period of time. This could give us real insights into what is troubling them both."

"So you are saying that nothing can be done until October?" queried Emily.

"I am not saying that. We have a playroom here, so we'll start this afternoon."

Dr Adamson rang a small bell on her desk, and a young woman in an attractive blue overall walked into the room from a door to their left. "Dorothy, please show Maggie and Jimmy the things in the playroom and, when they have settled down, we will come in and observe them playing."

The playroom was large and Jimmy and Maggie had it all to themselves. "Can we play with *any* of these toys?" asked Jimmy, hardly believing his luck.

"Of course you can!" laughed Dorothy. Jimmy ran immediately to the far corner of the room where he could see a model railway already set out. Soon he was guiding a little red engine with three carriages around the track, making chuffing noises as he went.

"Maggie, what do you want to do?"

"Can I draw on the blackboard?"

"You've got it all to yourself."

"Won't any more children come in and want to use it?"

Maggie began drawing a small picture at the edge of the board. There was Tudor Cottage and the well beside Grandpa Goodchild's back door. Then she put in the three cherry trees by the path in front of the barn, and the lawn going up the slope on the other side of the house. She soon became totally absorbed in what she was doing. The trees over by the hedge and the apple trees in the dell were faithfully reproduced, and then the garden fence across the front with its little wooden gate, only just big enough for a motorbike to get through.

"Maggie, why is your picture so small when you've got such a *big* board to draw on?" asked Dr Adamson. "Dorothy told you that you had it all to yourself."

"It's such a big space. I couldn't draw anything *that* big!"

"Why not?"

"Someone else might want it too, and I'm only used to drawing tiny pictures."

"Take this piece of chalk and draw me a big face on the other side of the board." Maggie tried hard to draw a big face, but it still took up only a fraction of the empty space on the large blackboard.

"Mrs Goodchild, why do you think Maggie is so restrained and seems too afraid to fill that blackboard?"

"I think it's my husband's influence. He is always telling us to be restrained, to be economical and not to take any more than we need. Also, he is not one to encourage spontaneity and exuberance in self-expression. As a three-year-old Maggie was just the opposite, and then a well-meaning doctor told him that she needed taking in hand, so he literally smacked all the exuberance and spontaneity out of her."

"Why didn't you intervene?"

"I tried to do so many times, and also suffered for my pains."

"What a pity! Do you think he is partly responsible for Jimmy's problems too?"

"No. I think Jimmy is under Ann's shadow. Ann is only eleven months younger and very sharp. Because *he* has a September birthday and Ann's is in August, both their birthdays fall in the same school year so they will always be in the same class. Ann had the chance to start school when she was four and is streets ahead of him already. She is probably brighter than Maggie, but doesn't have her tenacity."

"I must let you all go now. We'll make another appointment for next month."

"But you *must* let me pay for that session."

"No, definitely not. Your children need help and I know your means are limited. It is important for us to work with them here until we can get them in at the University. I will get in touch with the University myself, and they will write to you direct with the appointments. Once they have come up with the detailed assessments, then you will be back here again for us to discuss the results together."

"Thank you again for your help and understanding."

"Keep an eye on them both, and jot down anything about their behaviour you think might be significant."

"Yes, I'll do that."

"Until next month then. Goodbye."

⁓

"How are things going with the turning out?" asked John, when he came home on the evening after the visit to Dr Adamson.

"You know I had to take Maggie and Jimmy to Dr Adamson this afternoon, but I have made a start on the attic. Mrs Hurst has had Gracie for me all day."

"Why did you start there? Wouldn't it have been better to start on the things nearest to hand?"

"Not really, because we'll be using those things up to the last minute."

"Has anyone come from Nicholas's to look at the house yet?"

"No, not yet. They promised that the advert would be in the papers by next week."

The turning out was a thankless task. It wasn't just their own clutter they had to deal with, but all sorts of stuff left in the attic by previous generations, especially on Albert's side of the house. This area could only be accessed by climbing a ladder from Albert's bedroom. Emily had a problem with ladders and heights in general, but she didn't want John going up there or he would try to bring it all down before she had found anywhere to put it or the means of its disposal. "He may be a good carpenter and joiner, but he's a hopeless organiser," she thought to herself.

"Emily, I think we both ought to work together this evening as soon as the children have gone to sleep."

"But aren't you going to the prayer meeting tonight, John?"

"Oh! I forgot it was Tuesday."

"You need to be on your way in the next ten minutes."

While he was away at the Iron Room, Emily left Maggie in charge and decided to ask Ernie Hurst for advice. He was out in his garden mowing the lawn.

"Hello Emily, I'm afraid Rita is out this evening, gone to visit a friend."

"Actually, it's *you* I want to talk to. I need some advice. I'm starting to clear out the attic on Albert's side of the house. It's full of stuff from years ago. If John sees it, he will take ages sifting through it, deciding what he can salvage. I just want to get it all out and burn the lot before he even sees it."

"Well, I was thinking of lighting a bonfire myself. All I've got is garden rubbish, so I could get rid of a barrow-load for you if you like. What is it, old rugs and blankets?"

"Yes, that's it, and old sheets and other things that Ruth thought might come in handy one day."

"There's no time like the present. Let's get a load now."

Ernie's wheelbarrow was large and extra deep, and Ernie himself was a much stronger man than John. "Emily, *I'll* get the stuff down from the loft. I'm more used to ladders than you are. Do you want me to bring it just as it comes?"

"Yes. Can you see what you're doing or shall I get a torch?"

"I can see bundles of stuff all rolled up. They're jolly dusty, but quite easy to shift. Can you take them from me? They're not too heavy."

"I'll pile them up here by the bed for now."

Soon there were sufficient bundles lying on the floorboards to fill the barrow.

"We'll leave it at that for tonight. I'll come and get another load tomorrow if you like?"

"Can you come before seven? John's a funny old stick; he hates me asking favours of people."

"I've got some time off tomorrow. I could make a bonfire up here and you could watch it while I get the stuff down?"

"But your time is precious!"

"And so is your health!"

By the weekend the loft space behind Maggie's attic bedroom had all been cleared and the whole floor swept clean. Maggie could no longer hear the sound of mice scuttling around when she was lying in bed at night; they must have moved across to the barn. Surprisingly, John didn't even ask for details on how Emily had managed to get the job done so quickly. His thoughts were already turning towards his own house in Sonning Common and what he would like to do there once he had it to himself again.

The man from Nicholas' arrived on the Monday morning and Emily showed him around. He had brought a clipboard with him and was busily scribbling notes and drawing floor plans. He measured each room as they came to it, adding its dimensions to the plan.

"This house has possibilities but, in its present condition, it will only fetch about two thousand, if that."

"What about the land? We have three quarters of an acre here."

"Yes, but that wouldn't necessarily be a plus, especially for people looking for a weekend hideaway in the country. And people nowadays would certainly want electricity and a proper bathroom and lavatory, not a long-drop at the top of the garden!"

"Yes, it hasn't exactly been easy living out here in the sticks without any mod cons, plus four children and no transport."

"Now if anyone was into restoration, this property *would* be of interest. Above those false ceilings they would find the original oak beams, and in the sitting room, to the left of the front door, there's an ingle-nook behind that ugly old stove. This place must be about three hundred years old, or even more judging by the size of the bricks. If I had the money, I'd be tempted to have a go myself. It *could* be as pretty as a picture postcard, inside as well as out!"

Dr Bourne was actually rather relieved when he received the letter from Nicholas' saying that the owner, Mr J. Goodchild, wanted to move back into number 22 Newfield Road, and was giving him six months to find a new home. He had just lost his wife in childbirth, though his baby son had survived and he was paying a full-time nurse to look after him. His grief and remorse were made worse by the gossiping tongues all around him.

"Why did the silly man make Vivienne have Peter at home, when *she* wanted to have her baby in hospital, where there is specialist help at hand?" asked Ada Cotton in exasperation.

"He believes in all these newfangled ideas, natural childbirth and all that, but Vivienne apparently had a tough enough time with Judith, and he would have lost her *then* without the Caesarean," answered Lucy Piggott. "I don't know why he thought natural childbirth would solve all her problems – especially as they had to wait so long for Peter. He must have realised long ago that there was something not quite right with her inside."

"So, what was it that actually killed her?"

"Well, Ada, I *have* heard, but it seems a bit far-fetched to me, that her liver came away with the baby! I wouldn't have thought that was possible. The liver is a big organ."

"Where is Judith now?

"Judith has been sent to an aunt in Wiltshire, and he's given strict instructions that Judith is *not* to be told of her mother's death. When he told me that, I asked him why."

"What did he say?"

"'She will be told when the time is right.' I told him that the time will never be *right*. She ought to be told by the family *now* before she hears it later from the wrong person."

"What did he say to that?"

"He said it was none of my business. But I was thinking of poor little Judith. She's only eight, and now no mother."

It was less than three months later when the Bournes finally left

Sonning Common for an elegant terraced house near the centre of Malmesbury. Douglas Bourne's new practice was only a couple of streets away. Sadly, almost as soon as Judith arrived back in Sonning Common, a boy called Donald Fudge, who lived at the top of Newfield Road, made it his business to tell her about her mother.

"Judith, do you know where your mother is?"

"She's gone somewhere for a long holiday."

"No, she hasn't! She's *dead*, and they're too frightened to tell you."

"That's not true! Don't say such horrid things!"

"My mum read it in the Chronicle. They had the funeral at Peppard Church."

Judith burst into tears and ran to find Ada Cotton. "Auntie Ada, Donald Fudge says my mother is dead and everyone is afraid to tell me. Is that true?"

Ada's eyes filled with tears. Her voice shook as she put a comforting arm around the little girl's shoulders saying, "Come in and sit down, darling." Then she calmly led her towards her well-worn settee.

This was what Ada had been dreading all along. If ever she needed the help of the Almighty, she needed it now. "I'm sorry, it *is* true," she murmured. "Your daddy didn't want you to find out like that. He thought he would be able to tell you all about it himself when the time was ripe. But that *boy* got in first."

"Why *didn't* Daddy tell me straightaway?" Judith asked accusingly.

"I don't know, pet. I asked him the same question."

"What did he say?"

"He just said, 'It's none of your business.'"

They both heard Douglas Bourne arrive home and park the car in the front drive.

"Would you like me to take you home now?"

"No, I want to stay here with you."

"That's fine. You can stay here as long as you like, but I'd better go and talk to your father first."

The damage had already been done, so Ada Cotton had no intention of rubbing salt into his wounds. She spoke to him in matter-of-fact tones. "Judith has just heard about her mother from a boy up the road. His mother read about the funeral in the

Chronicle. Judith's very upset and it will take time for her to come to terms with the truth. She asked if she could stay with me for the time being. Pauline has gone to the Strattons otherwise she could keep her company while I get the tea ready. Anyway, helping me might take her mind off things. You could come too if you wanted to?"

"Actually, I would like that very much. I realise now just how badly I have handled the whole situation, and what a mess I've made of everything. If it wasn't for my pig-headedness, Vivienne could still be with us."

"Maybe, but maybe not. Anyway, Judith needs you now. ... So, I'll expect you over in about half an hour. ... Oh! I forgot to ask, how is Peter doing?"

"He's thriving under Annette's expert care. She is an excellent nurse and a very nice lady."

"Could you bring them over to tea, too? I've plenty of bread and cake."

Ada Cotton prepared a good spread and Annette brought some cold meat and salad which made it into a feast. Judith sat by Annette at the table, while Peter slept in his pram in the bedroom. Judith couldn't quite understand why Annette was looking after her brother and living in their house, instead of her mother.

"Judith, it's like this. Your little brother has lost his mother. I can't *be* his mother, but I have learnt how to look after little babies like Peter. That's my job, so I'll be looking after Peter and living in your house. I shall be looking after you and your daddy too, keeping the house clean and cooking your meals. So I am being paid as a housekeeper as well as Peter's nurse."

"So will you be doing *all* the things that my mother used to do?" Judith's lip quivered as she used the word 'mother'?"

"No, not all of them. I will do enough to make sure that you and your daddy have what you need and that Peter grows into a sturdy young lad."

"Auntie Ada. I think I would like to sleep in my own bed after all. Annette, where do *you* sleep?"

"In the bedroom downstairs with Peter. His cot is by the fireplace and my bed is right beside him."

"If I have a bad dream, can I come downstairs, too?"

"Yes, you come to me. Your daddy has to work and needs his sleep. I'll keep the hall light on."

As Ada cleared up the tea things after the Bournes had left, she was now much happier about Judith. "Annette will look after *her* as well as Peter," she told herself. "And perhaps, one day, she will take on Douglas himself and complete the family!"

September 1946

During the first week of my final school year, a boy from Standard Two came into our classroom with a note. Mr Lockyer read it and then looked across at me. I was now sitting in the top block, right by a window looking out onto the senior playground.

"Maggie Goodchild, Mrs Fisk wants a word with you; I hope you haven't been getting into mischief?"

"No Mr Lockyer. I have no idea what she wants." When I walked into the classroom and up to her desk she actually smiled at me, so I knew it wasn't trouble. She came straight to the point.

"I see the Bournes at number 22 Newfield Road are getting ready to move. Do you know whether your father is going to let it again, now the Bournes are going?"

"No, Mrs Fisk, he is not; we are going to live there ourselves."

"Thank you, Maggie. That's all I wanted to know."

Mr and Mrs Fisk lived in the top floor of Mrs Piggott's house, almost opposite Mrs Cotton's bungalow. They had their own little garden at the front of the spare plot between Auntie Ada's bungalow and Shalom where we were going back to live. This plot belonged to my father too, and it was my father who had put the air-raid shelter right in the middle to cut the plot in half. Though I don't think anyone had ever used it because there had been no bombing near Sonning Common.

Although the Goodchilds were getting ready to move and had hoped to move in before the end of September, they had had no firm offers for Tudor Cottage. Neither John nor David liked the idea of leaving the property empty, but Emily certainly didn't want another November moving day if she could help it! Both families were praying specifically about the matter with considerable urgency, expecting the answer to come through Nicholas' of Caversham, but it didn't. It was David's estate agent friend in Ruislip, Robert Jefferies, who found the buyer.

Mr Lionel Hazeldine was a wealthy businessman who lived in Eastcote. He had a particular interest in restoring old properties, especially in rural areas. He just happened to see a photograph of Tudor Cottage in the window of Robert Jefferies' office in the Ruislip High Street, and wondered if it could serve as a country retreat for his own family.

"Where exactly is Crowsley?" he asked Robert. "I've never heard of it."

"It's in South Oxfordshire, about five miles out of Reading. It's only a hamlet, and the nearest village of any size is Sonning Common."

"It sounds interesting."

"It needs some work to restore it to its former glory. Attractive old beams have been covered up to make the place warmer, and things like that. It also has no electricity or bathroom, hence the low price."

"I'd like to see it."

"Do you wish me to show you round?"

"If you trust me with the key, I'm sure I could find it myself."

"That's not necessary. The present occupants haven't moved out yet. Unfortunately they are not on the phone, but I have a neighbour's phone number. When would you like to view the property?"

"This coming Saturday would be good."

"Let me ring the Hursts and see if I can leave a message for the Goodchilds. Do you want to wait or can I call you at your office?"

"No, I have some other business to attend to. I'll go and do that and come back in an hour. You may have something for me by then."

Rita Hurst was at home when the call came through, and she went to find Emily as soon as she had received it.

"Some good news, Emily. I've just had a call from the estate agents in Ruislip. They've got a potential buyer who wants to come and see this place on Saturday."

"That *is* good news. John will be here to show him around."

"What time would you like him to come?"

"Morning *or* afternoon would be fine. On Saturdays we usually have our lunch about one. If he could avoid the lunch hour that would be helpful."

"I'll go and phone back."

"Let me come with you and then I can talk to Robert Jefferies myself."

⌇

The Hazeldines arrived mid-morning – Lionel and his wife Julie, and two teenage sons, Daniel and Clive. It was a perfect day to show off the countryside, with the leaves just beginning to turn and the native birds singing their hearts out in welcome.

"Do you hear the cuckoo in these woods?" asked Clive.

"Yes, we do, but you'll have to wait till April next year to hear them. They all left last month," answered Emily.

"Please forgive the muddle everywhere," apologised John, as they trouped through the front door into the small hall.

"Moving is always a mighty upheaval, isn't it?" answered Julie. "It won't be so bad for us. We haven't got to bring everything with us as we'll be starting from scratch setting this place up, if we decide to have it."

Emily and John showed them all round the property, starting with Grandpa Goodchild's part of the house. "As you will see, there have been two families living here, but I don't think it will be difficult to turn it back into one dwelling again."

When they came to the little bedroom which Jimmy had been occupying, Julie said, "This would probably make a good place for the bathroom."

"Or maybe the one next door at the front," answered Lionel. "We would need a passageway through here to the big bedroom beyond, and it might be easier to convert that into the bathroom."

"There is something else here on the landing I ought to show you now," said John. You see this door; it's not a cupboard but another staircase which comes up from the sitting room at the other side of the house."

"We could take this door away and stain the treads to match the other stairs," said Julie.

"You may like to keep the door at the bottom though, to avoid a draught. You've got three doors into the sitting room already, as you will see when you get there."

As they all walked through the various rooms together, the parents talked animatedly about what they might do with each room. But the boys were becoming restless and Daniel asked if they could walk around the garden.

"Of course you may," answered Emily. "Our four children are walking round the Triangle; they should be near Brooker's Farm by now. You might enjoy the farm more than the garden. Go down the lane and turn left at Honeysuckle Cottage and you should see them looking at the animals. Maggie is ten, Jimmy seven, Ann six and Gracie is four-and-a-half. I think the Brookers have some calves and a few lambs, but they might have gone to market by now."

"Yes, this house has possibilities. I like the setting very much," said Lionel over a cup of tea. "What do you say, Julie?"

"Yes, it would be a great place to relax in, once we've got all the work done."

"Don't worry, I know the right people to do it and they will do a very good job, revealing all its beams and other attractive features and sensitively blending in the bathroom, kitchen and other modern conveniences."

"I'd love to see it when it's finished," enthused John. "I'm a carpenter and joiner by trade, but seldom get any of the quality jobs that actually use my expertise. Shop-fitting is a soulless task; all has to be cheap and cheerful! Austin's seem to be getting more of that kind of work all the time."

"What kind of work do you enjoy most?" asked Julie.

"Work in churches, especially Anglican churches, where fine workmanship is valued. I made a special screen for Peppard Church – my first attempt at hand carving! Then there are fitted bookcases, and fancy items like wooden bowls, lamp stands of various kinds and other things that require hand carving and decorative designs. They take a long time to make and so work out quite expensive, and unfortunately folk would rather buy something mass produced than invest in quality workmanship."

"If I gave you a commission, would you make something for *me*?"

"Yes, I would; unless you wanted it in a hurry. I need to be able to take my time. We are moving back to Sonning Common so we won't be far away."

"I'll remember that."

"Ah! Here come the boys, we must be off. You'll be hearing from Robert Jefferies quite soon, I hope. Nice meeting you both."

Maggie and the others were walking behind Daniel and Clive, and Gracie seemed cross about something.

"Clive dropped my yo-yo and it doesn't work properly any more. Look! It's bent and goes all crooked."

"Here is half-a-crown," said Clive, pulling a coin out of his pocket. "Buy yourself another one; you can get a wooden one for that. The wooden one will be much stronger than that plastic one. Now, you *know* I'm sorry."

"You don't have to do that, Clive," interjected John.

"Yes, I do. I was showing off."

Chapter 17

A Hare in Winter

It was eerily silent in the sequestered wood, the squelching of my stiff wellington boots scarcely audible amid the deep drifts of soft snow. Just the place for a surprise encounter; yet when he materialised on the path before me, I stared at him in spellbound wonder: a mad March hare in his off-white winter overcoat, freezing as we each sized up the other. I noted the remnants of summer brown in his fur, his bulging eyes set sideways in his head, amazed at this timid creature taking time with me. Then he was off but left his tracks behind; two big, two small; two big, two small; he bounded away.

October was a busy month for the Goodchilds. In the middle of removal preparations, Emily had to drop everything to take Maggie and Jimmy to the University Psychology Department in London Road for two ten o'clock appointments. Catching the nine o'clock bus from the stop near the Bird-in-Hand meant that they had to leave the house just after half past eight. Emily hoped that follow-up appointments would be later in the day, but things might be easier from Sonning Common anyway.

Each child worked with two female second-year students. To Maggie and Jimmy, they looked like ordinary adults. Jimmy worked with Miss Price with the thick glasses and Miss Stevens with the curly blond hair; while Maggie worked with Miss Templeton with the short bobbed hair and fringe and Miss Collins with the red hair done up in a bun, which would keep coming undone. Both children related to them in the same way as they did to their teachers at school.

"Jimmy, why are you looking so frightened?" asked Miss Price. "I'm not going to bite you; we're going to play some games together and do some puzzles."

"I like puzzles, 'specially jig-saw puzzles!"

"While we do the puzzles, Miss Stevens is going to watch us and make sure we do it properly and don't cheat."

After that, Jimmy relaxed and treated it as a game. "It doesn't matter if you can't do everything. When you can't do something, I'll show you what to do, so that you can do it next time." He had to fit shapes into a board, build things with bricks, and look at a group of objects and decide which was the odd one out and he soon became totally absorbed in what he was doing. Jimmy was quite unaware that, while Miss Price was showing him what to do, Miss Stevens was writing a cross in the square on her paper instead of a tick.

Maggie wasn't frightened but apprehensive. She realised how important these assessments were, because they would affect the whole of the rest of her life. She wanted to go to the grammar school so badly, and knew that if these ladies told her that she wasn't good enough for the grammar school she would be devastated. She had some easy puzzles to do, like completing a picture. This was similar to a jigsaw puzzle except that you didn't match colours or shapes, but had to balance one side of the picture with what was shown on the other half. In the picture, she saw a group of animals in different poses all facing the same way. When she picked up the pieces she had to slot in, she realised they were the same animals but all facing the other way, so she knew exactly where she had to put them.

"Why did you arrange them like that, Maggie?" asked Miss Templeton.

"Can't you see? They are all looking at themselves in a mirror."

"Right, let's do a different kind of puzzle. Here are two pictures but they are not exactly the same. I want you to tell me where they are different." This time the animals were dressed up, but she needed to look at them and their clothes very carefully.

"This cat has lost a button on his jacket; this monkey's tie is yellow instead of red; this pig has one eye shut; this mouse has the wrong kind of tail; and this bear has a belt without a proper buckle; see *this* bit is missing. Oh! There's one more thing: this kangaroo has a joey in her pouch and that one has a bunny; look at its long ears!"

"Now, Maggie, I'm going to give you a really difficult one. Here are a lot of different shapes on this piece of paper. You have to look at them very carefully, and when you find two that are identical in every respect, that means *exactly* the same, draw a line between them like this. Do you understand what you have to do?"

"I think so; but some of them are *nearly* the same but not quite."

"You leave those out."

Maggie found that she had to concentrate very hard to match them up properly as they were often not the same way up and she had to turn the paper round to check that they were the same. She was so glad that everything was quiet in the room. When she had finished, she had time to look at them again and found a mistake. She had no rubber so she did small crosses along the line that was wrong, and carefully drew another line in the correct place.

"Time's up," announced Miss Templeton, as she came to the end of the line.

Maggie had other similar shapes and drawings to match up in different ways and the hour with Miss Templeton and Miss Collins went very quickly.

"Next week when you come, Maggie," said Miss Collins, "*I'll* be doing the talking and giving you some listening exercises and word puzzles of different kinds, instead of pictures and shapes."

While the two children were doing their intelligence tests, Emily wandered around the university grounds and then went into the refectory for a cup of tea. Nobody came up to her and asked her who she was, and she was even able to take a peek at the university library. She went to the English section and looked at some of the books on English literature. "That's what I would have studied if *I* had had the chance to go to university! At least I *have* had two stories published in the Christian Herald."

The following week, both children found their tasks more difficult. Jimmy couldn't recognise words he was supposed to know if they were out of context. Matching words to pictures, and even whole sentences to pictures, he found much easier. Meanwhile, Maggie was given some exercises she had never met before and had to be shown what to do before she could even make a start on the first one. Then Miss Collins described some everyday situations and Maggie had to say what was going on. The church service was easy; the fair was easy because she had been taken to a fair when she stayed at Chiseldon with Aunty Enid; but she had no idea about the funeral, even though she had seen Grandfather's dead body and had heard the word 'funeral'. No-one had ever taken the trouble to explain to her what actually went on at a funeral, nor why the doctor had to come when someone had died.

"Miss Collins, why does the doctor have to come when a person dies?" He can't bring him back to life again. Only Jesus can do that!"

"He has to make sure the person really *is* dead and then sign the death certificate."

"Can a person look like he's dead when he's not?"

"Yes, when he's in a state of deep unconsciousness because, say, he's had a serious head injury."

"But wouldn't you be able to see him breathing?"

"A doctor would, but *you* might not."

⁓

Doctor Adamson wrote a letter giving Emily the results of the intelligence tests:

... The tests reveal that James is of average ability for his age, so you must not expect the same of him as you do of Margaret or his younger sibling, Ann. It is important that you encourage and affirm him in all that he does, and foster any particular strengths you observe as he develops.

Margaret's results are interesting. She fell down on some everyday things that you would expect an eleven-year-old to know, and was able to do others that you would not expect anyone under sixteen to be able to do. She is definitely academically inclined and should be given a grammar school place if you can do something about helping her to improve her English and Mathematics.

However, from the play sessions here, I feel both children need to be encouraged to be more confident and secure in who they are. So I have arranged for them to attend play sessions at the university on Tuesday afternoons from 2 to 3.30 pm. You will be receiving an official letter from the university giving the details. If you take them yourself the first time, perhaps Maggie will be able to take her brother for the rest of the sessions. I would like to see them again in the New Year.

Yours faithfully,

J. Adamson

Emily was glad to hear from Dr Adamson and especially to discover that her own feelings about her children had been confirmed. But how was she to help Maggie with her English and Maths? She found the papers the cleric had sent from Uxbridge and tried to work through some of them herself. There were no problems with the English, but the Maths was more difficult because there was more than one way of setting things out and she certainly didn't want to confuse Maggie. "There's nothing for it, I'll have to go to a Reading bookshop and look at some Maths textbooks," she concluded. "Then, once we've moved, I must sit down with her and try to help her."

Moving day came at last. The Goodchilds finally moved on October the 31st, and this time the weather was relatively mild and the sun decided to shine. They needed two trips to get everything moved successfully. Maggie and Jimmy went ahead with John, while Emily stayed behind with Ann and Gracie, and tried to involve them in the final clear up. The Hursts also came to help.

"You know Rita, now it's time to go I'm beginning to realise how much I'm going to miss you both."

"Yes, but think about the electricity and having a proper bathroom and toilet. You won't know yourselves!"

"Yes, *that* will be wonderful!"

"We're going to have the same conveniences ourselves, when they come to do the work for the Hazeldines. That way both parties will get the jobs done a little cheaper. We talked to the Hazeldines when they made their second visit."

"Good for you!"

"They're planning to come down most weekends, so we should see quite a lot of them."

Meanwhile, when Maggie and Jimmy arrived at Shalom, they were surprised to see some stools in the sitting room made from the trunk of a tree.

"They're for you to sit on until the furniture arrives," said Den, one of the removal men. "If you sit down, I'll bring in some logs from the same tree to make a fire in this grate."

As he was laying the logs on the grate, both children noticed that one of his hands was deformed; instead of one thumb and four fingers, he had one finger only, the middle one.

"Are you kids looking at my hook?"

"What's happened to your hand?" asked Maggie.

"Nothing's *happened* to it. I was born with it like that. I can do lots of things with me 'ook!"

"If you put it in the flames like that, you'll burn it."

"No I won't! Look it's as tough as old boots. *You* feel it."

"It's tough like an elephant's skin."

"When did *you* feel an elephant's skin?"

"When I rode on one at London Zoo."

"Well, Maggie, I'd better go and help Joe, or I'll be in trouble."

Den and Joe began bringing in the bedroom furniture first, starting with the wardrobes and then the big double bed for the girls' room. Shalom was a semi-bungalow with only two bedrooms upstairs; it was much smaller than Tudor Cottage, so it was three in a bed from now on. Jimmy was lucky; he got a small double bed all to himself in the downstairs bedroom/dining-room. John and Emily had a double bed in the front bedroom. The single bed they had brought with them was left in pieces and put in one of the long cupboards off the bedrooms on either side of the house. Once the bedroom things had been unloaded, Den and Joe took the van back for the rest of the family and the furniture for the sitting room, the living-room and the hall, plus all the extra things which might come in handy one day; they could go in the garage because the family didn't have a car.

The Goodchilds weren't totally straight until Christmas, but Shalom was so much warmer than Tudor Cottage. John could walk to work, and the journey to school took only a quarter of an hour if the young Goodchilds didn't dawdle.

Well into the New Year, they were still congratulating themselves that *this* move had gone without a hitch, when they suddenly realised that the dining-room furniture they had originally loaned to the Bournes in 1939 was missing. They were preparing to entertain their first group of visitors and would have to use Jimmy's bedroom as the dining-room it was designed to be. But what had happened to the dining table, the six chairs and the sideboard? None of the items were in the house, nor were they in the garage. The Goodchilds couldn't seat a dozen people around the kitchen table, as there was only room to pull out one of the leaves and extend the table a little way. Without the second leaf, the table was far too small. The kitchen space was inadequate, even though an adjoining small scullery-cum-kitchenette housed the larder, electric stove and kitchen sink.

"Why didn't you notice that these things weren't here?" grumbled John.

"I suppose I'd got used to eating at the kitchen table at Crowsley," answered Emily. "Anyway, you made the furniture in the first place, why didn't *you* notice it wasn't here?"

At Malmesbury, a similar conversation was going on.

"Oh no!" groaned Douglas Bourne. "Annette, I've just realised we've brought the Goodchild's dining-room furniture with us. They let us use it because they wouldn't need it at Crowsley."

"Are you *sure* it's theirs? They haven't rung us up about it."

"I know. But it *is* theirs. They've probably forgotten about it too. I must get it sent back immediately."

January 1947

On the morning of Friday, January the 24th, we all woke to find that a thick blanket of snow had covered the garden, the road, and the field between us and the woods towards Shiplake Bottom. The bare branches of the beech trees were also lined with snow. That day we went to school in our wellington boots, and made snowmen in the playground.

However, over the weekend the temperatures plummeted and the snow fell continuously, accompanied by gale-force winds from the east. We were in for a long spell of ferocious cold. Ten foot drifts transformed the landscape and turned the countryside into a huge white maze. The River Thames froze over and there was a fuel crisis. As things got worse, my mother often said, "Thank goodness we aren't still at Crowsley!"

On February the 7th, Emanuel Shinwell, the minister of fuel and power, was forced to announce drastic measures. We had to switch off all our electricity between nine o'clock in the morning and midday, and again from two o'clock in the afternoon until four o'clock. It was usually on again by the time we arrived home from school. Snow fell every day until March the 16th. Coal was in short supply, but we could find logs in the frozen woods to burn on the kitchen stove.

Some of my friends owned toboggans, so on Saturdays we all trooped up to Peppard Common: Pauline from next door, Pat Stratton from Shiplake Bottom, and Florrie and Bob from next door on the other side. Mumsie would let me go with them, but not Jimmy, Ann or Gracie. On my first trip on the toboggan with Bob Larkin, Bob didn't steer properly, so, instead of speeding down the slope, we careered across it at an angle, landing face down in a deep snowdrift bordering some scrubby bushes.

"Now, don't you blubber! I can't bear little girls who make a scene."

"It just gave me a scare, that's all. I don't like snow in my face and it's hard to get out of this snow bank."

"Come on, give me your hand." None too gently he yanked me to my feet. As the afternoon wore on, we all became more skilful at managing the toboggans, making smooth paths through the uneven slopes. I wondered if we would ever have our own toboggan, but the answer was a very firm "No."

"Couldn't you make us one, Daddy? You once made us a rocking horse."

"No, Maggie, I could *not*. I have some lamp stands and bookcases to make, and I'm all behind with those orders already."

March 1947

Once the thaw began, the ice and snow melted into torrents. The River Thames, and the Kennet, Loddon, and Pang, were all overflowing and flooding the land around them. The great storm on March the 16th spread these flood waters far and wide. Nationwide, thirty-one English counties were affected by the flooding.

In the area around Sonning Common all the ditches overflowed. At the junction of Wood Lane and Woodlands Road the unmade-up road was completely flooded, and we had to go to school in our wellingtons. The Kirbys let us go through their back gate and use the path through to the front of the shop to avoid the deep water. Some silly children decided it was much more fun to chance the floods and arrived at school with water dripping out of their boots. Mr Ford was not amused at having to provide alternative footwear and to arrange for pairs of wet boots and woollen socks to be dried off before their owners could be sent back to their parents in the afternoon. The school secretary and nurse were annoyed too, as they had to leave their usual duties to undertake these tasks. The culprits were each given a note to take home to their parents, asking them to exercise more control over their unruly offspring.

Now we were installed in our own house again, unless the weather was really bad, Jimmy, Ann and I were expected to attend *all* the Sunday activities at the Iron Room: the Sunday School after breakfast at a quarter to ten, the Lord's Supper (which everyone called the 'morning meeting' because it didn't actually take place at suppertime, but at eleven o'clock in the morning), and the

Gospel Meeting after tea at half past six. In the afternoon, we were put to bed for a Sunday nap because our parents needed to rest. Gracie didn't come out with us in the evenings until she was five-and-a-half. My mother was glad to have some time to herself once she had put Gracie to bed.

As we now lived near the Iron Room, our father was given the job of getting there early to open up the hall. So, in the evening, we all left the house at five minutes to six. We had to turn left at the bottom of Newfield Road into Shiplake Bottom, then turn right up the footpath with the steps into Stoke Row Road. The Iron Room was on the right, half way between the top of Gravel Hill and the cross-roads by Peppard Common.

We liked going out in the evenings because Uncle Jock from Scotland started giving us some sweets in a tube as soon as the meeting was over. They were different from the boiled sweets and toffees we could get with our ration books. They were sort of fizzy and made our noses tingle. When Gracie realised that someone was giving *us* sweets, and not her, she became jealous and demanded to come out too.

"I like sweets, too. I want to go to meeting and have sweets."

"If we're going to have all this squabbling, I shall ask Uncle Jock to stop giving *any* of you sweets."

"No, Daddy, don't do that," said Ann. "You'll upset him; then we won't see him anymore. He's kind and I like the way he talks."

Somehow Jock Findlay found out that there were *four* Goodchilds, and the following Sunday he came with four tubes of sweets, and said to Ann, "Give these to your little sister. I don't want her to feel left out."

"Thank you, Uncle Jock; I'll make sure she gets them in the morning when she wakes up."

"Do you three girls all sleep in the same bedroom?"

"Yes," answered Ann. "In the same bed; Gracie sleeps in the middle, Maggie sleeps by the window and I sleep nearest the door. It's a very big bed."

"What happens when Gracie wants to get out in the night?"

"She clambers over me, but she doesn't wake me up!"

During the big freeze, none of us children went out on Sunday evenings. Once the thaw began, everywhere was very wet and slushy underfoot and my mother still didn't want any of us to go out until the roads and pavements were clear again. But, one wet evening, my father insisted that I go out and help him with the hymn books, so she let me go in my wellingtons and take my shoes to change into when I got there. My father sat at the front ready to play the harmonium, and I sat at the back with Uncle Jock, who came in late. Mr Lunn was preaching; he had a boring voice which droned on and on. I was beginning to nod off when Uncle Jock suddenly pinched me hard between my legs. I woke up with a start and nearly let out a squeal. Why did he hurt me like that instead of just tapping my arm?

From then on I did my best to pay attention, but when I glanced across at Uncle Jock, he had a very strange expression in his eyes. He didn't look cross but sort of hungry, as if he wanted something very badly. Then he stared hard at me and pinched me again in the same spot, but held on for longer this time, moving his other fingers all over the place. It wasn't nice at all! I was scared, and then remembered Revd. Priestley who had frightened me by the flower beds in Uxbridge Recreation Ground almost a year ago. Mumsie had told me later that Revd. Priestley wasn't a very nice man. Was Uncle Jock not a very nice man either? But he had been giving us all sweets; horrid men don't give children sweets do they? Or *do* they? Perhaps I've imagined it all! No! It still hurts.

At the end of the meeting, Uncle Jock was his normal self again. He pulled eight tubes of sherbet sweets out of his inside pocket, and said, "Now, Maggie, share these with the others, two for each of you."

"Thank you Uncle Jock," I answered, sweetly, as if nothing had happened.

"Now the weather is getting better, I'm going up to Scotland to see my mother. She's been very ill with pneumonia, so I'm going to stay with her for three or four weeks. She lives in Aberdeen."

"Is Aberdeen bigger than Reading?"

"Yes, it is; a lot bigger. I'll write to you all while I'm away. What number Newfield Road is it?"

"Number 22."

A week or so later we heard from Uncle Jock. Jimmy, Ann and Gracie had postcards with coloured photographs of Scotland and a short greeting and message on the back. Jimmy had a picture of the *Flying Scotsman*, Ann had one of *Edinburgh Castle*, and Gracie had one of fishing boats. I had a twenty-four page letter, fortunately the pad wasn't all that big and Uncle Jock's writing was large with round letters which were easy to read. I would much rather have had a postcard to put up alongside Gracie's and Ann's on the dressing table. I didn't always understand what he meant by some of the things he said about me. Why would he like to see me in a long frock with my hair loose and blowing in the wind? Or swimming like a mermaid in the sea?

"Has Uncle Jock written you an interesting letter," asked Mumsie.

"Not really; it's mostly about his family, not about Scotland. There are no pictures. His mother is better now, his youngest sister's having a baby, and his older brother has lost his wife. It is very sad; she got knocked down by a bus."

"Can I read the letter?"

"Yes, if you want to."

"You're right about it being a *long* letter," she answered, after reading it carefully. "Can I keep it for now to show Daddy?"

"Yes, but I don't think he'll have time to read it all!"

"I think he *will*."

"Mumsie, is something wrong?"

Emily was very unhappy about that letter. It wasn't the sort of letter that a man in his forties would normally write to an eleven-year-old girl. She showed it to John. He took several minutes wading through it.

"I just think it's rather flowery and foolish," answered John. "He expects her to understand when he's paying her a grown-up compliment about her hair, which I agree is more than she is capable of understanding, given the way we have tried to bring her up."

"Maggie, in her innocence, wouldn't pick up the innuendos. And it seems that you haven't either. I'm sure he has designs on Maggie which are not honourable. Why didn't he just send her a postcard like the others?"

"He knew that she would be able to read and understand a more grown-up letter than the others, that's all!"

"Maggie hasn't been herself since that Sunday she sat with him at the back of the hall. When she had her bath, she didn't want me to see her pubic area, as if she had something to hide. When I tried to question her, I could see she was afraid of something. I reckon he touched her inappropriately."

"Emily, what you are suggesting is libellous. Mr Findlay has shown a real interest in the Gospel. How can you suggest that he has tried to molest Maggie?"

"I want to keep her at home for a week or two. She can help look after Gracie."

On his return from Aberdeen, Jock Findlay thought it wise to keep away from the Iron Room for a couple weeks. It hadn't occurred to him immediately how the Goodchilds might have reacted to his writing such a long letter to Maggie and just brief notes to the others. What if Maggie had shown it to them? As naïve as they appeared to be, could they have suspected his real motives? When he did finally show up, he came into the hall with Marian Fowles and gave her his full attention, ignoring Ann and Jimmy completely. He didn't even ask them where Maggie was.

"Hello, Uncle Jock," they chorused as they ran up to him at the end of the meeting. "Thank you for our cards."

"Sorry children, I'm busy tonight and I haven't brought you any sweets. Come on Marian, you were going to show me that walk across the common." Ann and Jimmy were completely taken aback. What had they done to make him so cross?

~

February 1947

The snow was still on the ground when we took the first part of the Scholarship Exam. We took it in the school dinner room, while the rest of the school had a holiday. Mumsie thought we would be there till the afternoon, so gave me some beef sandwiches, which I ate in the break between the two papers we were given.

"Why have you come home so soon?" she asked when I arrived just as she was giving the other three their dinner.

"When we finished the two papers, they told us to go home."

"What have you done with your sandwiches?"

"I was hungry so I ate them in the break."

"Sorry Maggie, there's no dinner here for you."

"That's alright; I just want to go to sleep. Can I lie on top of the bed? Or should I take my clothes off and get right in?

"Take your jumper and skirt off and get right in. It's cold upstairs. You can tell me all about the exam when you wake up."

I must have slept for three or four hours. It was dark when I woke up again and heard Mumsie come into the bedroom with a cup of tea.

"How was the exam?"

"It was a bit like some of those things I did with the two ladies at the University, only I had to *write* the answers in pencil on the paper, and not say them out loud. Some of the questions were almost the same."

"Did you find the exam *very* hard?"

"Some of the questions were hard, and there wasn't enough time to do everything on the paper. The man in charge told us to go on to the next question if we were stuck. He said we could go back to the ones we'd missed at the end, if we had time. The first paper, we had picture puzzles to solve and the second paper was all words or figures."

"Were you worried about the exam beforehand?"

"A little bit. I do so want to go to the grammar school. We will get the results of this one quite soon. And we will only be allowed to take the second part if we pass the first part."

⌒

We took the second part of the exam just before the Easter holidays. There were seven of us who passed the first part, and our names were read out in assembly by Mr Ford: Pat Stratton and Stephen Miles from Standard Five; my deskmate Pam Hill; Christopher Aldridge, the nephew of Mrs Aldridge who used to teach Standard Two; David Morrison, whose mother taught us in Standard One; Helen James, who is the neatest writer in the class; and me. The second part was testing our ability in arithmetic and English and was really hard, especially the arithmetic. I couldn't work quickly enough and I often had no idea what I was expected to do, let alone come up with the right answer. There were some things on the English paper which I *could* do, like giving the meaning of some difficult words, completing proverbs, filling in the gaps left in a story with suitable words, and writing sensible answers to questions and vice versa. One thing I just couldn't fathom though was a code in figures which had to be turned into letters to give a message.

"That was easy-peasy, **1** is **a**, **2**is **b** and **26** is **z**," said Pam Hill as we were walking towards the school gate. "They have lots of puzzles like that in comics and quiz books."

"I'm not allowed to have comics and quiz books."

"Why ever not?"

"I don't really know. Probably because we can't afford them."

"You can always look at some of mine."

"It's a bit too late now, isn't it?"

"Silly! They're fun to read anyway. I'll bring you some."

Somehow, I knew already that I had not done enough to pass the scholarship, not even in the English paper, and the arithmetic was a total disaster.

Sometime in May, we were told in assembly, that only Stephen Miles had passed and won a place at Henley Grammar School. Christopher Aldridge was not upset because he had also taken an exam for the Blue Coat School in Sonning, and he was going there instead. I *was* upset and wondered how I was going to tell them at home. But during the day, from somewhere in my head, I heard a little voice telling me not to worry, that God had a plan for my life. So when I told Mumsie that I had failed the scholarship exam, I also told her about that little voice.

"Yes, Maggie, that's right, he has; and it will be a *good* plan."

A few days later, Mr Ford gave us an English lesson while Mr Lockyer had to go off and do something else. He told us he was going to give us a lesson on the **-ist family**. We all looked at him with blank expressions on our faces.

Then we realised he was talking about groups of words that end in **-ist**, like **typist**. So we all had to put our hands up and give him other words that end in **-ist**. I wasn't thinking carefully enough and came out with **drapist**, instead of **draper**. (There was a draper's shop on the parade at the bottom of Gravel Hill, before you turn up Sedgewell Road.) Mr Ford thought I was being silly on purpose. He handed me a sheet of paper, telling me to write out a hundred times, **I must not be silly in class**, and hand in the paper to him by tomorrow morning.

Normally, we were not supposed to be in school during the lunch hour, but there didn't seem to be anyone on duty so I sat down at my desk and started writing my lines. Then, horrors! I heard Mr Lockyer's voice in the corridor and Pat Stratton's mother was with him. I quickly laid myself down lengthways on the seat, hoping neither of them would look down and see me, and prayed that I wouldn't sneeze.

"I don't think that there is really anything we can do about it now. The examiners' word is final, Mrs Stratton."

"But you know how well Patricia has been doing since you put her up into Standard Five. Can't you appeal against the decision? Or get Mr Ford to do it for you?"

"No, I can't. They wouldn't take *my* recommendation. They would say that every school has its favourite scholars it would like to see go to a grammar school. There is still one glimmer of hope for Patricia. Once they have allocated places to all the children who have exceeded the agreed pass mark, there may be a few places left for those who are borderline cases. Patricia could get one of these places, but don't expect to hear anything just yet."

"Well, thank you for listening to me, Mr Lockyer."

"Don't give up yet, Mrs Stratton."

I heaved a sigh of relief, as they left the classroom, closing the door quietly behind them. I decided not to tell anyone about the conversation I had just heard. Maybe I was borderline, too? But, for now, I'd just get on with these lines.

Epilogue

I soon found out that I wasn't borderline; I had definitely failed the Scholarship because of that second paper. But, out of the blue, my parents received a letter saying that the examiners were 'interested' in my results and would they bring me to Henley for an interview. My mother came to school with me, and we showed the letter to Mr Lockyer, as I needed to take samples of my schoolwork to the interview with me. I told no-one else at school about the letter.

The date given was the last Wednesday of May at two-thirty, and the venue was the Henley Secondary School. We arrived at the Grammar School well before time, only to be told by Miss Hunt, the Senior Mistress, that we had come to the wrong place.

My mother apologized, and explained that she had thought the interview was for a *grammar* school place.

"It is. But we are a bit out-of-the-way up here, so the interviews are being held at the secondary school near the marketplace. You still have time to get there before they start. Maybe we shall see you both again?"

"We hope so."

There were about a dozen boys and girls and their mothers gathered in a large upstairs room. They all looked taller and older than I did. Almost as soon as we arrived, they started the interviews. We were each called into the little room with the examiner in alphabetical order, while our mothers chatted to one another as they waited. I was number five.

The lady who interviewed us was called Mrs Peel. She wore glasses, had brown curly hair and looked a bit younger than my mother. She smiled as I came into the room.

"So you are Margaret. I'm glad you found us without any bother."

"We did go to the wrong place first, because we didn't realise there were two schools, the Grammar School and the Secondary School."

"You weren't the only ones; but this interview *is* for the Grammar School. Why would *you* like to go to a grammar school?"

"I want to be a teacher when I grow up. I can't do that if I stay at Sonning Common Council School. I would have to leave school when I'm fifteen (it used to be fourteen but they've just put it up to fifteen) and get a job, and there would be no chance of going to a Teacher Training College without taking my School Certificate exams."

"I see, you've got that all worked out! Anyway, my job is to give you a few little tests and look at your schoolwork. We'll do the tests first. Here is a half-finished jigsaw puzzle. Can you complete it and then explain what is happening in the picture?" I couldn't believe my luck. It was exactly the same puzzle with the animals looking into a mirror that I had been given to do at the University, but I managed to stop myself telling Mrs Peel that I had seen it before. I knew exactly what to do with all the other tests too.

"Well, *they* didn't take you long! Now I'm going to ask you some questions. I'm going describe some everyday situations and I want you to tell me what is going on in each case." Again, these were similar to the problems I had been given to do at the University. There was the one about the doctor coming to certify a death, the people listening to a sermon in church, and the children at a fairground. One I hadn't heard before was about visiting a library; fortunately I had recently been to the Reading Library with my mother and found out what you had to do to take books out and what you had to do if you wanted to read reference books there at the library.

"Now it's time to look at your books. You haven't done very much in this arithmetic book yet. It's all very neat and tidy, and all the sums are ticked, but why didn't you bring a full one?"

"It was in Mr Lockyer's cupboard, and Mr Lockyer hadn't marked lots of the pages, so I didn't know if I had done the sums correctly or not. That's why I'm not very good at arithmetic."

"Oh dear! That's a shame. Now let's see your English book. Good, there's more for me to look at here. Do you know how to use a dictionary?"

"At home. But there are no dictionaries for us to use in the classroom. We have to ask Mr Lockyer if we don't know how to spell a word. Sometimes he says, 'Try and work it out for yourself. I'm busy.'"

"Why do you keep changing the way you write?"

"I can't make up my mind which style is best, sloping forward or upright. My father writes what he calls 'copperplate' with sloping writing and my mother writes with upright letters which are easier to read."

"So, that's the reason. Doesn't Mr Lockyer find it confusing?"

"He never says anything about it, unless there are too many crossings out."

"Thank you, Maggie, for showing me your work and answering all my questions. Your mother will be receiving a letter about the results of the interview in due course."

"Thank you, Mrs Peel."

"Goodbye Maggie."

It was about two weeks later when the letter came from the education office in Oxford. I was going to the grammar school after all, and I would be seeing Miss Hunt again! Did all grammar school teachers teach in a black gown? It would certainly keep the chalk dust off their ordinary clothes. I wouldn't be wearing one though, because I wanted to teach in a junior school.

"Mr Lockyer, I *am* going to the grammar school. I heard this morning," I said when I saw him in the corridor. "My mother has to write back to say that I'll take the place."

"Well done; but don't shout about it just yet, some of your friends are still upset that *they* didn't get in."

"No, I'll keep it all to myself." That was a very hard thing to do. But it wasn't long before Pat Stratton and Pam Hill had letters to say that they had won 'borderline' places. That left David Morrison and Helen James: David Morrison found out that the authorities were planning to open a technical school in Henley, so he could go there to prepare for a job in a bank, and Helen James wanted to be a hairdresser, so she didn't need a grammar school place anyway.

The last day of term arrived all too quickly. Somehow, I had hoped that the summer term 1947 could have gone on for ever. There were the extra-long playtimes in the warm summer sunshine when we performed handstands against the end wall of the junior corridor, did somersaults and cartwheels out on the school field and practised gymnastics on the climbing-frame. I climbed, swung, and rolled my supple little body around the top bar and jumped off with a soft landing on the asphalt below. Next term I would be at Henley Grammar School, and in two years' time I would be into my teens, and almost grown-up. Young ladies don't show their knickers in public, do they?

As a junior, I could win points for Sonning Common Council School in the area sports. I came second in the high jump by throwing myself over the bar, without worrying about whether I was doing the scissors or the western roll. Our team won the girls' relay and I was the one running the last lap towards the tape; I got the most cheers. At the grammar school, I would be one of the smallest girls in the school. With both parents under five foot three; there would be little chance for me ever to shine when it came to sports. I hoped Mr Ford would mention the area sports at our last school assembly. He was always talking about what the seniors were doing, and forgot all about the infants and juniors. As it was, it was only our class that ever went up to school assemblies, anyway.

We were all packed up and Mr Lockyer had talked to us for the very last time. Old Locky had been my teacher for the last two years, in both Standards Three and Four: Standard Three in the two rows nearest the corridor and Standard Four in the two rows nearest the windows. Everyone liked Old Locky; he was kind and always fair in the way he disciplined us. My deskmate Pam Hill was coming to Henley Grammar School with me; I did hope we would still be in the same class. Then we heard the bell.

"It's time to line up, class, said Mr Lockyer quietly. "Have a good holiday all of you. Pam and Maggie, we all wish you both well in your new school. Come back and see us sometime."

"We'll try," replied Pam, with a cheeky grin on her impish face.

"Thank you, Mr Lockyer," I answered primly, as we lined up by the door and filed along the corridor towards the school hall. It wasn't a real hall, but the Standard Five and Standard Six classrooms, with the sliding partition between them opened up. Mr Ford always stood in the middle with his back to the corridor and the rest of the staff stand opposite him. We filed into Standard Five classroom and stood in a line in front of the desks, and Standard Seven squeezed in with Standard Six.

Mr Ford made a big fuss of the Standard Seven folk who were leaving.

"Now, you are going out into the real world as young adults," enunciated Mr Ford. "We look forward to hearing from you as you find jobs and make your way in the workaday world." Each school leaver received a farewell handshake from the headmaster. Then, almost as an afterthought, he said, "There are also some juniors who are leaving us this term." There weren't any handshakes for us; he didn't say *who* we were or *why* we were leaving. Surely, to be given a grammar school place must bring some sort of honour to the school you are leaving? That's what I thought, anyway.

"Maggie, you're looking rather glum, what's the matter?" asked Mr Lockyer as we were walking back to the junior cloakroom."

"Mr Ford didn't say anything about us juniors leaving, nor about Pat Stratton and Stephen Miles. *We* didn't get any farewell handshakes."

"It's rather different for the seniors who are leaving. They are leaving the world of school for ever, *you* are not. Life will be very strange for them in the shop or office or factory, where they will be the youngest and the newest people in the workplace. It will be exciting, but very scary after the comfortable world of school. *You* are not making such a big change as they are, but yes, it *is* an important landmark for you. I do congratulate you on your success, and hope you will come back sometime to say 'hello' and tell me how you're getting on at Henley."

"Yes, I will. I promise."

"You have a lot more of life to live, Maggie, and a bigger, more exciting journey ahead of you: grammar school, then college, and finally satisfying work as a professional teacher when you reach the age of twenty or so. That's a very different prospect from that faced by today's school leavers. Do you understand what I'm saying?"

"I think so"

"Your parents must be very proud of you too. Good luck, Maggie."

I thought for a long time about what Mr Lockyer had said and I mentally went back over everything in my life leading up to that moment. He seemed keen to tell me that I had 'a lot more of life to live'. In my mind I could see the central characters in the story so far. I played a bit of a game with this, carefully placing all of them as a sort of photograph in my life so far. At the centre would be my parents and siblings, with my grandparents on either side of them. Uncle David, Auntie Nellie and my five cousins would be close by, as well as special family friends: Ada Cotton, Ernie and Rita Hurst, the Kings, Irene and Bert Long, Mrs Kirby, the Nielsen family, Auntie Frances Russell, and second cousins Auntie Edie and Uncle Ted.

My school friends: Helen James, Pam Hill and Pat Stratton, and favourite teachers like Mrs Morrison and Mr Lockyer would be in there too. I would have to include Mrs Claxton; perhaps in the bottom left-hand corner. I've never liked her, but she appears in the story so often. Then there are the Brookers, the Lunns, and the Fowles, and the German Prisoners of War, especially Fritz who gave us the mouth organs.

I've left out those horrid Maloneys who liked hurting people; also, the Reverend Priestley and Uncle Jock because they weren't what they pretended to be, and betrayed my trust. But, somehow, I'd like to put in the baby who died, right next to Gracie. I am sad that we never knew her.